CONTEMPORARY MUSICIANS

ISSN 1044-2197

CONTEMPORARY MUSICIANS

PROFILES OF THE PEOPLE IN MUSIC

**MICHAEL L. LaBLANC,
Editor**

VOLUME 2

Includes Cumulated Indexes

Gale Research Inc.

DETROIT • NEW YORK • FORT LAUDERDALE • LONDON

74160

STAFF

Michael L. LaBlanc, *Editor*

Peter M. Gareffa, *Supervising Editor*

David Collins, *Assistant Editor*

Robert Dupuis, Joan Goldsworthy, Anne Janette Johnson,
Kyle Kevorkian, Tim LaBorie, Jeanne M. Lesinski, Meg Mac Donald,
Robert Nagel, Calen D. Stone, and Elizabeth Thomas, *Contributing Editors*

Linda Metzger, *Senior Editor*

Jeanne Gough, *Permissions Manager*
Patricia A. Seefelt, *Permissions Supervisor (Pictures)*
Margaret A. Chamberlain, *Permissions Associate*
Pamela A. Hayes and Lillian Quickley, *Permissions Assistants*

Mary Beth Trimper, *Production Manager*
Marilyn Jackman, *External Production Assistant*
Arthur Chartow, *Art Director*
Cynthia Baldwin, *Graphic Designer*
C. J. Jonik, *Keyliner*

Laura Bryant, *Production Supervisor*
Louise Gagné, *Internal Production Associate*
Sharana Wier, *Internal Production Assistant*

Cover Illustration: John Kleber

Copyright © 1990
Gale Research Inc.
835 Penobscot Bldg.
Detroit, MI 48226-4094

ISBN 0-8103-2212-9
ISSN 1044-2197

Computerized photocomposition by
Roberts/Churcher
Derby Line, Vermont

Contents

Introduction

Fills the Information Gap on Today's Musicians

Contemporary Musicians profiles the colorful personalities in the music industry who create or influence the music we hear today. Prior to *Contemporary Musicians*, no quality reference series provided comprehensive information on such a wide range of artists despite keen and ongoing public interest. To find biographical and critical coverage, an information seeker had little choice but to wade through the offerings of the popular press, scan television "infotainment" programs, and search for the occasional published biography or expose. *Contemporary Musicians* is designed to serve that information seeker, providing in one ongoing source in-depth coverage of the important figures on the modern music scene in a format that is both informative and entertaining. Students, researchers, and casual browsers alike can use *Contemporary Musicians* to fill their needs for personal information about the artists, find a selected discography of the musician's recordings, and read an insightful essay offering biographical and critical information.

Provides Broad Coverage

Single-volume biographical sources on musicians are limited in scope, focusing on a handful of performers from a specific musical genre or era. In contrast, *Contemporary Musicians* offers researchers and music devotees a comprehensive, informative, and entertaining alternative. *Contemporary Musicians* is published twice yearly, with each volume providing information on 80 to 100 musical artists from all the genres that form the broad spectrum of contemporary music—pop, rock, jazz, blues, country, new wave, New Age, blues, folk, rhythm and blues, gospel, bluegrass, and reggae, to name a few, as well as selected classical artists who have achieved "crossover" success with the general public. *Contemporary Musicians* will occasionally include profiles of influential nonperforming members of the music industry, including producers, promoters, and record company executives.

Includes Popular Features

In *Contemporary Musicians* you'll find popular features that users value:

- **Easy-to-locate data sections**—Vital personal statistics, chronological career summaries, listings of major awards, and mailing addresses, when available, are prominently displayed in a clearly marked box on the second page of each entry.

- **Biographical/critical essays**—Colorful and informative essays trace each personality's personal and professional life, offer representative examples of critical response to each artist's work, and provide entertaining personal sidelights.

- **Selected discographies**—Each entry provides a comprehensive listing of the artist's major recorded works.

- **Photographs**—Most entries include portraits of the artists.

- **Sources for additional information**—This invaluable feature directs the user to selected books, magazines, and newspapers where more information on listees can be obtained.

Helpful Indexes Make It Easy to Find the Information You Need

Contemporary Musicians features a Musicians Index, listing names of individual performers and musical groups, and a Subject Index that provides the user with a breakdown by primary musical instruments played and by musical genre.

We Welcome Your Suggestions

The editors welcome your comments and suggestions for enhancing and improving *Contemporary Musicians*. If you would like to suggest musicians or composers to be covered in the future, please submit these names to the editors. Mail comments or suggestions to:

The Editor
Contemporary Musicians
Gale Research Inc.
835 Penobscot Bldg.
Detroit, MI 48226-4094
Phone : (800) 521-0707
Fax: (313) 961-6241

Photo Credits

Roy
Acuff

Singer, songwriter, violinist, and music publisher

"It's hard not to get a kick out of Roy Acuff and his Smoky Mountain Boys," announced Diane Zimmerman in the *New York Sunday News*. Labeled "The King of Country Music" by fans and peers alike, "Acuff hits the stage like greased Tennessee lightning," according to Zimmerman, "and he punctuates his renditions . . . with turns on the fiddle, the uk[ulele], and even the Yo-Yo. He even manages to leaven the heavy sentimentality of country music with a yeast of wry good humor that shows through off-stage as well as on." A fixture with his band, the Smoky Mountain Boys, at Nashville's famous Grand Ole Opry since 1938, and the first living performer elected to the Country Music Hall of Fame in 1962, Acuff is renowned for his renditions of "The Great Speckled Bird" and "The Wabash Cannonball."

Despite the fact that Acuff's father, Baptist preacher Neill Acuff, was an amateur fiddle player, Roy did not show much early interest in music except for singing in his father's church. Instead, he was the star actor and star athlete of his Knoxville, Tennessee, high school, performing in all of the school plays and winning a chance to play baseball for the New York Yankees when he graduated. While still in the organization's semipro leagues, however, Acuff was afflicted by a series of serious sunstrokes and had to give up his career in baseball. As Acuff stayed indoors recovering from his illness, he listened to his father's recordings of country-music artists Fiddlin' John Carson and Gid Tanner and the Skillet Lickers and learned to play the fiddle.

Acuff first put his new skills to use in an unusual way. In 1932 he joined Doc Hower's travelling medicine show, a troupe that put on skits and performed music in order to sell patent medicine—specifically, a product called Moc-A-Tan. Acuff toured with Doc Hower from the spring until the fall; when the touring season was over he formed a band called the Tennessee Crackerjacks. Soon he and the band were featured on local radio shows, and, after a name change to the Crazy Tennesseeans, they were offered a record contract from the now-defunct American Record Company. Acuff and the Tennesseeans' first recording session was in October 1936; one of the songs they put to wax, "The Wabash Cannonball," was probably the group's largest money-maker.

Another, "The Great Speckled Bird," a rather metaphysical gospel song based on a quotation from the Bible's Book of Jeremiah and written by a lyricist cryptically identified as the Reverend Gant, won Acuff and his band a great deal of attention in the country-music field. It also helped the Tennesseeans to the stage of the Grand Ole Opry in Nashville, Tennessee. When the group made their first appearance on the prestigious

Smoky Mountain Boys have also played with great success to European audiences.

After recording for labels such as Columbia, Vocalion, and Okeh, Acuff co-founded Hickory Records with Rose and has released songs for that company since 1957. Many attribute the label's success to the management of Mildred Acuff, Roy's wife, who became the driving force behind Hickory. In 1962 Acuff became the first living person elected to the Country Music Hall of Fame; the plaque put up in his honor cited his contributions in exposing new audiences to country music and in helping many fledgling performers in the field. Though he has continued to perform at the Opry and in concert, and has continued to release records through several decades, Acuff cut back his schedule after a 1965 car accident left him with broken collarbone, ribs, and pelvis.

Acuff's music stems solely from the mountain and gospel roots of country; once labeled "hillbilly" music, it

> *"Acuff hits the stage like greased Tennessee lightning and he punctuates his renditions . . . with turns on the fiddle, the uke, and even the Yo-Yo."*

is virtually untouched by the western influence that spread through the field in the 1940s and 1950s. Acuff revealed his own feelings about his art to a reporter for *Look* magazine: "The music is down to earth, for the home—not to get all hepped up and smoke a lot of marijuana and go wild about. The music is full of Christianity and sympathy and understanding. It helps make people better."

program in 1938, the Opry's radio audience was so impressed by Acuff's strong emotive interpretation of the song that they sent thousands of letters in praise of his performance. Within a year, Acuff had replaced Opry pioneer Uncle Dave Macon as the show's most prominent star, a position he retained for decades.

In 1939 the Crazy Tennesseans changed their name to the Smoky Mountain Boys because many, including Acuff, had begun to feel that the old name was derogatory to their home state. Though various group members came and went through the years, the name stuck, and Acuff and the Smoky Mountain Boys had a long string of country hits during the 1940s and 1950s, including "Wreck on the Highway," "Night Train to Memphis," "Will the Circle Be Unbroken," "Don't Make Me Go to Bed and I'll Be Good," "Beneath That Precious Mound of Clay," "I Saw the Light," and "Mule Skinner Blues." The 1940s also saw Acuff branch into music publishing. With Fred Rose, he founded Acuff-Rose, which became one of the world's largest country-music publishers. In 1948, at the urging of many, Acuff ran for governor of Tennessee on the Republican ticket. Campaigning by performing concerts with the Smoky Mountain Boys, he won the Republican primary, but he lost the election to Democratic incumbent and longtime friend Gordon Browning. Over the years Acuff and his band have done many concert tours; they have been especially conscientious about entertaining American servicemen overseas. Acuff performed for the troops during the Soviet Union's blockade of Berlin in 1949, and during the Korean and Vietnam Wars. He and the

Selected discography

Singles; on American

"Wabash Cannonball," 1936.
"The Great Speckled Bird," 1936.

Singles; on Vocalion; 1940s and early 1950s

"Steamboat Whistle Blues," "New Greenback Dollar," "Steel Guitar Chimes," "The Beautiful Picture," and "The Great Shining Light."

Singles; on Okeh; 1940s and early 1950s

"Wreck on the Highway," 1942.
"Night Train to Memphis," 1943.

Also released "Vagabond's Dream," "Haven of Dreams," "Beautiful Brown Eyes," "Living on the Mountain," "Baby Mine," "Ida Red," "Smoky Mountain Rag," "Will the Circle Be Unbroken," "When I Lay My Burden Down," "Streamline Cannonball," "Weary River," "Just to Ease My Worried Mind," "The Broken Heart," "The Precious Jewel," "Lyin' Women Blues," "Are You Thinking of Me, Darling?" "Don't Make Me Go to Bed and I'll Be Good," and "It's Too Late to Worry Anymore."

Singles; on Columbia; 1940s and early 1950s

"Beneath That Precious Mound of Clay," "It Won't Be Long," "Branded Wherever I Go," "Do You Wonder Why," "The Devil's Train," "The Songbirds Are Singing in Heaven," "I Saw the Light," "Unloved and Unclaimed," "Mule Skinner Blues," "Not a Word From Home," "Waiting for My Call to Glory," "I Called and Nobody Answered," "Golden Treasure," "Heartaches and Flowers," "Tennessee Waltz," "Sweeter Than Flowers," "Polk County Breakdown," "I'll Always Care," and "Black Mountain Rag."

Miscellaneous singles

"Fireball Mail," 1942.
"Low and Lonely," 1943.
"Pins and Needles," 1943.

Also released "Old Age Pension Check," "Yes, Sir, That's My Baby," "The Great Judgment Morning," "Mule Skinner Blues," and "All the World Is Lonely Now."

LPs

Roy Acuff, Harmony, 1958.

That Glory Bound Train, Harmony, 1961.
Hymn Time, MGM, 1962.
Best of Roy Acuff, Capitol, 1963.
American Folk Songs, Hickory, 1964.
Gospel Songs, Hickory, 1964.
Great Roy Acuff, Capitol, 1964.
King of Country Music, Hickory, 1964.
Once More, Hickory, 1964.
Songs of the Grand Ole Opry, Hickory, 1964.
The World Is His Stage, Hickory, 1964.
Smoky Mountain Boys, MGM, 1965.
The Voice of Country Music, Capitol, 1965.
Great Train Songs, Hickory, 1967.
Hall of Fame, Hickory, 1967.
Roy Acuff Sings Famous Opry Favorites, Hickory, 1967.
Roy Acuff Sings Hank Williams, Hickory, 1967.
Treasury of Hits, Hickory, 1969.
Roy Acuff Time, Hickory, 1970.
Roy Acuff's Greatest Hits, Volume 1, Elektra, 1978.
Roy Acuff's Greatest Hits, Volume 2, Elektra, 1979.

Sources

Books

Acuff, Roy, and William Neely, *Roy Acuff's Nashville: The Life and Good Times of Country Music,* Putnam, 1983.

Periodicals

Look, July 13, 1971.
New York Sunday News, December 5, 1971.

—Elizabeth Thomas

Bryan Adams

Singer, songwriter, guitarist

Bryan Adams "is arguably Canada's brightest male star," declared Nicholas Jennings in *Maclean's*. His 1985 album *Reckless* has sold more than ten million copies—impressive by any standard—but, as Jennings pointed out, Adams has enjoyed wider distribution "than any Canadian in history." He owes this distinction primarily to straightforward rock anthems like "Kids Wanna Rock" and ballads like "Heaven." Though some critics have dismissed Adams as a lesser version of rocker Bruce Springsteen, lacking the substance that the latter infuses into his songs, others have praised Adams's simplicity. "His music is about guys and girls. They're melodies that stick in your head," explained Pat Steward, Adams's drummer, to Jane O'Hara in another *Maclean's* article.

Adams was born on November 5, 1959, in Kingston, Ontario, Canada. His parents were former British citizens, and his father, Conrad Adams, came from a military family. This background, coupled with the fact that Conrad Adams served in the Canadian diplomatic corps, meant a childhood of moving from place to place for Bryan. He attended strict military schools in several countries, including England, Austria, Portugal, and Israel. Adams recalled for Steve Pond in *Rolling Stone* that "the discipline that they taught me in school was good, because I was able to focus on things—but I didn't realize that at the time. So I got sent to the headmaster a lot." When he turned sixteen, however, his parents separated, and he lived with his mother, Jane, in Vancouver, British Columbia.

Adams's early musical development is echoed, if not narrated, in the lyrics of his 1985 hit "Summer of '69": "I got my first real six-string / Bought it at the five-and-dime / Played it till my fingers bled / It was the summer of '69," as Pond quoted it. Though Adams was only ten at the time the song mentions, a year or two later, according to Pond, he *did* buy his first guitar and start learning to play it. As an adolescent, he pursued his rock goals with single-minded fervor. He explained to Pond: "In high school, I was too far into my music to even pay attention to girls."

At the age of sixteen Adams quit school and used the money his parents had saved for his higher education to buy a grand piano. He joined bands and played in nightclubs, supplementing his income by washing dishes, selling pet food, and working in record stores. "One summer night in 1976," Jennings related, "after hearing a local rock band perform in Surrey, B[ritish] C[olumbia], . . . Adams . . . strode boldly up to the group's producer and announced that he could sing better than its vocalist. He got an audition—and the job." Not long after that, Adams met up with Jim Vallance, who had formerly written songs for the Canadian rock group Prism. As

For the Record. . .

Full name, Bryan Guy Adams; born November 5, 1959, in Kingston, Ontario, Canada; son of Conrad (a diplomat) and Jane Adams.

Songwriter, with Jim Vallance, 1977—; recording artist, 1979—. Has performed in various charity concerts for organizations including Live Aid, Amnesty International, and the Prince's Trust.

Addresses: *Office*—c/o 406-68 Water St., #406, Vancouver, British Columbia, R2H 2M2, Canada.

O'Hara phrased it, "Vallance was looking for a singer, Adams was looking for a route to musical respectability, and the two hit it off immediately." The pair began writing songs together and recording demonstration tapes. Adams had a mild hit in 1979 with one of their products, the disco-styled "Let Me Take You Dancing," and they managed to sell some of their other creations to recording artists such as Joe Cocker, Juice Newton, and Bachman-Turner Overdrive. Adams and Vallance also won first a publishing contract and then a recording contract with A & M Records.

But Adams's first solo album, *Bryan Adams,* was unsuccessful. O'Hara explained: "On it his voice is high-pitched and the songs predictable." He wanted, according to O'Hara, to call his next effort "Bryan Adams Hasn't Heard of You Either," but settled for *You Want It, You Got It.* The album was a moderate success, selling five hundred thousand copies and earning Adams the privilege of opening concerts for rock bands like the Kinks, Loverboy, and Foreigner. However, it was Adams's third, *Cuts Like a Knife,* which pushed him to the level of rock stardom. The title song was a huge hit; the accompanying music video, involving a scantily clad woman and a gleaming knife, was considered controversial and attracted even more attention to Adams and his record. His 1985 release, *Reckless,* was even more popular, including the hits "Heaven" and "The Summer of '69."

Though he was selling records at a phenomenal rate and was a huge concert draw, Adams's songwriting had not gained the favor of most rock-music critics. O'Hara quoted a *Rolling Stone* reviewer: "Adams has typically produced the closest thing yet to generic rock 'n' roll, long on formal excellence but short on originality." Perhaps conceding a lack of depth in his many songs about painful love relationships, Adams told Pond that during one concert performance he thought, "'Man, I gotta sink my teeth into something else.' 'Cause I . . . had this desire to write something more *interesting* for myself." One of the results of this thought was the song Adams recorded to earn money for famine relief in Ethiopia, "Tears Are Not Enough." Another was his 1987 album *Into the Fire.* The disc includes a protest song about Native American land rights called "Native Son" and a contemplative number about a veteran of World War I titled "Remembrance Day." Still, despite refusing to allow the use of another song from *Into the Fire,* "Only the Strong Survive," in the film *Top Gun* because he felt the movie glorified war, Adams handles his newfound political principles gingerly. "I don't like politics being rammed down people's throats," he confessed to Jennings. "But there's a sensitive way of bringing up issues and making people think."

Selected discography

LPs

Bryan Adams, A & M, 1980.
You Want It, You Got It, A & M, 1981.
Cuts Like a Knife (includes "Cuts Like a Knife"), A & M, 1983.
Reckless (includes "Heaven" and "The Summer of '69"), A & M, 1985.
Into the Fire (includes "Into the Fire," "Rebel," "Native Son," "Remembrance Day," and "Only the Strong Survive"), A & M, 1987.

Other

Also released the 1979 single, "Let Me Take You Dancing."

Sources

Maclean's, August 5, 1985; July 6, 1987.
Rolling Stone, March 28, 1985; September 10, 1987.

—Elizabeth Thomas

Paul Anka

Singer, songwriter

Canadian-born singer and songwriter Paul Anka had his first hit record, "Diana," in 1957 when he was only fifteen years old. His was no one-shot teen novelty recording, either—Anka followed "Diana" with a string of hits that lasted into the early 1960s. When his popularity on the United States rock and roll scene faded, he began to aim his music at older, non-rock audiences and at his European and Asian fans, by whom he was greatly celebrated. A prolific writer, Anka also penned many hits for other recording artists, including Buddy Holly and Tom Jones, and he is responsible for the ballad standard "My Way," a huge success for both Frank Sinatra and Elvis Presley. In 1974 Anka scored a triumphant pop comeback with "You're Having My Baby" and has since pursued fame with other hits, including "I Don't Like to Sleep Alone," "There's Nothing Stronger Than Our Love," and "The Times of Your Life."

Anka was born July 30, 1941, in Ottawa, Ontario, Canada. His parents were immigrants from Lebanon who owned a successful restaurant frequented by Ottawa's show people. As a small child, Anka delighted in imitating popular singers and performing for neighborhood housewives, paperboys, and sanitation workers. He soon learned a little piano and taught himself how to play the guitar. Anka was generally uninspired by school, except for writing classes, and once intended to become either an actor or a writer, but the allure of music gradually swayed him from these early ambitions. When rock and roll began to flood the music world, Anka was only in his teens but nonetheless was convinced that he could create songs just as good, if not better, than the ones he was hearing on the radio. He began to compose, taking inspiration from Arabic chant melodies that his parents had brought with them from Lebanon and from the rhyming schemes of poet and playwright William Shakespeare.

Anka also formed a vocal trio called the Bobbysoxers with some friends; they played at local dances and at the Central Canada Exhibition of 1955. He also won a competition at the Fairmount Club in Ottawa, receiving as his prize a week's engagement at the club. Anka took his earnings from this and traveled to Los Angeles, California, in hopes that his uncle, Maurice Anka, a nightclub entertainer, could help him get his music published. Though a recording company there bought one of his songs, it didn't sell, and Anka had to work as a movie usher to earn his way back home to Ottawa.

In 1957, however, when Anka borrowed money from his father to go to New York City in hopes of publishing his music, he scored a resounding success. The fifteen-year-old performed a song he had written about his unrequited love for a girl three years older than himself,

wane, he began to concentrate on adult nightclub audiences, such as those who frequented New York City's Copacabana, Los Angeles, California's, Coconut Grove, and Las Vegas, Nevada's, Sahara. He toured Europe with great success, and focused more on his songwriting abilities. "I like to have four or five songs going at once," Anka explained to a writer for *Time* magazine. Among the hits he has composed for other artists, in addition to the stunning "My Way," is "She's a Lady," recorded by Welsh singer Tom Jones. Anka also wrote the theme for Johnny Carson's "Tonight Show."

But in 1974, Anka came back with a controversial hit of his own, "You're Having My Baby." Inspired by the

---

"Anka was generally uninspired by school, except for writing classes, and once intended to become either an actor or a writer."

Diana Ayoub, for the executives of ABC Paramount. The recording company was so excited by what they heard that, presumably because Anka was a minor, they asked his father to come to New York as soon as possible to sign a contract.

Anka's song, "Diana," was an enormous hit and sold over 8,500,000 copies, making it the second best-selling record ever, after crooner Bing Crosby's rendition of "White Christmas." Anka followed "Diana" with many other records that were snapped up by teenagers, including "You Are My Destiny" in 1958, "Lonely Boy" and "Put Your Head on My Shoulder" in 1959, and "Puppy Love," about his then steady date, actress Annette Funicello, in 1960. Anka also traveled across the United States and Canada with rock and roll acts like Buddy Holly, for whom he wrote "It Doesn't Matter Anymore," Chuck Berry, the Everly Brothers, and Fats Domino. And, as part of being considered a teen idol, he was persuaded by his manager to have plastic surgery on his nose, lost weight, and appeared in the films "Girls Town," "The Private Lives of Adam and Eve," and "Look in Any Window." Anka received little if any praise for his acting in these vehicles but fared better with critics in the 1962 film "The Longest Day," for which he also composed the music.

When the advent of British groups like the Beatles caused Anka's popularity with American teenagers to

childbearing experiences he shared with his wife, Ann de Zogheb, "Baby" includes the passage, as quoted by *Time,* "'Didn't have to keep it/ Wouldn't put you through it/ You could have swept it from your life/ But you wouldn't do it,'" that caused "both right-to-life and pro-abortion groups" to protest the song. "So did feminists," continued *Time,* "although *Baby* is rare among macho pop songs in that it acknowledges a woman's autonomy." Maureen Orth, commenting in *Newsweek,* labeled the song a "musical miscarriage" but quoted Anka's response to charges of sexism: "I can't hand out a pamphlet every time I write a song." Anka has since had other pop successes, including the mellow "The Times of Your Life," which began as a commercial jingle for Kodak film.

Selected discography

Major single releases

"Diana," ABC, 1957.
"I Love You, Baby," ABC, 1957.
"You Are My Destiny," ABC, 1958.
"Crazy Love," ABC, 1958.
"Let the Bells Keep Ringing," ABC, 1958.
"Midnight," ABC, 1958.
"Just Young," ABC, 1958.
"All of a Sudden My Heart Sings," ABC, 1958.

"I Miss You So," ABC, 1959.

"Lonely Boy," ABC, 1959.

"Put Your Head on My Shoulder," ABC, 1959.

"It's Time to Cry," ABC, 1959.

"Puppy Love," ABC, 1960.

"My Home Town," ABC, 1960.

"Something Happened," ABC, 1960.

"Hello, Young Lovers," ABC, 1960.

"I Love You in the Same Old Way," ABC, 1960.

"Summer's Gone," ABC, 1960.

"The Story of My Love," ABC, 1961.

"Tonight, My Love, Tonight," ABC, 1961.

"Dance On, Little Girl," ABC, 1961.

"Kissin' on the Phone," ABC, 1961.

"Cinderella," ABC, 1961.

"Love Me Warm and Tender," RCA, 1962.

"A Steel Guitar and a Glass of Wine," RCA, 1962.

"Every Night," RCA, 1962.

"Eso Beso," RCA, 1962.

"Love Makes the World Go 'Round," RCA, 1963.

"Remember Diana," RCA, 1963.

"Hello, Jim," RCA, 1963.

"Did You Have a Happy Birthday?" RCA, 1963.

LPs

Paul Anka (includes "Do I Love You"), Buddah, 1971.

Jubilation, Buddah, 1972.

Anka (includes "You're Having My Baby" and "One Man Woman—One Woman Man"), United Artists, 1974.

Feelings (includes "I Don't Like to Sleep Alone" and "There's Nothing Stronger Than Our Love"), United Artists, 1975.

Times of Your Life, United Artists, 1975.

The Painter, United Artists, 1976.

The Music Man (includes "Everybody Ought to Be in Love"), United Artists, 1977.

Sources

House and Garden, September, 1984.

Newsweek, February 24, 1975.

Time, December 8, 1975.

—Elizabeth Thomas

Count Basie

Pianist, bandleader

In his monumental second volume on the history of jazz, *The Swing Era,* Gunther Schuller delays his attempt to define swing until, some two hundred pages into the book, he introduces Count Basie in a section titled "The Quintessence of Swing." Schuller states: "That the Basie band has been from its inception a master of swing could hardly be disputed. . . . For over forty years [Basie] has upheld a particular concept and style of jazz deeply rooted in the Southwest and Kansas City in particular. It draws its aesthetic sustenance from the blues, uses the riff as its major rhetorical and structural device, all set in the language and grammar of swing."

Indeed, from the mid-1930s to the mid-1940s the "All-American Rhythm Section"—Walter Page, bass; Jo James, drums; and Freddie Green, guitar—combined with leader and pianist Count Basie to propel Basie's band from relative obscurity in a Kansas City nightclub to world renown as the leading purveyor of swing. Though blessed with an estimable array of soloists throughout the big band era, the Basie band originated an infectious pulse whose essence was a clean, unified, four-beats-to-the-bar swing. Though celebrated for the simplicity of the riff-oriented, call and response interaction of the brasses and reeds in its head arrangements, the band drew its virility from the rhythm section, even after Page and Jones left (c. 1948). Though energized in later years by brilliant writing and arranging, the Basie band housed a secret ingredient: the leader's quite but forceful insistence upon an uncluttered, swinging sound, anchored by the rhythm section and accented by his own "less is more" solos.

Page combined a walking bass line with fine tone and a correct choice of notes. Jones, dancing on the high hat cymbal rather than thumping on the bass drum, allowed the lively bass lines to breathe. Green, the latecomer, strummed the chords that inspired two generations of great soloists. Schuller says of Green that he is "a wonderful anacronism, in that he has (almost) never played a melodic solo and seems content to play those beautiful 'changes' night after night." Basie quarterbacked, accented, edited, filled, chorded, and prodded, often pitting the soloists against one another to expose their fire. And what a group of soloists it was: tenor saxophonists Lester Young (he of the lean, dry phrases, precursor of the "cool" school), Herschel Evans, Paul Gonsalves, Illinois Jacquet, Lucky Thompson, Charlie Rouse, and Don Byas; trumpeters Buck Clayton and Harry Edison; trombonists Vic Dickenson, Dicky Wells, Bennie Morton, and J.J. Johnson; and vocalists Jimmy Rushing, Helen Humes, and Billie Holiday. Later bands would include trumpeters Clark Terry and Thad Jones, trombonist Al Grey, and reedmen Eddie "Lockjaw" Davis, Frank Foster, Marshal Royal, and Frank Wess, and singer Joe Williams. Personnel changes in Basie's band were gradual as, from 1936 until his death in 1984 (with the exception of 1950-51, when it was reduced to an octet), Count Basie led the quintessential big swing band with which his name will always be associated.

From his Red Bank, New Jersey, home, Basie gravitated to the music parlors of 1920s Harlem, where he met fabled pianists James P. Johnson and Fats Waller, picking up some informal instruction on both piano and organ from the latter. As a piano soloist and accompanist to several acts, he worked his way to Kansas City with a troupe that became stranded there. After some service as a silent film organ accompanist, Basie played with several of the local bands including that of Bennie Moten, the area's best-known leader. Some time after Moten's death, Basie assumed command of the nucleus of that band in 1935, and with a nine-piece group embarked on a long run at the Reno Club, making it one of Kansas's City's hottest spots. A radio announcer there dubbed Basie "Count" and the title prevailed.

Jazz impresario John Hammond heard one of the band's regular broadcasts on an experimental radio station and helped to arrange bookings in Chicago and later New York. Basie increased the size of the band to thirteen pieces, trying to retain the feel of the smaller group, but initial reaction was disappointing. Finally, in 1937, several elements coalesced to launch the band on its nearly half-century of success. Freddie Green's guitar solidified the rhythm section. Booking agent Willard Alexander finessed an engagement at the Famous Door in the heart of New York's 52nd Street, a booking complete with a national NBC radio wire. Basie's Decca recordings—"One O'Clock Jump," "Jumpin' at the Woodside," "Swingin' the Blues," "Lester Leaps In" and others—began to catch on. As word fanned outward, Basie's band attracted wildly cheering audiences, often in excess of the capacity of the venues.

Basie's bands before and after the 1950-51 octet hiatus were quite different. The early band relied almost exclusively on head arrangements, those that often evolved over a period of time as the leader and the players experimented with short phrases (riffs) and accents that bounced from the trumpets to the reeds to the trombones, showcasing the parade of outstanding soloists. In the early 1940s the band benefited mightily from the writing and arranging of Buster Harding, Buck Clayton, and Tab Smith. Their work no doubt paved the way for the later band's heavy reliance upon brilliant writing and arranging, chiefly by Neal Hefti, Frank Foster, Ernie Wilkins, and Sam Nestico. It, too, showcased excellent soloists, but the Basie ensemble sound, now grown to sixteen pieces, was its hallmark and the rhythm section, with Basie and Green ever-present, was its heartbeat.

Prolific recording dates, tours to Europe and Asia, regular appearances at Broadway's Birdland, and an endless stream of dances, festivals, and concerts led to many honors for Basie and his band, including royal command performances in England and recognition by Presidents Kennedy and Reagan. In addition to some of the seminal hits, later audiences demanded to hear such new Basie staples as "Li'l Darlin'," "Cute," "Every Day I Have the Blues," "All Right, OK, You Win," and "April In Paris." Despite their differences, both bands exhibited a devotion to blues-based swinging and an uncluttered pulse; both also relied on effective use of dynamics, more subtle in the early band, more dramatic in the later, when Green's unamplified guitar chords often gave way to shouting brass.

Basie's bandstand demeanor appeared laid-back in the extreme—some called it laissez faire; others just plain lazy. Testimony of his bandmen and arrangers belie this. Perhaps Basie's greatest skill was that of editor, first in the matter of personnel, then in the selection of repertoire. As John S. Wilson quoted Basie in *The New York Times:* "I wanted my 13-piece band to work together just like those nine pieces . . . to think and play the same way. . . . I said the minute the brass got out of hand and blared and screeched instead of making every note mean something, there'd be some changes made." Basie told his autobiography collaborator, Albert Murray, "I'm experienced at auditions. I can tell in a few bars whether or not somebody can voice my stuff."

Francis Davis's *Atlantic* tribute column observed, "Basie apparently demanded of his sidemen a commitment to basics as single-minded as his own." The writers and arrangers for the later band became accustomed to

---

"Basie apparently demanded of his sidemen a commitment to basics as single-minded as his own."

Basie's editing out all material that he considered contrary to the ultimate goal: to swing. In the case of Neal Hefti's "Li'l Darlin'," Basie's insistence on a much slower tempo than Hefti had envisioned resulted in one of the band's greatest and most enduring hits. Basie's conducting arsenal included such simple movements as a pointed finger, a smile, a raised eyebrow, and a nod—all sufficient to shift the "swing machine" into high gear.

Though Basie's piano did surface significantly in later recordings with smaller groups, including piano duets with Oscar Peterson, he most often considered himself simply a part of the rhythm section. His spartan, unadorned solos, usually brief, cut to the essence of swing. With the full band, increasingly he was content to support and cajole soloists with carefully distilled single notes and chords of introduction and background. A genuine modesty about his pianistic skills combined with Basie's understanding of the role of the big-band piano to form his style. Several critics and musicologists have observed that Basie's spare playing inspired

such important artists as John Lewis, music director of the Modern Jazz Quartet, and Thelonious Monk, one of the architects of the Bop Era. Additionally, Mary Lou Williams and Oscar Peterson attest to Basie's influence upon their playing. As many mature jazz practitioners aver, great playing consists not only of the notes one chooses to play, but those that one leaves out. In this respect Count Basie stands out as the acknowledged master.

Whether viewed as its pianist, leader, composer, arranger, paymaster, chief editor, inspiration, or soul—Count Basie will always be inextricably associated with the Basie Band. Despite crippling arthritis of the spine and a 1976 heart attack, Basie continued to call the tune and the tempo until his death from cancer in 1984. It will be the burden of all big bands, past, present, and future, to stand comparison with the Basie band. It has been the standard for half a century. One reason may well be that Count Basie, he of the impeccable taste, was not only its leader, but the bands greatest fan. He would not permit it to play less than its best. He loved it so.

Selected discography

With Bennie Moten

The Complete Bennie Moten, Volumes 3/4, French RCA Victor.
The Complete Bennie Moten, Volumes 5/6, French RCA Victor.

As Leader

The Best of Count Basie, MCA.
The Indispensable Count Basie, French RCA Victor.
One O'Clock Jump, Columbia Special Products.
April in Paris, Verve.
Basie Plays Hefti, Emus.
16 Men Swinging, Verve.
88 Basie Street, Pablo.

With Dizzy Gillespie

The Gifted Ones, Pablo.

With Oscar Peterson

Satch and Josh, Pablo.

Sources

Books

Basie, Count, with Albert Murray, *Good Morning Blues,* Random House, 1985.
Chilton, John, *Who's Who of Jazz,* Time-Life Records, 1978.

Dance, Stanley, *The World of Count Basie,* Scribner, 1980.

Feather, Leonard, *The New Edition of The Encyclopedia of Jazz,* Bonanza Books, 1960.

McCarthy, Albert, *Big Band Jazz,* G. P. Putnam's Sons, 1974.

Rust, Brian, *Jazz Records 1897-1942,* 5th Revised and Enlarged Edition, Volume I, Storyville Publications, 1982.

Schuller, Gunther, *The Swing Era,* Oxford University Press, 1989.

Simon, George T., *The Big Bands,* Macmillan, 1967.

Periodicals

Atlantic, August, 1984.

down beat, July, 1984.

Ebony, January, 1984.

Newsweek, May 21, 1984; March 17, 1986.

New York Review of Books, January 16, 1986.

New York Times, April 27, 1984.

New York Times Book Review, February 2, 1986.

People, March 22, 1982.

Rolling Stone, June 7, 1984.

—*Robert Dupuis*

The Beatles

British pop/rock group

On February 7, 1964, the Beatles arrived at Kennedy International Airport in New York City, met by 110 police officers and a mob of more than 10,000 screaming fans. The British Invasion—and in particular, "Beatlemania"—had begun, and the "mop-topped" Beatles—John Lennon, Paul McCartney, George Harrison, and Ringo Starr—wasted no time in endearing themselves to American fans and the media, though many adults remained skeptical. According to the February 24, 1964, *Newsweek* cover story, the Beatles' music, already topping the charts, was "a near disaster" that did away with "secondary rhythms, harmony, and melody." Despite such early criticism, the Beatles garnered two Grammy Awards in 1964, foreshadowing the influence they would have on the future of pop culture.

Inspired by the simple guitar-and-washboard "skiffle" music of Lonnie Doengan and later by U.S. pop artists such as Elvis, Buddy Holly, and Little Richard, John Lennon formed his own group, the Quarrymen, in 1956 with Pete Shotton and other friends. Expertise helped

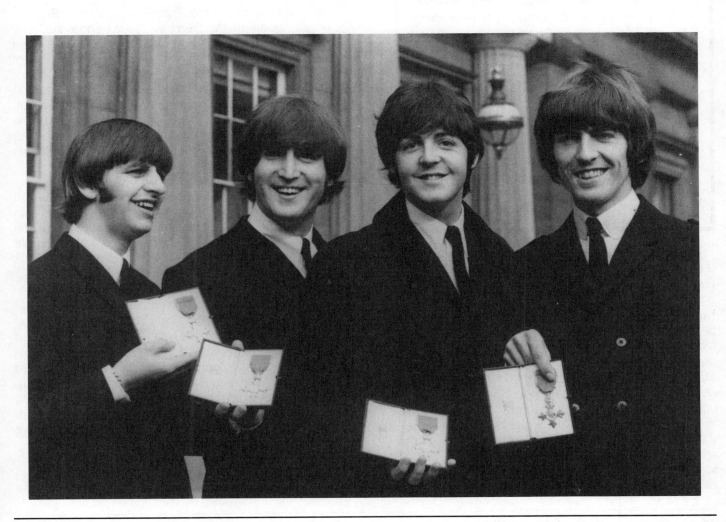

guitarist Paul McCartney, whom Shotton introduced to Lennon in 1957 at a church function, find a place in the band, and he in turn introduced Lennon to George Harrison. Only fourteen, Harrison, though a skilled guitarist, did not impress seventeen-year-old Lennon overmuch, but his perseverence finally won him a permanent niche in the developing ensemble. Stuart Sutcliffe, an artist friend of Lennon's brought a bass guitar into the group a year later. Calling themselves Johnny and the Moondogs, the band eventually won a chance to tour Scotland, backing a little-known singer, Johnny Gentle. Renamed the Silver Beatles, they were well-received, but the pay was poor, and the end of the tour saw the exit of a disgusted drummer and the arrival of Pete Best.

With the help of Welshman Allan Williams, club owner and sometime-manager for many promising bands playing around Liverpool in 1960, the Beatles found themselves polishing their act at seedy clubs in Hamburg, West Germany. Living quarters were squalid, working conditions demanding, but instead of splintering the group, the experience strengthened them. Encouraged by their audiences' demands to "make show," they became confident, outrageous performers. Lennon in particular was reported to have played in his underwear with a toiled seat around his neck, and the whole band romped madly on the stage. Such spectacles by the Beatles and another English band, Rory Storme and the Hurricanes, ultimately caved in the stage at one club. The Beatles' second trip to Hamburg, in 1961, was distinguished by a better club and a series of recordings for which they backed singer Tony Sheridan—recordings that proved critical in gaining them a full-time manager. At the end of that stay, Sutcliffe remained in Hamburg to marry, having ceded bass duties to McCartney. He died tragically the following spring, shortly after the Beatles joined up with Brian Epstein.

Intrigued by requests for Tony Sheridan's "My Bonnie" single, featuring the Beatles, record shop manager Brain Epstein sought the band at Liverpool's Cavern Club. Within a year of signing a managerial agreement with Epstein, the Beatles gained a recording contract from E.M.I. Records producer George Martin, and on the eve of success shuffled yet another drummer out, causing riots among Pete Best's loyal following. The last in a long line of percussionists came in the form of the Hurricanes' sad-eyed former drummer, Ritchie Starkey—Ringo Starr.

Despite initial doubts, Martin agreed to use Lennon and McCartney originals on both sides of the Beatles' first single. "Love Me Do," released on October 5, 1962, did well enough to convince Martin that, with the right material, the Beatles could achieve a number one record. He was proved correct. "Please Please Me," released in Britain on January 12, 1963, was an immediate hit. The biweekly newspaper *Mersey Beat* quoted Keith Fordyce of *New Musical Express,* who called the song "a really enjoyable platter, full of vigour and vitality," as well as Brian Matthew, then Britain's most influential commentator on pop music, who proclaimed the Beatles "musically and visually the most accomplished group to emerge since the Shadows." The Beatles' first British album, recorded in one thirteen-hour session, remained number one on the charts for six months.

The United States remained indifferent until, one month before the Beatles' arrival, E.M.I.'s U.S. subsidiary,

Capitol Records, launched an unprecedented $50,000 promotional campaign. It and the Beatles' performances on "The Ed Sullivan Show," which opened their first American tour, paid off handsomely. "I Want to Hold Your Hand," released in the United States in January of 1964, hit number one within three weeks. After seven weeks at the top of the charts, it dropped to number two to make room for "She Loves You," which gave way to "Can't Buy Me Love." As many as three new songs a week were released, until on April 4, 1964, the Beatles held the top five slots on the Billboard list of top sellers, anther seven in the top one hundred, and four albums positions including the top two. One week later, fourteen of the top one hundred songs were the Beatles'—a feat unmatched before or since.

Also in 1964, long before music videos had become commonplace, the Beatles appeared in the first of several innovative full-length feature films. Shot in black-and-white and well-received by critics, *A Hard Day's Night* represented a day in the life of the group. Its release one month before the Beatles began their second U.S. tour was timely. *Help,* released in July of 1965, was a madcap fantasy filmed in color. Exotic locations made *Help* visually more interesting than the first film, but critics were less impressed. Both albums sold well, though the U.S. versions contained fewer original songs, and *Help* was padded with pseudo-Eastern accompanying tracks.

The 1965 and 1966 albums *Rubber Soul* and *Revolver* marked a turning point in the Beatles' recording history. The most original of their collections to date, both combined Eastern, country-western, soul, and classical motifs with trend-setting covers, breaking any mold that seemed to contain "rock and roll." In both albums, balladry, classical instrumentation, and new structure resulted in brilliant new concepts just hinted at in earlier works like "Yesterday" and "Rain." Songs such as "Tomorrow Never Knows," "Eleanor Rigby," and the lyrically surreal "Norwegian Wood" made use of sophisticated recording techniques—marking the beginning of the end of the group's touring, since live performances of such songs was technically impossible at the time. The Beatles became further distanced from their fans by Lennon's comments to a London *Evening Standard* writer: "Christianity will go. It will vanish and shrink. I needn't argue about that, I'm right and will be proved right. We're more popular than Jesus Christ now. I don't know which will go first, rock 'n' roll or Christianity. Jesus was all right, but his disciples were thick and ordinary. It's them twisting it that ruins it for me." While the British dismissed the statement as another "Lennonism," American teens in the Bible Belt took Lennon's words literally, ceremoniously burning

Beatle albums as the group finished their last U.S. tour amid riots and death threats.

Acclaimed by critics, with advance sales of more than one million, the tightly produced "conceptual" album *Sgt. Pepper's Lonely Hearts Club Band* was perhaps the high point of the Beatles' recording career. No longer a "collection" of Lennon-McCartney and Harrison originals, the four-Grammy album was, in a stunning and evocative cover package, a thematic whole so aesthetically pleasing as to remain remarkably timeless. Imaginative melodies carried songs about many life experiences, self-conscious philosophy, and bizarre imagery, as in "A Day in the Life"—a quintessential sixties studio production. The Beatles' music had evolved from catchy love songs to profound ballads, social commentary, and work clearly affected by their growing awareness of and experimentation with Eastern mysticism and hallucinogenic drugs. Song like "Lucy in the Sky With Diamonds" were pegged as drug-induced (LSD), and even Starr's seemingly harmless rendition of "A Little Help From My Friends" included references to getting "high." Broadening their horizons

---

"[The Beatles] played the songs for the best time of our lives, and always will."

---

seemed an essential part of the Beatles' lives and, influenced greatly by Harrison's interest in Indian religion, the Beatles visited the Maharishi Mahesh Yogi in Bangor, Wales, in 1967. It was there that news of Brian Epstein's death reached them.

The group's next cooperative project was the scripting and directing of another film, *Magical Mystery Tour,* an unrehearsed, unorganized failure. Intended to be fresh, it drew criticism as a compilation of adolescent humor, gag bits, and undisciplined boredom. The resulting album, however, featured polished studio numbers such as McCartney's "Fool on the Hill" and a curiosity of Lennon's, "I Am the Walrus." The American LP added tracks including "Penny Lane," "Hello Goodbye," and "Strawberry Fields Forever," which were immortalized on short films broadcast by Ed Sullivan. Solo projects in 1967 and 1968 included the acting debuts of Lennon in *How I Won the War* and Starr in *Candy,* Harrison's soundtrack to the film *Wonderwall,* and Lennon's eventual release of his and Yoko Ono's controversial *Two Virgins* albums.

Growing diversity pointed to disintegration, the early

throes of which were evident in 1968 on the two-record set, *The Beatles,* the first album released by the group's new record company, Apple. The White Album, as it was commonly known, showcased a variety of songs, mostly disjointed, often incomprehensible. According to George Martin, as quoted in *The Beatles Forever,* "I tried to plead with them to be selective and make it a really good single album, but they wouldn't have it." The unity seen in earlier projects was nudged aside by individuality and what appeared to be a growing rift between Lennon and McCartney. Whereas the latter contributed ballads like "Blackbird," the former groundout antiwar statements, parodied the Maharishi, and continued to experiment with obscure production. Harrison, on the other hand, shone in "While My Guitar Gently Weeps," aided by Eric Clapton's tasteful guitar solo. Starr, for the first time, was allotted the space for an original, the country-western "Don't Pass Me By," which became a number-one hit in Scandinavia where it was released as a single. Overall, critics found the White Album a letdown after the mastery of *Sgt. Pepper,* though Capitol claimed it was the fastest-selling album in the history of the record industry.

Despite having little to do with its making, the Beatles regained some of their lost status with *Yellow Submarine,* an animated feature film released in July 1968. A fantasy pitting the big-eyed, colorfully clothed Beatles against the squattish Blue Meanies, the film was visually pleasing if not initially a big money-maker. The group spent minimal time on the music, padding it with studio-session throwaways and re-releases of "All You Need Is Love" and "Yellow Submarine" itself. The remainder of 1968 and 1969 showed the individual Beatles continuing to work apart. Starr appeared in the film *The Magic Christian,* and Lennon performed live outside the group with Yoko Ono, whom he had married, and the Plastic Ono Band.

After spending months filming and recording the documentary that would later emerge as the *Let It Be* film and album, the Beatles abandoned thirty hours of tape and film to producer George Martin. Since editing it down would make release before 1970 impossible, the album was put on hold. Instead, for the final time, the Beatles gathered to produce an album "the way we used to do it," as McCartney was quoted in Philip Norman's book, *Shout!* The result was as stunning in its internal integrity as *Sgt. Pepper* had been. Schisms seemed to vanish on *Abbey Road,* with all Beatles at their best. Lennon showed himself sardonic but controlled in "Come Together" and "I Want You—She's So Heavy," McCartney crooned ballads and doo-wop rockers alike in "Golden Slumbers" and "Oh! Darling!"; and Harrison surpassed both of them with "Here Comes

the Sun" and "Something," hailed by Lennon as the best track on the album. Starr, always in the background, provided vocals for "Octopus's Garden" and uncompromising and creative drumming throughout. Wrote Schaffner, "The musicianship is always tasteful, unobtrusive, and supportive of the songs themselves. . . . The Beatles never sounded more together." Yet another Grammy winner, it was a triumphal exit from the 1960s, and its declaration, "And in the end, the love you take is equal to the love you make," read like an epitaph until the "post mortem" release of the heavily edited *Let It Be.*

American producer Phil Spector took over the *Let It Be* clean-up project from George Martin in 1970. The resulting album, brought out after fifteen months of apathy, bickering, and legal battles, was a mixture of raw recordings, glimpses of the Beatles in an earlier era, and heavily dubbed strings and vocals—as on McCartney's "Long and Winding Road." Though most tracks were tightly and effectively edited, critics said the album lacked the harmony of earlier endeavors. According to Schaffner, Lennon later told *Rolling Stone,* "We couldn't get into it. . . . I don't know, it was just a dreadful, dreadful feeling . . . you couldn't make music . . . in a strange place with people filming you and colored lights." The film, which strove to show the Beatles as honestly and naturally as possible, gave further evidence of disintegration. Band members were shown quarreling, unresponsive to McCartney's attempts to raise morale. Said Alan Smith of the *New Musical Express,* quoted by Roy Carr and Tony Tyler in *The Beatles: An Illustrated Record,* "If the Beatles soundtrack album 'Let It Be' is to be their last, then it will stand as a cheapskate epitaph, a cardboard tombstone, a sad and tatty end to a musical fusion which wiped clean and drew again the face of pop music."

By the end of 1970, all four Beatles had recorded solo albums, and, in 1971, McCartney sued for the dissolution of the group. Throughout the seventies, promoters attempted to reunite them without success. The closest approximation of a reunion was Starr's *Ringo* album in 1973—though never together in the studio, Lennon, Harrison, and McCartney contributed music, vocals, and backing. Any lingering hope of a joint performance or album ended with the tragic murder of John Lennon on December 8, 1980. A year before, Neil Munro, in an *Oakland Press Sunday Magazine* article, provided what might make a fitting epitaph, setting the Beatles into their place in history: "Their musical imagination was startling. They lived on it. . . . They played the songs for the best times of our lives, and always will."

Selected discography

LPs

Introducing the Beatles, Vee Jay, 1963.
Meet the Beatles, Capitol, 1964.
The Beatles Second Album, Capitol, 1964.
A Hard Day's Night, United Artists, 1964.
Something New, Capitol, 1964.
The Beatles Story, Capitol, 1964.
Beatles '65, Capitol, 1964.
The Early Beatles, Capitol, 1965.
Beatles VI, Capitol, 1965.
Help, Capitol, 1965.
Rubber Soul, Capitol, 1965.
Yesterday . . . and Today, Capitol, 1966.
Revolver, Capitol, 1966.
Sgt. Pepper's Lonely Hearts Club Band, Capitol, 1967.
Magical Mystery Tour, Capitol, 1967.
The Beatles (White Album), Apple, 1968.
Yellow Submarine, Apple, 1969.
Abbey Road, Apple, 1969.
Hey Jude, Apple, 1970.
Tony Sheridan and the Beatles, Polydor, 1970.
Let It Be, Apple, 1970.
The Beatles 1962-1966, Apple, 1973.
The Beatles 1967-1970, Apple, 1973.

Rock 'N' Roll Music, Capitol, 1976.
The Beatles at the Hollywood Bowl, Capitol, 1976.
The Beatles Live! At the Star Club in Hamburg, Germany: 1962, Lingasong, 1977.
Love Songs, Capitol, 1977.
Rarities, Capitol, 1979.

Sources

Books

Carr, Roy and Tony Tyler, *The Beatles: An Illustrated Record,* Harmony Books, 1978.
Norman, Philip, *Shout! The Beatles in Their Generation,* Simon and Schuster, 1981.
Schaffner, Nicholas, *The Beatles Forever,* McGraw, 1978.
Schaumburg, Ron, *Growing up With the Beatles,* Harcourt, 1976.

Periodicals

Evening Standard (London), March 4, 1966.
Mersey Beat, January 31-February 14, 1963.
Newsweek, February 24, 1964.
Oakland Press Sunday Magazine, February 4, 1979.
Time, December 22, 1980.

—Meg Mac Donald

Tony
Bennett

Singer

Tony Bennett "is a deceptively low-key performer who can make the biggest hall seem intimate," according to Chet Flippo in *New York* magazine. "He also has unrivaled taste in song selection: He has long been known as the 'standard singer,' because any song he does becomes a standard. . . . His personal crusade has been to keep alive the music of composers like Richard Rodgers, Harold Arlen, and Jerome Kern, simultaneously retaining some of the fire of such torch singers as Billie Holiday and Lena Horne." Best known for his trademark song, "I Left My Heart in San Francisco," Bennett first rose to fame as a balladeer in 1950, with the quick hit "The Boulevard of Broken Dreams." He had many other successful releases during the next five years, but the advent of rock and roll—which he refused to be a part of—took away much of his popular audience until he recorded "San Francisco" in 1962. That hit permanently elevated Bennett to the level of major international entertainment figures such as Frank Sinatra, and he has been drawing crowds in the world's best nightclubs and concert halls ever since.

Bennett was born Anthony Dominick Benedetto on August 3, 1926, in Queens, New York. The death of his father when Bennett was nine years old left his family impoverished; his mother worked as a seamstress during the Great Depression to support them. When Bennett was old enough, his burgeoning vocal talents won him a job as a singing waiter at the Yukon, a prestigious New York City restaurant. Also interested in sketching and painting, the young man planned a future in commercial art, but World War II intervened. Bennett served in the infantry with the U.S. Army in Europe; throughout his hitch, he sang with various military bands. After the war he used the benefits to which he was entitled under the G.I. Bill to study voice at the professional school of the American Theatre Wing. At this time, Bennett began to land small nightclub engagements, but still had to supplement his income by working as an elevator operator at New York City's Park Sheraton Hotel.

Eventually, Bennett won a chance to appear on Arthur Godfrey's television show, "Talent Scouts." Even though he finished second to singer Rosemary Clooney on the program, the exposure led to a spot on comedian Jan Murray's "Songs for Sale," and to a 1950 Greenwich Village nightclub engagement with featured singer Pearl Bailey. Going by the stage name Joe Bari, Bennett so impressed comedian Bob Hope, who was an audience member, that Hope had him sing at his own show at the Paramount Theatre. As Bennett told interviewer Ben Gross in the *New York Sunday News,* "Right then and there, [Hope] announced that my name thereafter would

For the Record. . .

Born Anthony Dominick Benedetto, August 3, 1926, in Queens, New York, N.Y.; son of John (a tailor) and Anna (a seamstress; maiden name, Suraci) Benedetto; married Patricia Ann Beech, February 11, 1952 (divorced, 1971); married Sandra Grant, December 29, 1971 (marriage ended, 1979); children: (first marriage) D'Andrea, Daegal (son); (second marriage) Joanna, Antonia.

During teens worked as a singing waiter in Queens, N.Y.; employed as an elevator operator; nightclub performer, c. 1948—; recording artist, 1950—. Hosted own television variety show, summer, 1956; appeared in motion picture *The Oscar*, 1965. Also an artist, exhibits paintings under name Anthony Benedetto.

Awards: Numerous gold records; recipient of two Grammy Awards, for best record of the year and for best male solo vocal performance, both 1963, both for "I Left My Heart in San Francisco"; named variety performer of the year, 1964, by the American Guild of Variety Artists.

be Tony Bennett and that I'd accompany him on his nationwide tour."

Meanwhile, Bennett had made a demonstration record of a song called "The Boulevard of Broken Dreams" and submitted it to Mitch Miller, an executive at Columbia Records. Miller liked what he heard, and immediately offered the young singer a recording contract. "Boulevard" became Bennett's first hit, and although its time on the charts was short lived, it was quickly followed by two million sellers—"Because of You," and a pop rendition of country artist Hank Williams's "Cold, Cold Heart." As Flippo pointed out, the latter was quite an achievement for Bennett, because "he was the man who sang the first country-and-western crossover smash hit."

Bennett continued to score gold records throughout the first half of the 1950s, including "Rags to Riches" and "Stranger in Paradise" in 1953, but the new sounds of rock and roll took his young audience away from him in the latter half of the decade. He told Flippo: "The change came in 1955. No, it wasn't just Elvis [Presley]. All of a sudden, everybody was impressed by Detroit and the idea of obsolescence. . . . They didn't want records that would last, they didn't want lasting artists, they wanted *lots* of artists. It became like a supermarket: Go with the next, the next. So they started discarding people like me and [bandleader] Duke Ellington and [composer] Leonard Bernstein."

But Bennett continued playing smaller clubs, and at one such engagement at San Francisco, he was looking for a number with local appeal when he stumbled upon the song by Douglass Cross and George Cory that became his ticket to lasting success. Of course, he recorded "I Left My Heart in San Francisco" in 1962, and it sold over 1,500,000 copies. The song also won Bennett two Grammy Awards from the National Academy of Recording Arts and Sciences in 1963—one for best record of the year, and another for best solo vocal performance by a male singer—and became a classic standard of American popular music. Bennett followed up "San Francisco" with three other hits: "I Wanna Be Around," "The Good Life," and "This Is All I Ask." He became a featured performer at the best clubs, such as New York City's Copacabana, The Dunes in Las Vegas, and Chez Paree in Chicago. As Flippo noted, Bennett's "popular appeal cuts across all class lines." After a gap in his recording career because of differences with Columbia, he issued the album *The Art of Excellence*

> *"I Left My Heart in San Francisco" permanently elevated Bennett to the level of major international entertainment figures such as Frank Sinatra.*

on that label in 1986, garnering much critical applause: among others, Eric Levin of *People* magazine called it "superb."

Bennett has also been successful with his other creative talent, art. He signs his real name, Anthony Benedetto, to his paintings; they sell well, and he has exhibited his work in major galleries in every city he tours as a singer. Singing, however, will probably be Bennett's forte for a long time. As he explained to Levin, "My teachers, when I was young, taught me how to save my voice. Most singers peak out when they're around 35. But I have this ambition to actually sing better as I get older." Musician and singer Ray Charles echoed for Levin Bennett's prediction of future success. "There are just a few male singers in this world who I feel can sing forever—Perry Como, Sinatra, if he wants to, and Tony Bennett," declared Charles. "Tony has such an even flow of all his notes, and they're so effortlessly produced. He's always had the tools, but his maturity is that what he thinks of, he can do easier now. I'm happy he's recording again, because it's always good to listen to goodness."

Selected discography

Singles; released by Columbia

"The Boulevard of Broken Dreams," 1950.
"Because of You," 1951.
"I Won't Cry Anymore," 1951.
"Cold, Cold Heart," 1951.
"Blue Velvet," 1951.
"Solitaire," 1951.
"Here in My Heart," 1952.
"Have a Good Time," 1952.
"Rags to Riches," 1953.
"Stranger in Paradise," 1953.
"There'll Be No Teardrops Tonight," 1954.
"Cinnamon Sinner," 1954.
"Can You Find It in Your Heart," 1956.
"Happiness Street," 1956.
"From the Candy Store on the Corner to the Chapel on the Hill," 1956.
"Just in Time," 1956.
"The Autumn Waltz," 1956.
"One for My Baby," 1957.
"In the Middle of an Island," 1957.
"I Am," 1957.
"Ca, c'est l'amour," 1957.
"Young and Warm and Wonderful," 1958.
"Firefly," 1958.
"Smile," 1959.
"Climb Ev'ry Mountain," 1959.
"I Left My Heart in San Francisco," 1962.
"I Will Live My Life for You," 1963.
"I Wanna Be Around," 1963.
"The Good Life," 1963.
"Spring in Manhattan," 1963.
"This Is All I Ask," 1963.
"True Blue Lou," 1963.
"Don't Wait Too Long," 1963.
"The Little Boy," 1963.
"When Joanna Loved Me," 1964.
"It's a Sin to Tell a Lie," 1964.
"A Taste of Honey," 1964.
"Who Can I Turn To?" 1964.
"If I Ruled the World," 1965.
"Fly Me to the Moon," 1965.
"Love Theme From The Sandpipers," 1965.
"Georgia Rose," 1966.
"For Once in My Life," 1967.

LPs

I Left My Heart in San Francisco, Columbia, 1962.
The Art of Excellence, Columbia, 1986.

Also has released over eighty other albums, including *Tony Sings for Two, Alone Together, Tony Bennett Sings a String of Harold Arlen, Blue Velvet, My Heart Sings, In Person, Mr. Broadway, I Wanna Be Around, This Is All I Ask, Don't Wait Too Long, The Many Moods of Tony Bennett,* and *Tony Bennett at Carnegie.*

Sources

Jet, September 15, 1986.
New York, May 11, 1981.
People, June 23, 1986.

—Elizabeth Thomas

Bunny Berigan

Trumpeter, bandleader

Bunny Berigan was *the* trumpet phenomenon as he blazed his way across New York's Depression-wracked 1936 music scene. He was the inspiration for three of CBS Radio's popular small groups; the nucleus of innumerable jazz record sessions; the heart and soul of the combo that captivated patrons at the Famous Door and other 52nd Street (Swing Street) night spots. Often playing his trumpet for seventy hours a week, Berigan literally rushed from studio to studio, fawned upon by listeners, coveted by producers, respected by musicians, and revered by fellow-trumpeters. Sturdily built and matinee-idol handsome, Berigan had the unique combination of skills that made him welcome at virtually any musical session, from a Victor Young-led classical program to the most challenging of the "cutting sessions" that attracted jazz players. Those who heard and played with Berigan are virtually unanimous in listing the qualities that endeared him to musicians and listeners alike: a gorgeous, full tone throughout the range of the horn; fluent technique; a compositional approach that flows naturally while making each phrase a logical part of a whole; a sense of time and drama; and a gut-level communication of searing emotion.

Illustrative of the assessment of Berigan's peers, Jack Teagarden, the legendary trombonist, told this story: "I thought Bunny was one of the finest trumpet players in the world. And I'll tell you another wonderful compliment, and it really means a lot because it comes from a guy who does a little bit of braggin'—let's say he's his own best publicity agent—Wingy Mannone. He used to say, 'Now me and Louis' [Armstrong]—he even put himself before Louis—'me and Louis is the best trumpet players.' About that time Bunny came to town and was playing at one of the hotels with Hal Kemp. I said, 'Wingy, why don't you go down and hear this new fellow, Bunny Berigan, and see what you think?' I saw Wingy on the street the next day and asked him if he'd gone to see the new boy. He said, 'Yup. Now there's three of us: me, and Louis Armstrong, and Bunny Berigan.'"

Several of Berigan's sidemen from his own band re-called trumpeter Harry James standing in the audience frequently, drinking in Berigan's ideas and sound. Guitarist Tom Morgan recalled that James was reluctant to follow Berigan in soloing at some of the frequent jam sessions that ensued when more than one big band appeared in the same town. Drummer Zutty Singleton liked to tell of one such trumpets-only session in Philadelphia that ended early: when Bunny finished working his way through several explosive choruses, none of the other trumpeters would play. Trumpeter Pee Wee Irwin often expressed his amazement at Berigan's massive tone: "like a cannon shot . . . sheer body of sound." In 1941, Louis Armstrong wrote a letter

For the Record. . .

Full name, Bernard Roland Berigan; born November 2, 1908, in Hilbert, Wis.; died of complications resulting from chronic alcoholism, June 2, 1942; son of William (a candy and tobacco route salesman) and Mary "Mayme" (a musician and housewife; maiden name, Schlitzberg) Berigan; married Donna McArthur (a dancer and housewife), May 25, 1931; children: Patricia (born July 23, 1932), Joyce (born April 22, 1936). *Education:* Attended public schools (to approximately 10th grade) in Fox Lake and Madison, Wis.

Trumpeter with Hal Kemp Orchestra, 1930-31; member of CBS studio house band, 1931-36; member of Paul Whiteman Orchestra, 1933; featured soloist with various ad hoc recording groups, 1933-37; member of Benny Goodman Orchestra, 1935; regular performer at the Famous Door and other 52nd street nightclubs, 1935-36; featured performer on innovative jazz radio program, "Saturday Night Swing Club," 1936-39; member of the Tommy Dorsey Orchestra, 1937, and 1940; leader of the Bunny Berigan Orchestra, 1937-42.

Awards: Voted best hot trumpet in *Metronome* poll, 1937; recorded with *Metronome* all-star band, 1939; Berigan's "I Can't Get Started" one of first ten recordings inducted into National Academy of Recording Arts and Sciences (NARAS) Hall of Fame in recognition of excellence in recordings made before its first Grammy Awards, 1975; dedication of Wisconsin State Historical Society marker in Fox Lake, Wis., 1976; inducted into the Wiscousin Performing Artists Hall of Fame, 1985.

to *down beat,* in which he responded to their request to name his favorite trumpeter: "First I'll name my boy Bunny Berigan. . . . To me Bunny can't do no wrong in music."

Berigan arrived at this lofty position in the esteem of his fellow-musicians and in the hearts of an adoring public at a relatively early age. He was not yet twenty-one when he moved to New York from Madison, Wisconsin, in September, 1929, to play with Frank Cornwell's band at Janssen's original Hofbrau at Broadway and 52nd Street, where he soon established himself as the new voice to be heard. He also met his wife-to-be, Donna McArthur, who was an adagio dancer in the show. Before long, he joined the popular Hal Kemp band. Shortly thereafter, with the Depression entering its second half-year, the band departed for a tour of England, Belgium, and France.

Berigan left the Kemp band in early 1931 in favor of one of the most coveted of jobs, one proffered without benefit of a formal audition. He joined the house band at CBS, principally on the strength of his playing in local jam sessions with "Radio Row" standouts of the day. From that point, Berigan recorded hundreds of tunes with the Dorsey brothers, the Boswell Sisters, Bing Crosby, and an array of other, frequently bad singers, rendering the usually insipid songs of the day under the leadership of a variety of names, many of which were pseudonyms. Not only was Berigan playing some of the most innovative jazz of the day, he was a producer's dream: a lead and solo trumpter who could sight-read parts, eliminating the need for costly second and third takes. On much of this recording Berigan remains buried in anonymity, but the discerning listener can hear his strong, driving lead playing, which sometimes breaks out into an eight- or sixteen-bar solo that transforms the whole performance with its fresh and daring jazz voice.

Berigan joined the orchestra of Paul Whiteman, the extremely popular so-called "King of Jazz," in early 1933, taking over the chair once held by another trumpet legend, Bix Beiderbecke. A year of touring with this quasi-jazz, quasi-symphonic group provided a good income, but little chance for jazz expression, a need Berigan met in the recording studios and at jam sessions. When he left Whiteman and returned to the CBS studios, Berigan quickly increased his public following as the mainstay of three separate jazz-oriented groups that were given daily exposure. Recording sessions found him playing with Benny Goodman, Mildred Bailey, Frankie Trumbauer, and other jazz stars, usually in small group settings.

When Goodman began to form a big band, he turned to Berigan to provide the necessary spark, by doubling as both lead trumpeter and jazz soloist. Goodman's fabled 1935 cross-country trip nearly proved disastrous for the band, but finally culminated in triumph at Los Angeles's Palomar Ballroom. There, wild throngs of fans, won over through hearing Goodman on the three-hour "Let's Dance" radio program from New York, catapulted Goodman from relative obscurity to royalty—the "King of Swing." Berigan was largely responsible for the excitement generated; by all accounts, Berigan's electric solos and crackling lead trumpet provided the perfect complement to the leader's own sparkling solo work and the arrangements of Fletcher Henderson and others. Pianist Jess Stacy summed up Berigan's contribution: "Bunny was the mainstay. With his reputation and ability he helped sell the band. He was something else!"

Berigan left the Goodman band while it was still playing in Los Angeles, returning to a rich recording and radio studio schedule in New York. His first sides as a band leader, recorded on December 13, 1935, featured a small group, Bunny Berigan and His Blue Boys; seven sessions under his own name followed in the next fourteen months, using groups of differing configurations. Concurrently with some of these latter sessions, Berigan played and recorded with the Tommy Dorsey big band, an alliance that was marked by brevity, bombast, and brilliance.

Within a month of joining Dorsey, Berigan recorded two of the calssic trumpet solos of all time, on "Song of India" and "Marie." Indeed, more than half a century later the Tommy Dorsey ghost band still plays "Marie," with the brass ensemble playing a transcribed note-for-note version of the Berigan solo. His three-month stint with Dorsey ended in an argument between Berigan and the temperamental leader, whereupon Berigan formed his own big band, one that would virtually occupy Berigan's full time for the remainder of his life. The new band began asupiciously with a Victor recording contract launched on April 1, 1937; a weekly radio program; and an engagement a the prestigious Penn-

---

When Bunny finished working his way through several explosive choruses, none of the other trumpeters would play.

---

sylvania Hotel. As part of its fifth recording session the band did "I Can't Get Started," still regarded as one of the true masterpieces of recorded jazz. It became Berigan's theme song, and the band's only hit record.

As fast-paced 1937 drew to a close for the band, rapid and regular turnover of personnel foreshadowed some of the pessimism that encroached. Berigan, never a business-oriented leader, became the dupe of unscrupulous management. Moreover, an old problem, alcoholism, dogged Berigan and he acquired a new label: unreliable. In spite of the leader's brilliance and the excitement generated by his band in person, choice bookings and the pick of the tunes to record increasingly went to rival leaders Dorsey, Goodman, Artie Shaw, and Gene Krupa.

From mid-1938 on, Berigan waged a battle against booze and bad business in which he never achieved the upper hand. Bankruptcy forced his return to the Tommy Dorsey band for a period from March to August, 1940, during which he sparked that group once again

with his solo and lead work. Ten separate recording sessions, many featuring vocals by a young Frank Sinatra, have preserved some of Berigan's excellent playing in this second Dorsey stint. Re-forming a band almost immediately upon leaving Dorsey, Berigan spent the remainder of his life trying to earn his way out of debt, playing a schedule of punishing one-nighters almost exclusively, and making occasional attempts to beat the disease whose complications ultimately claimed his life on June 2, 1942, at age thirty-three. A few days prior to his death, his once-powerful body ravaged by illness, Berigan was still able to give a command performance of "I Can't Get Started" that thrilled listeners, critics, and, most of all, his band.

Selected discography

[All of Berigan's issued recordings were 78s except for several that were done for various transcription companies. The original 78s are items coveted by collectors and, when found, command high prices. What follows is a selected list of LP re-issues that are available to some degree.]

Swinging '34: Bill Dodge and His All-Star Orchestra, (includes "Junk Man," "Dinah," "I Gotta Right to Sing the Blues," "Love is the Sweetest Thing," "I Just Couldn't Take it, Baby," "Ol' Pappy," "Old Man Harlem," "Keep on Doin' What You're Doin'," "Nobody's Sweetheart Now," "Ain'tcha Glad?," "Basin Street Blues," "Tappin' the Barrel," "Dr. Heckle and Mr. Jibe," "Georgia Jubilee," "Texas Tea Party," "Honeysuckle Rose," "Holiday," "Emaline," "Sweet Sue—Just You," "A Hundred Years from Today," "Riffin' the Scotch," "Your Mother's Son-in-Law," "Love Me or Leave Me," "I Can't Give You Anything But Love, Baby"), Melodeon, c. 1970.

The Indispensable Bunny Berigan, (includes selections by Bunny Berigan and His Orchestra, unless otherwise indicated: "Honeysuckle Rose" and "Blues" [Jam Session at Victor]; "'Cause My Baby Says It's So," "Swanee River," "All God's Chillun Got Rhythm," "Frankie and Johnny," "Mahogany Hall Stomp," "Turn On That Red Hot Heat," "A Study in Brown," "I Can't Get Started," "The Prisoner's Song," "Mama, I Wanna Make Rhythm," "Black Bottom," "Russian Lullaby," "Azure," "The Wearin' of the Green," "Livery Stable Blues," "High Society," "Rockin' Rollers' Jubilee," "Sobbin' Blues," "Jelly Roll Blues," [the next group of five Bix Beiderbecke compositions are by Bunny Berigan and His Men, a group of nine men from the Orchestra, as is the sixth tune] "In a Mist," "Flashes," "Davenport Blues," "Candlelights," "In the Dark," "Walkin' the Dog;" "Blue Lou" and "The Blues" [Metronome All-Star Band]; "There'll Be Some Changes Made," "Little Gate's Special," "Peg O' My Heart," "Night Song," "Ain't She Sweet?"), French-issued RCA, c. 1980.

Time-Life Giants of Jazz series—Bunny Berigan (Includes "Them There Eyes" [with Hal Kemp]; "Everybody Loves My Baby" [with the Boswell Sisters]; "Me minus You" [with Connee

Boswell]; "Is That Religion?" [with Mildred Bailey]; "She Re-
minds Me of You" [with Paul Hamilton]; "Troubled" [with
Frankie Trumbauer]; "In a Little Spanish Town" [with Glenn
Miller]; "Solo Hop" [with Miller]; "Nothin' But the Blues" [with
Gene Gifford]; "Squareface" [with Gifford]; "Sometimes I'm
Happy" [with Benny Goodman]; "The Buzzard" [with Bud
Freeman]; "Tillie's Downtown Now" [with Freeman]; "Keep
Smilin' at Trouble" [with Freeman]; "Willow Tree" [with Mildred
Bailey]; "You Took Advantage of Me" [Bunny Berigan and His
Blue Boys]; "I'm Coming, Virginia" [Blue Boys]; "Blues" [Blue
Boys]; "Let Yourself Go" [Bunny Berigan and His Boys];
"Swing, Mr. Charlie"; "I Can't Get Started" [His Boys]; "Did
I Remember?" [with Billie Holiday]; "One, Two, Button Your
Shoe" [with Holiday]; * All remaining tunes are Bunny Berigan
and His Orchestra unless otherwise designated * "That Foolish
Feeling"; "Mr. Ghost Goes to Town" [with Tommy Dorsey];
"Blue Lou"; "Song of India" [with Tommy Dorsey]; "Marie"
[with Tommy Dorsey]; "Mahogany Hall Stomp," "I Can't Get
Started," "The Prisoner's Song," "Mama, I Wanna Make Rhythm,"
"Black Bottom," "The Wearin' of the Green," "I Cried for You,"
"Jelly Roll Blues," "Davenport Blues," "Blue Lou" [with the
Metronome All Star Band]), Time-Life, 1982.
The Complete Bunny Berigan, Volume 1 (includes all selections
by Bunny Berigan and His Orchestra: "You Can't Run Away
From Love Tonight," "'Cause My Baby Says It's So," "Care-
lessly," "All Dark People Are Are Light on Their Feet," "I'm
Happy, Darling, Dancing with You," "Swanee River," "All
God's Chillun Got Rhythm," "The Lady from Fifth Avenue,"
"Let's Have Another Cigarette," "Roses in December," "Moth-
er Goose," "Frankie and Johnny," "Mahogany Hall Stomp,"
"Let 'er Go," "Turn on That Red Hot Heat," "I Can't Get
Started," "The Prisoner's Song," "Why Talk About Love?,"
"Caravan," "A Study in Brown," "Sweet Varsity Sue," "Gee But
It's Great to Meet a Friend," "Ebb Tide," "Have You Ever Been
in Heaven?," "Mama, I Wanna Make Rhythm," "I'd Love to Play
A Love Scene," "I Want A New Romance," "Miles Apart"),
RCA, 1982.
Bunny Berigan 1931, (includes "I Can't Get Mississippi Off My
Mind," "I Apologize," "Beggin' for Love," and "Parkin' in the
Moonlight" [with the Dorsey Brothers Orchestra]; "In the Merry
Month of Maybe," "How the Time Can Fly," "At Your Com-
mand," "When Yuba Plays the Rhumba on the Tuba," "Bub-
bling Over with Love," "Now You're In My Arms," "Fiesta,"
"Have You Forgotten?," "Dancing with the Daffodils," and
"Love Is Like That" [probably with the Freddie Rich Orchestra];
"When the Moon Comes Over the Mountain" and "Neverthe-
less" [with Sam Lanin and His Orchestra], Shoestring, 1983.
Tommy Dorsey and His Orchestra, Featuring Bunny Berigan,
(includes "Losers, Weepers," "Easy Does It," "Boog It," "East
of the Sun," "Dark Eyes," "I'm Nobody's Baby," "Sweet Lor-
raine," "Symphony in Riffs"), Fanfare, c. 1985.
The Complete Bunny Berigan, Volume 2 (includes all selections
by Bunny Berigan and His Orchestra): "A Strange Loneliness,"
"In a Little Spanish Town," "Black Bottom," "Trees," "Russian
Lullaby," "Can't Help Lovin' Dat Man," "Piano Tuner Man,"
"Heigh-Ho," "A Serenade to the Stars," "Outside of Paradise,"

"Downstream," "Sophisticated Swing," "Lovelight in the Star-
light," "Rinkatinka Man," "An Old Straw Hat," "I Dance Alone,"
"Never Felt Better, Never Had Less," "I've Got a Guy," "Moon-
shine Over Kentucky," "Round the Old Deserted Farm," "Azure," "Somewhere with Somebody Else," "It's the Little Things
That Count," "Wacky Dust," "The Wearin' of the Green," "The
Pied Piper," "Tonight Will Live," "And So Forth"), RCA, 1986.

Sources

Books

Case, Brian, and Britt, Stan, *The Illustrated Encyclopedia of
Jazz,* Salamander Books Ltd., 1978.
Chilton, John, *Who's Who of Jazz,* Time-Life Records, 1978.
Chilton, John, and Sudhalter, Richard M., *Giants of Jazz: Bunny
Berigan,* Time-Life Records-Books, 1982.
Condon, Eddie, *We Called it Music,* Holt, 1947.
Feather, Leonard, *The New Edition of The Encyclopedia of Jazz,*
Bonanza Books, 1960.
Keepnews, Orrin, and Grauer, Bill Jr., *A Pictorial History of Jazz,*
Crown, 1955.
McCarthy, Albert, *Big Band Jazz,* G.P. Putnam's Sons, 1974.
Rust, Brian, *Jazz Records 1897-1942,* 5th Revised and Enlarged
Edition, Volumes 1 and 2, Storyville Publications, 1982.
Simon, George T., *The Big Bands,* Macmillian, 1967.
Wilson, Bob, *Beauty, Drive, and Freedom* (unpublished mono-
graph), c. 1958.

Periodicals

Collier's, January 20, 1956.
down beat, August, 1935; March 15, 1940; September 1, 1941;
July 1, 1942.
Metronome, July 1935; October, 1943.
New Yorker, November 8, 1982.
New York Times, June 3, 1942.
Philadelphia Bulletin-Enquirer, April 10, 1928.
Variety, February 12, 1936.

Other sources

Much of the material included in the Berigan entry comes from
research by contributing editor Robert Dupuis for his soon-to-be
published book, . . . *STARTED: The Unfinished Life of Bunny
Berigan* (Louisiana State University Press). Included in this research are personal interviews with Berigan's widow, Donna
Berigan Burmeister; his daughters, Patricia Slavin and Joyce
Berigan; his sister-in-law, Loretta Berigan; and musicians who
worked with Berigan in one capacity or another, including Joe

Bushkin, Jess Stacy, Jack Sperling, Joe Dixon, Joe Lipman, Gene Kutch, Johnny Blowers, Tom Morgan, George Quinty, and Clif Gomon. Some interview material has been loaned by Deborah Mickolas, Tom Cullen, Bozy White, and Norm Krusinski. The interview with Jack Teagarden was loaned by John Grams, from his program on radio station WTMJ, Milwaukee.

—Robert Dupuis

Leonard Bernstein

Composer, conductor, pianist

Leonard Bernstein is an immensely talented American conductor, composer, pianist, and educator who has made significant contributions to the realms of both classical and popular music through numerous concerts, compositions, recordings, television appearances, and classes. He is one of the best-known American composers and the first American-born conductor to regularly conduct European orchestras.

Born on August 25, 1918, in Lawrence, Massachusetts, Bernstein is the eldest of three children born to Samuel and Jennie Resnick Bernstein, Russian-Jewish immigrants. Though he was named Louis by his parents, at age sixteen Bernstein legally changed his name to Leonard to distinguish himself from other Louis Bernsteins in the family. Bernstein attended Boston's highly competitive Latin School and, despite his father's wish that he work for the family cosmetic business, studied piano, beginning at the rather late age of ten, with Helen Coates and later Heinrich Gebhard. In 1935 Bernstein enrolled at Harvard University, where he studied music with Edward Ballantine, Edward Brulingame Hill, A. Tillman Merritt, and Walter Piston, as well as philosophy, aesthetics, literature, and philology. After earning a B.A. in 1939, Bernstein studied with a number of renowned musicians at the Curtis Institute of Music in Philadelphia: Isabella Bengerova, Renee Longy, Randall Thompson, and Fritz Reiner. During the summers of 1940 and 1941 Bernstein studied conducting with the celebrated conductor Sergei Koussevitzky at the Berkshire Music Center at Tanglewood. Koussevitzky recognized Bernstein's talent and in 1942 appointed him his assistant.

At this time Bernstein worked for a music publisher, arranging popular songs, transcribing band pieces, and notating jazz improvizations, which were published under the pseudonym Lenny Amber. He ocassionally conducted Boston ensembles and became the assistant conductor under Arthur Rodzinski of the New York Philharmonic. On November 14, 1943, when Bruno Walter, who was scheduled to conduct the orchestra's nationally broadcast concert, suddenly became ill, Bernstein substituted for him with such success that his career was launched.

From 1944 to 1950 Bernstein served as guest conductor to seven major orchestras and replaced Leopold Stokowski as music director of the New York City Symphony Orchestra, a position Bernstein held from 1945 to 1948. During his tenure with the orchestra, Bernstein conducted primarily twentieth-century works by European and American composers and proved to be an effective proponent of American music, which was largely ignored until his intervention. Bernstein's compositions of this period include his *Symphony No. 1, "Jeremiah,"* which premiered in 1944 under his own

in Milan, Italy, when in 1953 he directed the celebrated soprano Maria Callas in Cherubini's *Medea*. After a year as co-director under Dimitri Mitropoulos, in 1958 Bernstein acceded to the directorship of the New York Philharmonic Orchestra. Bernstein adapted a thematic approach to organizing concert programs and premiered works by American composers. With the orchestra, he produced many recordings and toured widely, including the Near East, Japan, Alaska, and Canada. The orchestra attracted record crowds. Bernstein's *Symphony No. 3, "Kaddish,"* premiered in 1963, and the following year Bernstein took a sabbatical leave to experiment with composing using twelve-tone serial techniques. He did not find this popular technique to his liking and the product of this period, the *Chichester Pslams,* is a re-affirmation of his belief in tonality. At this time Bernstein also considered writing another musical, but was unable to settle on an appropriate project. To devote more time to composing, in 1969 Bernstein

> *Approaching music intellectually, but with passion, Bernstein believes that as a conductor, he must intimately understand the intent of the composer and the culture in which he or she lived in order to "recompose" the work on stage.*

direction and the ballet *Fancy Free,* which later became the basis for the critically acclaimed Broadway musical "On the Town." Bernstein was also active as a pianist, and in 1949 performed the solo part in his own *Symphony No. 2, "The Age of Anxiety."*

In 1951 Bernstein married his longtime friend, Chilean actress Felicia Montealegre Cohn. That same year Koussevitzy died, and Bernstein replaced him as director of the orchestra and conducting departments at the Berkshire Music Center. He was also appointed professor of music at Brandeis University, a position he held until 1955. While at Brandeis and in the late 1950s Bernstein continued to compose works for the stage, including the one-act opera *Trouble in Tahiti,* the Broadway musical "Wonderful Town," the comic operetta *Candide,* and the monumentally sucessful Broadway musical "West Side Story." He also composed the film score for *On the Waterfront,* starring Marlon Brando.

In the 1950s and 1960s, Bernstein achieved international stature as a conductor. He was the first American to conduct at the famous opera venue Teatro alla Scala,

resigned as the permanent conductor, though he was given the permanent title "laureate conductor" and thus allowed to conduct ocassionally.

In the 1970s and 1980s, Bernstein often guest-conducted the Vienna Philharmonic and the Israel Philharmonic Orchestra, with which he has made recordings and television appearances. His *Mass,* a work commissioned by the John F. Kennedy family for the opening of the Kennedy Center for the Performing Arts, was premiered in 1971, and his ballet based on a classic Jewish legend, *The Dybbuk,* was first performed in 1974 with choreography by Jerome Robbins, who had choreographed *West Side Story*. After many months of work on a musical about life in the White House, "1600 Pennsylvania Avenue," which was lambasted by critics, Bernstein gave up composing musicals. In 1977 tragedy struck when his wife Felicia died from cancer.

In 1980 Bernstein began the challenging project of

concert performances, and television and record recordings of Richard Wagner's opera *Tristan and Isolde*. After a busy concert season in 1982, Bernstein focused his attention on the opera *A Quiet Place (Tahiti II)*, which premiered in 1983. After visiting Europe again in late 1983 for concerts and recordings, Bernstein opened a concert tour with the Vienna Philharmonic Orchestra and conducted in a series of guest appearances. He then went to Milan, where a revised version of *A Quiet Place* became the first American opera to be performed at Teatro alla Scala. Bernstein continued to revise this work for some time afterward, and for the fiftieth anniversary of the Israel Philharmonic he composed *Jubilee Games*.

Approaching music intellectually, but with passion, Bernstein believes that as a conductor, he must intimately understand the intent of the composer and the culture in which he or she lived in order to "recompose" the work on stage. Sometimes his interpretations have been considered self-indulgent, and commentators have long criticized what they consider to be overly exuberant conducting gestures, but by and large he is acclaimed wherever he appears. Bernstein has become especially well known for his interpretations of the works of Mahler and Wagner, which include recordings of the complete cycle of Mahler symphonies. Since he first took to the podium, Bernstein has made over four hundred recordings, for which he has received many Grammy nominations and awards.

Bernstein has also been the recipient of numerous awards for his work as a composer and educator. In the 1970s and 1980s music festivals were held in his honor, and the arrival of his seventieth birthday was feted with numerous performances of his works. Bernstein calls himself both a compulsive composer and educator. In 1954 he produced a series of television lectures about music that were published a year later as *The Joy of Music*. Subsequent television shows were regularly shown on network television, among them fifty-two talks for young listeners (published as *Leonard Bernstein's Young People's Concerts for Reading and Listening*) and a series of Harvard lectures (published as *The Unanswered Question: Six Talks at Harvard*). Bernstein has published a number of other informative books and regularly conducts workshops at Tangelwood for promising conducting students.

Though Bernstein refuses to be associated with any single orchestra in his later years, he has spent more time conducting than composing—yet composing is never far from his mind. His 1988 composition, *Arias and Barcarolles*, is only one of several songs cycles he plans to compose, which he has hinted may evolve into an opera. At a press conference a week before his seventieth birthday, Bernstein expressed his thankfulness for the opportunities he has enjoyed throughout his career and his desire for more years during which to use the talents with which he has been so abundantly blessed.

Compositions

Pslam 149 (for voice and piano), 1935.
Music for the Dance, No. 1, No. 2, 1938.
Scenes from the City of Sin (eight minitures for piano, four hands), 1939.
The Peace (music for the play by Aristophanes), 1940.
Symphony No. 1, "Jeremiah," 1942.
Seven Anniversaries (piano solo), 1943.
Fancy Free (ballet), 1944.
On the Town (musical comedy), 1944.
Hashkivenu (for cantor [tenor], four-part choir and organ), 1945.
Afterthought (for voice and piano), 1945.
Facsimile (ballet), 1946.
Choreographic Essay for Orchestra, 1946.
La Bonne Cuisine (four "recipes" for voice and piano), 1947.
Ssimchu na (Hebrew folk song for four-part choir and piano or orchestra), 1947.
Re'ena (Hebrew folksong for choir and orchestra), 1947.
Rondo for Lifey (for trumpet and piano), 1948.
Elegy for Mippy I (for horn and piano), 1948.
Elegy for Mippy II (trombone solo), 1948.
Waltz for Mippy III (for tuba and piano), 1948.
Fanfare for Bima (for trumpet, horn, trombone, and tuba), 1948.
Symphony No. 2, "The Age of Axniety" (symphony for piano and orchestra), 1949.
Prelude, Fugue and Riffs (for solo clarinet and jazz ensemble), 1949.
Peter Pan (stage music, lyrics by Bernstein), 1950.
Yigdal (Hebrew liturgical melody for choir and piano), 1950.
Trouble in Tahiti (opera in one act), 1950.
Five Anniversaries (piano solo), 1951.
Silhouette: Galilee (for voice and piano), 1951.
Wonderful Town (musical comedy), 1953.
Serenade (after Plato's *Symposium;* for violin solo, string orchestra, harp and percussion), 1954.
On the Waterfront (music for the film), 1954.
On the Waterfront (symphonic suite from the music for the film), 1955.
Salome (music for Oscar Wilde's dream, for chamber orchestra and vocal solo), 1955.
Candide (comic operetta), 1956.
West Side Story (musical), 1957.
The First Born (two pieces for voice and percussion for the drama by Christopher Fry), 1958.
West Side Story (symphonic dances for orchestra), 1960.
Symphony No. 3, "Kaddish" (symphony for orchestra, mixed choir, boys' choir, speaker and soprano solo), 1963.

Chichester Psalms (for choir, boy's solo, and orchestra), 1965.

Shivaree (for double brass ensemble and percussion), 1969.

Mass: Theater Piece for Singers, Players and Dancers, 1971.

Dybbuk (ballet music and two orchestral suites), 1974.

By Bernstein (a revue with songs written for earlier shows but not used in them), 1975.

1600 Pennsylvania Avenue: A Musical about the Problems of Housekeeping, 1976.

Songfest (a cycle of American poems for six singers and orchestra), 1977.

Slava! (overture for orchestra or symphonic band), 1977.

Divertimento (for orchestra), 1980.

A Musical Toast (for orchestra), 1980.

Touches (piano solo), 1981.

Halil (Nocturno for solo flute, string orchestra and percussion), 1981.

A Quiet Place (opera in four scenes), 1983.

A Quiet Place (a new version with *Trouble in Tahiti* as part of Act II), 1984.

Jubilee Games (two movements for orchestra), 1986.

Prayer (for baritone and small orchestra), 1986.

My Twelve-Tone Melody, 1988.

Arias and Barcarolles (piano four hands and singers), 1988.

Selected discography

Original compositions

Candide, Columbia.
Chichester Psalms, Columbia.
Divertimento, DG.
The Dybbuk (full ballet), Columbia.
Fancy Free, Columbia.
Mass, Columbia.
On the Town, Columbia.

On the Waterfront (film score), Decca.
A Quiet Place, DG.
Songfest, DG.
Symphonic Dances from West Side Story, Columbia.
Symphonic Suite from On the Waterfront, Columbia.
Symphony No. 1, "Jeremiah," DG.
Symphony No. 2, "The Age of Anxiety," DG.
Symphony No. 3, "Kaddish," Columbia.
Trouble in Tahiti, Columbia.
West Side Story (complete), DG.
Wonderful Town, Columbia.

Sources

Books

Gottlieb, Jack, *Leonard Bernstein: A Complete Catalogue of His Works,* Amberson Enterprises, 1978.

Gradenwitz, Peter, *Leonard Bernstein: The Infinite Variety of a Musician,* Oswald Wolff Books, 1987.

Gruen, John, and Ken Hyman (photographer), *The Private World of Leonard Bernstein,* Viking Press, 1968.

Peyser, Joan, *Bernstein: A Biography,* Beech Tree Books, 1987.

Periodicals

Berkshire Eagle, August 18, 1988; August 21, 1988.
Boston Globe, August 18, 1988.
Hackensack Record, September 13, 1987.
Los Angeles Herald Examiner, August 4, 1986; January 22, 1987.
Miami Herald, June 26, 1988.
Newark Star-Ledger, January 22, 1989.
Pittsburgh Press, September 12, 1984.

—*Jeanne M. Lesinski*

Ruben Blades

Singer, songwriter

R uben Blades is probably the best-selling performer of Latin salsa music in recent years. Though he most often sings in Spanish and is extremely popular with Latin Americans, he has gone beyond salsa's usual, primarily Hispanic audience to reach listeners from all cultural and ethnic backgrounds. Critics, and Blades himself, attribute his enormous success to the quality of his lyrics. As Pete Hamill phrased it in *New York* magazine, "Blades does not write jingles for teenagers, or moony ballads of self-pity and abandonment; his songs are about people, one at a time, and their universal problems; they're about exile, too, and brutality and the loss of political innocence; they're about the struggle to be decent."

At the same time, the stories Blades tells in his songs are backed with a salsa beat, designed for dancing. Blades feels that adding content to the salsa form answers a deep need in the Hispanic community. He explained to Hamill: "The radio and the songs were becoming companions of so many people. And sporadically, when a song would come on and *speak,* and talk about something more than *mira-mira*-let's-dance-baby-let's-dance, it struck a chord, a very sensitive spot in the audience." With his songs, and with his straightforward, unflashy image, he wishes to fight stereotypes generally associated with Hispanic performers—not only among the English-speaking members of his audiences, but among Hispanics themselves.

Blades was born in Panama City, Panama, on July 16, 1948. His father was a police officer, his mother sang and acted in radio soap operas; but he was most deeply influenced by his paternal grandmother, Emma. "Emma was some woman," Blades recounted for Hamill. "She had a character and a half. . . . She practiced yoga, she was a Rosicrucian, she was into spiritualism, she levitated, she was a vegetarian when nobody had even thought about it." His grandmother used to take him to the theater to watch American films, and, he told Eric Levin of *People,* she "instilled in me the desire for justice and truth."

During Blades's childhood and adolescence, "justice and truth" seemed almost synonymous with things American. He remembers being captivated by early American rock and roll along with many of his friends. "We didn't understand the words, but there was some kind of *thing* in there. Something we could intuitively associate—I guess—with what we were: kids," he explained to Hamill. Then, as Hamill reported, "Blades and his friends began singing doo-wop together, searching out buildings in Panama City that had echoes under the stairs, school bathrooms, anyplace that might help them sound like the new songs they were

Full name, Ruben Blades, Jr.; born July 16, 1948, in Panama City, Panama (first came to the U.S. in 1969); son of Ruben (a police officer) and Anoland (a radio actress and singer/pianist) Blades; married, wife's name, Lisa. *Education:* Law degree, University of Panama, 1974; Master of Law, Harvard University, 1985.

Performed in various Latin groups in New York City and Panama beginning in 1969; solo performer and recording artist, 1982—. Appeared in films, including *Crossover Dreams, The Last Fight,* and *Waiting for Salazar.* Wrote scores for films, including *When the Mountains Tremble* and *Caminos Verde,* and a play, *The Balcony.* Author of political columns for Panamanian newspapers.

Awards: Named Best Ethnic/International Act and Best Latin Act by the *New York Post,* 1986.

Addresses: *Record company*—Elektra, 962 N. La Cienega, Los Angeles, Calif. 90069.

hearing on the radio." They sang in English, and Blades also sang in English when he joined his brother's band in 1963. In this latter experience he sang Frank Sinatra standards like "Strangers in the Night." But shortly afterwards Blades stopped singing in English, turning away from his interest in American music in shock and disgust, when Americans' refusal to fly the Panamanian flag alongside their own over a Canal Zone high school (the law designated that both flags be flown) sparked a riot that killed twenty-one and wounded almost five hundred Panamanians. The incident affected him so profoundly, Blades believes, because, as he told Hamill, "until then the North Americans were always the good guys. We knew that from the movies, didn't we? They were the guys we'd seen kicking the Nazis, beating the bad guys. And all of a sudden, you had them on the other side, and they were shooting at you! It was a big disappointment." So he immersed himself in Latin music instead, listening to the creations of Joe Cuba, Ismael Rivera, and the Cortijo y Su Combo.

While Blades was serious about his musical ambitions, playing with various Latin bands during the late 1960s, he was also serious about his academic career. He entered the University of Panama to work on a law degree, and when offered a chance to replace one of the members of the Joe Cuba band, refused it to remain in school. Ironically, the following year the Panamanian military closed the university due to student unrest, and Blades went to New York City to work on his music. He cut an album with Pete Rodriguez, *De Panama a Nueva York,* for which he wrote all but one of the songs. Yet when the University of Panama was reopened, Blades returned to finish his degree.

Afterwards, Blades served for a short time as an attorney for the Bank of Panama and worked to rehabilitate prisoners, but in 1974 he returned to New York to further his musical career. Though he started off in the mailroom of New York's Fania Records, a company that specializes in Latin-American music, he quickly graduated to singing salsa with the Ray Barretto band. Then, in 1976, Blades became a songwriter and vocalist for the Willie Colon Combo, with whom he began to record the thoughtful songs that have made him famous. *Metiendo Mano,* his first effort with the Combo, featured one of Blades's most popular songs, "Pablo Pueblo," which sympathetically portrays a tired working man. *Siembra,* released in 1977, was distinguished by "Pedro Navaja," a Spanish adaptation of "Mack the Knife." Blades stirred up controversy in 1980 with the song

> *"Blades does not write jingles for teenagers, or moony ballads of self-pity and abandonment; his songs are about people . . . about the struggle to be decent."*

"Tiburon" (Spanish for "shark"), which depicted interventionists as endlessly hungry sharks. The song was banned by Miami's most popular Latin-music radio station, and Blades was branded a Communist. He told Fred Bouchard in *down beat,* however, that the song was neutral: "My contra-intervention themes are not directed exclusively to the U.S. policy in Latin America, but include the Russians in Afghanistan and the British in Argentina."

In 1982 Blades left the Colon Combo to strike out on his own with *Maestra Vida,* an album "obviously inspired," according to Hamill, by the stories of Colombian author Gabriel García Márquez. Soon afterwards, in an attempt to get his musical message to a wider audience, he signed with the mainstream record company Elektra. Blades's first release for them was the immensely popular *Buscando America,* which not only drew rave reviews from critics but sold more than three hundred thousand copies—"remarkable for a Latin record," testified Bill Barol in *Newsweek. Buscando* featured more of Blades's story songs, particularly "El Padre Antonio y el Monanguillo

Andres," about an outspoken pacifist priest gunned down in his church with one of his altar boys, and "GDBD," which describes a secret policeman who has been assigned to make political arrests preparing for his day's work. In 1985 Blades released *Escenas,* which included a duet with popular singing star Linda Ronstadt, "Silencios." Though Blades has been including printouts with English translations of his songs since *Buscando,* he did not record in English until his 1988 album *Nothing But the Truth.*

But Blades is not merely a singer-songwriter. He drew praise from film critics in 1985 for his starring performance in *Crossover Dreams,* an independent motion picture about a Latin singer whose attempts to go mainstream alienate his family and friends, leaving him nothing to return to when his efforts fail. He has also acted in the film *Waiting for Salazar,* and provided musical scores for the documentaries *When the Mountains Tremble* and *Caminos Verdes.* Blades's goals are not limited to the entertainment fields, either. He writes political columns for a Panamanian newspaper and intends to return to Panama in the future and run for political office, perhaps even president. He took time off from the music business in 1985 to obtain a Master of Law degree from Harvard University, in part so that no one can say he is just an entertainer with no background for politics.

Selected discography

With the Willie Colon Combo; on Fania Records

Metiendo Mano (includes "Pablo Pueblo"), 1976.
Siembra (includes "Pedro Navaja"), 1977.
Canciones del Solar de los Aburridos, 1982.

Solo LPs

Maestra Vida, Fania, c. 1982.
Buscando America (includes "El Padre Antonio y el Monanguillo Andres," "Desapariciones," "GDBD," "Decisiones," and "Todos Vuelven"), Elektra, 1984.
Escenas (includes "Silencios," "La Sorpresa," "Tierra Dura," "Cuentas del Alma," "Cancion del Final del Mundo," and "Muevete"), Elektra, 1985.
Nothing But the Truth, Elektra, 1988.

Also recorded, with Pete Rodriguez, *De Panama a Nueva York,* c. 1969.

Sources

down beat, January, 1986.
Newsweek, September 9, 1985.
New York, August 19, 1985.
People, August 13, 1984.
Time, July 11, 1988.

—*Elizabeth Thomas*

Laura Branigan

Singer

Laura Branigan burst upon the popular-music scene in 1982 with her hit single "Gloria." Though "Gloria," from the album *Branigan,* took months to climb to the upper regions of the pop charts, its rise was steady. The song began to gain popularity in the dance clubs Branigan toured in her efforts to promote it, and ended up, in the words of a *Harper's Bazaar* critic, "the year's summer beach anthem." Branigan received a Grammy nomination for Best Pop Vocal Performance, and has since confirmed her star status with hits like "Solitaire," "Self-Control," and "Shattered Glass."

Branigan grew up in Brewster, New York, a suburb of New York City. Though singing seemed to run in her family—her grandmother had studied opera in Ireland, and both her parents had good voices and led the family in singing at the dinner table—Branigan had no ambitions to pursue a vocalist's career in her youth. In high school she was extremely shy; she did, however, enjoy singing harmony with friends and performing in her church choir. To help Branigan overcome her shyness, one of her teachers persuaded her to try out for the school musical in her senior year. Branigan did, won the lead in *Pajama Game,* and discovered her calling. She reminisced for a *Seventeen* interviewer: "It was amazing. Once I was up there, I felt a tremendous confidence. I realized this was my way of expressing myself—and that was it."

After graduating from high school in 1975, Branigan enrolled at the American Academy of Dramatic Arts in New York City to prepare for her new vocation. At first she commuted from her parents' home, but then she moved to Manhattan and worked as a waitress to pay her rent and tuition. Branigan found in waitressing a form of preparation for performing that wasn't available in her classes. "In dealing with people all the time," she told *Seventeen,* "I learned how to make them comfortable, and that helped me a lot to overcome my shyness. And I learned how to ignore hecklers."

Meanwhile, Branigan was also trying to break into the music business. After landing a job as a backup singer for Canadian folk artist Leonard Cohen and touring Europe with him, she decided to become a soloist. Knowing that her chances would be better if she had a good manager, she sought one. Sid Bernstein, who had managed talents such as the Rascals and the Bay City Rollers and had promoted the Beatles' first U.S. appearance, listened to Branigan sing in 1977 and agreed to help her become a star. According to Sarah Crichton in *Harper's,* Bernstein started Branigan slowly, first featuring her in concerts held in his office for his friends, and gradually inviting record producers to these informal gatherings. At first, this tactic was unsuccessful. Branigan recalled in *Seventeen:* "Everyone said, 'Well, you don't really sound like anyone else.' That meant that [I] really didn't fit in."

Finally, in 1979, Branigan auditioned for Ahmet Ertegun, the chairman of Atlantic Records, and he signed her. An initial album session produced mixed results—Atlantic was unsure what style best suited their new talent. Eventually the company hired Jack White, a German producer famous for his efforts in what Crichton labels the "Euro-pop approach." White selected the songs for what would become Branigan's debut album, including "Gloria," which had been a hit in Italy a few years previous. Before the single was released, White introduced Branigan to manager Susan Joseph. After talking to her, the singer became convinced that Joseph could represent her interests much better than Bernstein. Branigan switched managers, but while she

did indeed become a star under Joseph's guidance, she also became the object of a $15 million breach-of-contract lawsuit by Bernstein.

Despite this controversy, what *Seventeen* designated as Branigan's "smoky vibrato" voice struck a chord with pop audiences. The success of "Gloria" was followed in 1983 by another European-style hit, "Solitaire," originally done by another artist in France, and in 1984 Branigan had a smash with the title track from her third album, *Self-Control.* Though she has made her reputation by belting out danceable numbers, Branigan has also had success with ballads such as 1987's "Power of Love." She has modeled herself most after French torch singer Edith Piaf, and revealed her goal as a singer to *Harper's Bazaar:* "I want to touch people's hearts, to get right down to their souls."

Selected discography

Branigan (includes "Gloria"), Atlantic, 1982.
Branigan II (includes "Solitaire"), Atlantic, 1983.
Self-Control (includes "Self-Control"), Atlantic, 1984.
Touch (includes "Power of Love" and "Shattered Glass"), Atlantic, 1987.

Sources

Harper's, July, 1983.
Harper's Bazaar, December, 1983.
People, July 18, 1983.
Seventeen, April, 1984.

—*Elizabeth Thomas*

James Brown

Singer and songwriter

In *The Rolling Stone Illustrated History of Rock & Roll*, critic Robert Palmer credits James Brown with taking rhythm and blues and " . . . pulling it away from show business sophistication and back into the orbit of the black churches from which it ultimately derived." Popularly known as "The Godfather of Soul," Brown was born into extreme poverty in 1933 in Georgia. While growing up, he worked every odd job he could to earn an extra buck, from picking cotton and shining shoes to boxing and semi-pro baseball, striving to become something respectable.

Brown's ambitions, however, led him astray and into an 8- to 16-year stint at the Alto Reform School (Toccoa, Georgia) in 1949 for armed robbery. After three and a half years, Brown found himself and, with the help of his friend Bobby Byrd, he was paroled. Once out, Brown joined Byrd's singing group, the Gospel Starlighters, which soon became the Flames and switched to rhythm and blues. Federal Records executive Ralph Bass found the group in Macon, Georgia, and brought them north to sign with his label in January of 1956. Brown soon began to assume control and renamed the band James Brown and the Famous Flames (Don Terry, Syd Keels, Nash Knox, Floyd Scott and Byrd). They released their first single that same year, "Please, Please, Please." Bass told Arnold Shaw, "When Syd Nathan (of the King label, a subsidiary of Federal) heard 'Please, Please, Please,' he thought it was a piece of [crap]. He said that I was out of my mind to bring Brown from Macon to Cincinnati—and pay his fare. And we put out that first record on Federal, not King. But then after 'Please' began to sell and made the charts—that was in 1956—Syd sang a different tune . . . Brown was way ahead of his time. He wasn't really singing R & B. He was singing gospel to an R & B combo with a real heavy feeling . . . He wasn't singing or playing music—he was transmitting feeling, pure feeling."

It would take another two years and ten more singles for Brown to climb the charts again. "Try Me" became a huge hit and helped to usher in the age of soul music. Prior to this, the band had been imitating other groups like the Midnighters, the Drifters, and the Five Royals. Realizing that their own material was just as good, Brown asked Nathan if he could record with his own touring band (the J.B.s), but was denied. So, under the name of Nat Kendrick and the Swans, they released 1960's instrumental hit "(Do the) Mashed Potato" on another label. Former tour manager Alan Leeds told *Rolling Stone* that Brown would "make them suffer until they needed a James Brown record so badly that they'd take whatever he gave them." King relented and soon Brown was back with the label and recording with his own band.

For the Record. . .

Born June 17, 1928 (some sources cite May 3, 1928; others cite May 3, 1933) in Pulaski, Tenn. (some sources cite Augusta, Ga.); mother's name, Susie; married to Adrienne "Alfie" Rodriguez (a hair stylist and makeup artist).

Incarcerated in Alto Reform School, Toccoa, Ga., 1949-52; was a boxer and a semi-pro baseball player, c. 1953-55; lead singer in gospel group the Gospel Starlighters, c. 1955, group changed name to Famous Flames and format to rhythm and blues, 1956, became James Brown and the Famous Flames, c. 1956. Appeared in motion picture "Ski Party," 1965. Formerly owned and was president of J.B. Broadcasting, Ltd., James Brown Network, James Brown Productions, and seventeen publishing companies. Incarcerated in State Park Correctional Center, Columbia, S.C., 1988—.

Awards: Winner of Grammy Award for best rhythm and blues recording, 1965, for "Papa's Got a Brand New Bag," and for best male rhythm and blues performance, 1986, for "Living in America"; inducted into Rock and Roll Hall of Fame, 1986.

Addresses: *Home*—Beech Island, S.C. *Current residence*—State Park Correctional Center, 7901 Farrow Rd., Columbia, S.C. 29203.

The Famous Flames honed their live shows to perfection by playing one-night stands throughout the South. The word took years to spread, but by 1963 *James Brown Show Live at the Apollo* was number 2 on *Billboard*'s album charts. The James Brown Revue had become the tightest, most spectacular rhythm and blues act ever. The musicians were fined by Brown for anything less than razor-sharp precision while "Mr. Dynamite" himself virtually defined the standard for showmanship.

Future performers like Mick Jagger, Otis Redding, Michael Jackson, Prince, Wilson Pickett, and Terrence Trent D'Arby would all "borrow" extensively from Brown's repetoire, but no one could equal his acrobatics and sheer energy. His "Please" finale found him on his knees, seemingly spent, while the Flames would drape a cape over his shoulders and help to lead him offstage. But he would only get a few feet before the cape was hurled off and he fell back to the floor, gripping the microphone and pleading once again. After a few rounds of this, most audiences were literally too drained to expect any more.

By 1964 though, Brown was fed up with King's weak promotional abilities and decided to release a batch of tunes on the more substantial Mercury label, Smash. "Out of Sight" was an immediate hit and Brown's popularity soared as English groups began to cover his tunes and style. And, after a year-long court fight with King, Brown won the right to control almost every aspect of his career. In 1965 he recorded "Papa's Got a Brand New Bag," probably the epitome of Brown's sound, influential not only during the '60s but the '70s as well: shucking rhythm guitars, choppy bass lines, one-chord vamps and a horn section that blasted like a roll of fire-crackers. Solos were nearly out of the question; rhythm was the key.

By 1971 Brown was managing his own career and even had his own record company. His insistence on control had both positive and negative aspects though. Brown could craft a song down to the most minute detail by actually singing the way he wanted parts to be played to each musician (and at one point the band totaled 30 members!). Sometimes he took credit for ideas he did not originate but made into his own, which has caused resentment among members like Byrd, who co-wrote many of the hits. Nevertheless, as Brown's associate Bob Patton told *Rolling Stone*, "If you took James away, the band could play the tunes, but they didn't have the spark. He made the engine run. Damn near burn it out sometimes."

During the racially-tense period of the 1960s, Brown became somewhat of a spokesman for blacks. He preached through songs like "Say It Loud—I'm Black and I'm Proud," "Don't Be a Dropout," and "I Don't Want Nobody to Give Me Nothin." He even received a personal thanks from President Lyndon Johnson for calming rioters down with a television appearance. His social position was elevated also by his astute business dealings, which included ownership of fast-food franchises, radio stations, a booking agency, publishing companies, and a Lear jet. He became, according to *The Illustrated Encyclopedia of Rock*, "the first and most potent symbol of black America."

Calling himself the Minister of New Super Heavy Funk, Brown helped create the funk music movement, spawning artists like Sly and the Family Stone, Earth, Wind & Fire, and Parliment Funkadelic. Brown's own style was too raw though to be lumped in with the techno-slick groups of the 1970s. And, when disco appeared later on, Brown "was unable to lighten up his groove enough to get disco's sense of propulsion," wrote Tom Smucker in *The Rolling Stone Illustrated History of Rock & Roll*, but the influence he had is still very obvious. Even rap music relies heavily on Brown's recordings for its samplings, and, as Brown told *Rolling Stone*'s Michael Goldberg, "The music out there is only as good as my last record." Indeed, other artists need pretty good aim to shoot as well as Brown. Robert Christgau described the *Revolution of the Mind* LP as being "so hot that anybody but JB will have trouble dancing to it."

With over 114 charted singles ("I Want You So Bad," "I'll Go Crazy," "I Got You (I Feel Good)," "It's a Man's Man's Man's World," "Cold Sweat," "The Popcorn," and "Sex Machine" are just a few) to his credit and one of the best live shows (still), Brown has earned the title of "The Hardest Working Man in Show Business." He told *Rock 100,* "I have no personal life at all. I spend all my time keeping JB together." Though he never really left the music scene, Brown was back in the spotlight with his first Top Ten pop song in 18 years with 1986's "Living in America." And that same year he was also inducted into the Rock and Roll Hall of Fame.

"If you took James away, the band could play the tunes, but they didn't have the spark. He made the engine run. Damn near burn it out sometimes."

But Brown's personal life has received just as much attention. He reportedly owes the U.S. government $9 million in taxes and he has been alleged to beat up his wife Adrienne (she called it a publicity stunt in *Rolling Stone:* "We sold newspapers.") But on September 24, 1988, Brown entered an insurance seminar in Augusta, Georgia, with a shotgun, which resulted in a police chase and many bullet holes in his car. The next day he was again arrested, and subsequently convicted of driving under the influence of the drug PCP. With good behavior, Brown could end his six-year term in prison by 1991. "I'll tell you, it's like an omen," he told *Rolling Stone.* "As a kid in that prison, I found myself. An omen in my life. The same place I'm at right now. That was the beginning of my life, in 1950. This is the beginning of my life again. An omen."

Selected discography

Sex Machine, King, 1970.
Super Bad, King, 1970.
Sho Is Funky Down Here, King, 1971.
Hot Pants, Polydor, 1971.
Revolution of the Mind, Polydor, 1971.
Soul Classics, Polydor, 1972.
There It Is, Polydor, 1972.
Get on the Good Foot, Polydor, 1972.
Black Caesar, Polydor, 1973.
Slaughter's Big Rip-Off, Polydor, 1973.
Soul Classics Volume II, Polydor, 1973.
The Payback, Polydor, 1973.
Hell, Polydor, 1974.
Reality, Polydor, 1974.
Sex Machine Today, Polydor, 1975.
Everybody's Doin' the Hustle and Dead on the Double Bump, Polydor, 1975.
Hot, Polydor, 1975.
Get Up Offa That Thing, Polydor, 1976.
Bodyheat, Polydor, 1976.
Mutha's Nature, Polydor, 1977.
Jam/1980's, Polydor, 1978.
Take a Look at Those Cakes, Polydor, 1978.
The Original Disco Man, Polydor, 1979.
Gravity, CBS, 1986.
I'm Real, CBS, 1988.

Sources

Books

Christgau, Robert, *Christgau's Record Guide,* Ticknor & Fields, 1981.
Dalton, David, and Lenny Kaye, *Rock 100,* Grosset & Dunlap, 1977.
The Illustrated Encyclopedia of Rock, compiled by Nick Logan and Bob Woffinden, Harmony Books, 1976.
The Rolling Stone Illustrated History of Rock and Roll, edited by Jim Miller, Random House/Rolling Stone Press, 1976.
Shaw, Arnold, *Honkers and Shouters,* Macmillan, 1978.

Periodicals

Rolling Stone, April 6, 1989.

—Calen D. Stone

Glen Campbell

Singer, guitarist

Singer-instrumentalist Glen Campbell became country music's most popular performer in the years when rock and pop styles threatened to steal Nashville's audience permanently. From 1967 until 1972, the well-groomed Campbell turned out a series of winsome country hits such as "Gentle on My Mind," "By the Time I Get to Phoenix," and "Wichita Lineman," and starred in his own network television show. Throughout his career—but especially in the late 1960s—Campbell has projected a clean-cut, All-American persona that has stood in sharp contrast to the prevalent "outlaw" image in country and rock. Some critics feel that this middle-of-the-road style has provided Campbell with a steady audience, those listeners dissatisfied with protest songs and wild instrumentation. *TV Guide* contributor Cleveland Amory summed up Campbell's appeal in 1969 when he called the performer "a big, blond, . . . farmboy-charmboy type," a handsome but honorable idol for women. Campbell himself has never fought that characterization. He told *Time* magazine that his approach has always been "simplicity." He added: "If I can just make a forty-year-old housewife put down her dish towel and say 'Oh!'—why then, man, I've got it made."

The seventh son of a seventh son, Glen Travis Campbell was born near the tiny town of Delight, Arkansas, in 1936. His large family (eventually twelve children in all) suffered severe poverty but managed nevertheless to enjoy singing and playing music together. Young Glen picked cotton in the fields beside his brothers and father "for $1.25 a hundred pounds," he told *Newsweek*. He received his first guitar, from the Sears catalogue mail order, when he was only four. Surrounded by musical uncles and siblings, he soon learned to play well enough to land occasional professional work. By six he was appearing on local radio stations, and when he entered his teens and his family relocated to Houston, he expanded to nightclub engagements. Campbell left high school in the tenth grade, telling *Newsweek:* "I woke up in school one day and saw that they weren't teaching me how to play and sing, so I quit." At twenty he joined his uncle Dick Bill's band, the Sandia Mountain Boys, then working in Albuquerque, New Mexico. "It was a good training ground," Campbell told the *New York Post,* "because we played everything from 'Liza' to 'Sundown' to 'Tumblin' Tumbleweed' and gospel songs." The Sandia Mountain Boys were a modest local success, performing five days per week on the radio and once weekly on television, in addition to their live shows.

Campbell left his uncle's band in 1958, largely because he felt he was singled out for undue persecution. Forming his own group, Glen Campbell and the Western Wranglers, he continued to perform mainly in the

Full name, Glen Travis Campbell; born April 22, 1936 (some sources say 1938), in Delight, Ark.; son of John Wesley (a farmer) and Carrie Dell (a homemaker; maiden name Stone) Campbell; married Diane Kirk, 1954 (divorced, 1958); married Billie Jean Nunley, September 20, 1959 (divorced, 1976); married Sarah Barg Davis, 1977 (divorced, 1980); married Kimberly Woollen, 1982; children: (first marriage) Debby, (second marriage) Kelli, Travis, Kane, (third marriage) Dillon, (fourth marriage) Cal, Shannon, Ashly. *Education:* Attended schools in Arkansas and New Mexico.

Country-western and pop singer and instrumentalist, 1953—. Member of Sandia Mountain Boys (Albuquerque, New Mex.), 1956-58; member of Glen Campbell and the Western Wranglers, 1958-60; studio instrumentalist, 1960-67, recorded with Frank Sinatra, Nat King Cole, Dean Martin, Elvis Presley, the Beach Boys, the Mamas and the Papas, among others.

Solo performer of country-western vocals and instrumentals, 1967—, recorded first solo vocal album, *Gentle on My Mind,* 1967. Recorded with Capitol Records, 1967-83, Atlantic Records, 1983—. Host of network television shows, including "Shindig," 1964, "The Summer Smothers Brothers Show," 1968, "The Glen Campbell Good Time Hour," 1969-71, and "Glen Campbell Music Show," 1981. Star of films "True Grit," 1969, and "Norwood," 1970. Co-sponsor of Glen Campbell-Los Angeles Open Golf Tournament.

Awards: Grammy Awards for best country and western male vocalist and best contemporary male vocalist, both 1967, both for "Gentle on My Mind"; Entertainer of the Year Award from Country Music Association and Artist of the Year Award from Music Operators of America, both 1967; Grammy Awards for album of the year, best male vocalist, and best contemporary male vocalist, all 1968, all for *By the Time I Get to Pheonix;* TV Personality of the Year citation and Entertainer of the Year Award, both from Great Britain Country Music Association, both 1969; recipient of eleven gold albums.

Addresses: *Agent*—Triad Artists, Ltd., 10100 Santa Monica Blvd., 16th Floor, Los Angeles, Calif. 90067.

Albuquerque area until 1960. Then, with his second wife, he struck out for Hollywood, hoping to become a star. His first years in Hollywood were frustrating ones, during which he found few paying gigs. Eventually, however, he earned a reputation as a talented studio musician and began doing background guitar for a wide variety of recordings. At one time or another, Campbell played behind Elvis Presley, Frank Sinatra, Nat King Cole, the Mamas and the Papas, and Dean Martin, to name only a few. In 1965 he had done so much studio work with the Beach Boys that he actually went on tour with them, substituting for the ailing Brian Wilson. Campbell has estimated that he was earning about $100,000 per year for background work in the mid-1960s, but he still wanted stardom on his own terms. In 1961 he had two minor solo hits, "Turn Around—Look at Me" and "Too Late To Worry—Too Blue To Cry," and Capitol Records signed him to a long-term contract. When Capitol failed to market his recordings aggressively, he decided to quit studio musicianship and "work on Glen Campbell."

A country ballad by John Hartford called "Gentle on My Mind" launched Campbell as a solo performer in 1967. The Capitol single hit number one on the country charts and made the Billboard Top Forty as well. Campbell quickly followed that recording with Jimmy Webb's "By the Time I Get to Phoenix," another ballad of love and loss. Both "Gentle on My Mind" and "By the Time I Get

> *Campbell has projected a clean-cut, All-American persona in sharp contrast to the prevalent outlaw image in country and rock.*

to Phoenix" earned Campbell Grammy Awards, and in 1967 he was chosen Entertainer of the Year by the Country Music Association. Television soon brought Campbell to a wider audience. After co-hosting "The Summer Smothers Brothers Show" successfully in 1968, he was offered his own prime-time network variety show, "The Glen Campbell Good Time Hour." Expressly non-political in a volatile era, Campbell's show quickly entered the Nielsen Top Ten; it offered country music, mild comedy, and mainstream guest stars, with Campbell an affable, satin-and-rhinestone-clad master of ceremonies. The show was cancelled in 1971, and Campbell turned to touring, earning in excess of $30,000 per appearance in America and abroad. His hits of the 1970s include "I Knew Jesus before He Was a Superstar," "Galveston," and "Rhinestone Cowboy."

In recent years Campbell's private life has undergone more scrutiny than his professional work. His tumultuous relationship with country star Tanya Tucker provided grist for the gossip mills in the early 1980s, with tales of extravagant spending and public brawls. Then, in

1983, he unexpectedly wed dancer Kim Woollen, his fourth wife. They have three children, and Campbell has five other children by his previous marriages. Campbell continues to record and tour, his most recent major success being the album *Southern Nights*. When asked the secret of his success after so many years of struggle, Campbell told the *Country Music Encyclopedia:* "One year I played in 586 sessions, and of all those records there were only three hits. I sat down and analyzed what the trouble was with the others. There was a lot of good music there, but out of all those singles I worked on that year only three of them had lyrics that meant something!" Campbell concluded: "The main thing that makes for a hit song is that it tells a story; you get caught up in the lyrics." An accomplished instrumentalist, Campbell needed only the right ingredient—the ballad—to propel him to stardom. His "story formula" that rescued him from the anonymity of studio work has assured him a permanent place in country music's top ranks.

Selected discography

Singles

"Turn Around—Look at Me," Crest, 1961.
"Too Late to Worry—Too Blue to Cry," Capitol, 1961.
"Burning Bridges," Capitol.
"I Gotta Have My Baby Back," Capitol.

LPs

The Astounding Twelve-String Guitar of Glen Campbell, Capitol.
Gentle on My Mind, Capitol.
By the Time I Get to Phoenix, Capitol, 1968.
Wichita Lineman, Capitol, 1968.
Galveston, Capitol, 1968.
Oh Happy Day, Capitol, 1968.
(With Bobbie Gentry) *Bobbie Gentry and Glen Campbell,* Capitol, 1970.
Dream Baby, Capitol, 1971.
Rhinestone Cowboy, Capitol, 1975.
Southern Nights, Capitol, 1977.

Glen Travis Campbell, Capitol.
I Knew Jesus, Capitol.
I Remember Hank Williams, Capitol.
I'll Paint You a Song, Capitol.
The Last Time I Saw Her, Capitol.
Glen Campbell Live, Capitol.
Only the Lonely, Capitol.
Try a Little Kindness, Capitol.
(With Anne Murray) *Anne Murray—Glen Campbell,* Capitol.
Arkansas, Capitol.
Houston, Capitol.
Bloodline, Capitol.
Reunion, Capitol.
(With Tennessee Ernie Ford) *Ernie Sings and Glen Picks,* Capitol.
Words, Capitol.
Album, Capitol.
More Words, Capitol.
Turn Around, Look at Me, Ember.
This is Glen Campbell, Ember.
That Christmas Feeling, Capitol.
Two Sides of Glen Campbell, Starline.
20 Golden Greats, Capitol.

Sources

Books

The Illustrated Encyclopedia of Country Music, Harmony, 1977.
Shestack, Melvin, *The Country Music Encyclopedia,* T. Crowell, 1974.
Stambler, Irwin, and Grelun Landon, *The Encyclopedia of Folk, Country, and Western Music,* St. Martin's, 1969.

Periodicals

Newsweek, April 15, 1968.
New York Times, August 4, 1968.
People, May 4, 1968; January 31, 1983.
Post (New York), January 25, 1969.
Sunday News Magazine (New York), April 6, 1969.
Time, January 31, 1969.

—Anne Janette Johnson

Rosanne Cash

Singer, songwriter

One of country music's "New Women," Rosanne Cash is an outspoken proponent of the progressive, rock-oriented country style. The eldest daughter of Johnny Cash has been performing since she was eighteen, recently forging a name for herself outside the shadow of her famous father. "On her last five albums," writes Steve Pond in *Rolling Stone,* "Cash has been carving out her own niche, singing a distinctive mixture of new rock songs, old ballads and the odd country tune; hers is a tougher, hipper version of the country-rock hybrid that Linda Ronstadt once pursued." Cash herself jokingly calls her sound "Punktry," an unlikely fusion of country and punk rock that challenges traditional boundaries in form, content, and even language. Still, Cash told Alanna Nash in *Behind Closed Doors: Talking with the Legends of Country Music,* she feels that her roots are firmly based in the country sound. "The music I'm doing is a natural progression of where country music is going," she said. "It's lyrically oriented, which is what country music has always been, it's logical music, it's simple . . . maybe some of it does have a harder edge, but I consider myself a country artist."

"Nobody likes the kids of famous people," Cash told *People* magazine. "It's particularly hard if you go into the profession where the parent has been very successful. But if that's where your talent lies, it's dumb not to pursue it. Doctors' children become doctors. It shouldn't be all that strange that Johnny Cash's child likes to sing." Rosanne Cash was born in Memphis, the first child of Johnny Cash and his first wife, Vivian Liberto. Cash says little about her childhood, except to note in *Stereo Review* that her father "was bigger than life, . . . because of his image and because he was not home a lot. 'Conquering hero' is a good term for it." Cash has admitted that her father's alcohol and drug problems—and his raging ambition—further distanced him from his family. She was twelve years old when her parents divorced.

A rebellious teen growing up in southern California, Cash began to experiment with drugs when she was fourteen. She has described her musical tastes at the time as "the same stuff most kids listened to" in California, including the Beatles. She was also influenced by the folk sound of Joni Mitchell, James Taylor, and two "old folkies," Tom Rush and Eric Andersen. At eighteen, right out of high school, she joined her father's entourage and began to travel and perform with him. This, she said in *Stereo Review,* was a mixed blessing. "It was a good learning ground," she admitted, "to watch *him* work, but I was so protected I couldn't get any objectivity about *my* work. I got to the point where I was doing a couple of songs, but it was still playing for his crowd and it was still cute for his daughter to be up

For the Record. . .

Born c. 1955 in Memphis, Tenn.; daughter of Johnny (a country singer) and Vivian (Liberto) Cash; married Rodney Crowell (a record producer and songwriter), 1979; children: Hannah, Caitlyn, Chelsea. *Education:* Attended Vanderbilt University and the Lee Strasberg Drama School.

Began performing as a backup singer for Johnny Cash's road show, c. 1973; solo performer, 1978—. Signed with Columbia Records, 1979.

Addresses: *Agent*—Side One Management Agency, 1775 Broadway, 7th Floor, New York, NY 10019.

there, you know—the crowds thought, 'Oh, how sweet,' no matter how bad you were. At some point, you have to fall on your face."

After three years on tour with her father, Cash did not fall on her face, but she did question her viability as a solo performer. Finally she quit the show and enrolled in Vanderbilt University, where she majored in English and drama. The following year she moved to Hollywood to study in Lee Strasberg's noted drama school, hoping to become an actress. Although she was too shy to study with Strasberg directly, she did take courses with his associates, describing the experience as "great . . . like therapy." Cash left the drama school after six months because Ariola Records, a German company, offered her a recording contract. She travelled to Munich to cut the album, facing bitter disappointment when the German producers forced "stiff arrangements" on her. Still, one cut on the album attracted the attention of Rich Blackburn of Columbia Records, and he agreed to allow Cash and her fiance, producer/songwriter Rodney Crowell, to make an album that would fit their own creative standards.

The album, *Right or Wrong,* was deemed a critical success by both country and rock critics. "It had a no-nonsense feel to it," writes Noel Coppage in *Stereo Review,* "with Rosanne's warm, moist, round tones supported by strikingly clean and lyrical electric-guitar fills and breaks before arrangements that touched bases with Austin and Los Angeles but were captives of neither." Subsequent Cash albums have built on this rock-country fusion, utilizing rock rhythms and melodies but maintaining the country tradition of the highly personal ballads about heartbreak, infidelity, and reconciliation. As a husband and wife team, Cash and Crowell have produced most of Cash's albums and have contributed original songs to all of them. The

songs that Cash writes are based on her own marriage as well as on her addiction to cocaine, a condition that forced her to seek hospital treatment in 1985. Reflecting on her chart-topping album *Rhythm and Romance,* which contained songs about the near-dissolution of her marriage, Cash told Alanna Nash: "I have to pick songs that I feel relate to me personally. I don't think I could ever just do a song for ulterior motives. It's a real emotional process with me." Coppage observes that such a daring exploration of personal feelings gives added force to Cash's music. The critic writes: "The result, I think, . . . reflects the spirit of pushing on through growing pains. Any listener making any sort of attempt to live an examined life can hardly help identifying with the humanity [Cash] projects."

Daring humanity and progressive sound—these best describe the Rosanne Cash repertoire. It is Cash's independence from Nashville's dictates, however, that

---

Cash jokingly calls her sound "Punktry," an unlikely fusion of country and punk rock.

---

has helped to earn her a place among country music's "New Women." Cash told Alanna Nash: "There's a formula in Nashville about how you should make records, how you should relate to your audience, how much you should tour. The whole thing is a package deal. They might as well turn it into a handbook and give it to you as you enter the business. And I *just don't buy it!* I don't buy it at all! I think there's individual ways to approach life and success." The mother of three children (one adopted), Cash prefers not to tour. She lives quietly with her family in a spacious log home near Nashville, content to confine her creativity to songwriting, recording, and an occasional concert or television appearance. Cash told *Esquire* magazine: "Country music might have chosen me, rather than the other way around. I think I'm helping move country to the next logical step. You see, country-music listeners are much more sophisticated now. So much has happened since Hank Williams. They're more world-wise, more cosmopolitan, I guess. My music is that, I think—country, but world-wise."

Selected discography

Right or Wrong, Columbia, 1980.
Somewhere in the Stars, Columbia.

Seven Year Ache, Columbia.
Rhythm & Romance, Columbia, 1985.
King's Record Shop, Columbia, 1987.
Hits 1979-1989, Columbia, 1989.

Sources

Books

Nash, Alanna, *Behind Closed Doors: Talking with the Legends of Country Music,* Knopf, 1988.

Periodicals

Esquire, July, 1981.
Newsweek, August 12, 1985.
People, September 6, 1982.
Rolling Stone, February 25, 1988.
Stereo Review, May, 1981.

—Anne Janette Johnson

Toni Childs

Singer, songwriter

Toni Childs "delivers . . . evocative, evanescent music that allows you to immerse yourself and drift away," according to *Rolling Stone* critic Steve Pond. With the release of *Union,* her 1988 solo debut album, she has been favorably compared to rock and folk artisans such as Van Morrison, Joan Armatrading, and Phoebe Snow. "You notice her voice first," explained Pond. "It's full, deep and flexible . . . her album's commanding centerpiece." Childs has been classified by many reviewers as ranking alongside other female folk stars coming into the spotlight in the late 1980s, such as Suzanne Vega and Tracy Chapman, and with the likes of them is credited with the resurgence in popularity of serious women singer-songwriters. "She makes music," asserted Jay Cocks of *Time,* "that catches the sweet, scary feelings, all the uncertainty and release, that can come when the sun goes down."

Childs was born in southern California. Her early years, spent there and in small towns in Arkansas, Oklahoma, and Kansas, were not especially conducive to developing her musical talents—her parents were strict Christian fundamentalists who forbade her to listen to rock or pop music, "or even go to the movies. There was a lot I missed out on," she confided to Cocks. She was also unhappy in school, due to a dyslexic reading disorder that went undiagnosed and caused her to be placed in classes for slow learners. But despite her troubles, Childs's aptitude for music began to show through; she started writing songs when she was fourteen. Because she did not know how to play a musical instrument at the time (later she learned guitar and bass), she tried to write a musical solely for voice; the story concerned a mermaid. "I just locked myself in my bedroom for two weeks," she told a *Seventeen* interviewer, "and scribbled it out."

When Childs was fifteen, however, she could no longer stand her repressive family environment. There had been other problems as well; when she was twelve, the man she thought was her biological father divorced her mother—before he left he revealed that he had only been stepfather to Childs and her brothers, and that a man who had been introduced as a friend of the family was their real father. Her mother remarried again, and Childs did not get along well with her second stepfather. She told *Seventeen* that he "didn't have a good grip on who he was. You love your mother, you want to make her life better, but after a point you can't really help, and you have to go." So she left home. She worked odd jobs to live; she served as a nanny, and did chores in a commune that fed her for her work. Childs began listening to rock then, too, and found herself admiring the work of David Bowie, Led Zeppelin, and Pink Floyd.

For the Record. . .

Born 1957, in southern California. Singer, songwriter, 1974—; founder of group Toni and the Movers, 1979; worked for Island Music in the early 1980s; solo recording artist and concert performer, 1988—. Signed with A & M Records, 1985.

Addresses: c/o A & M Records, 1416 N. La Brea, Los Angeles, CA 90028.

One night, at about the same time, Childs was in a southern California roller rink and the band performing there allowed her to see what her voice sounded like through a microphone. "I sounded like somebody who could *really* sing!" she recalled for *Seventeen.* A few years later, Childs began singing with rock bands herself, and by 1979 was the leader of Toni and the Movers. As John Milward put it in an article for *Mademoiselle,* the group "was for [Childs] the living out of a loud, raunchy rock-and-roll fantasy, complete with skunk-drunk performances and plenty of LSD." The band was not very successful, and its leader was arrested on drug charges for her efforts to earn money for the band. Childs spent three months in a federal prison, with fellow inmates like former members of the infamous Charles Manson family, and heiress-turned-brainwashed terrorist Patricia Hearst. The experience reformed her: "It was a very big scare-the-hell-out-of-me situation," she told Cocks.

A short time after this, Childs gave up on Toni and the Movers and went to England, where she worked for Island Music. The company's heavy involvement with African and West Indian rhythms and musical forms deeply influenced Childs, and when she returned to California to sign a recording contract with A & M Records in 1985 she knew that the album she would create for them would incorporate these influences. On the same day that she signed with A & M, however, she moved in with musician David Ricketts, of the duo David and David. He would become *Union*'s associate producer, and helped Childs write many of the album's songs; further, the ups and downs of Child's sixteen-month love affair with him would serve as the basic theme of the album.

Union took three years to complete, partially because

Childs and Ricketts searched in countries such as Zambia and Swaziland to obtain what Marianne Meyer termed in *Rolling Stone* "the perfect atmospheric washes and ethnic accents." As Meyer reported, A & M "was understandably nervous about their new signing's traveling the globe in search of something she couldn't quite describe," but Childs and Ricketts found two African choirs to use on *Union,* and the album's critical and popular success have more than made up for the difficulties of its production. *Union* has launched two hits, "Don't Walk Away," lauded as "electrifying" by *Seventeen,* and "Stop Your Fussin'," which *People* described as a "slinky Caribbean samba." Other songs on the album that have drawn praise are "Let the Rain Come Down," in which, according to Pond, "Childs sounds downright triumphant, buoyed by her faith in the renewal that comes with time and distance and a cleansing rain"; and "Walk and Talk Like Angels," which *People* called "as warm, dry and stirring as a desert breeze." Overall, concluded Pond, "*Union* is an album about the precarious dynamic between men and women. . . . And . . . the album is suffused with a sense of peace and restfulness." Childs intends to record a second album, this time working with Indian and Indonesian rhythms.

Selected discography

Union (contains "Don't Walk Away," "Walk and Talk Like Angels," "Stop Your Fussin'," "Dreamer," "Let the Rain Come Down," "Zimbabwae," "Hush," "Tin Drum," and "Where's the Ocean"), A & M, 1988.

Also recorded a single with Toni and the Movers.

Sources

Mademoiselle, September, 1988.
People, June 27, 1988.
Rolling Stone, June 2, 1988; January 26, 1989.
Seventeen, January, 1989.
Time, June 6, 1988.

—Elizabeth Thomas

Dick Clark

Rock music promoter

Dick Clark has spent over thirty years as the host of the longest-running musical variety show in U.S. history, "American Bandstand." Clark has given many of rock and roll's brightest stars their first national television exposure and is credited with being one of the most important early promoters of rock music. Rock pioneers who made their television debuts on Clark's show include Buddy Holly and Chuck Berry, and Clark's influence has extended into the latter days of rock and pop, giving him the privilege of hosting the first television appearances of more modern superstars, such as Prince and Madonna. Clark has also branched out from strictly musical ventures into more general areas of television and film production and has gained a respected reputation with the heads of major networks for delivering successful projects on time and within budget limitations. As Nikki Finke Greenberg summed up in *Newsweek,* "In every aspect of the business, Clark shows himself to be a committed, hardworking professional."

Born Richard Wagstaff Clark on November 30, 1929, in Bronxville, New York, his childhood ambition was to work in radio. This ambition intensified when his older brother, Bradley, was killed in World War II, leaving Clark to fight grief and loneliness by listening to radio programs like "Make Believe Ballroom" and "Battle of the Baritones." His parents encouraged his interest and at the same time helped bring him out of depression by taking him to live radio shows and advising him to join the school dramatic clubs. Clark became popular in high school, serving as class president and being voted "Man Most Likely to Sell the Brooklyn Bridge."

When Clark was in his late teens, his father took a job managing a relative's radio station in Utica, New York. The young man worked at the station, WRUN, taking care of the mimeographing and the mailroom. When a weather announcer went on vacation, Clark was allowed to substitute; eventually he was promoted to broadcasting station breaks and reading the news on the AM affiliate. In 1946, Clark matriculated at Syracuse University. Though his major was advertising, he took a minor in radio, and served as a disc jockey on the university's student radio station, WAER-FM. Just before his graduation he did weekend work as a news announcer and disc jockey for a country-music segment on a commercial Syracuse station.

Soon after Clark graduated in 1951, he returned to Utica and took a job at a small television station. WKTV was such a tiny setup that Clark found himself involved in almost every facet of its operation, including writing commercials and changing scenery backdrops. More importantly, he was the host of a country-music program called "Cactus Dick and the Santa Fe Riders."

Full name Richard Wagstaff Clark; born November 30, 1929, in Bronxville, New York; son of Richard (a salesman and radio-station manager) and Julia Clark; married Bobbie Mallery, 1952 (divorced, 1961); married Loretta Martin (a secretary), 1962 (divorced, 1971); married Kari Wigton (a secretary), 1977; children: (first marriage) Richard, Jr.; (second marriage) Duane, Cindy. *Education:* Graduated from Syracuse University in 1951.

Worked in the mailroom of radio station WRUN, Utica, N.Y., c. 1945; disc jockey at WAER, and news announcer and disc jockey at WOLF, both in Syracuse, N.Y., 1946-51; worked as a news announcer, music-show host, and at various other jobs at television station WKTV, Utica, N.Y., 1951; music-show host, WFIL Radio, Philadelphia, 1952-56; host of "Bandstand" on WFIL-TV, Philadelphia, 1956; host of nationwide "American Bandstand" on ABC, 1957-c. 1988; host of various game shows, including "The $25,000 Pyramid." Founder of various music and television business ventures, including Dick Clark Productions, SRO Artists, Sea Lark, January Music, Swan Records, and Dick Clark's Caravan of Stars. Has produced and appeared in films and authored books, including an autobiography.

Awards: Four Emmy Awards—one for "American Bandstand," c. 1982, two for hosting "The $25,000 Pyramid," c. 1978 and c. 1985, and one for coproducing *The Woman Who Willed a Miracle.*

Addresses: *Residence*—Malibu, Calif.; and New York, N.Y.; *Office*—Dick Clark Productions, 3003 W. Olive Ave., Burbank, CA 91505.

But in 1952, Clark saw a better career opportunity and moved to Philadelphia to work at radio station WFIL. He knew the station had a television affiliate, and exposure in Philadelphia was a step up from exposure in Utica. He was soon given his own daily radio show, "Dick Clark's Caravan of Music." The young disc jockey continued successfully at the station for a few years. Meanwhile, WFIL's television affiliate had spawned a popular afternoon music program called "Bandstand." When one of its hosts, Bob Horn, went on vacation in 1955, Clark took his place. And when Horn was jailed for drunk driving the following year, Clark became the show's permanent host.

Within a year, Clark's presence had helped transform "Bandstand" into Philadelphia's best-known daily television show, and the American Broadcasting Corpora-

tion (ABC) chose to pick it up for nationwide viewing. The name was changed to "American Bandstand," but the program kept its format of dancing teenagers, record playing, and star appearances and interviews. "American Bandstand" was so successful nationally that not only did Clark receive fan mail, but so did many of the show's regular dancers. Singers and musicians of the caliber of Bill Haley, Jerry Lee Lewis, Johnny Mathis, and Neil Sedaka came to lip-sync their latest hits before the program's cameras. The dancers started national dance crazes such as the twist, the Watusi, and the stroll. Clark also did a weekly nighttime program which traveled to cities throughout the United States; one of these editions of "The Dick Clark Saturday Night Show," done in Atlanta, was also one of the first racially integrated rock concerts in the South and was picketed by the Ku Klux Klan.

"American Bandstand" would provide Clark with a steady income for over thirty years, but he did not stop there. He invested heavily in the music industry, forming the music-publishing firms Sea Lark and January

---

> *Dick Clark is credited with being one of the most important early promoters of rock music.*

Music and starting Swan Records. He had to divest himself of these businesses, however, at the request of ABC, when he came under investigation by a U.S. Congress subcommittee during the payola scandal of the late 1950s and early 1960s. *Payola* referred to the taking of money for playing new records, and though Clark did not do this, his holdings in the music business were perceived as a conflict of interest.

Though the program was still going strong in the 1960s, Clark himself lost interest in music during the psychedelic era. He began to branch out into other areas of television, including game shows like "Missing Links" and "The Object Is." He also appeared in movies and produced such films as *Psych-Out, The Savage Seven,* and *Killers Three.* As Clark tried to become a larger force in the television industry, however, the youthful good looks that enabled him to be a convincing host for his teen-oriented show worked against him. As Greenberg reports, "for many years he couldn't get anyone to take him seriously." Clark told her that he "would leave a meeting, bang his fist against a wall and say, 'They don't know how *smart* I am.'"

Eventually, in the late 1970s, he began to close large deals with the major television networks. Meanwhile, Clark became the host of "The $25,000 Pyramid," a game show. At one time, according to Christopher P. Andersen in *People,* "only he simultaneously [hosted] hit shows on all three networks and in syndication." His production company has also been responsible for ratings-grabbing specials, and television films like *Elvis, Murder in Texas, Copacabana,* which featured pop star Barry Manilow, and *The Woman Who Willed a Miracle,* which earned Clark an Emmy Award as coproducer. Though he is now seen as a major figure in television, who can be counted on to produce shows that get good Nielsen ratings, Clark has garnered some criticism for the lack of quality in his productions. He claims he provides what the television audience wants, and gave this rebuttal to Greenberg: "If I were given the assignment of doing a classical-music hour for PBS, it would be exquisite and beautifully done." Clark's other productions include the 1985 box-office film *Remo Williams: The Adventure Begins,* and the annual special "Dick Clark's New Year's Rockin' Eve." He also cofounded United Stations, the second largest radio network in the United States.

On the subject of his youthful appearance, which has lasted for decades, "America's oldest living teenager" told Andersen, "It's . . . like being a female sex symbol. They're constantly told how wonderful they look, but it gets to be a drag after a while, because someday the looks have gotta go. It would be nice to be allowed to age gracefully." Apparently, Clark has begun to do just that, relinquishing his role as host of "American Bandstand" to a younger man in 1988.

Sources

Books

Clark, Dick, *Rock, Roll, and Remember,* Crowell, 1976.

Periodicals

Newsweek, August 18, 1986.
People, January 27, 1986.

—Elizabeth Thomas

Phil Collins

Drummer, singer, songwriter, producer

Pop music superstars often strive for the gaudy, flamboyant effect. Phil Collins, a plain, balding rock drummer, would rather let his songs speak for him. Since the late 1970s Collins has served as the lead singer for the British rock band Genesis, and he has simultaneously enjoyed a dramatic solo career complete with Grammy Awards and a long string of Top Ten hits. The affable Collins has also achieved a measure of critical respect beyond the bounds usually accorded to pop musicians; many of his mysterious, wrenching songs about heartbreak and suspicion are hailed for their revolutionary use of rhythm. *New York Times* correspondent Stephen Holden notes that Collins has "defined a new relationship between rock rhythm, singing and songwriting in which . . . shifting multicolored drum textures determine the music's emotional as well as its rhythmic climate." Holden adds: "As both a songwriter and an instrumentalist, . . . Collins is especially adept at sustaining a mood of suspense, often heavily tinged with menace. His shadowy song lyrics are suffused with . . . dread and the suggestion of passions so pent-up they could explode violently, though they never do."

Ever since Collins began his solo work, observers have speculated that he would eventually leave Genesis. Collins has proven them wrong, managing to write, record, and tour with the group regularly. Collins is candid, however, about how much his individual success means to him. "I feel like I'm in the middle, reaching out to do lots of little things," he told *Rolling Stone* magazine. "One of the things I do is Genesis. Another is producing other people's records. . . Another thing I do is play on other people's records. But the main thing is *my* records." These solo albums, including *Hello, I Must Be Going* and *No Jacket Required,* have sold in excess of six million copies worldwide, assuring their creator fame and fortune. "I make more money on my own than I do with Genesis," Collins admitted, "so the bottom line, mercenary level is that there's no reason for me to be in Genesis except that I enjoy it. But, honestly, in the end, I'm doing something on my own, my little self, and that's the most gratifying of all."

Phil Collins has been passionately involved with music since his early childhood. The youngest of three children, he was born in the affluent London suburb of Hounslow in 1951. By the time he was five, Collins was experimenting with drums, and his parents bought him a full drum set when he was ten. At first both of his parents seemed inclined to push him in other directions—his father toward a nine-to-five office job and his mother toward an acting career. Collins agreed to try his hand at acting, joining the prestigious Barbara Speake Stage School in 1964. From there he received several professional dramatic roles, including one as the Artful Dodger in a London stage production of *Oliver!* He still preferred music, though, so in 1967—against his mother's wishes—he dropped out of school to work as a rock drummer.

Growing up in Great Britain, Collins was naturally influenced by such groups as the Beatles and the Who. He was equally fascinated, however, by the Motown music of the Supremes, the Four Tops, and the Temptations. When he began to make his own music, he incorporated the black American rhythm and blues and soul sounds, modifying them to fit the circumstances of his white, middle-class background. By 1970 Collins had earned a reputation as an able studio drummer, so he was asked to audition for an up-and-coming "art rock" group, Genesis. Collins won the audition and began a long tenure in "comfortable anonymity, hidden behind the drums, as the group built its reputation around the flamboyance and theatrics of its leader-'auteur,' Peter Gabriel," according to Rob Hoerburger in the *Chicago Tribune.* Genesis's somewhat unique style combined American influences such as folk and soul with long, brooding symphonic suites and allegorical rock operas. Just as the group began to experience a high level of success in Britain and Europe, Gabriel quit to pursue a solo career. The other members of Genesis—Collins, Mike Rutherford, and Tony Banks, decided to keep performing as Genesis.

Genesis auditioned more than one hundred lead singers in an effort to replace Gabriel as the British press declared the group "dead and buried." Finally Collins, who had never considered singing lead, realized that he was as able as any of the performers he had auditioned. He took over both the performing and the songwriting duties, realizing that changing tastes necessitated a more upbeat, less cerebral style. In 1978 Collins came to a momentous decision—Genesis would have to reach out to an American audience through an extended tour. That choice, he admits, cost him his first marriage, since his wife resented the long separations required by the music business. A long divorce proceeding ensued that left Collins "demoralized, bitter, alone and, eventually, rich," to quote Hoerburger in *Rolling Stone.* Although his intentions were anything but mercenary, Collins began to write intensely personal songs about the breakup of his marriage—ballads that were quite different in style and emotion than any of his Genesis work. He recorded the songs on his first solo album, *Face Value,* released in 1981.

Face Value was more successful than any of the Genesis albums had been, reaching the top ten on the *Billboard* album chart and spawning two hit singles, "I Missed Again" and "In the Air Tonight." Amidst rumors of the breakup of Genesis, Collins returned to the group with new songs for it as well. Late in 1981 Genesis released *Abacab,* its first million-seller, and embarked on a lengthy, multi-million dollar international tour. Only when the tour ended did Collins return to solo work with his next hit album, *Hello, I Must Be Going.* He also offered his talents as a producer and arranger to several other artists, including Frida Lyngstrom of Abba, Eric Clapton, and Philip Bailey of Earth, Wind, and Fire. Collins and Bailey were particularly pleased when their duet, "Easy Lover," topped both the pop and soul charts.

By 1985 Collins had scored a string of hits, both with Genesis and on his own. Still, critics made much of his bald, paunchy appearance—sometimes to the exclusion of serious commentary on his work. In *Rolling Stone,* for instance, Hoerburger wrote: "The pop audience was primed for its own Cabbage Patch Kid, and Collins, with his catchy, smartly produced music, fit the bill; he was homely, and he sold." *No Jacket Required,* Collins's 1985 album, forced reviewers to take the artist

Aaron Copland

Composer

"To a composer, music is a kind of language," Aaron Copland opens the first volume of his autobiography, *Copland: 1900 Through 1942.* "Behind the written score, even behind the various sounds they make when played, is a language of the emotions. The composer has it in his power to make music speak of many things: tender, harsh and lively, consoling and challenging things." With his language, Copland has given America its language, a language of its land and its people, of its history and its myths. It is an indigenous American language spoken with emotion and understanding for the common American man.

Aaron Copland was born on November 14, 1900, in Brooklyn, New York. He showed an affinity with music early in life, composing songs when he was only eight-and-a-half years old. His formal training, however, did not begin until he was thirteen. Although this is an "old" age at which to begin musical studies, Copland's desire and tenacity expedited his musical training. At fifteen, he took piano lessons from Leopold Wolfsohn, and at seventeen began studying composition with Rubin Goldmark, remaining under his tutelage for the next four years.

The young Copland's modernist tendencies conflicted with Goldmark's conservatism, however, and in 1921 Copland escaped to France to study at the newly formed Conservatoire Americain at Fountainebleau. Composition studies there with Paul Vidal continued along the same musical idiom as Goldmark's, and Copland didn't find release until, upon a friend's urging, he visited the harmony class of Nadia Boulanger. It was a pivotal moment, one that wasn't lost on the perceptive budding composer. He recounts in *Copland:* "[Boulanger's] sense of involvement in the whole subject of harmony made it more lively than I ever thought it could be. She created a kind of excitement about the subject, emphasizing how it was, after all, the fundamental basis of our music, when one really thought about it. I suspected that first day that I had found my composition teacher."

While Copland studied in Paris for the next three years with Boulanger, his senses developed amid what Donald Henahan, writing for the *New York Times Book Review,* labeled "an artistic hotbed." Figures like the surrealist Andre Breton, expatriate writers T. S. Eliot and Ezra Pound, painters Georges Braque and Max Ernst, and composers Francis Poulenc and Darius Milhaud eschewed the past in search of a new aesthetic voice. Copland relates in his autobiography: "The air was charged with talk of new tendencies, and the password was originality—anything was possible. . . . Tradition was nothing; innovation everything." This thoroughly modernist atmosphere pervaded Copland, and informed his first orchestral work, *Grogh* (1922-25).

For the Record. . .

Born November 14, 1900, in Brooklyn, N.Y.; son of Harris Morris (owner of a department store) and Sarah (Mittenthal) Copland. *Education:* Studied music (piano) privately under Leopold Wolfsohn, Victor Wittgenstein, Clarence Adler, and Ricardo Vines; studied composition with Rubin Goldmark, 1917-21, with Nadia Boulanger at Fontainbleau School of Music, 1921, and in Paris, 1921-24.

Composer, 1924—. Lecturer on contemporary music at New School for Social Research, 1927-37, and at Harvard University, 1935, and 1944; assistant director of Berkshire Music Center, 1940; Charles Eliot Norton Professor of Poetry at Harvard University, 1951-52; public lecturer throughout the United States.

Awards: First composer to receive Guggenheim Foundation fellowship, 1925, renewed, 1926; awarded $5,000 for *Dance Symphony* by RCA Victor, 1930; Pulitzer Prize in Music, 1945, for *Appalachian Spring;* New York Music Critics Circle Award, 1945, for *Appalachian Spring,* and 1946, for *Third Symphony;* received Academy Award for musical score for *The Heiress,* 1950; recipient of gold medal from American Academy of Arts and Letters, 1956; Edward MacDowell Medal, 1961; Presidential Medal of Freedom, 1964; National Medal of the Arts, 1986; awarded Congressional Gold Medal, 1986.

Addresses: *Office*—c/o Boosey & Hawkes, 24 West 57th St., New York, NY 10019.

Upon returning to the United States in 1924, Copland intended to compose music in an American voice. "I was very conscious of how French composers sounded in comparison with the Germans, and how Russian [Igor] Stravinsky was," Copland explained many years later to Edward Rothstein of the *New York Times.* "I became very preoccupied with writing serious concert music that would have a specifically American flavor." Before he left France, Copland had been asked by Boulanger to compose an orchestral piece for organ for her upcoming tour as soloist with several American orchestras. The completed piece, *Symphony for Organ and Orchestra,* raised more than a few eyebrows at its premiere in New York. It was a time when, as Arthur Berger in his biography on Copland explained, "the public at large regarded a modern composer as something of a naughty boy by whom it was both amused and shocked." Walter Damrosch, conductor of the New York Symphony, turned to the audience at the completion of the symphony and gave the now famous remark, "If a young man at the age of twenty-three can write a symphony like that, within five years he will be ready to commit murder." Although critics both praised and panned the new work, Copland subsequently found that it had more of a European style than an American one. For his next two works, *Music for the Theater* (1925) and the *Piano Concerto* (1926), he incorporated American jazz. But this attempt at an American sound was too manufactured, and Rothstein admitted that "however influenced [Copland] was by cross rhythms and metrical freedom, one can hear, particularly in the concerto, how much more jazz was a 'sign' of things American, rather than a personal expression."

In addition to his own music, Copland propagated the American voice by championing the works of other young American composers at the time. He joined the League of Composers, became good friends with the eminent composer and proponent of modern music Serge Koussevitzky, and maintained and enhanced contacts with fellow composers such as Virgil Thomson and Roy Harris. In 1928, along with Roger Sessions, he founded the Copland-Sessions Concerts, which for several years offered New York audiences an opportunity to hear contemporary American music. In *Copland,* Thomson succinctly defined Copland's activities at that time: "Aaron was president of young American music, and then middle-aged American music, because he had tact, good business sense about colleagues, and loyalty."

With his increased activity in the modern music society came an increasingly complex quality in his music. Audiences were perplexed by his *Symphonic Ode* (1929) and subsequent works, not because of their dense structuring, but, ironically, because of their leanness, angularity, and spaciousness. Copland points out in his autobiography that "one can hear in the *Ode* the beginnings of a purer, non-programmatic style, an attempt toward an economy of material and transparency of texture that would be taken much further in the next few years in the *Piano Variations,* the *Short Symphony,* and *Statements for Orchestra.*" Julia Smith, in her biography *Aaron Copland,* argued that this shift occurred because Copland was "a man of his time, reflecting the spirit and mood of his age through his music," its sparseness reflecting "the disillusion-filled depression years of the early thirties."

This "abstract" period did not last long, however, as Copland continued to change his style (a characteristic he maintained throughout his career). Influenced by the social and political climate of the 1930s, he sought a way to lift the spirits of the American public, as well as heighten its musical knowledge. Some forty years later Copland told John Rockwell of the *New York Times,*

"There was a problem with the public then. Composers were writing music that people were lost with. Writing music with a greater appeal was a kind of challenge for me. The usual assumption is that if you're working with simple materials, it's very easy. But that's not necessarily true."

His first work in the new "popular" style was *El Salon Mexico* (1936). Inspired by a trip to Mexico, specifically a dance hall in Mexico City, the work was grounded on Mexican folk melodies. This marked the beginning of his movement toward the incorporation of regional melodies in an attempt to capture, as he says in *Copland*, "that electric sense one gets sometimes in far-off places, of suddenly knowing the essence of a people—their humanity, their shyness, their dignity and unique charm." Copland next looked to New England and Shaker hymnody and cowboy songs to capture the American "essence" that he had sought since his return from France in the early 1920s. The consequent simpler, plainer style that brought wide public approval also resulted in derisive comments from colleagues who felt Copland was betraying his art. In a letter to Arthur Berger, reprinted in *Copland*, the composer explained and defended his movement: "What I was trying for in the simpler works was only partly a larger audience; they also gave me a chance to try for a home-spun musical idiom similar to what I was trying for in a more hectic fashion in the earlier jazz works. . . . I like to think that I have touched off for myself and others a kind of musical naturalness that we have badly needed."

In this new style Copland composed works for such diverse settings as high schools, *The Second Hurricane* (a play-opera, 1937) and *Outdoor Overture* (1938); plays, *The Five Kings* (1939) and *Quiet City* (1939); and radio broadcasts, *Music for Radio* (1937) and *Letter From Home* (1944). In addition, he tried to educate the public musically—in general and to his own efforts—by publishing two books, *What to Listen for in Music* (1939) and *Our New Music* (1941). But two areas for which he is most widely recognized, which yield the Coplandesque sound most often associated with him, are film scores and ballets.

After having written the score for the documentary film *The City* (1939), Copland attracted the attention of Hollywood. He scored five movies: *Of Mice and Men* (1939), *Our Town* (1940), *North Star* (1943), *The Red Pony* (1948), and *The Heiress* (1949). His determination to provide quality music that enhanced the action on the screen without overwhelming it has given a touchstone for film music since. He admits in his autobiography that for "some in Hollywood my music was strange, lean, and dissonant; to others it spoke with a

new incisiveness and clarity." For Wilfrid Mellers of the London *Times Literary Supplement*, Copland's film scores were more than just incisive: "There's point in the fact that in his film scores for *Of Mice and Men* and *Our Town* he produced perhaps the finest film music ever, honouring rural America by way of an intelligent subservience to a mechanized medium." Hollywood didn't fail to recognize these achievements. Copland received an Academy Award nomination for best dramatic film score for his first three motion pictures and was eventually given the Oscar for *The Heiress*.

His achievements in film music were not only matched by his work for ballets but were surpassed. Smith declared that "by means of the ballet form, Aaron Copland has expressed the strength, power, and conviction of our American traditions, marking them with a definitiveness of contemporary musical language never before achieved by an American composer. In so doing, he has laid the cornerstone of an American national art, established a recognizably American musical idiom." Copland's most famous works are the two

---

Copland has given America its language, a language of its land and its people, of its history and its myths.

---

cowboy ballets—*Billy the Kid* (1938) and *Rodeo* (1942)— and his masterpiece, *Appalachian Spring* (1944). This work, composed for choreographer Martha Graham (who chose the title from a Hart Crane poem), won the Pulitzer Prize for music in 1944 and the New York Music Critics' Award as the outstanding theatrical composition of 1944-45. Of it, S. L. M. Barlow, quoted by Smith, wrote, "Here were the tart herbs of plain American speech, the pasture, without the flowers of elocution,. . . the clean rhythms . . . the irony and the homespun tenderness that, in a fine peroration, reached a sustained exaltation."

During this time of simplicity, Copland also produced works—*Piano Sonata* (1941), *Violin Sonata* (1943), and *Third Symphony* (1946)—in a more severe tone. As Copland indicated throughout his career, he never abandoned one style for another. And as Henahan explained, "He still wanted to be respected by what he called 'the cultivated audience that understands a sophisticated musical language.'" Copland's subsequent works of the 1950s and 1960s, works like *Piano Fantasy* (1957), *Connotations* (1962), and *Inscape*

(1967), pleased only a small following. In the early 1970s, he left composing for the conductor's podium. Joseph McLellan, in the *Washington Post Book World*, defined Copland's stature: "At that point, Copland had become a sort of national monument—a status that requires one simply to exist, to be visible and to do what has been done before."

According to Copland's long-time friend Harold Clurman, quoted in *Copland,* the composer's only uttered ambition was "to be remembered." In his autobiography Copland states that Stravinsky was important to him because "Stravinsky proved it was possible for a twentieth-century composer to create his own tradition." Copland is important for this very reason—he has created and given America its tradition. Mellers declared: "There is no music which conveys the big-city experience more honestly than Copland's; which is more compassionately human in its acceptance of spiritual isolation while being responsive to the thoughts and feelings of average men and women; which attains, through tension, a deeper calm. In his music, we can detect the neat, bland-eyed, rugged-souled early Americans of a Copley portrait, after they have lived through the physical and nervous stresses to which a machine age has submitted them."

Writings

What to Listen for in Music, 1939.
Our New Music, 1941.
Music and Imagination, 1952.
Copland on Music, 1960.
The New Music 1900-1960, 1968.
Copland: 1900 Through 1942, 1984.

Selected compositions

Grogh (ballet), 1922-25.
Symphony for Organ and Orchestra, 1924.
Music for the Theater, 1925.
Dance Symphony, 1925.
Piano Concerto, 1926.
First Symphony, 1928.
Symphonic Ode, 1929.
Piano Variations, 1930.
Short Symphony, 1933.
Statements for Orchestra, 1935.
El Salon Mexico, 1936.
The Second Hurricane (play-opera), 1937.

Music for Radio, 1937.
Billy the Kid (ballet), 1938.
Outdoor Overture, 1938.
The Five Kings (incidental music for play), 1939.
The Quiet City (incidental music for play), 1939.
The City (documentary film), 1939.
Of Mice and Men (film), 1939.
Our Town (film), 1940.
Piano Sonata, 1941.
Lincoln Portrait, 1942.
Rodeo (ballet), 1942.
Fanfare for the Common Man, 1942.
North Star (film), 1943.
Violin Sonata, 1943.
Appalachian Spring (ballet), 1944.
Letter from Home, 1944.
Third Symphony, 1946.
The Red Pony (film), 1948.
Concerto for Clarinet, 1948.
The Heiress (film), 1949.
Twelve Poems of Emily Dickinson, 1950.
The Tender Land (opera), 1954.
Symphonic Ode, 1955.
Piano Fantasy, 1957.
Orchestral Variations, 1958.
Connotations, 1962.
Music for a Great City, 1963.
Emblems for a Band, 1964.
Inscape, 1967.
Duo for Flute and Piano, 1971.
Three Latin American Sketches, 1971.
Night Thoughts for Piano, 1972.

Sources

Books

Berger, Arthur, *Aaron Copland,* Oxford University Press, 1953.
Copland, Aaron and Vivian Perlis, *Copland: 1900 Through 1942,* St. Martin's, 1984.
Smith, Julia, *Aaron Copland: His Work and Contribution to American Music,* Dutton, 1955.

Periodicals

New York Times, November 12, 1975; November 9, 1980; September 9, 1984.
New York Times Book Review, September 30, 1984.
Times Literary Supplement, November 2, 1984.
Washington Post Book World, September 30, 1984.

—Rob Nagel

Elvis Costello

Singer, songwriter, guitarist, producer

Elvis Costello has emerged from the punk-rock movement of the late 1970s to become one of the most critically acclaimed artists in contemporary music. While bands like the Sex Pisols and the Clash may have burned more furiously in the beginning, they did, nevertheless, burn out. Costello, on the other hand, definitely had longer range goals in mind, forsaking the mind-numbing three-chord drone and leather garb for a more melodic, yet still powerful, sound and knock-kneed Buddy Holly appearance. In fact, his looks have probably done more than his music to endear him to fans. "He is so much the perfect rock critic hero that he even looks like one of us," wrote Dave Marsh in *Rolling Stone,* "scrawny, bespectacled and neurasthemic, doesn't know when to shut up, bone-dull onstage." Still, his crafty lyrics and my-way-or-the-highway attitude are the main reasons for Costello's noteriety.

Born Declan MacManus, he gained an early introduction to the music world through his father, a singer with the Joe Loss Orchestra, and by the time he was eleven the Beatles' fan club enjoyed his membership. In 1971, when he was sixteen, he moved out of his family's home and began working as a computer programmer at England's Elizabeth Arden cosmetic factory. During the evenings he played bluegrass with Flip City in the pubs of Liverpool. By day he peddled demos of his own songs to countless English record companies, sometimes even playing acoustic guitar and singing for the execs. In 1974 he met Nick Lowe, staff producer and artist for Stiff Records, and in two years Costello was signed to the label.

With the aid of Clover, a California country-rock band, and Lowe producing (as he would the next four LPs), Costello recorded his debut LP in 1977, *My Aim Is True.* With his first single, "Less Than Zero," released in April, the album became America's hottest-selling import of the year. The combination of rockabilly, country, rock and biting lyrics also made it the first New Wave LP to break the American Top 50. After his debut in San Francisco, Costello stated in *Rolling Stone* that "revenge and guilt" were the driving force behind his lyrics. "Those are the only emotions I know about and that I know I can feel. Love? I dunno what it means, really, and it doesn't exist in my songs."

After the Sex Pistols bailed out on "Saturday Night Live" television appearance, Costello agreed to fill in and play "Less Than Zero." Once his segment began, however, he switched songs on the producers and played "Radio, Radio," a scathing commentary on media manipulation which would appear on his next album, *This Year's Model.* He may not have looked as menacing as Johnny Rotten, but when Costello sneered "I want to bite the hand that feeds me," he seemed just as eager to let his feelings towards the establishment be heard. But, as Marsh pointed out in *Rolling Stone,* "given the proper amount of publicity, it is possible that 'Radio, Radio' could destroy Costello's career."

The album also featured the Attractions, Costello's newly formed backup band that included Bruce Thomas on bass, Steve Nieve on keyboards, and Pete Thomas on drums. They provided support on tunes like "Pump It Up" while Costello delivered more of his patented lyrics ("Sometimes I almost feel like a human being"). "For all his surface cockiness, Costello is a man who's trembling underneath," wrote Kit Rachlis in *Rolling Stone,* "a man so suspicious of the world that it doesn't matter whether you're bearing gifts or a blackjack, because *he*'s not convinced it makes a difference."

Costello's third album, *Armed Forces,* included more biting words on "Oliver's Army," the reggae-tinged "Watching the Detectives," and the rumbling "(What's So Funny 'bout) Peace, Love and Understanding." As Mikal Gilmore stated in *Rolling Stone,* [Costello's] "songs seem to be subterfuge: communiques that create the illusion of disclosure while masking the artists' true passions and disillusions." The tour to support the album was a particularly memorable, and violent, one to be sure. After a botched performance in Columbus, Ohio, a drunken Costello ended up in a barroom fight with the Steven Stills and Bonnie Bramlett entourage after he called Ray Charles "nothing but a blind, igno-

rant nigger". (Oddly enough, Costello had been hired by Rock Against Racism, an organization founded in England in the mid-1970s, to headline a 1978 anti-Nazi rally in London.) Death threats followed Costello for the remainder of the tour while his manager, Jake Riviera (the one who coined the name Elvis Costello), and the roadies assumed the role of a goon squad. The band was also heavily into drinking and other vices that caused their playing to be at a nearly breakneck speed and blurred the impact of many of the tunes. Nearly a decade after the Charles incident, Costello told *Rolling Stone* that "there's a tremendous amount of fun in terrorizing people that are so thick-skinned."

After slamming one of the forefathers of soul music, Costello turned right around and released his own version with the LP *Get Happy.* With over twenty tunes packed between the grooves, the album seemed to be a rapid succession of stop-and-go bursts that had Costello's tortured voice as a common denominator. "This is the singing of a man who's so depressed that his bitterness is the one thing that keeps him sane,"

> ## "[Elvis Costello] is so much the perfect rock critic hero that he even looks like one of us."
> ### —Dave Marsh

Tom Carson wrote in *Rolling Stone.* Also in 1980 he released *Taking Liberties,* a collection of B-sides, British album cuts, and unreleased tracks intended for the diehard fan. "By ceremoneously gift-wrapping his trash, "wrote Debra Rae Cohen in *Rolling Stone,* "the artist treats himself with an archivists' reverence usually reserved for the dead."

The initial impact of Costello was beginning to wear off and the music began to settle down, even though his lyrics were as rich as ever. On *Trust* he explored more of the Dylan-styled double meanings, while *Almost Blue* was a hearty helping of country music, pure and simple. Artists like George Jones and Johnny Cash have covered Costello tunes, as have Roy Orbison, Chet Baker, and Dusty Springfield. Costello continued to release an average of one album per year with eight Top 40 LPs in the 1980s. Critics loved his *Imperial Bedroom,* but *Punch the Clock,* which contained his only single to break the Top 40, "Everday I Write The Book," and *Goodbye Cruel World* were deemed a little awkward and uneven by critics.

In 1986 Costello put the Attractions on hold for all but one tune when he recorded *King of America* with a pickup band christened the Confederates (James Burton, Ronnie Tutt, and Jerry Scheff). With that done, he brought the Attractions back for the burning rocker, *Blood and Chocolate,* in order to satisfy demand for something a little harder. The tour to support both albums alternated between the Confederates, the Attractions, and solo acoustic sets by Costello. In addition, an audience participation device called the Spinning Songbook was employed. "I see myself sort of increasingly veering towards a kind of rock 'n' roll Three Stooges," Costello told the *Detroit Free Press.*

During 1987 he began to collaborate with Paul McCartney, writing songs which would eventually appear on *Spike,* Costello's 1989 release that included help from Roger McGuinn, Chrissie Hynde, and the Dirty Dozen Brass Band. It was also his first full album without the Attractions. Like most of his records, it may not outsell the big guns like Madonna or Prince, but then again, he'll never be confused with those types either. "We're not in the same game, are we?," he said to David Wild of *Rolling Stone.* "The truth is, I would rather do it my way and lose money."

Selected discography

My Aim Is True, Columbia, 1977.
This Year's Model, Columbia, 1978.
Armed Forces, Columbia, 1980.
Taking Liberties (B-sides and unreleased tracks), Columbia, 1980.
Trust, Columbia, 1981.
Almost Blue, Columbia, 1981.
Imperial Bedroom, Columbia, 1982.
Punch The Clock, Columbia, 1983.

Goodbye Cruel World, Columbia, 1984.
The Best of Elvis Costello and the Attractions, Vol. I, Columbia, 1985.
Blood and Chocolate, Columbia, 1986.
King of America, Columbia, 1986.
Spike, Warner Brothers, 1989.

Also producer of records, including *The Specials,* 1979; *East Side Story* (for the Squeeze), 1981; and *Rum, Sodomy, and the Lash* (for the Pogues), 1985.

Sources

Books

Christgau, Robert, *Christgau's Record Guide,* Ticknor & Fields, 1981.
The Rolling Stone Illustrated History of Rock and Roll, edited by Jim Miller, Random House/Rolling Stone Press, 1976.
The Rolling Stone Record Guide, edited by Dave Marsh with John Swenson, Random House/Rolling Stone Press, 1979.

Periodicals

Detroit Free Press, April 21, 1989.
Detroit News, April 21, 1989.
Guitar Player, March, 1987.
Interview, February, 1989.
Lansing State Journal, April 13, 1989.
People, June 9, 1986.
Rolling Stone, November 3, 1977; January 12, 1978; May 18, 1978; June 29, 1978; March 22, 1979; April 5, 1979; May 17, 1979; April 17, 1980; December 11, 1980; April 2, 1981; June 1, 1989.

—*Calen D. Stone*

Fats Domino

Singer, songwriter, pianist

After hearing rock pioneer Fats Domino in a 1985 concert in his native Louisiana, Ben Sandmel declared in *down beat* that "a classic rock originator can still be heard in peak form." Sandmel praised Domino for his "indifference to current trends," and related that "Domino sticks to his own vintage sound and repertoire. The instrumentation and arrangements are totally unchanged—no young, disco rhythm sections, for instance." In short, Domino successfully pleases audiences with the same rhythm-and-blues-based music he helped bring to the public's attention with his 1950 hit, "The Fat Man." Credited with playing rock and roll years before the phrase was invented, Domino's non-threatening performance style—called "childlike" and "almost asexual" by Sandmel—helped popularize the new music with mainstream audiences of both blacks and whites. Writing most of his own material, Domino consistently held high positions in either the rhythm and blues or the popular charts for twelve years, keeping his audience singing and dancing with hits like "Blueberry Hill," "Ain't That a Shame," and "Whole Lotta Lovin'."

Born Antoine Domino in 1928, in New Orleans, Louisiana, to a family that would eventually include nine children, he became interested in playing the piano in his youth. He taught himself most of the popular piano styles of his time, including ragtime, blues, and boogie-woogie. Later, during his public career, Domino became known for blending these styles to arrive at some of the basic rock rhythms still used by contemporary performers in the field. But Domino almost missed his chance to effect such influence. Working in a bedspring factory as a young man, one of his hands was injured by a heavy spring, requiring several stitches and making it doubtful that he would be able to use it again. As Gene Busnar reported in his *It's Rock'n' Roll,* however, "through exercise and determination, [Domino] reacquired almost full use of the hand and was able to continue with his piano playing."

In 1949, Domino was playing piano at New Orleans' Hideaway Club for three dollars a week. Lew Chudd, head of the independent Imperial record company in Los Angeles, was seeking new talent to get his label on the charts when he saw Domino play. Chudd signed the young artist, and with Imperial's Dave Bartholomew, Domino penned the song that became his first rhythm and blues hit and established him as "Fats" from then on—"The Fat Man." Noting the appropriateness of the lyrics to Domino's 5-foot-5-inch, 224-pound frame, Ed Ward remarked in *Rock of Ages: The Rolling Stone History of Rock and Roll:* "What better song to introduce the young singer than the one he opened with, the one that said, 'They call, they call me the Fat Man/Because I weigh two hundred pounds.'" As Ward reported, "'Fat Man' took off, winning Imperial some prominence in the

For the Record. . .

Real name, Antoine Domino; born February 26, 1928, in New Orleans, La.; married, wife's name, Rosemary; children: Antoinette, Antoine III, Andrea, Andre, Anatole, Anola, Adonica, Antonio. *Religion:* Roman Catholic.

Worked on an ice truck and in a bedspring factory to support himself early in music career; played with various musicians at numerous venues, including the Hideaway Club in New Orleans, 1949; signed recording contract with Imperial Records, 1950; concert performer, 1950—.

Awards: More than 20 gold records; inducted into Rock and Roll Hall of Fame, 1986; recipient of Grammy Lifetime Achievement Award, 1987.

Addresses: *Residence*—New Orleans, LA. *Office*—c/o Steve Cooper Willard Alexander Agency, 9229 Sunset Blvd., 4th Floor, Los Angeles, CA 90069.

rhythm-and-blues world and, more important, on its charts."

Domino continued to provide Chudd and Imperial with cajun-accented rhythm and blues hits through the next five years, such as "Rockin' Chair," "Goin' Home," and "You Done Me Wrong," but he did not cross over into the popular charts until he released his 1955 "Ain't That a Shame." With his 1956 string of successes, comprised of "I'm in Love Again," a unique version of "My Blue Heaven," "Blue Monday," and his rendition of an old Louis Armstrong recording, "Blueberry Hill," Domino became a standard attraction in traveling rock and roll shows. As Busnar explained, "Most of Fats' songs were less raw and sexually explicit than most other blues-based singers. He was, therefore, more acceptable to the pop audience. Domino was the only successful rhythm and blues singer to have consistent popularity in the pop charts without greatly changing his style." But if his singing and stage personality is mild, "his keyboard work is *right there,*" as Sandmel put it. Domino was also one of the first black performers to be featured in popular music shows, starring with other rock and roll greats like Buddy Holly and the Everly Brothers.

Domino was hot on the rhythm and blues and pop charts through the early sixties, scoring with hits like "Whole Lotta Lovin'," "I'm Ready," "Be My Guest," "Walking to New Orleans," and "Let the Four Winds Blow." But, like that of many other American rock pioneers of the 1950s, Domino's popularity declined

with the introduction of British and psychedelic rock in the 1960s. He left Imperial for ABC in 1963, and had a moderate hit with "Red Sails in the Sunset," but did not reach the charts again except for a modest success with his version of the Beatles' "Lady Madonna" in 1968. He finally stopped recording, he told Hans J. Massaquoi in *Ebony,* because companies wanted him to update his style. "I refused to change," Domino explained. "I had to stick to my own style that I've always used or it just wouldn't be ME."

Meanwhile, in the 1960s Domino began to concentrate his performance efforts in Las Vegas. Playing under contract at the Flamingo Casino there, however, he began to pass the time between shows in the gambling room, starting with the slot machines and soon advanc-

---

Domino successfully pleases audiences with the same rhythm-and-blues-based music he helped bring to the public's attention with his 1950 hit, "The Fat Man."

---

ing to the crap tables. As Massaquoi reported, during a ten year period Domino lost approximately two million dollars gambling, losing as much as one hundred and thirty thousand dollars in one night. He began to realize he had a problem, and through will power was able to taper off until, he told Massaquoi, he was cured of the expensive habit in 1972.

With the nostalgia craze for the 1950s that swept the United States in the late 1970s, Domino experienced a resurgence in popularity. Though he spends more time near his New Orleans home with his wife, Rosemary, and their eight children, he still performs in rock revival shows throughout the country. As Sandmel concluded, "As pure entertainment, Domino's deceptively simple gems [are] beyond improvement."

Compositions

Composer of numerous songs, including "Let the Four Winds Blow," "Walking to New Orleans," "Ain't That a Shame," "Blue Monday," "The Fat Man," "I Want to Walk You Home," "I'm Gonna Be a Wheel Someday," "I'm Walkin'," "and "Whole Lotta Loving."

Selected discography

Single releases; for Imperial, except as noted

"The Fat Man," 1950.
"Korea Blues," 1950.
"Every Night About This Time," 1950.
"Rockin' Chair," 1951.
"Goin' Home," 1952.
"How Long," 1952.
"Goin' to the River," 1953.
"Please Don't Leave Me," 1953.
"Rose Mary," 1953.
"Something's Wrong," 1953.
"You Done Me Wrong," 1954.
"Don't You Know," 1955.
"Ain't That a Shame," 1955.
"All by Myself," 1955.
"Poor Me," 1955.
"Bo Weevil/Don't Blame It on Me," 1956.
"I'm in Love Again/My Blue Heaven," 1956.
"When My Dreamboat Comes Home/So Long," 1956.
"Blueberry Hill," 1956.
"Blue Monday," 1956.
"What's the Reason I'm Not Pleasing You?" 1957.
"I'm Walkin'," 1957.
"Valley of Tears," 1957.
"It's You I Love," 1957.
"When I See You," 1957.
"What Will I Tell My Heart," 1957.
"I Still Love You," 1957.
"Wait and See," 1957.
"The Big Beat," 1957.
"I Want You to Know," 1957.
"Yes, My Darling," 1958.
"Sick and Tired/No No," 1958.
"Little Mary," 1958.
"Young School Girl," 1958.
"Whole Lotta Lovin'," 1958.
"Coquette," 1959.
"Telling Lies," 1959.
"When the Saints Go Marching In," 1959.
"I'm Ready," 1959.
"Margie," 1959.
"I Want to Walk You Home," 1959.

"I'm Gonna Be a Wheel Some Day," 1959.
"Be My Guest," 1959.
"I've Been Around," 1959.
"Country Boy," 1960.
"If You Need Me," 1960.
"Tell Me That You Love Me," 1960.
"Before I Grow Too Old," 1960.
"Walking to New Orleans," 1960.
"Don't Come Knockin'," 1960.
"Three Nights a Week," 1960.
"Put Your Arms Around Me, Honey," 1960.
"My Girl Josephine," 1960.
"Natural Born Lover," 1961.
"Ain't That Just Like a Woman," 1961.
"What a Price," 1961.
"Shu Rah," 1961.
"Fall in Love on Monday," 1961.
"It Keeps Rainin'," 1961.
"Let the Four Winds Blow," 1961.
"Rockin' Bicycle," 1961.
"Jambalaya," 1961.
"I Hear You Knockin'," 1961.
"You Win Again," 1962.
"Ida Jane," 1962.
"My Real Name," 1962.
"Dance With Mr. Domino," 1962.
"Did You Ever See a Dream Walking?" 1962.
"There Goes (My Heart Again)," 1963.
"Red Sails in the Sunset," ABC, 1963.
"Lady Madonna," Reprise, 1968.

Sources

Books

Busnar, Gene, *It's Rock'n'Roll*, Messner, 1979.
Ward, Ed, Geoffrey Stokes, and Ken Tucker, *Rock of Ages: The Rolling Stone History of Rock and Roll*, Summit Books, 1986.

Periodicals

down beat, March, 1985.
Ebony, May, 1974.

—Elizabeth Thomas

Sheena Easton

Singer

Scottish pop singer Sheena Easton first became known in the United States through her hit single "Morning Train." Though this record, and her rendition of "For Your Eyes Only" from the James Bond film of the same title, sold successfully, she did not win the respect of rock and pop critics until 1984, with the release of the controversial "Strut" and "Sugar Walls." These two risqué songs enlivened her middle-of-the-road image, and she has since gone on to have a smash duet with pop/funk superstar Prince, 1987's "U Got the Look."

Born Sheena Shirley Orr and raised near Glasgow, Scotland, the young singer was married to fellow singer and actor Sandi Easton when she made her first real entrance into the entertainment field in 1979. Easton entered and won a singing competition sponsored by the British Broadcasting Corporation (BBC). Her prize included a marketing strategy and image development package that was also covered on camera for the contest's audience, which, as Christopher Connelly reported in *Rolling Stone* in 1985, "led to the charge that Easton had little or no say in her career." She told the critic: "People called me a mindless cretin of pop, a manipulated puppet. It made it look like everyone tells this poor kid what to do, but it never showed *my* decision-making process. It's taken five years for people to know that I *do* make my own decisions."

Despite Easton's complaint about what the handling of her early career did for her image, her popular success was unquestionable. Her 1980 debut single, "Morning Train," about a housewife who stays home and loyally waits for the daily return of her commuting husband, must have touched a chord with many fans, for it sold well. Easton also had moderate success with the change-of-pace follow-up song, "Modern Girl," which concerned a sexually liberated young woman proud of her lack of attachment to any particular man. But she quickly showed her ability with a ballad when she was chosen to record the theme from "For Your Eyes Only," the 1981 film adventure of author Ian Fleming's famous spy character, James Bond.

From there, however, Easton's career went into a brief decline. Never especially favored by music critics, Easton was blasted for her duet with country singer Kenny Rogers, a remake of rocker Bob Seger's "We've Got Tonight." Connelly, for instance, labeled her interpretation "shrieking and insensitive"; it was, however, a popular success. And she had other hits, including "When He Shines," and "You Could Have Been With Me." But in the mid-1980s, Easton decided to toughen her image and try for "a harder sound," as Connelly put it. She had difficulty, though, finding the right material, she confided to Connelly. "It was like getting blood out

For the Record. . .

Full name, Sheena Shirley Orr, born c. 1959 near Glasgow, Scotland; married Sandi Easton (a singer and actor), 1978 (divorced c. 1979); married Rob Light (a musical manager), 1984 (divorced December 1986). *Education:* Attended Royal Scottish Academy of Music and Drama.

Solo recording artist and concert performer, c. 1980—.

Addresses: c/o MCA Records, 100 Universal City Plaza, Universal City, CA 91608.

of a stone. . . . The great rock songs would go straight to [rock singer] Pat Benatar."

Finally, in 1984, Easton's luck began to change. She was given a demo tape of "Strut," which she decided to record, and one of her recording engineers, David Leonard, asked Prince to write a song for her. The pop star obliged with "Sugar Walls," and both songs became hits. In addition to gaining a critical reevaluation with the tough-sounding danceable tunes, Easton also generated some controversy. "Strut" features hints of sadomasochism with its lyrics about leather, but according to Richard Sanders in *People,* "Sugar Walls" was branded pornographic by the Parents Music Resource Center, a group which favors putting ratings on records similar to those applied to films. The song was also banned from several radio stations. The attention focused on "Sugar Walls," however, probably only served to increase public demand for the record.

Easton's newfound success gained an added boost in 1987. After setbacks such as an album of ballads not being released because of a change of management on the part of EMI, her recording company, and her second divorce, she won a four-week role on the popular television series "Miami Vice." Though she had studied acting at the Royal Scottish Academy of Music and Drama, she had difficulty persuading the show to let her try out. When she did audition, she impressed the series' people favorably, but she was not their first choice—she got the part when the chosen actress became ill. Easton also added to her lists of accomplishments that year a hit duet with Prince, "U Got the Look," which Sanders lauded as "notable for its deep funk groove and single-entendre lyrics." In 1988, she released the album *The Lover in Me.*

Selected discography

Singles

"Morning Train," EMI, c. 1980.
"Modern Girl," EMI, c. 1980.
"For Your Eyes Only," EMI, 1981.
"When He Shines," EMI, 1981.
"You Could Have Been With Me," EMI, 1981.
"Strut," EMI, 1984.
"Sugar Walls," EMI, 1984.

Also recorded "We've Got Tonight" with Kenny Rogers, and "U Got the Look," in 1987 with Prince.

Albums

You Could Have Been With Me, EMI, 1981.
Money, Madness, and Music, EMI, 1982.
Best Kept Secret, EMI, 1983.
A Private Heaven, EMI, 1984.
The Lover in Me, MCA, 1988.

Sources

People, November 22, 1982; November 23, 1987.
Rolling Stone, May 9, 1985.

—Elizabeth Thomas

Duke Ellington

Bandleader, composer, pianist

Duke Ellington was eulogized as "the supreme jazz talent of the past fifty years" by critic Alistair Cooke in a 1983 issue of *Esquire.* A prolific composer, Ellington created over two thousand pieces of music, including the standard songs "Take the A-Train" and "It Don't Mean a Thing (If It Ain't Got That Swing)" and the longer works *Black, Brown, and Beige, Liberian Suite,* and *Afro-Eurasian Eclipse.* With the variously named bands he led from 1919 until his death in 1974, Ellington was responsible for many innovations in the jazz field, such as "jungle-style" use of the growl and plunger, and the manipulation of the human voice as an instrument—singing notes without words. During the course of his long career, Ellington was showered with many honors, including the highest civilian award granted by the United States, the Presidential Medal of Freedom, which was presented to him by President Richard M. Nixon in 1969. "No one else," concluded Cooke, "in the eighty- or ninety-year history of jazz, created so personal an orchestral sound and so continuously expanded the jazz idiom."

Born Edward Kennedy Ellington in Washington, D.C., on April 29, 1899, to a middle-class black family, he was exposed to music at an early age. Both his father—who made blueprints for the navy and served as a White House butler—and his mother could play the piano. The Ellingtons were strongly religious and hoped that if their son learned piano he would later exchange it for the church organ, but at first he was uncooperative. At the age of six young Ellington labeled his piano teacher "Miss Clinkscales" and, according to *Esquire,* "was her poorest pupil," the only child to forget his part in her yearly piano recital. As he grew older Ellington became interested in drawing and painting, and won a prize from the National Association for the Advancement of Colored People (NAACP) for a poster he created, but continued his music lessons because he noticed that pretty girls tended to flock around piano players.

Ellington began to take the piano more seriously as a high-school student and learned much from his school's music teacher, Henry Grant. When he was fifteen Ellington worked after school in a soda shop; the experience led him to write his first jazz song, "Soda Fountain Rag." At about this time, he also acquired the nickname Duke. There are many stories explaining how Ellington obtained the moniker, but the most prevalent says that he had a young, elegant, social-climbing friend who felt that admission into his circle demanded that Ellington have a noble title, and the label stuck. Ellington dropped out of high school to pursue his musical career, playing in jazz bands by night and supplementing his income by painting signs during the

For the Record. . .

Full name Edward Kennedy Ellington; born April 29, 1899, in Washington, D.C.; died May 24, 1974; son of James Edward (a butler, carpenter, and blueprint maker) and Daisy (Kennedy) Ellington; married Edna Thompson, July 2, 1918 (separated); children: Mercer. *Education:* High-school dropout.

Worked in a soda shop and as a sign painter in his youth; began playing in jazz bands c. 1917; served as a U.S. Navy and State Department messenger during World War I; began leading his own band c. 1919; performed in Washington, D.C., and New York City during the 1920s, and various other cities throughout the world beginning in the 1930s; concert performer and recording artist with his various bands until his death of cancer in 1974. Appeared in and/or wrote scores for films, including *Check and Double Check,* 1930, *Anatomy of a Murder, Paris Blues,* and *Assault on a Queen.*

Awards: Received numerous awards, including the French Legion of Honor, the President's Gold Medal, the Presidential Medal of Freedom, several Grammys, an Academy Award nomination for the score of *Paris Blues.*

day. Often he managed to persuade club owners to let him paint the signs announcing the group's engagement.

Influenced by the style of earlier jazz artist Doc Perry, Ellington continued to work on his piano playing and, after the end of World War I, formed his own band. Critics note that it was his band, rather than his piano, that was his true instrument. He composed, not so much with a particular instrument in mind, but rather thinking of the current band member who played that instrument, suiting the music to the style of the player. Though the turnover rate in Ellington's band was not high, due to the band's longevity many musicians and singers played with Ellington over the years: Toby Hardwick, Elmer Snowden, William Greer, Barney Bigard, Wellman Braud, Harry Carney, Johnny Hodges, Bubber Miley, Joe Nanton, Cootie Williams, Adelaide Hall, and Billy Strayhorn are among the more notable. Ellington and his band began playing local clubs and parties in Washington, D.C., during the early 1920s, but soon moved to New York City, where they secured a three-year engagement at the popular Cotton Club.

During the 1920s and 1930s, Ellington branched out into writing musical revues, such as *Chocolate Kiddies,* a success in Germany; playing in Broadway musicals, such as the 1929 *Show Girl;* and appearing with his band in motion pictures, such as the 1930 Amos and Andy feature *Check and Double Check.* Later Ellington composed scores for films and was nominated for an Academy Award for the music of *Paris Blues* (1961). But during the 1930s he was also experimenting with the infusion of Latin American elements into jazz; perhaps the most famous example of this work is his "Caravan." In 1939 Strayhorn joined Ellington's band, beginning a composition partnership that lasted until Strayhorn's death in 1967. The band's horizons expanded geographically in the 1930s as well—Ellington on tour was well received not only by audiences throughout the United States, but also in Europe.

In 1943 Ellington helped set up an annual jazz concert series at New York City's Carnegie Hall. The series lasted until 1955, and Ellington was deeply involved with it each year. He used the yearly event to premiere new, longer works of jazz that he composed. For the first concert, Ellington introduced *Black, Brown, and Beige,* a piece in three sections that represented symphonically the story of blacks in the United States.

> *Critics note that it was Ellington's band, rather than his piano, that was his true instrument.*

"Black" concerned black people at work and at prayer, "Brown" celebrated black soldiers who fought in the American Revolution, and "Beige" depicted the black music of Harlem. Other Carnegie Hall debuts included *New World a-Comin',* about a black revolution to come after the end of World War II, *Liberian Suite,* commissioned by the government of Liberia to honor its centennial, *The Tattooed Bride,* and *Night Creature.*

During the mid 1960s Ellington and his band, ever innovative, started to perform jazz-style sacred-music concerts in large cathedrals throughout the world. The first was in San Francisco's Grace Episcopal Cathedral in 1965 and included *In the Beginning God.* He featured different songs at his 1968 concert in New York City's Episcopal Cathedral of St. John the Divine. Ellington also presented his sacred music at St. Sulpice in Paris, Santa Maria del Mar in Barcelona, and Westminster Abbey in London.

Duke Ellington was active as a performer and composer until his death of lung cancer on May 24, 1974, in New York City. Though his audiences constantly demanded such old standards as "Mood Indigo" and "In a Sentimental Mood," Ellington preferred to look ahead and develop new songs for his band. One of his last was "The Blues Is Waitin'." After his death, his only son, Mercer Ellington, who had been serving as the band's business manager and trumpet player, took over its leadership. But Ellington will always be remembered, in the words of Phyl Garland in *Ebony* magazine, for "the daring innovations that [marked] his music—the strange modulations built upon lush melodies that ramble into unexpected places; the unorthodox construction of songs . . . [and] the bold use of dissonance in advance of the time."

Selected discography

Shorter works; recorded primarily on Reprise and RCA

"Black and Tan Fantasy," 1927.
"East St. Louis Toodle-Oo," 1927.
"Creole Love Call," 1927.
"Hot and Bothered," 1928.
"Mood Indigo," 1931.
"It Don't Mean a Thing (If It Ain't Got That Swing)," 1932.
"Sophisticated Lady," 1933.
"Drop Me Off at Harlem," 1933.
"In a Sentimental Mood," 1935.
"Caravan," 1937.
"Empty Ballroom Blues," 1938.
"Concerto for Cootie," 1939.

Also recorded "Soda Fountain Rag," "Take the A-Train," "Solitude," "I Got It Bad and That Ain't Good," "When a Black Man's Blue," "Rockin' in Rhythm," and "The Blues Is Waitin'."

Longer works; recorded primarily on Reprise and RCA

Creole Rhapsody, 1931.

Reminiscing in Tempo, 1935.
Black, Brown, and Beige, 1943.
New World a-Comin', 1943.
The Deep South Suite, 1946.
Liberian Suite, 1947.
The Tattooed Bride, 1948.
Harlem, 1951.
Night Creature, 1955.
Festival Suite, 1956.
Suite Thursday, 1960.
My People, 1963.
Golden Broom, 1964.
Green Apple, 1964.
In the Beginning God, 1965.
The River, 1970.
Afro-Eurasian Eclipse, 1970.
Toga Brava, 1973.

Also recorded *Shakespearian Suite*, *The Far East Suite*, and *New Orleans Suite*.

Sources

Books

Ellington, Duke, *Music Is My Mistress*, Doubleday, 1973.
Jewell, Derek, *Duke: A Portrait of Duke Ellington*, Norton, 1977.

Periodicals

The Crisis, January, 1982.
Ebony, July, 1969.
Esquire, December, 1983.
The Progressive, August, 1982.

—Elizabeth Thomas

Gloria Estefan

Singer

Gloria Estefan has become the leading force behind the Miami Sound Machine, a Latin-influenced pop band with a series of spicy dance hits. Born in Cuba but raised in Miami, the sultry Estefan had to overcome crippling shyness in order to perform; she blossomed just at the moment when her group began to write songs in English. Today, Estefan is not only the principal singer in the Miami Sound Machine, but also the band's manager of group operations. Together, Estefan and her partners—husband Emilio Estefan, Jr., Enrique Garcia, and Juan Marcos Avila—have forged a "bright, salsafied pop" that has given Americans a new dance beat, to quote *People* contributor Linda Marx.

The members of Miami Sound Machine, Estefan included, were born in Cuba. Their families became refugees to America during the revolution that brought Fidel Castro to power. In Gloria Estefan's case, her father was a bodyguard to dictator Fulgencio Batista's family; after moving to the United States he worked for the American military. Her mother had been a schoolteacher in Cuba, so after learning English—and teaching it to young Gloria—she earned a master's degree and went back to work. Gloria was placed in charge of the housekeeping at an early age, thus binding her to her home at a time when other children were forming social ties. She told *People* that she spent hours listening to the radio. "I would sit in my room and sing Top 40 songs and teach myself how to play guitar enough to accompany them," she said.

A career in pop music was not even a dream for Estefan. The shy young woman attended a Catholic girls' school and the University of Miami, where she majored in psychology. In 1975 she joined a local band, the Miami Latin Boys, and began to perform more or less as a hobby. Three years later she married the group's percussionist, Emilio Estefan, and their combo, renamed the Miami Sound Machine, began to attract attention.

For more than six years the Miami Sound Machine was better known outside the United States than within it. The group's straightforward Spanish-language pop music became a hit in Latin America, and in the early 1980s Estefan and her partners were packing soccer stadiums in Peru, Ecuador, Panama, and Guatemala. They also cut an album that sold one million copies in Europe but did very little business in America. "It was kind of strange," Estefan told the *Detroit Free Press*. "We'd play those [big] shows, then come back to Miami where we were just a local club band."

At the same time, Estefan was wrestling with her shyness. *Detroit Free Press* correspondent Gary Graff claims that the singer "used to try to hide behind the

For the Record. . .

Born c. 1958 in Havana, Cuba; daughter of a bodyguard to Fulgencio Batista and a schoolteacher; married Emilio Estefan, Jr. (a musician), 1978; children: Nayib. *Education:* University of Miami, B.A. in psychology.

Joined group Miami Latin Boys, 1975; name changed to Miami Sound Machine; other members are Enrique Garcia, Juan Marcos Avila, and Emilio Estefan, Jr. Toured Latin America and Europe numerous times, 1976-84, had several hit albums in Spanish. Had first million-selling American album, *Primitive Love,* 1986. Represented United States at the Pan American Games, 1987.

Addresses: *Record company*—Epic Records, 51 W. 52nd St., New York, NY 10019.

congas rather than dance in front of them." Estefan told Graff: "I remember I used to stand there and clutch the microphone and close my eyes and look down. I tried to be as inconspicuous as possible—with a spotlight on me. I'd videotape myself, and I hated it. I used to sit on the sofa and look through my fingers at the tape and just cringe." Estefan changed by a sheer act of will, and just in time—group member Enrique Garcia started to write English lyrics for the Miami Sound Machine.

In 1986 Estefan's band finally found an American audience. The album *Primitive Love* sold more than a million copies and produced three hit singles, "Conga," "Bad Boys," and "Words Get in the Way." A subsequent release, *Let It Loose,* contained the number one single "1-2-3." Suddenly, the Miami Sound Machine was in demand, and Gloria Estefan—married and mother of a son—found herself cast as a sex symbol. "Now that's something I never expected to be," she told Graff. "But I see where it could happen. And [husband] Emilio's been working very hard for that image. . . . He's a businessman and he knows that image is going to help us sell records."

That image may *help* to sell records, but it is hardly enough in and of itself to guarantee success. Estefan bolsters her "sex symbol" looks with a velvety soprano voice and a dramatic flair that adds pitch to the up-tempo numbers. Her accomplishment is so striking that the group she fronts has been renamed once again: it is now Gloria Estefan and the Miami Sound Machine. "People think that was my idea," Estefan told Graff, "but it really wasn't. The record company wanted me to have an identity." Estefan's professional identity is certainly assured, with two gold albums and more than five hit singles to her credit.

When not on tour, Estefan lives in Miami with her husband and son, Nayib. Her band has been honored in its hometown by having a major street named after it—Miami Sound Machine Boulevard. Estefan told *People* that the television show "Miami Vice" has "conjured up images of drugs and violence. We're goodwill ambassadors for [Miami]." The singer told *Teen* magazine that she has become successful because both her mother and grandmother were independent women who worked hard for their achievements. "I've grown up," she said, "with a very strong example that women can really do anything they want to."

Selected discography

Eyes of Innocence, Epic.
Primitive Love, Epic, 1985.
Let It Loose, Epic, 1987.

Sources

Detroit Free Press, August 1, 1988.
People, October 27, 1986.
Teen, October, 1988.

—Anne Janette Johnson

The Everly Brothers

Singers, songwriters, guitarists

The Everly Brothers, Phil and Don, have been summed up as "two primordial presences from the dawn of rock history, without whose precise vocal harmonics . . . there would have been no McCartney and Lennon, no Simon and Garfunkel, no California country-rock sound" by Jim Jerome of *People* magazine. Singers on their parents' country radio show since childhood, the Everly Brothers crossed over to the field of popular music with their 1957 smash, "Bye, Bye, Love." Soon renowned for the harmonious blending of their voices, they had a string of hits in the late 1950s and early 1960s that included "Wake Up, Little Susie," "Bird Dog," "Cathy's Clown," and "I'll Do My Crying in the Rain." Though the popularity of British groups and psychedelic rock in the later 1960s diminished the demand for the Everly Brothers' music, they continued to play small concerts and release recordings together until 1973. At that time, they separated for ten years, not speaking to each other. In 1983, however, they reunited, garnering much critical acclaim for their new albums, and for their concert performances.

Don, the eldest, was born in 1937 in Brownie, Kentucky; Phil was born in 1939 in Chicago, Illinois. Their parents, Ike and Margaret Everly, landed a country music radio show in Shenandoah, Iowa, in 1945. Don was the first brother to join the show, featured in his own spot, "The Little Donnie Show." As he revealed to Kurt Loder in *Rolling Stone,* "I'd sing three or four songs, read a commercial, and go home." When Don was eight and Phil was six, the youngest brother was brought into the act, and they sang as a duo. Both brothers agree that their father, Ike, taught them everything they know about singing and guitar playing, and that his style influenced them deeply. Don Everly told Loder that "Country's not the right word for what [Ike Everly] played. It was more uptown, more honky-tonk. I'll tell you the right word for it: blues. White blues."

By the 1950s, however, live radio music shows were on the way out and the brothers knew that recordings, concerts, and television appearances had become the way to establish a musical career. Ike brought his sons to the attention of guitarist Chet Atkins, who placed songs that Don had written with country stars Kitty Wells and Anita Carter. With the royalty money this provided, Don and Phil set off for Nashville to audition for a recording contract. There, they cut a record for Columbia in 1956 called "Keep A' Lovin' Me," but it did not catch on with the public. Finally, the Everlys met up with Wesley Rose, who was the president of Acuff-Rose, a music publishing company. Rose told the brothers he would get them a record deal if they would sign on with Acuff-Rose as songwriters. Phil and Don agreed, and Rose introduced them to Archie Bleyer, who owned

Don's full name, Isaac Donald Everly; born February 1, 1937, in Brownie, Ky.; Phil born January 19, 1939, in Chicago, Ill.; sons of Ike and Margaret Everly (musicians who hosted their own radio show); Don married Sue Ingraham (divorced, 1961); married second wife, Venetia Stevenson (divorced); married third wife, Karen Prettyman (divorced); children: three girls, one boy; Phil married Jackie Ertel (divorced); married second wife, 1971 (divorced); children: (first marriage) Jordan, Patricia, Mickey; (second marriage) Christopher.

The brothers appeared with parents as "The Everlys" on country music radio program in Shenandoah, Iowa, during the late 1940s; Don wrote and sold songs to Kitty Wells and Anita Carter during the early and mid-1950s; performed as the Everly Brothers, 1956-73; each persued solo careers until reunited in 1983. Hosted ABC-TV variety program for ten weeks, 1970.

Awards: Inducted into Rock and Roll Hall of Fame, 1986.

Addresses: (**Don**) *Residence*—Nashville, TN. *Office*—c/o 10100 Santa Monica Blvd., #1600, Los Angeles, CA. (**Phil**) *Residence*—Los Angeles, CA. *Office*—c/o 10414 Camarillo St., North Hollywood, CA 91602.

Cadence, a New York-based record label. Bleyer was looking to branch out into the field of country music at the time, and eagerly signed the Everly Brothers. He liked the material that Phil and Don had written themselves, but he offered them a song written by the husband and wife team Boudleaux and Felice Bryant, "Bye, Bye, Love."

Thus began a long and profitable association. Though the Bryants' song had already been turned down by several country artists, the Everly Brother's 1957 recording of it not only became a country smash but reached number two on the pop music charts. Phil and Don followed "Bye, Bye, Love" with another Bryant composition, "Wake Up, Little Susie." "Susie" quickly shot up the charts, but was soon banned in Boston and other United States cities because it was deemed too suggestive. Ironically, the song's lyrics describe an innocent episode in which two teenagers on a date fall asleep watching a boring movie at the drive-in, and fear parental and peer suspicions about why they broke their curfew. Undaunted by their brush with notoriety, the Everly Brothers continued to put out hit records for the Cadence label, including the 1958 efforts "All I Have to Do Is Dream," "Bird Dog," and "Problems"; and the 1959 singles "Poor Jenny" and "Till I Kissed You."

In 1960, the Everly Brothers left Cadence for Warner Brothers, and had their biggest hit, "Cathy's Clown," a song that they wrote themselves. But, though Phil and Don had many more hits in the early 1960s, like "Walk Right Back," "Ebony Eyes," and "That's Old-Fashioned," their days in the upper part of the charts were numbered. The change of style that took place in the mid-1960s (ironically vanguarded by the Beatles, who were deeply influenced by the Everly Brothers' use of harmony) decreased the demand for traditional American rock and roll. Though they continued to perform and cut records into the 1970s, tensions began to develop between the brothers—their business keeping them so constantly together—and in their individual personal lives. Both brothers suffered from drug abuse problems, but Don's dependence on the then-legitimate Ritalin drug therapy led him into deeper trouble than Phil experienced. After twice attempting suicide, Don was committed to a mental hospital and given electroshock therapy. Both brothers experienced multiple divorces; Don, three, and Phil, two. Finally, Don told Phil that their performances at Knott's Berry Farm near Los Angeles, California, in July, 1973, would be their last. Though Don had conquered his Ritalin dependence, according to Loder he showed up for one of the shows so drunk that "a Knott's manager stopped the show midway through the second of three scheduled sets. Phil, furious, stormed offstage, smashing his guitar to the floor before disappearing."

Don decided it was time to reunite and make a comeback in 1983. Phil, having as little success as his brother had as a solo artist, agreed. Ten months later they gave a much-publicized reunion concert at the Royal Albert Hall in London, England, which was videotaped and shown on the Home Box Office cable network. The critics raved. "Once the Everlys buried the hatchet . . . it was as if they had never been away. Their fusion of sweet Appalachian harmonies, rock arrangements and lyrical sentiment . . . seemed, indeed, as powerful as ever," announced Jerome.

After the reunion concert, the brothers recorded their first studio album in ten years, *EB '84,* which also met with enthusiastic critical response. *EB '84* featured a song donated to the Everlys by Paul McCartney, "On the Wings of a Nightingale," which Loder in a *Rolling Stone* review lauded as "almost impossibly perfect." Loder went on to declare that on *EB '84* the Everlys "truly never have sounded better," and concluded that "these are voices so rich, and so symbiotically attuned to each other, that their effect seems to go beyond simple artistry and to resonate instead on a cellular level."

In 1986, the Everlys told Jay Cocks of *Time* that they were now settled and comfortable in their new performing relationship. Phil explained: "Don and I are infamous for our split, but we're closer than most brothers. Harmony singing requires that you enlarge yourself, not use any kind of suppression. Harmony is the ultimate love." As Cocks concluded from their 1986 album *Born Yesterday*, "The Everlys are back. They are back to stay. Back, and as good as ever. And rock 'n' roll just doesn't get any better than that."

Selected discography

Major single releases

"Keep A' Lovin' Me," Columbia, 1956.
"Bye, Bye, Love," Cadence, 1957.
"Wake Up, Little Susie," Cadence, 1957.
"This Little Girl of Mine," Cadence, 1958.
"All I Have to Do Is Dream," Cadence, 1958.
"Claudette," Cadence, 1958.
"Bird Dog," Cadence, 1958.
"Devoted to You," Cadence, 1958.
"Problems," Cadence, 1958.
"Love of My Life," Cadence, 1958.
"Take a Message to Mary," Cadence, 1959.
"Poor Jenny," Cadence, 1959.
"Till I Kissed You," Cadence, 1959.
"Let It Be Me," Cadence, 1960.
"Be-Bop-a-Lula," Cadence, 1960.
"Like Strangers," Cadence, 1960.
"Cathy's Clown," Warner Brothers, 1960.
"Always It's You," Warner Brothers, 1960.
"So Sad," Warner Brothers, 1960.
"Lucille," Warner Brothers, 1960.
"Walk Right Back," Warner Brothers, 1961.
"Ebony Eyes," Warner Brothers, 1961.
"Temptation," Warner Brothers, 1961.
"Stick With Me, Baby," Warner Brothers, 1961.
"Don't Blame Me," Warner Brothers, 1961.
"Muskrat," Warner Brothers, 1961.
"I'm Here to Get My Baby Out of Jail," Cadence, 1962.
"Crying in the Rain," Warner Brothers, 1962.
"That's Old-Fashioned," Warner Brothers, 1962.

LPs

The Everly Brothers, Cadence, 1958.

Songs Our Daddy Taught Us, Cadence, 1958.
The Everly Brothers: Their Best, Cadence, 1959.
The Fabulous Style of the Everly Brothers, Cadence, 1960.
It's Everly Time, Warner Brothers, 1960.
A Date With the Everly Brothers, Warner Brothers, 1960.
Both Sides of an Evening, Warner Brothers, 1961.
Instant Party, Warner Brothers, 1962.
Golden Hits, Warner Brothers, 1962.
Christmas With the Everly Brothers, Warner Brothers, 1962.
The Everly Brothers Sing Great Country Hits, Warner Brothers, 1963.
Very Best of the Everly Brothers, Warner Brothers, 1965.
Rock'n' Soul, Warner Brothers, 1965.
Gone, Gone, Gone, Warner Brothers, 1965.
Beat and Soul, Warner Brothers, 1965.
In Our Image, Warner Brothers, 1965.
Two Yanks in England, Warner Brothers, 1965.
The Everly Brothers Sing, Warner Brothers, 1967.
Roots, Warner Brothers, 1968.
The Everly Brothers Show, Warner Brothers, 1970.
Stories We Could Tell, RCA, 1972.
Pass the Chicken, RCA, 1973.
EB '84, Polydor, 1984.
Born Yesterday, Polydor, 1986.

Don Everly

Don Everly, Ode, 1971.
Sunset Towers, Ode, 1974.
Brother Juke Box, Hickory, 1977.

Phil Everly

Star Spangled Springer, RCA, 1973.
Phil's Diner, Pye, 1974.
Mystic Line, Pye, 1975.
Phil Everly, Elektra, 1979.

Sources

Books

Busnar, Gene, *It's Rock'n'Roll,* Messner, 1979.

Periodicals

People, January 23, 1984.
Rolling Stone, September 13, 1984; May 8, 1986.
Time, March 17, 1986.

—Elizabeth Thomas

John Fogerty

Singer, songwriter, guitarist

John Fogerty is "a great American songwriter, with the clean-cut narrative gifts of [rock pioneer] Chuck Berry, the honesty of [country star] Hank Williams and the rave-up musical skills of a perfesser in a Saturday night juke joint," declared Jay Cocks of *Time*. Perhaps best known as the driving force behind what Jim Miller of *Newsweek* labeled "the best American rock band of its era," Creedence Clearwater Revival, Fogerty, with his writing, lead guitar, and vocals, led the group to prominence during the late 1960s and early 1970s. With the other members of Creedence, he is responsible for rock classics such as "Proud Mary," "Bad Moon Rising," and "Who'll Stop the Rain." After Creedence disbanded in 1972, Fogerty's first attempt at making a solo career for himself was only moderately successful. In the mid-1970s he became embroiled in legal battles with Fantasy, Creedence's record label, and an accounting firm that had allegedly mishandled his funds; embittered, he dropped out of the music scene for approximately nine years. In 1985, however, Fogerty resurfaced with a new album, *Centerfield*—in addition to the smash title-track paean to baseball, it includes the hits "The Old Man down the Road" and "Rock and Roll Girls."

The multitalented Fogerty began his musical career while still in junior high in El Cerrito, California. He got together with fellow students Stu Cook and Doug Clifford to form a group called the Blue Velvets. They were later joined by Fogerty's older brother Tom and performed in the San Francisco Bay area. The young men also made a few recordings on small local labels such as Kristy and Orchestra, but these efforts did not sell. In 1964, however, the Blue Velvets landed a contract with Fantasy Records in nearby Berkeley. A year later, the group had changed its name to the Golliwogs, but they were still unable to make a hit record. Fantasy lost interest in them, but when Saul Zaentz bought the label, he encouraged the Golliwogs to come back, though he suggested the group find itself a better name. Thus, in 1968, Creedence Clearwater Revival was born.

Creedence's first hit single was a 1968 revision of a song by Dale Hawkins, with John Fogerty singing the lead—"Suzie-Q." After that, the band primarily kept to recording Fogerty's original compositions. In 1969 Creedence had several chart hits, including "Proud Mary," "Bad Moon Rising," "Lodi," "Green River," and "Commotion." They followed these up with 1970's "Who'll Stop the Rain," "Looking Out My Back Door," and "Run through the Jungle," which Cocks credited as one of "the first songs about Viet Nam that sounded as if [it] could have been sung by the soldiers as well as peace marchers." In 1971, however, tensions arising from John Fogerty's artistic domination of the group led Tom Fogerty to leave it. Though John Fogerty subsequently shared the songwriting tasks with the remaining members, and completed a successful European tour with them, Creedence finally broke up in 1972.

When John Fogerty became a solo artist, he released the country-flavored *Blue Ridge Rangers* in 1973. Through the use of overdubbing different tracks during the recording process, he played all of the instruments and sang all of the vocals himself. Fogerty's efforts were rewarded with borderline-hit status for the album's single "Hearts of Stone." He released a few more albums, but none enjoyed the popularity of his work with Creedence.

Fogerty stopped recording in the mid-1970s, however, when legal disputes with Fantasy and his accounting firm began to take up much of his time. "There was an anvil over my head," Fogerty told Cocks. "Writing, the music, my understanding of 'arrange' and 'produce' were gone." But he planned to make a comeback when the legal battles were over, and he continued to practice daily. "I knew that if I kept working on the music, not getting somebody else to play bass or anything for me, that if I somehow understood the music again the way I did in the beginning, when it was so personal, when I did it with my own two hands, I knew that somehow each of the motions would help release me," Fogerty explained to Cocks.

Finally, in the early 1980s, Fogerty began to write songs again. He composed what would become *Centerfield* in roughly five and a half months and took the results to Warner Brothers Records. According to Cocks, Fogerty asked Lenny Waronker, the president of the company, "How does a 39-year-old has-been rock singer get you to listen to his records?" Waronker was more than agreeable to listening and was impressed by Fogerty's material—*Centerfield* was on its way.

Most critics raved about the 1985 release, on which

Fogerty again played all the instruments himself; most of them also noted its relationship to the swampy-sounding Creedence repertoire. "Fogerty's new music [is] like rediscovering a long-lost friend," Miller observed, and Kurt Loder of *Rolling Stone* proclaimed it "a near-seamless extension of the Creedence sound and a record that's likely to convert a whole new generation of true believers." *Centerfield* rose quickly on the album charts, hitting the Top 10 in only three weeks. "The Old Man down the Road," the first single from the album, "sounds like nothing else on the radio," applauded Cocks, "a swampy, spooky piece of back-country funk about a mojo man who becomes a figure of mystery, and of death." Another hit, "Rock and Roll Girls," was praised by Loder as "a rather spectacular demonstration of what can still be done with three shitty chords and a blatzing sax." Of course, the album's title song, in which Fogerty uses his love of baseball as a metaphor for his joy in making music, has become not only a hit record but a standard anthem played in baseball stadiums across the United States. Other interesting cuts from *Centerfield* include "Big Train," a tribute to the old

> "Fogerty's music seems timeless . . . torn out of some imaginary territory in rock's persistent past."

rockabilly sound of Sun Records, and "Zanz Kant Danz," which, Loder speculates, may be an attack on the former head of Fantasy Records, Saul Zaentz.

Though Loder complained that some of *Centerfield*'s material is dated, Cocks argued that Fogerty's music seems "timeless . . . torn out of some imaginary territory in rock's persistent past." Miller concluded that "Fogerty's sensibility has an enduring popular appeal," and hailed him as "the once and future poet laureate of the pop single."

Selected discography

With Creedence Clearwater Revival; on Fantasy Records

Creedence Clearwater Revival (includes "Suzie-Q"), 1968.
Bayou Country (includes "Proud Mary" and "Born on the Bayou"), 1969.
Green River (includes "Green River," "Bad Moon Rising," "Lodi," "Commotion," and "Wrote a Song for Everyone"), 1969.

Willy and the Poor Boys (includes "Down on the Corner" and "Fortunate Son"), 1969.

Cosmo's Factory (includes "Travelin' Band," "Who'll Stop the Rain," "Up around the Bend," "Run through the Jungle," "Looking Out My Back Door," and "Long As I Can See the Light"), 1970.

Pendulum (includes "Have You Ever Seen the Rain?" and "Hey, Tonight"), 1970.

Mardi Gras (includes "Sweet Hitchhiker" and "Someday Never Comes"), 1972.

Solo LPs

Blue Ridge Rangers (includes "Hearts of Stone"), Fantasy, 1973.

Centerfield (includes "Centerfield," "The Old Man down the Road," "Rock and Roll Girls," "Searchlight," "I Saw It on TV," "Big Train," "Mr. Greed," "I Can't Help Myself," and "Zanz Kant Danz"), Warner Brothers, 1985.

Eye of the Zombie, Warner Brothers, c. 1986.

Also recorded *John Fogerty* and *Hoodoo* with Asylum Records in the early 1970s.

Sources

Newsweek, February 18, 1985.
Rolling Stone, January 31, 1985; March 14, 1985.
Time, January 28, 1985.

—*Elizabeth Thomas*

Aretha Franklin

Singer

Aretha Franklin has reigned as the "Queen of Soul" for more than twenty years. One of the first female performers to inject the rhythms and intensity of black gospel music into the pop format, Franklin has been hailed as the finest, most enduring soul singer of a generation by black and white audiences alike. A long series of personal setbacks—divorces, fear of flying, shyness, and the shooting death of her father—have failed to dim Franklin's career or her popularity. She is one of a very few artists who have had million-selling albums in three decades, one of an even smaller group of performers who could, in her mid-forties, reach out to the hip, predominately teenage MTV audience. "No great singer is more self-effacing than Aretha Franklin," writes Mark Moses in the *New Yorker,* "and that's a matter of imagery as well as of music. Her meaning as a popular icon is elusive. The Queen of Soul doesn't bear up comfortably under the steady weight of myth. . . . Her notorious offstage reclusiveness and timid manner bespeak an anonymous homebody rather than a sheltered deity. . . . The contours of her career have the ups and downs you'd expect of someone who has worked as long as she has, but often the highs are as inexplicable as the lows. Every four years or so over the last twenty, Franklin has experienced 'comebacks' that have never registered with much authenticity, partly because she had never gone away."

A *Time* magazine reporter once observed that Franklin "does not seem to be performing so much as bearing witness to a reality so simple and compelling that she could not possibly fake it." Such onstage sincerity and verve no doubt stem from Franklin's background in evangelical gospel music. The daughter of an immensely popular Baptist minister, Reverend C. L. Franklin, Aretha grew up on the edge of the Detroit ghetto, with only her religious beliefs and several siblings to protect her from the debilitating atmosphere. When she was seven her father took over the duties at the New Bethel Baptist Church, and she joined the choir with her sisters. She also taught herself to play the piano when she was eight, and she was able to absorb the passion of gospel by listening to the private performances of houseguests such as Mahalia Jackson, Clara Ward, James Cleveland, B. B. King, Lou Rawls, and Sam Cooke. Still, life in the Franklin home was not particularly happy. Aretha's mother deserted the family when the singer was six. The Reverend Franklin traveled often, leaving his children in the care of housekeepers. As soon as she was able, Aretha began to take trips with her father, singing behind his powerful preaching. She recorded her first album in 1956, when she was only fourteen.

From her teens Franklin exhibited the personality traits that have shaped her performing career. Shy and

For the Record. . .

Born March 25, 1942, in Memphis, Tenn.; daughter of Clarence L. (a minister and gospel singer) and Barbara (Siggers) Franklin; married Ted White (a businessman), 1961 (divorced); married Glynn Turman, April 11, 1978 (divorced, 1984); children: (first marriage) Clarence, Edward, Teddy. *Education:* Attended schools in Detroit, Michigan. *Politics:* Democrat. *Religion:* Baptist.

Gospel singer, 1952-61, performing as member of her father's traveling Baptist ministry; recorded first album of gospel music in 1956. Rhythm and blues/soul vocalist, 1960—; signed first with Columbia Records, 1961, transferred to Atlantic Records, 1967, transferred to Arista Records, 1980. Has given numerous live performances in America and Europe, including a special command performance for the birthday of England's Queen Mother. Appeared in film "The Blues Brothers," 1980, and in Showtime television special, "Aretha," 1986.

Awards: Grammy awards for best female rhythm and blues vocal performance, 1967, 1968, 1969, 1970, 1971, 1972, 1973, 1974, 1981, 1985, 1987, Grammy awards for best rhythm and blues recording, 1967, for best soul gospel performance, 1972, and for best rhythm and blues duo vocal (with George Michael), 1987, for "I Knew You Were Waiting"; American Music Award, 1984.

Addresses: *Home*—8450 Linwood St., Detroit, Mich. 48206.

her style is identified." Franklin's first Atlantic release, *I Never Loved a Man,* was her first million-seller. The title single and two other cuts—"Respect" and "Baby, I Love You" also went gold. From near obscurity, Franklin became an overnight star who was named "top female vocalist of 1967" by every major trade magazine in the music business. She also won the first of a record eleven Grammy awards for best female rhythm and blues performer.

I Never Loved a Man was followed by a string of similarly successful albums and singles, produced in rapid succession between 1968 and 1973. Haas sums up the components of Franklin's style that contributed to her phenomenal success: "The authority of her phrasing let her run lyrics into a seamless scat while still juicing all the meaning from each word, duck around the beat and stock a song with sexy tension, and go from a conversational inflection to an opulently musical one in midline or from fragile breathiness to a slow-vibratoed fullness of tone that could upend small objects." The critic also notes that Franklin projected a

> *"Franklin has experienced 'comebacks' that have never registered with much authenticity, partly because she had never gone away."*

sometimes morose offstage, she would be transformed into a dynamo by the gospel music she so loved. She quickly became a favorite on the gospel circuit, but in 1960 she decided to move into pop music. Traveling to New York City, she signed a contract with Columbia Records. As a *Time* correspondent notes, however, the producers at Columbia "never quite distilled her true essence," channeling her into stereotyped pop arrangements, jazz standards, and old Broadway melodies. Not surprisingly, Franklin decided not to renew her Columbia contract when it expired, even though the nine albums she had cut had sold moderately well. Instead, she moved to Atlantic Records, then a pioneering outfit for rhythm and blues with a playlist that included Wilson Pickett, Ruth Brown, and Ray Charles.

At Atlantic, writes Charlie Haas in *Esquire,* "something happened that had been absent not only from the Columbia recordings but from previous soul music as a whole: Aretha Franklin's mature voice and delivery. With Jerry Wexler, Arif Mardin, and Tom Dowd producing and arranging, she made the series of albums by which

sassier, more sexually-aware and confident image than most of her contemporaries in the business. "Though she could put a victimized-woman song over—chillingly," Haas declares, "the main persona she built, in the lyrics she wrote and chose, was far from the virgin victim. . . . Franklin's character, underwritten by her usually eccentric and always precisely right style, was a self-knowledgeable woman who had wised up in the course of a few affairs without losing any of her sensuality, who had begun to see love not just as a thrill but as a pragmatic bargain." This persona is particularly evident in Franklin's two biggest hits, "Respect" and "You Make Me Feel Like a Natural Woman."

The mid- to late-1970s were a difficult time for soul music in general, as the rigid beat of disco held sway. Franklin was one of many singers who suffered a declining audience during the period. Her professional woes were compounded by a series of personal problems—her father was rendered comatose by a shooting during a burglary in his home, and her first marriage failed. Then, just as her career was beginning to rebound under the Arista label, Franklin was involved in an incident aboard a small airplane that caused her to fear flying. Some observers feel that only the need to pay her father's expensive hospital bills kept Franklin recording during the early 1980s. The Reverend Franklin died in 1984, never having recovered consciousness after the shooting. The following year Aretha recorded the album that can legitimately be called her "comeback" project—*Who's Zoomin' Who*, a snappy work reminiscent of her early material. Though well into her forties, Franklin cavorted elegantly through several "Who's Zoomin' Who" videos that became immensely popular on MTV and helped two singles, "Freeway of Love" and the title tune, top the pop charts. "I wanted something that kids would enjoy," Franklin told *Newsweek*, "something that would span the age gap, but not leave older fans behind. The soul is still there."

Franklin is still bothered by her fear of flying, so much of her work is accomplished in or near Detroit, her home base since 1982. Her recent hit single, "I Knew You Were Waiting (For Me)," paired her with George Michael, a pop singer seemingly from another generation altogether. In the wake of that success, Franklin has returned to her first and lasting love—gospel, with the release of a dramatic double album, *One Lord, One Faith, One Baptism*. As Franklin once remarked in *Time*, "My heart is still there in gospel music. It never left." Franklin does not intend to leave pop music's ranks permanently, however. She told *Newsweek* that she sees singing—any kind of singing—as a means of escape. "It does get me out of myself," she said. "I guess you could say I do a lot of traveling with my voice." Mark Moses pays homage to the Queen of Soul in his *New Yorker* essay, calling Aretha Franklin "both the statesman shouldering history and the woman wishing herself back to childhood . . . as if there were no extremes that her wide, rippling voice could not reconcile."

Selected discography

Aretha, Columbia, 1961.
Electrifying, Columbia, 1962.
Tender Moving and Swinging, Columbia, 1962.
Laughing on the Outside, Columbia, 1962.
Unforgettable, Columbia, 1964.
Songs of Faith, Columbia, 1964.
Running Out of Fools, Columbia, 1964.
Yeah, Columbia, 1965.
Soul Sister, Columbia, 1966.
Queen of Soul, Columbia, 1967.
Greatest Hits, Columbia, 1967.
I Never Loved a Man, Atlantic, 1967.

Once in a Lifetime, Atlantic, 1967.
Aretha Arrives, Atlantic, 1967.
Lady Soul, Atlantic, 1968.
Greatest Hits, Volume 2, Atlantic, 1968.
Live at Paris Olympia, Atlantic, 1968.
Aretha Now, Atlantic, 1968.
Soul 69, Atlantic, 1969.
Today I Sing the Blues, Atlantic, 1969.
Aretha Gold, Atlantic, 1969.
I Say a Little Prayer, Atlantic, 1969.
This Girl's in Love with You, Atlantic, 1970.
Spirit in the Dark, Atlantic, 1970.
Don't Play That Song, Atlantic, 1970.
Live at the Fillmore West, Atlantic, 1971.
Young, Gifted, and Black, Atlantic, 1971.
Aretha's Greatest Hits, Atlantic, 1971.
Amazing Grace, Atlantic, 1972.
Hey Hey Now, Atlantic, 1973.
Let Me into Your Life, Atlantic, 1974.
With Everything I Feel in Me, Atlantic, 1975.
You, Atlantic, 1975.
Sparkle, Atlantic, 1976.
Ten Years of Gold, Atlantic, 1976.
Sweet Passion, Atlantic, 1977.
Almighty Fire, Atlantic, 1978.
La Diva, Atlantic, 1979.
Aretha, Arista, 1980.
Aretha Gospel (rerelease of 1956 debut album), Sugar Hill, 1984.
Who's Zoomin' Who, Arista, 1985.
Aretha After Hours, Columbia, 1987.
Love All the Hurt Away, Arista, 1987.
The Great Aretha Franklin: The First 12 Sides, Columbia, 1988.
One Lord, One Faith, One Baptism, Arista, 1988.
Through the Storm, Arista, 1989.

Sources

Books

Stambler, Irwin, *Encyclopedia of Pop, Rock, and Soul*, St. Martin's, 1974.

Periodicals

Ebony, October, 1967.
Esquire, March, 1982.
Newsweek, August 26, 1985.
New Yorker, February 1, 1988.
New York Post, October 28, 1967.
People, February 23, 1981; October 14, 1985.
Time, January 5, 1968; June 28, 1968.

—Anne Janette Johnson

Peter Gabriel

Singer, songwriter

Peter Gabriel has had a long career in music. As one of the founding members of the British band Genesis, he helped it gain a reputation for artistic rock music and performances. When he left the group in 1975, it stood on the brink of popular success—a success it would go on to fully attain. But Gabriel, too, has done well. The cult following of Genesis's early days continued to support the solo efforts of its former leader; then Gabriel broadened his appeal with hits like the haunting "Games without Frontiers" and the New Wave-flavored "Shock the Monkey." He attained huge popularity, however, and four Grammy nominations, with his 1986 album, *So,* and its smash chart hit, "Sledgehammer."

Gabriel, born May 13, 1950, grew up on a farm in Woking, England, and had a childhood with "piano lessons, dancing lessons, riding lessons, every sort of lesson," he told Steve Pond of *Rolling Stone.* He was also sent as a boy to England's Charterhouse public school—the equivalent of a very prestigious private school in the United States. There he met Tony Banks, Mike Rutherford, and Anthony Phillips, with whom he would later put together Genesis. At first, however, the four youths were merely friends who shared a love of rhythm-and-blues music, particularly the work of Otis Redding. Charterhouse was a very strict school, and both radios and record players were contraband items, so the friends had to meet secretly to indulge their musical tastes.

Yet by the time Gabriel and his companions began to compose and play their own music as Genesis, the product was quite different from the songs they once risked punishment to hear. Critics considered Genesis's early output eclectic and intellectual—progressive rock. The band used keyboards and synthesizers as prominent parts of their recordings. Under Gabriel's leadership—he wrote most of the songs and sang the lead—Genesis was perhaps too eccentric for the general pop audience and didn't have chart hits. They did, however, achieve a loyal cult following that idolized Gabriel. "I used to get quite a few letters from people I visited with my psychic body," he revealed to Pond, "or told to do all sorts of things with a song." Gabriel also helped make Genesis concerts into spectacular shows, featuring impressive lighting effects and with its lead singer in costume—occasionally wearing dresses.

Genesis began to gain an audience in America with their 1973 album, *Selling England by the Pound;* they followed this with the critically acclaimed *The Lamb Lies Down on Broadway,* a double-sided concept album that chronicles the strange adventures of a man named Rael in New York City. But it was during the production of *Lamb* that Gabriel came into conflict with the rest of the band. He and his wife, Jill Moore, whom he had also met while a student at Charterhouse, had their first child; the birth was attended by many severe complications. The infant, Anna, had caught an infection in the womb, was born with fluid in her lungs, and was not expected to live—she came through the danger, however, with no lasting ill effects. Consequently, Gabriel spent much of his time with his wife and daughter, and the other members of Genesis resented the time not spent completing *Lamb*. By 1975, Gabriel had left the group. Disillusioned by the music business, he spent approximately two years "puttering in his garden," in Pond's words, until he began recording again in 1977.

Gabriel's first three solo albums were all entitled *Peter Gabriel*. The first two were a struggle, but the third exhibited a new interest in the rhythms of African music and the use of drum machines. Atlantic Records, which had released Gabriel's first two albums, felt that the sound of the third was too unconventional to find an audience and refused to have anything to do with it. So Gabriel went to Mercury Records, which did want the album. "Games without Frontiers," a single from the third *Peter Gabriel* disc, became a hit, and, as Gabriel succinctly gloated to Pond, "Atlantic's regretted it." His next album, *Security,* released by Geffen, was also a success.

So, Gabriel's 1986 effort, "is shot through with hurt and hope," declared *Time*'s Jay Cocks. The singer-songwriter confided to Pond that many of the songs on the album, such as "In Your Eyes," "That Voice Again," and "Don't Give Up," were written during a period of separation from his wife; *So* is thus more emotionally open than his previous work. "I wanted some of this album to be more direct," he explained. "Over the past few years . . . I tended to hide from some things, both personal and in my music. And so, if you like, it was part of a coming-out

process." As Pond reported, fans have responded well to this new, more intimate Gabriel, but the overwhelming success of *So* is perhaps more attributable to the innovative video that accompanied the hit "Sledgehammer." "It started with a video," Pond asserted. "It started with singing vegetables and dancing chickens, with model trains circling Peter Gabriel's skull as he sang about lust in a series of luridly silly metaphors."

Gabriel is also deeply committed to the political issue of human rights and has been involved in benefits for Amnesty International and anti-apartheid causes. This aspect of the musician is reflected in *So* by the song "Biko," a tribute to Steven Biko, a black South African activist who died under mysterious circumstances while in police custody. Cocks credited Gabriel with finding "a resonance in Biko's death that goes beyond outrage or simple protest" and added that there is "no resisting either [the song's] heat or its true moral force. *Biko* is . . . full of ghosts that will haunt any political present."

Selected discography

LPs; with Genesis

In the Beginning, Mercury, 1968.
Trespass, Impulse, 1970.
Nursery Cryme (includes "Musical Box" and "Return of the Giant Hogweed"), Charisma, 1971.
Foxtrot (includes "Watcher of the Skies" and "Supper's Ready"), Charisma, 1972.
Selling England by the Pound (includes "I Know What I Like"), Charisma, 1973.
The Lamb Lies Down on Broadway, Atlantic, 1974.

Solo LPs

Peter Gabriel (includes "Solsbury Hill"), Atlantic, 1977.
Peter Gabriel, Atlantic, 1978.
Peter Gabriel (includes "Games without Frontiers"), Mercury, 1980.
Security, Geffen.
So (includes "Sledgehammer," "In Your Eyes," "That Voice Again," "Red Rain," "Don't Give Up," and "Biko"), Geffen, 1986.

Sources

Rolling Stone, January 29, 1987.
Time, February 2, 1987.

—*Elizabeth Thomas*

Guns n' Roses

Rock group

With sales of more than eight million albums in less than two years, Guns n' Roses has become the latest heavy-metal phenomenon. *Rolling Stone* contributor Rob Tannenbaum calls the group "the world's most exciting hard-rock band . . . young, foolhardy, stubborn, cynical, proud, uncompromising, insolent, conflicted and very candid about their faults." A generation of teens has flocked to the Guns n' Roses banner, celebrating the group's fiery, belligerent, and cynical music and the members' frankly self-destructive lifestyles. "There's always an audience for wild-eyed hellions with electric guitars," writes John Milward in the *Philadelphia Inquirer*. "The Guns n' Roses difference is that youths somehow sense that these guys' raucous sounds are more genuine than those of their heavy-metal peers. They're reckless kids who have stumbled onto a career, and they seem so out of control that you can't help believing the most scandalous stories. They're stupid enough to live out each and every rock-and-roll cliche but talented enough to spike their best songs with that same 80-proof energy."

Tannenbaum notes that "the Gunners" engage in antics "revolving around booze, drugs and women; they trumpet their music as 'rebellious'; and they claim to play for 'the kids.'" However, unlike other metal bands, whose older members base their images on fantasy rather than the daily reality of adolescence, Guns n' Roses draws frankly on "the unfocused rage and pervasive doubt, the insecurity and cockiness, the horniness and fear" of the teen years. Tannenbaum concludes: "The Gunners' songs don't hide the fact that they're confused and screwed up." This darkly honest look at adolescence stems from the youth of the band members themselves—all are under twenty-eight, and all have undergone their own personal periods of manic behavior. "Our attitude epitomizes what rock & roll is all about," said lead guitarist, Slash. "We . . . bleed and sweat for it, you know? We do a lot of things where other bands will be, like, 'Get the stunt guy to do it.'"

Guns n' Roses came together in the scruffy hard-rock scene of Los Angeles early in 1985. Two of the founding members, singer Axl Rose and guitarist Izzy Stradlin, grew up together in Lafayette, Indiana, where Rose in particular had a reputation for violence and juvenile delinquency. They were joined in Los Angeles by Slash, a native of Great Britain whose artist parents worked in Hollywood, and Duff "Rose" McKagan, a former resident of Seattle. The group was rounded out by drummer Steven Adler, the only married member. According to Tannenbaum, once the members met in California, "they played, they fought, they got high, they toyed with the idea of forming bands with names like Heads of Amazon and AIDS. They finally settled on Guns n' Roses, combining the names of two bands that various members had been involved in, L.A. Guns and Hollywood Rose."

Club ads for Guns n' Roses shows often read "FRESH FROM DETOX" or "ADDICTED: ONLY THE STRONG SURVIVE." The group members lived together in a tiny studio apartment, with no bathroom, shower, or kitchen; most of the money that came in was spent on drugs and alcohol. In 1986 they signed a contract with Geffen Records, but for many months thereafter they could find neither a manager nor a producer—even among those working with other heavy-metal bands. Finally Mike Clink, an engineer who had worked with Heart and Eddie Money, agreed to produce a Guns n' Roses album. *Appetite for Destruction* was released in 1987, promptly drawing criticism for its violent lyrics and its sexually graphic cover. The band found it difficult to get airtime on Top 40 radio and MTV until one of the album cuts, "Sweet Child o' Mine," got grass-roots support from rock fans. Guns n' Roses drew further attention when they opened for Aerosmith on a 1987 national tour. By the time the tour ended—almost a year after *Appetite for Destruction* had been released, the album went platinum and hit the *Billboard* Top Five.

"No law says that rock and rollers have to be good role models," writes Milward, "but the blue-noses of the Parents Resource Music Committee couldn't have

> *"If the Gunners go beyond what the Stones sang about, it's because times are rougher; they are a brutal band for brutal times."*

dreamed up a group with such exploitative bad attitudes as Guns n' Roses. *Appetite for Destruction* unspools like a cheesy movie about the Hollywood lowlife . . . [portraying] a wicked, corrupting world and [suggesting] that it only makes sense to have some fun on your way to hell." The same theme runs through *G n' R Lies*, a more recent album; its best-known cut, "Used to Love Her, but I Had to Kill Her," has drawn protests from numerous fronts. The members of Guns n' Roses certainly face a dilemma when they perform—while proud of their own violent antics, they try not to incite their audiences to similar behavior. "I guess we are playing with fire," Duff told *Rolling Stone*. "I would seriously hate for anything to happen [to the fans], but we're not the kind of guys to really change our ways."

Tannenbaum describes Guns n' Roses as "a musical sawed-off shotgun, with great power but erratic aim. . . . They . . . bring to mind the early Rolling Stones, who won a similar notoriety for singing about spite and hostility. And if the Gunners go beyond what the Stones sang about, it's because times are rougher; they are a brutal band for brutal times. Unlike the Stones, they don't keep an ironic distance between them and their songs." Admitting to alcoholism, drug abuse, sexual excesses, and violent brawling, the members of Guns n' Roses see their lifestyles as "part of the energy we put out," to quote Slash in *Rolling Stone*. Milward observes that the group has never apologized for a reputation "that embraces sex and drugs and rock and roll with a casual abandon that makes earlier rock decadents seem responsible." The critic concludes: "Years ago, the Who sang of a 'teenage wasteland,' but they saw it from a distance. Not so Guns n' Roses— they were born there, and that's why the kids accept them as their own."

Selected discography

Live Like a Suicide (EP), Geffen Records, 1986.
Appetite for Destruction, Geffen Records, 1987.
G n' R Lies (contains cuts from *Live Like a Suicide),* Geffen Records, 1988.

Sources

Philadelphia Inquirer, February 16, 1989.
Rolling Stone, November 17, 1988.

—*Anne Janette Johnson*

Woody Guthrie

Singer, songwriter, guitarist

"Woodrow Wilson Guthrie was a short, wiry guy with a mop of curly hair under a cowboy hat, as I first saw him. He'd stand with his guitar slung on his back, spinning out stories like Will Rogers, with a faint, wry grin. Then he'd hitch his guitar around and sing the longest long outlaw ballad you ever heard, or some Rabelaisian fantasy he'd concocted the day before and might never sing again," Pete Seeger described Woody Guthrie in his 1967 eulogy in *Life* magazine.

Guthrie, Seeger claimed, wrote more than 1000 songs. Many of them, like "This Land is Your Land," "So Long, It's Been Good to Know You," and "This Train Is Bound for Glory," have become American folk song standards. Many were written only for the moment to enliven a union hall rally or to entertain the hobos and dust bowl refugees he traveled with. Most were never intended for publication or the recording studio. He was also an avid collector of American folk songs, and many of his own songs consisted of original lyrics written to traditional melodies. This prolific writer and itinerant troubadour became a legend in his own time and helped usher in the folk music revival of the 1950s and 1960s.

His skills are succinctly assessed by Murray Kempton in the *New York Review of Books:* "As composer he was more collector than creator; the tunes that provide royalties to his heirs represent the mining of traditional themes rather than the search for fresh ones. His vocal range was severely limited; his tones were dry and his voice had the harsh and distancing timbre that Klein [in his biography of Guthrie] captures nicely when he says that listening to Guthrie was like biting into a lemon."

Kempton also suggested that Guthrie's status as a legendary folk hero belies the reality of the artist's life. He was not a dirt farmer, his family were townsfolk. Although he hung out with hobos, he eventually shied away from boxcar travel because hitching rides on the highway was much safer. He earned his meals picking songs in saloons, not picking fruit in the fields with the dust bowl refugees whose plight he described in song. "The roving life was a choice rather than a necessity, and more a flight from family tragedy than from otherwise hopeless poverty," Kempton concluded.

Guthrie was born July 14, 1912, in Okema, Oklahoma. His father, Charles, had a successful real estate business, but his business failed when more aggressive traders moved in on the heels of an oil boom. His mother, Nora, showed signs of increasing mental instability during Guthrie's youth and she was committed to a state mental institution after a fire (which she may have started) severely burned Charles. When Charles left town, Guthrie, at age 14, was left to drift on his own. He and his older brother Roy took up residence with a poor family and he attended high school, worked at

Full name, Woodrow Wilson Guthrie; born July 14, 1912, in Okemah, Okla.; died of Huntington's chorea, October 3, 1967, in Queens, N.Y.; son of Charles Edward (in real estate) and Nora Belle (a housewife; maiden name, Tanner) Guthrie; married first wife, Marry Jennings, October 28, 1933 (divorced); married second wife, Marjorie Mazia Greenblatt (a dancer and teacher), November 13, 1945 (divorced); married Anneke (Marshall) Van Kirk, 1953 (divorced); children (first marriage) Gwendolyn Gail, Carolyn Sue, Bill Rogers (died, 1962); (second marriage), Cathy Ann (died, 1947), Arlo Davy, Joady Ben, Nora Lee; (third marriage) Lorina Lynn. *Education:* Attended Brooklyn College.

Held a variety of odd jobs, including newsboy, junk collector, milkman, shoe shiner, service station attendant, sigh painter, and real estate agent; appeared with cousin, Jack Guthrie, on daily radio programs on KFVD, Los Angeles, beginning 1937; also appeared on radio programs broadcast out of New York City; performed in waterfront saloons, picket lines, migratory camps, army camps, union halls, on ski rows, and at country fairs, dances, rodeos, and carnivals; recording artist, 1940—; also author of books, including autobiography, *Bound for Glory,* and of numerous articles for newspapers and magazines, including *People's World* and the *Daily Worker. Military service:* U.S. Merchant Marine, 1942-45; U.S. Army Air Forces, 1945-46.

Awards: Fellowship from Julius Rosenwald Fund, 1943, to "write books, ballads, songs, and novels that will help people to know each other's work better."

the building of the Bonneville and Grand Coulee dams. His biographer, Joe Klein, called this the most productive period of his life—in one month he wrote nearly a song per day, including the last of his dust bowl ballads, "Pastures of Plenty," a song than many consider his best. He occasionally joined Pete Seeger and Lee Hays in performances by the Almanac Singers, a song collective which, as they were described by *The Progressive,* "attempted to translate folk sources into materials that would inspire working people to create a socialist America through their unions."

Guthrie wrote more than songs. He wrote two major autobiographical works as well as songbooks. He was an occasional journalist and an avid letter writer; he wrote in book margins, drew and scribbled on calendars, notebooks, and endless scraps of paper. Joe Klein tells of being overwhelmed by a room of file cabinets filled with unpublished material when Marjorie, Guthrie's second wife, agreed to let him write Guthrie's definitive biography.

Guthrie's best-received book, *Bound for Glory,* an autobiography of his early years, was published in

> *"[Guthrie's] roving life was a choice rather than a necessity, and more a flight from family tragedy than from otherwise hopeless poverty."*

1943. It is a vivid tale told in the artist's own down-home dialect, with the flare and imagery of a true storyteller. *Library Journal* complained about the "Too careful reproduction of illiterate speech." But Clifton Fadiman, reviewing the book in the *New York Times,* paid the author a fine tribute: "Some day people are going to wake up to the fact that Woody Guthrie and the ten thousand songs that leap and tumble off the strings of his music box are a national possession like Yellowstone and Yosemite, and part of the best stuff this country has to show the world."

Guthrie was first recorded in 1940 by Alan Lomax, who had become enamored with rural southern folk music while traveling the South with his father, John Lomax, who was making archival recordings of the music of Southern black prisoners. In 1940, Lomax, who was assistant director of the Archive of Folk Song at the Library of Congress, recorded a collection of Guthrie interviews and songs for the Library. The recordings

odd jobs, and learned to play harmonica. A couple of years later he hit the road, a pattern that would be repeated throughout his life.

Guthrie learned many old-time songs by listening to his mother sing, but generally, his immediate family was not musically inclined. He was taught to play guitar by his uncle Jeff Guthrie and worked with him on a short-lived traveling show. Later, in 1937, he had a radio show with his cousin Jack Guthrie on KFVD in Los Angeles. He moved to New York and was popular on several "hillbilly" radio shows that were popular at the time but he left the radio business when he was not allowed to perform his more sensitive, politically-oriented songs.

In 1941 he was employed briefly by the Bonneville Power Administration in Oregon to write songs about

were eventually released in 1964 by Electra. These recordings are essential Guthrie listening. Also in 1940, Victor Records recorded another vital collection, the *Dust Bowl Ballads*.

In 1944 Moses Asch, a recording pioneer with a love for American folk music, arranged a series of recording sessions at which Guthrie, backed occasionally by Cisco Houston, Sonny Terry, and Leadbelly, recorded over 150 original and traditional folk songs. Many of these early recordings were released on Asch's Folkways label and are still available today, including three volumes of children's songs called *Songs to Grow On*.

The last 15 years of Guthrie's life were spent in the hospital suffering from the degenerative effects of the inherited disease Huntington's chorea. During this time, the 1950s and 1960s, folk music became a major trend and Guthrie became a living legend, his bedside visited by aspiring folk singers like Bob Dylan, who celebrated the man in his "Song to Woody." On one weekend visit home he taught Arlo Guthrie, his son from his second marriage and a successful folk singer in his own right, the radical verses he had written to "This Land is your Land," which he felt were in danger of being lost now that the song was being suggested as a replacement for the "Star Spangled Banner" as the national anthem.

As the songwriter lay dying, slowly losing the use of his limbs, his ability to speak and focus his eyes, his songs began to achieve the wide recognition they deserved. Popular folk performers like the Weavers, Joan Baez, and Peter, Paul and Mary were recording Woody Guthrie songs. One of the last songs Guthrie wrote, about a year after he had entered the hospital, was "I Ain't Dead Yet." The song is symbolic of his indomitable spirit—which refused to give up when faced with life's many hardships—and his penchant for turning hardship into song.

Selected discography

Bound for Glory, Folkways.
This Land is Your Land, Folkways.
Woody Guthrie Sings Folk Songs (2 volumes), Folkways.
Poor Boy, Folkways.
Songs to Grow On (3 volumes), Folkways.
Cowboy Songs (with Cisco Houston), Stinson.
Folk Songs (with Cisco Houston), Stinson.
Woody Guthrie: Library of Congress Recordings, Elektra, 1964.
Columbia River Collection, Rounder, 1987.
Dust Bowl Ballads, Folkways.

Sources

Books

Guthrie, Woody, *Bound for Glory*, Dutton (originally published 1943).
Klein, Joe, *Woody Guthrie: A Life*, Knopf, 1980.

Periodicals

New York Review of Books, February 19, 1981.
Life, April 2, 1967.
Library Journal, March 15, 1943.
New Yorker, March 20, 1943.
The Progressive, February, 1981.

—*Tim LaBorie*

Merle Haggard

Singer, songwriter, guitarist

Merle Haggard has been called the "poet laureate of the hard hats" because he is an intense, dedicated artist who happens to write and perform traditional country songs. Haggard holds the record, after Conway Twitty, for the most number-one country singles—hardly a year has passed since 1963 when he has not had at least one original hit. According to Tim Schneckloth in *down beat* magazine, Haggard "is playing a very personal brand of music that is strongly rooted in the American past, music that synthesizes the work of long-departed artists from virtually every field of American popular music. . . . Like much art Haggard's work is complex, operating on a number of different levels. A listener can come into the show totally cold, never having heard of Haggard or his many sources, and still be impressed by . . . Haggard's expressive singing and concisely powerful songwriting. But there are other things going on. Beyond the level of pure entertainment, strands of American music are being woven together in a totally organic manner. . . . [The] music seems completely natural to the players and the singers on the stage."

A *Time* magazine correspondent observes that, in the midst of country music's "booming supermarket of traditional goods and new brands, teaser displays and soaring profits," Haggard "stands virtually alone as a pure, proud and prominent link between country's past and present. He is not about to record with a couple of dozen violins to woo the easy-listening audience or hire a rock band to turn on the kids. Haggard has wide enough range and appeal already." That appeal has been recognized with a staggering array of awards from the Nashville music industry as well as the respect of peers like Johnny Cash, Willie Nelson, and Kris Kristofferson. Critics such as *Atlantic* essayist Paul Hemphill call Haggard "one of the few genuine folk heroes in American popular music today," a writer-songster who is "gifted with an ability to capture the life of the common man with a certain dignity."

Most country musicians sing about hard lives of poverty, prison, and privation. Haggard is the rare artist who has actually lived that life. Before he was born his parents were forced to abandon their Oklahoma farm and join the Depression-era migration to California. Haggard was born in 1937 in a railroad boxcar his father had converted into a house near Bakersfield, California. The Haggard family had slightly better fortune than many "Okies" who found themselves on the West Coast— James Haggard got regular work with the railroad and did carpentry on the side. Young Merle was particularly close to his father and was left at loose ends when the elder Haggard died in 1946. Within five years, while he was still a young teen, Haggard was skipping school and indulging in petty crime. "The trouble with me," he told *Newsweek,* "was that I started taking the songs I was singing too seriously. Like Jimmie Rodgers, I wanted to ride the freight trains. As a result, I was a general screw-up from the time I was 14."

Haggard escaped from juvenile homes no less than seven times, travelled up and down the West Coast doing odd jobs here and there, and fathered four children in a short-lived marriage. When he wasn't in trouble he could sometimes be found picking guitar in small clubs and dance halls—he had taught himself to play after his mother showed him several basic chords. In 1957 he and his friends tried to burglarize a Bakersfield bar; he was arrested and sent to San Quentin for a six-month to fifteen-year stay. At first Haggard continued his antisocial behavior in the rough prison. The turning point came when he spent his twenty-first birthday in solitary confinement, listening to the agonies of the inmates on the nearby death row. "I'm not so sure it works like that very often," he told *Atlantic,* "but I'm one guy the prison system straightened out. I know

damned well I'm a better man because of it." Released from solitary, Haggard volunteered for the prison's most difficult jobs. He also played in a prison band and got to meet his idol, Johnny Cash. When he was paroled at twenty-three, he returned to Bakersfield, determined to make good.

By 1960 Bakersfield had earned the nickname "Nashville West," having become a minor but significant center for the production of country music. Haggard soon found regular work as a backup guitarist at the clubs in Bakersfield and Las Vegas. In 1962 he met an energetic Arkansan named Fuzzy Owen, who became his manager and mentor in the business. Owen coached Haggard on his singing and songwriting, setting high standards that the young performer struggled to meet. Owen had bought Tally Records, a tiny production company, and in 1963 he recorded Haggard's first singles. The second of these, "Sing Me a Sad Song," made the country charts, and their following release, "All My Friends Are Gonna Be Strangers," made the country Top 10. Overnight, according to Hemphill, "the doors blew open" for Haggard. Capitol Records offered him a contract, and—in what would become typical Haggard fashion—the artist agreed to the deal only if Capitol would buy Tally Records and make Fuzzy Owen his manager. Capitol agreed. Hemphill notes that Haggard assembled a band, "started writing his own stuff, running into Hollywood to record, hitting the top of the charts with every release, turning them into albums, and became by 1968 one of the top stars in country music with a fanatical following in America's factories and bars and prisons. . . . He was, to that forgotten mass out there between New York and Los Angeles, relevant."

That relevance became charged with political meaning in 1969 when Haggard released his two biggest sellers, "Okie from Muskogee" and "The Fightin' Side of Me," songs that affirmed a middle-American pride in America at a moment of national turmoil. "Okie" in particular "was the making of Haggard," to quote the *Time* reporter. "The song put [him] into the millionaire class, which he did not mind. It also earned him a reputation as a spokesman for the right wing, which he did." For several years Haggard struggled with the superpatriotic image his best-known songs attached to him, only emerging from "Okie's" shadow when the Vietnam War ended and the nation became less polarized. Haggard told *down beat* that, of all the songs he has written, "Okie from Muskogee" was the one that had "about 18 different messages. . . . Anything that becomes as big as that song did has got to have something more than a beer belly mentality to it. I didn't even know what it had myself. I got to analyzing it later and realized that it could be taken any number of ways, one of which is from a pride standpoint. Of course, a lot of people think that you have to have a beer gut mentality to be proud of a particular thing. In other words, you should be ashamed to be proud."

The critics expected Haggard to follow "Okie" with a string of patriotic hits that would capitalize on the mood of his blue-collar audience. Haggard surprised them, though, by returning to his standard themes—the hard life of the working man, the prisoner, and the disappointed lover. *Esquire* contributor Bob Allen notes that Haggard's songs prove him to be "a writer and singer of remarkable range and sensitivity. There are, in fact, few popular musicians today who have, in the clear, simple meter of the workingman, embraced so many dimensions of the American experience. In Haggard's songs, one hears the country's history, mythopoeic personas (the freight-riding drifter, the honest workingman, the condemned fugitive), and musical heritage. . . . These songs stand as stunning synapses of memory and emotional revelation, and are as simple and concise in their imagery as they are universal in their sweep." More and more, Haggard began to pay homage to his stylistic forebears; since 1980, for instance, he has played a major role in the revival of western swing music and has, with his band the Strangers, created a new genre, country jazz. Schneckloth contends that in his twenty years as a singing star Haggard "has become almost symbolic of the purist, professional, no-nonsense approach to performing rooted American music."

In recent years Haggard has had to struggle with artistic malaise and professional burnout, especially evident in his lack of enthusiasm for touring. In *Behind Closed Doors: Talking with the Legends of Country Music,* he told Alanna Nash that he suffers from "physical and mental fatigue. And boredom, or complacency, or whatever—doin' the same thing." He added: "A lot of people don't realize that what goes along with this glamour and these high points that the people witness—the big nights at the [Country Music Association] and this and that—are just a small percentage of the life that's involved. The main part of this life is a twenty-year bus ride." Still, Haggard has been able to rejuvenate himself by working with other artists—like Willie Nelson—and by experimenting onstage with his highly regarded band. Nash perhaps best sums up the complicated character of Haggard when she calls him the "restless, conflicted, dislocated itinerant poet [who] has eschewed an array of wives and children for the lure and the loneliness of the road." Nash also quotes the award-winning singer himself, who admits wistfully: "My character will probably pay in the end for not experiencing those soft and beautiful parts of life I've heard other people sing about in their songs."

Selected discography

Strangers, Capitol, 1965.
(With wife, Bonnie Owens) *Just between the Two of Us,* Capitol, 1966.
Best of Merle Haggard, Capitol, 1968.
Okie from Muskogee, Capitol, 1969.
Same Train, a Different Time, Capitol, 1970.
A Tribute to the Best Damned Fiddle Player in the World, Capitol.
Land of Many Churches, Capitol, 1972.
I Love Dixie Blues, Capitol, 1974.
Serving 190 Proof, MCA, 1979.
I'm Always on a Mountain When I Fall, MCA.
My Farewell to Elvis, MCA.
Songs for the Mama That Tried, MCA.
Rainbow Stew—Live at Anaheim Stadium, MCA, 1980.
(With Willie Nelson) *Pancho and Lefty,* Epic, 1983.
Amber Waves of Grain, Epic, 1985.
Big City, Epic, 1985.
Merle Haggard: His Best, MCA, 1985.
It's All in the Game, Epic.
Kern River, Epic.
A Friend in California, Epic, 1986.
Out Among the Stars, Epic, 1986.
Songwriter, MCA, 1986.
That's the Way Love Goes, Epic.
Going Where the Lonely Go, Epic.
(With George Jones) *A Taste of Yesterday's Wine,* Epic.
Back to the Barrooms/The Way I Am, Epic, 1987.
(With Nelson) *Seashores of Old Mexico,* Epic, 1987.
(With Nelson and Jones) *Walking the Line,* Epic, 1987.
Chill Factor, Epic, 1988.
Merle Haggard's Greatest Hits, MCA, 1988.

Sources

Books

Haggard, Merle, *Sing Me Back Home* (autobiography), Times Books, 1981.
Nash, Alanna, *Behind Closed Doors: Talking with the Legends of Country Music,* Knopf, 1988.

Periodicals

Atlantic, September, 1971.
down beat, May, 1980.
Esquire, September, 1981.
Look, July 13, 1971.
Newsweek, June 18, 1973.
People, November 23, 1981.
Time, May 6, 1974.
Washington Post, August 13, 1974.

—Anne Janette Johnson

George Harrison

Singer, songwriter, guitarist

George Harrison is perhaps best known as one-fourth of what was probably the most popular and influential quartet in the history of rock, the Beatles. In 1958 Harrison joined John Lennon and Paul McCartney to form the core of what would—after name changes such as the Quarrymen and the Silver Beatles, the entrances and exits of members Stu Sutcliffe and Pete Best, and the final addition of drummer Ringo Starr—become the renowned English group. When the Beatles followed up their phenomenal success in their native country by taking American pop fans by storm in 1964, Harrison was with his fellow band members for U.S. concert appearances and their celebrated television introduction on "The Ed Sullivan Show." Throughout the changing trends in rock that the late 1960s brought, the Beatles remained not only popular but were acclaimed as serious, innovative musicians. Harrison helped influence the group with his explorations into Eastern music and religion, but the Beatles' breakup in 1970 gained him greater exposure for his own compositions, previously shadowed by those of Lennon and McCartney. Harrison has had mixed success as a solo artist; his first album, 1971's *All Things Must Pass,* was highly praised and included the hit single "My Sweet Lord," but his "finest since," according to Anthony DeCurtis in *Rolling Stone,* is his 1987 effort, *Cloud Nine.*

Harrison was born February 25, 1943, in Liverpool, England. He grew up in a public housing project, and was a mediocre student. Harrison's early efforts at guitar playing were somewhat futile—he bought a guitar as a young adolescent, but found he couldn't understand the chording patterns. While he was experimenting with one of the screws, the instrument fell apart. In frustration Harrison hid the guitar in the closet and turned his efforts to the trumpet, where he met with a similar lack of success. Eventually one of his older brothers repaired the guitar, and on his next attempts Harrison managed to learn a few chords. After that he practiced diligently, listening to recordings of famed guitarists Chet Atkins and Duane Eddy in order to perfect his style. At roughly the same time, Harrison became friends with Paul McCartney, a fellow student at the Liverpool Institute, and the two young musicians often took their guitars and went camping together in the country. Later, of course, Harrison would join the band that McCartney had formed with John Lennon.

Though during the Beatle years Harrison's musical compositions often took a back seat to those of Lennon and McCartney, he was always an integral part of what was happening to the group. The Beatles's legendary musical apprenticeship in Hamburg, Germany, came to a premature end partly due to the fact that the Hamburg police found out that Harrison was under eighteen and therefore ineligible to work in a foreign

Born February 25, 1943, in Liverpool, England; son of Harold (a school bus driver) and Louise Harrison; married Patricia Ann Boyd (a model and actress) on January 21, 1966 (divorced 1977); married Olivia Arias (a secretary) in 1978; children: Dhani (a son by second marriage).

Lead guitarist, singer, songwriter; apprentice electrician in Liverpool; joined group that eventually became the Beatles in 1958; stayed with them until group's dissolution in 1970; solo performer, 1970—; member of the Traveling Wilburys, 1988.

Appeared in motion pictures *A Hard Day's Night* and *Help!*; provided voice for animated film *Yellow Submarine;* co-owner of film production company Hand Made Films; organized charity concert for Bangladesh, 1971.

Awards: Grammy Awards and British Songwriters' Guild Award with the Beatles; made member of the Order of the British Empire, 1965.

Addresses: *Home*—Friar Park Rd., Henley-on-Thames near London, England; *Office*—c/o Warner Bros. Records, Inc., 3300 Warner Blvd., Burbank, CA 91505.

country. At the time of their appearance on "The Ed Sullivan Show," polls showed Harrison to be the most popular Beatle with American audiences. In the late 1960s, as DeCurtis phrased it, "Harrison led the Beatles to Maharashi Mahesh Yogi and transcendental meditation." Fascinated by the work of Indian musician Ravi Shankar, he also learned to play the sitar. And, while they were no match in number to the group's Lennon-McCartney efforts, Harrison's compositions for the Beatles included impressive hits such as "Something," "Taxman," "Here Comes the Sun," "I Need You," and "While My Guitar Gently Weeps."

Right after the Beatles broke up, Harrison was perhaps the most visible of the four musicians. He released the three-album set, *All Things Must Pass,* the following year. Harrison explained to DeCurtis that years of his songs coming second in priority to those of Lennon and McCartney left him with a lot of material: "By the time *All Things Must Pass* came, it was like being constipated for years, then finally you were allowed to go." In 1971 he was asked by his friend Shankar to organize a benefit concert for famine relief in Bangladesh; Harrison complied, and brought together many of the current rock stars of the day for a successful effort. "The Concert for Bangladesh," as it was called, was the

forerunner for the "Live Aid" efforts of the 1980s for famine relief in Ethiopia.

But then Harrison fell on relatively hard times. Perhaps because the orchestra of Indian musicians accompanying him was judged too esoteric for most audiences, his 1974 American tour was a failure. And in 1976, "My Sweet Lord," his biggest hit from *All Things Must Pass,* cost him $587,000. According to Steve Dougherty of *People* magazine, Harrison was found guilty of "'subconsciously plagiarizing' the Chiffons tune *He's So Fine*" with the song. His divorce from actress and model Patti Boyd in 1977, and the assassination of Lennon in late 1980, were personal blows to Harrison. Though his tribute to Lennon, "All Those Years Ago," on *Somewhere in England* brought him back into the musical spotlight, his reaction to his friend's death gave rise to rumors that Harrison had become a recluse. He admitted to Dougherty, "I am leery about big crowds of people. If somebody comes rushing up in the street, it does go through your mind." But the rumors, Harrison

> *At the time of their appearance on "The Ed Sullivan Show," polls showed Harrison to be the most popular Beatle with American audiences.*

declared, are unfounded. "All it is, really, is that I just don't go to discos where the gossip columnists hang out. . . . But I was going out all the time. I go out with friends, go to dinner, go to parties. It's all a joke."

Harrison has also become involved in filmmaking. Of course, as a Beatle, he appeared in the motion pictures *A Hard Day's Night* and *Help!,* and provided the voice for the cartoon image of himself in the animated film *Yellow Submarine,* but in the 1980s he has busied himself as the co-owner of the production company Hand Made Films. The company has brought to the screen popular works such as *Monty Python's Life of Brian* and *Time Bandits.* Harrison told Dougherty: "We tend to do low-budget movies that nobody else will do."

Musically, Harrison has been very active in the late 1980s. His 1987 album, *Cloud Nine,* produced hits with the singles "Got My Mind Set on You," lauded by DeCurtis as a "cocky, early-rock kicker"; "When We Was Fab," a recollection of being a Beatle; and "Devil's

Radio," which DeCurtis described as an "assault on gossip journalism." He also joined in 1988 with musical acquaintances Bob Dylan, Tom Petty, Jeff Lynne, and the late Roy Orbison to form the Traveling Wilburys. The Wilburys's first album, *Volume One,* became a huge chart success.

Selected discography

All Things Must Pass (includes "My Sweet Lord," "Isn't It a Pity," "Beware of Darkness," "Ballad of Sir Frankie Crisp," and "What Is Life"), Apple, 1971.
Living in a Material World, Apple, 1973.
Dark Horse (includes "Bye Bye, Love"), Apple, 1974.
Extra Texture, Apple, 1975.
33 1/3 (includes "Crackerbox Palace"), Dark Horse, 1976.
George Harrison, Dark Horse, 1979.
Somewhere in England (includes "All Those Years Ago" and "Blood From a Clone,") Warner Brothers, 1981.

Gone Troppo, Warner Brothers, 1982.
Cloud Nine (includes "Got My Mind Set On You," "When We Was Fab," "Devil's Radio," "Just for Today," "Someplace Else," "Breath Away From Heaven," "This Is Love," "That's What It Takes," "Fish in the Sand," and "Wreck of the Hesperus"), Warner Brothers, 1987.
(With the Traveling Wilburys) *Volume One,* Warner Brothers, 1988.

Sources

Books

Harrison, George, *I, Me, Mine,* Simon & Schuster, 1980.

Periodicals

People, October 19, 1987.
Rolling Stone, October 22, 1987.

—*Elizabeth Thomas*

Jimi Hendrix

Singer, songwriter, guitarist

Without a doubt, Jimi Hendrix will be remembered as the most innovative electric guitarist of all time. In a professional career that lasted less than a decade, he created music that still sounds as fresh and breathtaking today as it did when he took the pop world by storm in 1967. As producer Alan Douglas told *Guitar World,* Hendrix "essentially established the school and nobody's graduated from the school yet. Consequently, he is the only reference."

Hendrix picked up the guitar at age eleven and was soon playing with local rock groups as a teenager in his hometown of Seattle, Washington. He left school at sixteen and, with the permission of his father, joined the Army a year later as a paratrooper. But that career ended after he was injured on his twenty-sixth jump, forcing him to be discharged. While in the service he befriended bassist Billy Cox and the two jammed together and swapped guitar licks. Hendrix absorbed the music of the blues masters like Muddy Waters, Howlin' Wolf, Albert and B.B. King, and Lightnin' Hopkins, and even went so far as to sleep with his guitar because he had heard that his idols had done the same. (The blues influence was very deep; check out his song "Red House").

Once out of the Army he began concentrating on music and hit the chitlin circuit as a backing guitarist for a host of popular rock and rhythm and blues artists: Little Richard, Jackie Wilson, the Isley Brothers, Curtis Knight, Wilson Pickett, Ike and Tina Turner, King Curtis, and James Brown. Hendrix also teamed with Cox in the King Kasuals, providing support for performers including Slim Harpo and Nappy Brown. During this period, from around 1962-1964, he began incorporating trademark crowd-pleasers (playing the guitar with his teeth, behind his back, and between his legs) and could just as easily peel off a Charlie Christian-styled jazz lick, a scorching rocker, or a low-down blues.

Hendrix hit New York in 1964, changing his name to Jimmy James and fronting his own band called the Blue Flames. Fellow guitarist John Hammond, Jr., heard them playing at a dingy little club called the Cafe Wa in Greenwich Village and asked Hendrix to join his group, but their eventual collaboration at the nearby Cafe Au Go Go lasted only a few weeks. "I knew there was no way he was going to be my guitar player," Hammond told *Guitar Player.* "He was his own star." Others—including the Beatles, Bob Dylan, and the Animals—caught wind of the new hot-shot guitarist who made colleagues feel embarrassed that they had even picked up the instrument.

Chas Chandler (former Animals' bassist) convinced Hendrix to come back with him to London, where the music scene was really taking off. On the promise that he would get to meet Eric Clapton, Hendrix agreed and headed overseas to search for the proper backup band. The rhythm section auditions produced Mitch Mitchell, a free-form jazz flavored drummer, and Noel Redding, a guitarist who switched to bass for the job. In just three weeks the Jimi Hendrix Experience was formed and playing live. Managers Chandler and Michael Jeffrey had the trio frizz their hair and dress as outlandishly as possible to create a stir as their first single, "Hey Joe," went all the way to Number 6 on the U.K. charts in 1967. An appearance on the British television show "Ready, Steady Go" followed before their next single, "Purple Haze," set the world on its ear with Hendrix's distorted guitar assault.

Beatle Paul McCartney persuaded Monterey Pop Festival officials to book Hendrix despite the fact his first album had not even been released yet. His perform-ance transformed the twenty-four-year-old into a immediate superstar. While noted for being shy and unassuming offstage, Hendrix's showmanship floored the Monterey audience as he pulled out all the stops following the Who's thunderous set and finalized the gig by burning his guitar onstage. Amazingly (or foolishly), the Jimi Hendrix Experience was then booked as the opening act for the Monkees 1967 U.S. tour but, as the two acts appealed to totally different audiences, it was a short-lived venture. Supposedly, Hendrix's management team concocted a false story that the Daughters of the American Revolution had Hendrix banned. Regardless, his debut LP, *Are You Experienced?*, was soon commanding listeners' attention with an exciting new sound: "The Wind Cries Mary," "Third Stone From the Sun," "Fire," "Foxy Lady," the two previously releases singles, and five more tunes. *Guitar Player* 's Jas Obrecht called it the "most revolutionary debut album in rock guitar history."

Hendrix had literally reinvented the electric guitar's potential and became its first true innovator since Chuck Berry. Although earlier in his career Hendrix could play ambidextrously, he eventually settled on using a right-handed Fender Statocaster restrung upside down and played left-handed. He manipulated the tone and volume controls (which were now on top) to make unique effects and became the first to fully realize the vibrato arm's usefullness by creating dive-bombing shrieks and bending full chords. He custom shaped the bar himself in order to obtain a three-step variation instead of the stock bar's one step. His rapid-fire flicking of the toggle switch produced a bullet-spitting rattle ("Machine Gun") while his huge hands allowed for extreme reaches and funky chordings.

Compared to contemporary guitarists, Hendrix's use of special electronic effects seems very limited. His basic setup included a Univibe (to simulate a rotating speaker), a wah-wah, and a fuzz-box. They key, however, was to channel this through a stack of screaming Marshall amplifiers with the volume wide open. Hendrix harnessed the feedback whereas others had barely been able to control it. His ability to play clean leads and distorted rhythm simultaneously is still a mystery. Like John Coltrane on the tenor sax, Hendrix expanded the boundaries of his instrument like no one before or since.

In 1968 Chandler quit and Jeffrey became sole manager of the Experience, an arrangement which troubled Hendrix until his death (almost twenty years later, Hendrix's estate is still a financial nightmare). He released his second LP, *Axis: Bold as Love,* which contained more of his magical sounds on tunes like "Little Wing," "If 6 Was 9," "Castles Made of Sand," and "EXP." His third album, the double set *Electric Ladyland,* was released just nine months later and displayed Hendrix's flair for studio tricks and included guest musicians that included Steve Winwood and Jack Cassidy.

Larry Coryell told *Guitar World* that Hendrix "had a Christ-like appeal; he was more than just a guitar player, he was a personality." As his first three LPs went gold, Hendrix began getting caught up in the superstar trappings. The band became consumed by drinking, pill-popping, and dope smoking while Hendrix's voracious sexual appetite was fueled by a constant barrage of hangers-on. "In a way, Jimi's ego fed off it; but in the end the necessity and constant pressure to be Jimi Hendrix took much more out of him," Redding stated in *Musician.* "Everyone took, took, took from Jimi. The only things they gave were drugs." By mid-1969 the Experience had disintegrated. They played their last show on June 29th at the Denver Pop Festival, the same month their *Smash Hits* LP was released (featuring their first and only Top 20 single, "All Along the Watchtower").

In August of 1969 Hendrix played the Woodstock Festival with an assemblage of fellow musicians and created a triumph of improvisation on "The Star Spangled Banner," complete with exploding bombs and electronic warfare. Pressured by black militant groups, but wanting no part of politics, Hendrix formed the all-black Band of Gypsys with former Army pal Bill Cox on bass and Buddy Miles on drums. Although the group lasted only a few months, a live performance was captured on the *Band of Gypsys* LP. Hendrix went next with the lineup of Cox and Mitchell for the Isle of Wight Festival and his final performance at the Isle of Fehmarn in West Germany on September 6, 1970. Twelve days later Hendrix died after inhaling his own vomit caused by barbiturate intoxication.

Debates continue as to whether or not Hendrix was washed up musically just prior to his death. Some say that he could not perform at all, which is not surprising given his physical state. Others point out that he was experiencing a sort of musical rebirth and was very excited about future projects which included moving towards jazz and avant garde areas. He had also expressed an interest in utilizing big-band musicians and classical concepts in addition to learning music theory. An idea of where Hendrix was headed can be heard on *Nine To The Universe,* released in 1980 and filled with some very unique studio jams.

Since 1974 producer Alan Douglas has been in charge of releasing all posthumous Hendrix material. However, his first two efforts, *Crash Landing* and *Midnight Lightning,* received the outrage of purists who were upset that Douglas had stripped the recordings of everything but Hendrix's guitar and then hired studio musicians to play the missing parts over. Even so, with the general public so hungry for Hendrix's genius, *Crash Landing* became a Top Ten LP. After a few more less than satisfactory LPs, Douglas finally came across with two fine compact disc versions of vintage Hendrix, *Live at Winterland* and *Radio One.* But, with dozens of bootleg LPs available, Hendrix will also be remembered as one of the most ripped-off and artistically abused artists of all time.

The aura of Hendrix still lives: guitarists like Robin Trower and Stevie Ray Vaughan pay their respects to the master while turning on new generations to his music. Others, like Randy Hansen's Machine Gun, go so far as to try and recreate Hendrix's image and sound note-for-note, but the aping seems futile, as some of the material just cannot be reproduced even today. A film biography has also been in the works for some time but finding an actor to fill the lead is proving troublesome.

Speculation exists as to what Jimi Hendrix would be playing were he still alive. Sadly, the best answer to that

> *"I wasn't surprised at all when Hendrix died. You knew he was going to die just by listening to his music. It was all there, he had done it [all] and he almost had to die to finalize it."*
> —*Roy Buchanan*

question probably came from the late Roy Buchanan in *Rolling Stone,* "I wasn't surprised at all when Hendrix died. You knew he was going to die just by listening to his music. It was all there, he had done it [all] and he almost had to die to finalize it."

Selected discography

Are You Experienced?, Reprise, 1967.
Axis: Bold As Love, Reprise, 1968.
Electric Ladyland, Reprise, 1968.
Smash Hits, Reprise, 1969.
Band of Gypsys, Capitol, 1970.
Otis Redding/Jimi Hendrix Experience at Monterey, Reprise, 1970.

Released posthumously

The Cry of Love, Reprise, 1971.
Rainbow Bridge, Reprise, 1971.
Hendrix in the West, Reprise, 1972.
War Heroes, Reprise, 1972.
Sound Track Recording From the Film "Jimi Hendrix," Reprise, 1973.
Crash Landing, Reprise, 1975.
Midnight Landing, Reprise, 1975.
The Essential Jimi Hendrix, Reprise, 1978.
The Essential Jimi Hendrix, Volume Two, Reprise, 1979.
Nine to the Universe, Reprise, 1980.
The Jimi Hendrix Concerts, Reprise, 1982.
Kiss the Sky, Reprise, 1985.
Band of Gypsys 2, Capitol, 1986.
Jimi Plays Monterey, Reprise, 1986.
Live at Winterland, Rykodisc, 1987.
Radio One, Rykodisc, 1988.

Sources

Books

Christgau, Robert, *Christgau's Record Guide,* Ticknor & Fields, 1981.
Dalton, David, and Lenny Kaye, *Rock 100,* Grosset & Dunlap, 1977.

Evans, Mary, and Tom Evans, *Guitars, From the Renaissance to Rock,* Facts on File, 1977.
Harris, Sheldon, *Blues Who's Who,* Da Capo, 1979.
Henderson, David, *'Scuse Me While I Kiss the Sky/The Life of Jimi Hendrix,* Bantam, 1978.
Hopkins, Jerry, *Hit and Run: The Jimi Hendrix Story,* Perigree/Putnam, 1983.
Knight, Curtis, *Jimi,* Praeger, 1974.
Kozinn, Allan, Pete Welding, Dan Forte, and Gene Santoro, *The Guitar: The History, The Music, The Players,* Quill, 1984.
The Illustrated History of Rock, compiled by Nick Logan and Bob Woffinden, Harmony, 1977.
The Rolling Stone Illustrated History of Rock and Roll, edited by Jim Miller, Random House/Rolling Stone Press, 1976.
The Rolling Stone Record Guide, edited by Dave Marsh with John Swenson, Random House/Rolling Stone Press, 1979.
Sampson, Victor, *Hendrix,* Proteus, 1984.
Welch, Chris, *Hendrix,* Delilah/Putnam, 1978.

Periodicals

Guitar Player, September, 1975; June, 1980; November, 1982; June, 1983; January, 1987; June, 1987; February, 1989; May, 1989.
Guitar World, September, 1985; March, 1988.
Musician, August, 1986; September, 1986.
Rolling Stone, December 2, 1976; November 16, 1978.

—Calen D. Stone

Julio Iglesias

Singer, songwriter

Spanish-born singer Julio Iglesias has sold more albums than any other singer in the world—over one hundred million as of 1984. He started out singing in Spanish and winning audiences from his homeland and from Latin American countries. Then Iglesias branched into singing in Portuguese, Italian, French, German, Japanese, and English, gaining fans throughout Europe and Asia, and finally in Great Britain and the United States. Though he did not catch on until the early 1980s with non-Hispanic American audiences—traditionally difficult for foreign acts—when he did, he broke through in a big way, filling concert halls in New York, Los Angeles, and other major U.S. cities. His popular 1984 album *1100 Bel Air Place* included duets with many American music celebrities, notably the hit "To All the Girls I've Loved Before," recorded with country singer Willie Nelson.

Iglesias, whose full name is Julio José Iglesias de la Cueva, was born September 23, 1943, in Madrid, Spain. The son of a prominent physician, Iglesias had a comfortable childhood. His parents sent him to Catholic school, where his grades were mediocre at best and he did not measure up to the standards of the choir. Instead, he began to excel at soccer. Though as he grew older Iglesias became more concerned with his studies and aimed at Spain's diplomatic service, he continued to play soccer and earned a membership at the age of sixteen in the junior reserve squad of the prestigious Real Madrid Club de Futbol.

When Iglesias was about twenty years old and working towards a law degree, however, his hopes for a future as a soccer star were dashed by a near-fatal automobile accident. The encounter with a runaway truck that forced his car off the road left him paralyzed from the chest down. But Iglesias was determined not to use a wheelchair, and worked at physical therapy almost unceasingly. And during the long months of his recovery, one of his nurses presented him with a guitar in an effort to take his mind off his disabilities. Iglesias began trying to play along with the songs he heard on the radio; when he had learned to do that, he began composing his own. While still crippled, he watched a telecast of a music festival competition with his mother and told her that someday he himself would win one.

Not long after Iglesias regained the use of his legs (he still retains a slight limp from the accident), he began to push himself towards that goal. On a trip to England to improve his English, he composed the song "La Vida sigue igual" (title means "Life Goes on as Usual"), and used it to win the 1968 Benidorm Song Festival on the Spanish Mediterranean coast. This was the first step on Iglesias's way to international stardom, but although he continued to enter contests such as 1970's Eurovision

Festival, for which he wrote the song "Guendoline," he devoted most of his time to completing his law degree in accordance with his parents' wishes. When he finished, though, he concentrated on his singing career with great fervor. Iglesias won 1972's Eurovision contest; by that time he had signed a contract with Alhambra Records and was being heard not only throughout Europe but in Latin America, Romania, Japan, and the Middle East.

Since then Iglesias has released over one hundred albums; he averages roughly eight in a year. He has gained a reputation as a Latin-lover-type sex symbol though he has been married and divorced and has three children. Iglesias's biggest fans are mostly women over twenty-five; his appeal was explained by Italian psychologist Erika Kaufmann to Gerald Clarke in *Time:* "He rouses middle-aged women, especially the depressed ladies with no dreams. When he sings, they come alive." But Iglesias's phenomenal success is not merely the result of filling the needs of lonely females. "Behind Iglesias's undeniable mystique," asserts Jim Miller in *Newsweek,* "lies an astonishing amount of sheer hard work." He often spends over nine months a year in recording studios, doing many takes of each song until he is completely satisfied, frequently working into the early hours of the morning. "The result," lauded Miller, "is records that shimmer in the mind like the memory of a Mediterranean sunset."

Despite switching to the larger CBS International record company in about 1980, Iglesias still found it diffi-

cult to get through to an English-speaking audience. When it happened, it began by accident—British tourists in Europe brought Iglesias's records home with them. They circulated among British disc jockeys and received airplay, and Iglesias became the first Hispanic singer to have a number one song in England—a Spanish-language version of Cole Porter's "Begin the Beguine." CBS took notice, and prepared to release Iglesias albums in English. The company also planned to promote the singer in the United States. Iglesias began appearing at events with American celebrities, on American television talk shows. After former U.S. President Ronald Reagan and his wife Nancy saw him in a Washington, D.C., performance, he received invitations to sing at the White House.

> The encounter with a runaway truck that forced his car off the road left Iglesias paralyzed from the chest down.

By the time Iglesias released *1100 Bel Air Place,* he had already become well-known in the United States. The album featured duets with stars like Diana Ross, the Beach Boys, and the Pointer Sisters. While some critics, such as Lynn Van Matre in the *Chicago Tribune,* denigrated Iglesias's multi-genre approach as an attempt to please too many diverse tastes, it proved effective. His biggest American splash, perhaps, was made in the country music audience. "To All the Girls I've Loved Before," his duet with Willie Nelson, rose to the top ten of *Billboard*'s music charts. With the addition of fans in the United States, Iglesias's world conquest was complete.

Selected discography

Como el Alamo al camino, Alhambra, 1972.
Julio Iglesias, Alhambra, 1972.
Soy, Alhambra, 1973.
A Mexico, Alhambra, 1975.
El Amor, Alhambra, 1975.
America, Alhambra, 1976.
A mis 33 anos, Alhambra, 1977.
Emociones, Alhambra, 1978.
Hoy, CBS, 1980.
De nina a mujer, CBS, 1981.
El Disco de oro, CBS, 1981.

Momentos, CBS, 1982.
Julio, CBS, c. 1983.
1100 Bel Air Place (includes "To All the Girls I've Loved Before"),
    CBS, 1984.

Sources

Books

Daly, Marsha, *Julio Iglesias,* St. Martin's, 1986.

Periodicals

Chicago Tribune, February 26, 1984.
Ladies' Home Journal, August, 1985.
Newsweek, July 11, 1983.
Time, September 10, 1984.

—*Elizabeth Thomas*

INXS

Australian rock group

oted for their blend of rock and funk, Australia's INXS is still composed of the same members who started the band in 1977—Michael Hutchence, Tim, Andrew, and Jon Farriss, Kirk Pengilly, and Garry Gary Beers. After struggling for years on the Australian pub scene, the group began to attract international attention in the early 1980s and had what Rob Tannenbaum labeled in *Rolling Stone* a "breakthrough hit" in the United States with 1986's "What You Need." This taste of fame was small, however, compared to the phenomenal popularity INXS experienced after the release of their 1987 album *Kick*. Aided by wide music video exposure on networks such as MTV, *Kick*'s first single, "Need You Tonight," thrust INXS, and especially lead singer Hutchence, into the limelight. As critic Cathleen McGuigan announced in *Newsweek*, INXS has "a hard-driving, irresistibly danceable sound and a sexy, live-for-the-moment attitude—tempered with just a dash of social consciousness." She concluded that the band possessed "all the right ingredients for late '80s success."

Perhaps part of the reason that INXS has remained

Band started in 1977 as the Farris Brothers; briefly called the Vegetables; became INXS (pronounced "in excess") in 1979; consists of Michael Hutchence (born c. 1960, in Sidney, Australia; father's occupation: an importer; mother's occupation: a make-up artist; unmarried; home—Hong Kong) lead vocals, also group's lyricist, appeared in film *Dogs in Space*; Tim Farriss (born c. 1958, in Perth, Australia; married with two sons; home—Sidney, Australia) lead guitar; Andrew Farriss (born c. 1959, in Perth, Australia; unmarried; home—Sidney, Australia) keyboards, group's primary composer; Jon Farriss (born c. 1961, in Perth, Australia; unmarried; home—Hong Kong) drummer; Kirk Pengilly (born c. 1959; unmarried, one daughter; home—Sidney, Australia) guitar, saxophone; Garry Gary Beers (born c. 1957; unmarried; home—Sidney, Australia) bass; musical speciality: rock-funk, pop.

Addresses: *Record company*—c/o Atlantic Records, 75 Rockefeller Plaza, New York, N.Y. 10019.

intact long enough to reach that pinnacle is that half of the group is composed of family members. Tim Farriss on lead guitar, Andrew Farriss playing keyboards and writing most of the group's music, and Jon Farriss on drums, are all brothers. The Farrisses grew up in Perth, Australia, where their early interest in music was supported by their parents. Tim, the eldest, told Anthony DeCurtis of *Rolling Stone:* "When we were really young, we used to stand around with tennis rackets and mime records, the three of us. . . . Like 'Don't Sleep in the Subway' and 'Mr. Pleasant,' by the Kinks—and the Monkees, even Herb Alpert!" Later, their father bought them instruments "and made sure that we could play them, that we got taught," Tim added. By the time the Farrisses had moved to Sidney and all of INXS's members had joined together, Jon Farriss explained to DeCurtis, their parents were still "exceptionally helpful in accommodating everything we needed. If Kirk's parents or someone's parents were against it, they'd have them over to stay the night so they'd feel really kosher about it. They'd allow us to play until eleven at night so we could develop."

Michael Hutchence was born in Sidney, but spent much of his childhood in Hong Kong while his father was in the import business. During a return to Sidney at the age of fourteen, he met Andrew Farriss, and, after Farriss rescued Hutchence from the persecutions of a neighborhood bully, the two became good friends. As Hutchence confided to Tannenbaum, the relationship

was based on "hang[ing] around living rooms and record[ing] obscure music on this four-track recorder and try[ing] to impress girls with this." Despite the fact that Hutchence moved to Los Angeles, California, a year later—his mother became a make-up artist there after his parents were divorced—the boys remained in contact with each other through a steady correspondence. After a year in the United States, Hutchence returned yet again to Sidney. He recalled for DeCurtis: "The day I got back, I rang Andrew, and he said, 'Yeah, great, come around.' It was funny . . . . Most people fifteen, you split them up for a while and they come back completely different people. We still had a strong friendship."

Hutchence and Andrew Farriss began playing in a band that also featured bassist Garry Gary Beers; meanwhile, Tim Farriss, who, according to Tannenbaum, had been "a Christian youth-group leader until a copy of Roxy Music's *For Your Pleasure* 'changed [his] life,'" was performing in a group that included guitar and

> *INXS has "a hard-driving, irresistibly dancable sound and a sexy, live-for-the-moment attitude—tempered with just a dash of social consciousness."*

saxophone player Kirk Pengilly. In 1977 after both groups broke up, the five young men joined together, and invited Jon Farriss, the youngest, to serve as their drummer. Though they were not yet INXS—early names included the Vegetables and the Farriss Brothers—all concerned felt sufficiently committed to the new combination to move to Perth rather than lose Jon, who, because of his age, had to go with his parents when they decided to return to the family's earlier home. When Jon graduated from high school in 1979, the band decided to come back to Sidney and start playing in pubs—and used its moniker for the first time. Tim Farriss recounted for Steve Dougherty in *People:* "Our record company suggested 'In Excess.' But without a record out, it seemed people came to shows if your name was really big on your posters. We wanted ours huge, so we shortened it [to INXS]."

While playing pubs throughout Australia, where audiences were so rough that success was based on whether or not a band was peppered by hurled beer bottles, INXS also managed to release a few albums, including *INXS* and *Underneath the Colours*. They had attracted more widespread attention (and better arenas for their concert performances) by 1984, when they recorded *The Swing* and its single "Original Sin." Featuring the controversial theme of interracial love, "Original Sin" was denied airplay by many radio stations. INXS followed *The Swing* with *Listen Like Thieves,* which included the hit song "What You Need." But most critics agree that 1987's *Kick* is the band's best effort. In addition to the hit "Need You Tonight," songs like "Devil Inside"—which Hutchence has been known to dedicate in concerts to televangelist Jimmy Swaggart—and "Guns in the Sky" help make up *Kick*. Though Hutchence, who writes the words to most of the group's songs, made clear to DeCurtis that he was "not a great political lyricist" and that he dislikes "knee-jerk politics," "Guns in the Sky" is a protest song against the United States' proposed Strategic Defense Initiative.

The success of *Kick* and the sex-symbol status that it has gained Hutchence as INXS's lead singer have led to speculation that he would separate from the band. True, he has outside interests—he was featured in the Australian film *Dogs in Space,* in which he played what Dougherty described as "a feral, half-naked junkie who spends most of his time crawling around the floor of a squalid commune." But Garry Gary Beers assured

DeCurtis that Hutchence "has gone out of his way to make us all realize that INXS is his number-one priority. I feel more confident in him than ever." Hutchence himself summed up the band's probable future for DeCurtis: "We've got a lot more to say, a lot more to do and a lot more songs to write."

Selected discography

INXS, Atco, 1980.
Underneath the Colours, Atco, 1982.
The Swing, Atco, 1984.
Listen Like Theives, Atlantic, 1985.
Kick (includes "Need You Tonight," "Devil Inside," "New Sensation," and "Guns in the Sky"), Atlantic, 1987.

Also released *Dekadance* and *Shabooh Shoobah.*

Sources

Newsweek, April 11, 1988.
People, July 11, 1988.
Rolling Stone, January 14, 1988; June 16, 1988.

—*Elizabeth Thomas*

Rick James

Singer, songwriter

Funk star Rick James has been hailed as "the cornrow-braided sultan of street music" by Eric Levin of *People*. Perhaps best known for his 1981 dance hit "Superfreak," he has been writing songs professionally since the early 1970s and recording since the later years of that decade. *Street Songs*, the album that includes "Superfreak," has sold over four million copies; his combined album sales are in the area of ten million copies. James has also received attention for his secondary vocals on comedian Eddie Murphy's singing debut, the hit single "Party All the Time," and is credited with the discovery of pop singer Teena Marie.

James, whose original surname was Johnson, was born into a poor family. His father, James, worked in a foundry in Buffalo, New York, but left his wife and seven children when Rick was six years old. According to Levin, Betty, the singer's mother, then became a numbers runner to support her family. She made quite a bit of money at this illegal undertaking, enough so that by the time Rick was eight she was able to buy a house in a white neighborhood. There, the black family suffered from racial prejudice. James told Levin: "We had to fight our way home from school every day."

When James was in high school, he was active in sports, lettering in both basketball and football. But he was also beginning to write songs, and he liked this better than the more structured pastimes of team athletics, so he spent much of his time singing in bands. In 1966, however, though he was only fifteen, James began to worry about being drafted and sent to Vietnam. Thinking to evade this fate, he lied about his age and entered the U.S. Navy reserves—reserve members usually being the last to see active duty. But his attendance at reserve meetings was irregular at best, and as punishment he was assigned to a ship headed for Vietnam. James decided to run away to Canada.

He wound up in Toronto, where he again became involved with music. In the various groups he sang for, he met fellow artists who would become members of bands like Steppenwolf and Buffalo Springfield. Because James feared the Navy would catch up with him, he sometimes performed under the alias Ricky James Matthews, Matthews being the surname of one of his girlfriends at the time. James also met rock musician Neil Young during his stint in Toronto, and together they started a group called the Mynah Birds. In 1971 the Mynah Birds signed a contract with Motown Records, but the company insisted that James come back to the United States and turn himself in to the Navy before he began recording.

The result was that James spent approximately eight months in a Navy prison. He escaped once with three others, but returned to finish his sentence two months later. James told Levin that prison strengthened him: "I went in there a pitiful form of human being, and I came out 180 pounds of rock." While he was incarcerated, the Mynah Birds deal fell through, but he still had a job writing songs for Motown. James spent several years in this position, but in 1978 he recorded his debut album, *Come Get It,* along with his first hit single, "You and I."

James was unable to handle his overnight success. He confided to Levin: "In 1978 I *spent* $1 million on cars, wine, women and booze." He also did hard drugs, and though he continued producing successful albums, he wound up with hepatitis and large debts due to his abusive lifestyle. As of 1982 James told Levin he had

given up all drugs except marijuana; as of 1987 *Jet* magazine reported that James had become a born-again Christian. In that article James was quoted as saying, "God has saved me from overdosing and all kinds of different experiences," but "God has not told me to stop rocking." Critic David Hiltbrand of *People,* however, complained that on the singer's 1988 release, *Wonderful,* "his usual creativity [had] deserted him." But James came back with a different style in 1989, trading in his long braids for a 1950s-era pompadour on the video for his medley remake of "This Magic Moment/Dance with Me," from the album *Rock, Rhythm, and Blues.*

Selected discography

Come Get It (includes "You and I"), Motown, 1978.
Street Songs (includes "Superfreak"), Motown, 1981.
Throwin' Down, Motown, 1982.
Wonderful (includes "Wonderful," "Judy," "Sexual Luv Affair," "I Believe in U," "Tight," and "Loosey's Rap"), Reprise, 1988.
Rock, Rhythm, and Blues (includes "This Magic Moment/Dance with Me"), Warner Brothers, 1989.

Sources

Jet, February 9, 1987.
People, November 22, 1982; August 8, 1988.

—Elizabeth Thomas

Jean-Michel Jarre

Composer, keyboardist

Jean-Michel Jarre's flowing and melodic synthesizer music is so calming that his album *Oxygene* was played on Dutch radio and television throughout the two days in 1977 that South Moluccan terrorists held Dutch passengers hostage on a train. *Interview,* which reported this event, called *Oxygene* "perfect background music for life." Although this was the French composer's first album, he was familiar with the power that music can exert when playing a supporting role— his father is Maurice Jarre, a highly successful composer of music for film soundtracks. The influence was not immediate, though, for his parents separated when he was young. His father moved to Hollywood, where he solidly established himself with the well known "Laura's Theme" from the movie *Doctor Zhivago* and the score for *Lawrence of Arabia.* Concerning the influence of his father on his music, Jarre told *Interview:* "My mother and father split when I was six years old. She never remarried and I only saw my father once or twice a year. He moved to Hollywood. But I played piano when I was five and I saw his movies, so maybe that was an influence."

Jarre studied French literature at the University of Paris and while there joined the Groupe de Recherches Musicales founded by French sythesizer specialist Pierre Schaeffer. He also studied at the Conservatoire de Paris but found his professional educational experience stifling. He set up a home recording studio and began to pursue his own musical directions. At age 22 he wrote a ballet score, *Aor,* which was successfully produced at the Paris Opera. *Oxygene* was released in 1977 and became one of the top-selling albums in Europe and the first record by a French composer to reach the number one position on the British charts. The album is a model for the form of synthesizer music that has been referred to as "Space Music." *down beat* appropriately described *Oxygene* in space terminology: "[the album provides] a languid aural journey through the galaxy in 4/4—a big bottom sound thuds portentiously over the hum of the old spaceship's motor; asteroids shoot past; a meteor shower washes away the stars twittering in the high register."

In 1986 Jarre was invited to Houston to be part of a celebration of the city's sesquicentennial and the twenty-fifth anniversary of NASA's Johnson Space Center. His "City in Concert" presentation was described by *Stereo Review:* "On April 5, 1986, more than a million people filled Houston's parks, bridges, highways, and streets to witness a synchronized mystical, pyrotechnic, and laser-projection extravaganza that actually turned the city and its skyline into one gigantic stage." The album *Rendez-vous* is a live recording of this show. Jarre performed with a seven-member band; one song is dedicated to astronaut/musician, Ron McNair, who

For the Record. . .

Son of Maurice Jarre (a composer of film soundtracks); first wife was in public relations work; married second wife, Charlotte Rampling (an actress), October 7, 1978; children: (first marriage) Emillie; (second marriage) David-Alexis. *Education:* Attended the University of Paris and the Conservatoire de Paris.

Recording artist, 1977—. Has also composed a ballet score, *Aor.*

Addresses: c/o Olga Horstig-Primuz, 76 Champs Elysees, Paris 75008, France.

was to play saxophone at the concert but had died earlier that year in the tragic *Challenger* space shuttle disaster.

Jarre is not a prolific musician. While many artists try to produce an album each year, he has five major releases in ten years. But with each one he pushes his art a little farther to offer something unique. With *Magnetic Fields* he abandoned the romanticism of *Oxygene* to explore what a *down beat* reviewer called "a world of ethnic rhythms with a battery of synthesized percussion sounds that stack up in polyrhythmic spiral." With *Zoo Look* he teamed up with Laurie Anderson, who pushed the "world rhythm" concept one step further by contributing vocal material in over twenty rare languages including Balinese, Sioux, Quechua, and Gabonese. *down beat* called the album "a keyboard album of vocal music, a contradiction in terms made possible by the wonders of digital technology." Jarre had taken Anderson's vocal contributions, and through sampling techniques, entered them as sounds into his Fairlight and Emulator synthesizers, ready to be played back like any other instrumental sound.

In his search for new sounds, Jarre experiments with new musical instruments. "Each generation must invent a new range of instruments for their new music," he told Steven Gains in *Interview.* "We are still less clever than the composers of the seventeenth century. We still use clarinets, violins, and pianos that were invented by furniture and instrument makers with the complicity of the musicians of the time." The Rhythmin' Computer, and instrument he had built to his own specifications, can be heard on *Oxygene.*

Jarre also has his own ideas about music. His creations come primarily from within himself, rooted in his own imagination and feelings, not in what he learned in school. He is mistrustful of traditional categories and of the system of music training that enforces right and wrong approaches to music. "We are the only society with a written musical code," he told Gaines. "There is none in sculpture, or painting—only music, and not in China or Africa, either, only in the West. That's the reason people stopped considering music as an abstract expression or an intellectual art." Jarre has created a new form of music on entirely new instruments. His instruments create sounds never heard before, and mimic the sounds from cultures that few of his listeners will ever experience. His music is the sound of the future, built on the sounds of the world at large, and cast in the form of his own musical ideas.

Selected discography

All sections released by Polydor/Dreyfus

Oxygene, 1977, reissued, 1987.
Magnetic Fields, 1979, reissued, 1987.
Equinox, 1979, reissued, 1987.
Zoo Look, 1985, reissued, 1987.
Rendez-vous, 1986.
The Essential Jean-Michel Jarre, 1986.

Sources

down beat, May, 1978; September, 1982; April, 1985.
Interview, January, 1978.
People, December 5, 1977.
Stereo Review, April, 1979; December, 1986; May, 1985.

—Tim LaBorie

Billy Joel

Singer, songwriter, pianist

Billy Joel has had a huge impact on the popular music genre during the 1970s and 1980s. Beginning with his 1973 hit "Piano Man," and continuing through smash successes like 1977's "Just the Way You Are," 1978's "Big Shot," 1980's "It's Still Rock and Roll to Me," and 1986's "This Is the Time," the singer-songwriter has consistently met the changing demands of the pop audience. Joel seems equally comfortable with ballads or hard-driving rockers, broadening his appeal still further. Over his prolific career, his talents in composition, singing, and playing the piano have garnered him several platinum albums and other honors, including two Grammy awards in 1978.

Joel, born William Martin Joel in the Bronx, New York, on May 9, 1949, began to display his musical talents early, banging on the family piano at the age of two. By the time he was four his mother noticed that he enjoyed listening to Mozart, and decided to get him piano lessons. Though Joel's lessons lasted twelve years, he found time as a teenager for other pursuits—he was a member of a street gang and participated in bantamweight boxing. He told Anthony DeCurtis of *Rolling Stone* that he attributes the attraction of these rougher activities to his father's leaving the family when he was seven: "I missed having a father very much. I went out and did crazy things to discover what my masculinity was. . . . Stupid stuff."

Though Joel's early musical training was classical, as a teenager his taste changed under the influence of rock. He liked the Motown sound, and accorded psychedelic rocker Jimi Hendrix genius status, but he was particularly entranced by the Beatles. Though DeCurtis noted similarities in style between Joel's *Nylon Curtain* album and the materials of ex-Beatle John Lennon, Joel claims that he modeled himself most as a singer-songwriter after ex-Beatle Paul McCartney. In 1968 Joel began playing with a local Long Island band called the Hassles; they played in bars and clubs, their performances primarily composed of renditions of Beatles and Rolling Stones hits. The Hassles did, however, record two albums, but their success was too moderate to prevent Joel from supplementing his income by harvesting oysters, painting houses, and writing occasional rock criticism for *Changes* magazine. Around 1970 the Hassles broke up, and Joel founded a duo called Attila with the group's drummer, Jon Small. Attila made an album, too, but fame remained elusive.

Finally, in 1972 Joel released his first solo album, *Cold Spring Harbor.* He was under contract with Family Productions, and apparently the recording was shoddily handled. Due to a mix-up in *Cold Spring*'s mastering stage, the speed was accidentally bumped from 33 1/3 rpm to 33 2/3, making Joel's singing voice come out too

For the Record. . .

Full name, William Martin Joel; born May 9, 1949, in the Bronx, New York; son of Howard (an engineer) and Rosalind (a secretary; maiden name, Nyman) Joel; married Elizabeth (divorced c. 1983); married Christie Brinkley (a model); children: (second marriage) Alexa Ray.

Singer, songwriter; performed with the Hassles, 1968-79; performed with and founded group Attila, 1970; played piano in lounges in Los Angeles, Calif., under pseudonym Bill Martin; solo concert performer and recording artist, 1972—. Wrote rock criticism for *Changes,* painted houses, and harvested oysters, late 1960s-early 1970s.

Awards: Winner of several platinum albums; two Grammy Awards for "Just the Way You Are," (one for best record; the other for best song), both 1978; named Best New Male Vocalist by *Cashbox* magazine, 1974.

Addresses: *Home*—375 N. Broadway, Jericho, N.Y. 11753. *Office*—Columbia Records, 51 W. 52nd St., New York, N.Y. 10019.

high. While trying to extricate himself from his agreement with Family, Joel left for the West Coast to spend time in Los Angeles, playing piano in a cocktail lounge under the alias Bill Martin. Meanwhile, a song from one of Joel's live performances to promote *Cold Spring* had been recorded and was being played on FM radio stations. Clive Davis of Columbia Records saw potential in the song, "Captain Jack," about a heroin addict in the suburbs, managed to find Joel, helped him out of his ties to Family, and signed him to a recording contract.

Thus the way was paved for the release of Joel's first successful album, 1973's *Piano Man.* The popular title track was a somewhat autobiographical rendition of his experiences as a lounge player; the disc also included "Captain Jack" and other narrative songs like "The Ballad of Billy the Kid." Because of the strong story content of *Piano Man,* Joel was perceived by many as an artist in the tradition of narrative singer-songwriter Harry Chapin. This perception was reinforced by Joel's next album, *Streetlife Serenade.* Some critics liked *Streetlife,* such as Steven Gaynes in the *New York Sunday News,* who affirmed that it "actually meets the standards set by its predecessor," being "heavily stocked with those stinging lyrics Joel is so brilliant at." But the album was not as well-liked as *Piano Man* with the record-buying public. Neither was Joel's next album, *Turnstiles,* though it included a song likely to

become a Manhattan standard, "New York State of Mind."

Apparently, hiring Phil Ramone as his producer provided the magic to revitalize Joel's career. The first of Joel's albums that Ramone worked on was *The Stranger,* which spawned four hit singles: "Just the Way You Are" and "She's Always a Woman," romantic love ballads, the energetic "Movin' Out," and the controversial "Only the Good Die Young." The latter drew flak from Roman Catholics because it portrayed a teenage boy criticizing his Catholic girlfriend's religion in order to persuade her to have sex with him. Joel claims that he did not intend to be anti-Catholic; he told Eve Zibart in the *Washington Post:* "The point is lust. When you're young and sexually crazed, you'll tell anybody anything. . . . *Don't listen to your parents, don't listen to your religious upbringing. . .*"

Most of Joel's albums after *The Stranger* produced hits as well. Notable among them are the new-wave influenced "It's Still Rock and Roll to Me," from *Glass Houses;* "Allentown," a song about the difficulties of the

> *Joel claims that he modeled himself most as a singer-songwriter after ex-Beatle Paul McCartney.*

working-class unemployed from *The Nylon Curtain* that brought him Allentown, Pennsylvania's key to the city; and "Uptown Girl," concerning a love relationship that crosses class boundaries, from *An Innocent Man*—an album which, according to DeCurtis, "seems like a valentine" to model Christie Brinkley, the woman Joel married after he divorced his first wife, Elizabeth. Joel explained to DeCurtis that his first marriage was troubled by the fact that Elizabeth served as his manager: "She was more focused on my career than I was. . . . It was fruitful and successful in terms of what the music business is supposed to be, but it was ultimately damaging in terms of a relationship."

Since his remarriage to Brinkley, and the birth of their daughter, Alexa Ray, Joel has slowed his career pace somewhat. He plans to cut down on his concert tours, and eventually to retire from the performance aspects of music in favor of more songwriting and production. As he told DeCurtis, "it's sort of like being an athlete. Eventually, you have to become a coach. It's just a natural extension."

Selected discography

(With the Hassles) *The Hassles,* United Artists, 1968.

(With the Hassles) *Hour of the Wolf,* United Artists, 1969.

(With Attila) *Attila,* Epic, 1970.

Cold Spring Harbor, Family Productions, 1972.

Piano Man (includes "Piano Man," "Captain Jack," "The Ballad of Billy the Kid," and "Travelin' Prayer"), Columbia, 1973.

Streetlife Serenade (includes "The Entertainer"), Columbia, 1974.

Turnstiles (includes "Summer, Highland Falls," "Say Goodbye to San Francisco," and "New York State of Mind"), Columbia, 1976.

The Stranger (includes "Just the Way You Are," "Movin' Out," "She's Always a Woman to Me," and "Only the Good Die Young"), Columbia, 1977.

52nd Street (includes "Big Shot," "Half a Mile Away," "My Life," "Honesty," "Until the Night," "Stiletto," "Zanzibar," and "Rosalinda's Eyes"), Columbia, 1978.

Glass Houses (includes "It's Still Rock and Roll to Me," "You May Be Right," and "Don't Ask Me Why"), Columbia, 1980.

Songs in the Attic, Columbia, 1981.

Nylon Curtain (includes "Allentown," "Pressure," and "Goodnight, Saigon"), Columbia, 1982.

An Innocent Man (includes "An Innocent Man," "Uptown Girl," and "Keepin' the Faith"), Columbia, 1983.

The Bridge (includes "This Is the Time" and "You're Only Human"), Columbia, c. 1986.

Sources

Books

McKenzie, Michael, *Billy Joel,* Ballantine, 1985.

Periodicals

New York Sunday News, September 29, 1974.
People, January 10, 1983.
Rolling Stone, November 6, 1986.
Washington Post, October 8, 1978.

—Elizabeth Thomas

Quincy Jones

Producer, composer, arranger,
trumpeter, and bandleader

Quincy Jones is, quite simply, one of the world's most admired record producers. An award-winning jazz musician in his own right, Jones has overseen the creation of a staggering array of albums, film and television scores, big-band tunes, and pop music, featuring some of the entertainment industry's biggest stars. As David Breskin notes in *Life* magazine, however, commercial success is not the best measure of Jones's accomplishments. "It is range that distinguishes Jones," writes Breskin. "He has worked with everyone from Louis Armstrong to Eddie Van Halen, Billie Holiday to Diana Ross, [Frank] Sinatra . . . to [Bruce] Springsteen. No one in the history of contemporary American music has cut so wide a path."

A child prodigy who was performing professionally at the age of fifteen, Jones has literally done it all in the music business, from supplying scores to Count Basie and Sarah Vaughan to recording his own work on albums such as the platinum-selling *Sounds . . . and Stuff Like That,* to engineering one of the biggest-selling records in history, Michael Jackson's *Thriller.* Critics and clients alike seek Jones out for his dedication to perfection, his affability, and especially, his talent for making memorable music. "Quincy Jones on a roll is something to see," says David Ritz in *Rolling Stone.* "No one knows exactly what it is, but in an insecure, neurotic business, where the *Billboard* charts are revered like the Bible and everyone's looking for a savior, Quincy's flaming hot. . . . He's an enthusiast who thrives under a barrage of creative challenges and who exhibits uncanny emotional control as he moves from one high-minded hustle to another. With everyone around him going nuts, Quincy has a gift for staying steady, even as he picks up the tempo and drives his crew—singers, secretaries and sidemen—to faster speeds."

The hectic routine suits Jones just fine. He has lived most of his life at a pace that would exhaust all but the hardiest adventurers. One in a family of nine children, Jones was born in Chicago and raised in Seattle by his father, a carpenter, and a stepmother. Unlike many musicians, who come upon their training by listening to parents or relatives play, Jones learned the trumpet in public school. He showed an unusual aptitude for the instrument, and for music in general, so much so that by thirteen he was sending arrangements to Count Basie and performing with a professional dance band. Jones's best friend at the time was another young talent, Ray Charles. "Ray would play at clubs, . . . and I also played all over town, and then we'd get together at the Elks Club after hours to play bop," Jones remembered in *down beat.* "In the clubs or at dances, you'd have to play schottisches [Scottish dances], pop songs, r & b, and so on, but when we played at the Elks Club, that

Full name Quincy Delight Jones; born March 14, 1933, in Chicago, Ill.; son of Quincy Delight (a carpenter) and Sarah Jones; married third wife, Peggy Lipton (an actress), 1974 (divorced, 1986); children: (first marriage) Jolie, (second marriage) Martina-Lisa, Quincy III, (third marriage) Kidada, Rashida. *Education:* Attended Seattle University, Berklee School of Music (now Berklee College of Music), and Boston Conservatory; also studied arranging in Paris with Nadia Boulanger.

Composer, arranger, trumpeter, and bandleader, 1950—. Member of Lionel Hampton Orchestra, 1950-53; toured Europe with his own big band, 1953-60, while providing orchestra arrangements for Frank Sinatra, Dinah Washington, Count Basie, Sarah Vaughan, and Peggy Lee; organizing member of Dizzy Gillespie Orchestra for the Department of State, 1956; music director, Barchlay Disques (Paris), 1956-60.

Named music director of Mercury Records, 1961, produced first hit record, Leslie Gore's "It's My Party," 1963, promoted to vice-president, 1964. Independent composer and conductor, 1965—, providing scores for numerous television shows and feature films, including *The Pawnbroker,* 1964, *In Cold Blood,* 1967, *Cactus Flower,* 1969, *The Hot Rock,* 1972, *The Wiz,* 1978, and *The Color Purple,* 1985.

Recorded with A & M Records, 1969-80, founded Qwest Records, 1981. Producer of albums, including Michael Jackson's *Off the Wall* and *Thriller,* George Benson's *Give Me the Night,* Frank Sinatra's *L.A. Is My Lady,* and Patti Austin's *Every Home Should Have One.* Producer of single "We Are the World," special song to aid famine victims in Ethiopia, 1986. Winner of fifteen Grammy Awards and numerous other citations for musical excellence.

Addresses: *Other*— 10880 Wilshire Blvd. #2110, Los Angeles, Calif. 90024.

He studied under scholarship at Boston's Berklee College of Music and later travelled to Paris to learn scoring under the renowned Nadia Boulanger. Throughout the 1950s Jones wrote big-band tunes, performed in Europe with his own group or with Dizzy Gillespie's band, and produced records for Barchlay Disques, a Parisian company. He returned to the United States in 1960 to work as one of the first black executives in a major recording firm, Mercury Records. He was promoted to vice president of Mercury in 1964.

Jones broke yet another color barrier in 1965 when he became the first black composer to be accepted by the Hollywood establishment. He began to score motion pictures such as *In Cold Blood, In the Heat of the Night,* and *Cactus Flower,* as well as television shows such as "Ironside" and "Sanford and Son." Meanwhile he continued to record his own and others' work, first for Mercury, then for A & M Records, and finally, in 1980, for his own company, Qwest Records. Although he appreciated every sort of music from Bach to Basie, Jones began to show a pragmatic streak—he was as willing to produce pop music as he was to create original jazz. "I had all the five-star *down beat* reviews I could use," he told *Rolling Stone.* "Hey, man, I wasn't going to be intimidated by a pure art trip. My new motto was . . . 'Let's dance.' Not that I didn't love the art. Loved it to death. Still do and always will. . . .[But] I'm as silly as any kid and wanna stay that way. The kids hear it straight and clean. They know who's jiving and who ain't."

In 1978 Jones worked on the orchestration for the film *The Wiz.* The movie was not a great success, but it brought Jones together with Michael Jackson, and the two established a professional rapport. Jackson hired Jones to produce a 1981 album, *Off the Wall,* that went platinum. Two years later the team paired again to work on *Thriller.* Jones admitted in *down beat* that he had great trepidations about *Thriller.* "We cut nine songs, at first, and had it finished, and *then* threw four out to get four more that were *really* strong," he said. "That's a nice psychological thing to do, because you're competing with yourself. We had just come off an album that sold eight million [*Off the Wall*], and it's scary to go back in after that kind of home run. Our thinking was, 'If we could just catch up with *half* of this thing, we'd be happy,' and little did we know it'd do what it did." *Thriller* has sold more than forty million copies worldwide; it won Jones three Grammy awards and the continued respect of his peers in the industry. Two years later he was given the monumental task of organizing and directing more than thirty top stars for the "We Are the World" recording, created to provide relief for Ethiopian famine victims.

was for us." Jones told *Rolling Stone* that he was getting a snobbish attitude about his art until Charles settled him down and gave him a direction for his future. "A blind man said to me, 'Listen to everything you can, and don't play the fool by putting ropes around yourself,'" Jones said. "That was Ray Charles teaching me, a know-nothing fourteen-year-old squirt, how to write music."

The "know-nothing squirt" managed to land a job with the prestigious Lionel Hampton Orchestra when he was still in his teens. After a few years of touring, however, Jones decided to seek more formal musical training.

Much has been written about Quincy Jones's style,

substance, and production methods. A *U.S. News and World Report* correspondent writes: "Not only is almost no one else in the business so widely admired, but Jones still manages to bring new vigor and curiosity to each job—a rarity in a jaded industry." Breskin describes Jones's "signature sound" as "warm rhythms, lush synthesizer textures, extravagant yet uncluttered string-and-horn orchestrations, a touchable presence to the vocals. All played by a cast of hundreds and recorded with an ear for infinitesimal detail." The critic concludes that Jones is "the Cecil B. DeMille of record production . . . loved for his street humor, his thoughtfulness and his hard-won joie de vivre." Jones's own analysis is simpler. His method, he told *Rolling Stone*, is to "take the tune home and live with it for days. Live with it in all forms—as a demo, rhythm track, with and without vocals. When it starts boring me, I throw it away. When it starts haunting me, I start considering it. Patience, man. This recording business is about patience—and keeping things relaxed."

Quincy Jones is, quite simply, one of the world's most admired record producers.

If Jones seems to embrace life more enthusiastically than most, it is due in part to an illness that almost killed him in 1974. That year he underwent several dangerous operations for brain aneurisms—his friends at one point gave up hope. Jones not only survived, he also brought a new philosophy to his work and his personal life. "Coming from a jazz background," he told *Life*, "you spend half your life trying to be real hip. It was pathetic how hip I was! But the operation put a lot of things in close-up. A lot of corny things that didn't count before took on a significance." Today Jones continues to be involved in myriad projects, including a massive history of black music that has consumed him for years. He told *Life* that his days are like "running through hell with gasoline drawers on," but he thrives on the pressure. His work, he concluded in *Rolling Stone*, is "an obsession. But producing is always an obsession. Fact is, I'm obsessed with this whole business. That's why I'm so happy, and why I'll be up half the night trying to figure things out."

Selected discography

Brand New Bag, Mercury.

Ndeda, Mercury.
The Dude, A & M.
The Best of Quincy Jones, A & M.
Sounds . . . and Stuff Like That, A & M.
I Heard That, A & M.
Mellow Madness, A & M.
Body Heat, A & M.
You've Got It Bad, Girl, A & M.
Smackwater Jack, A & M.
Gula Matari, A & M.
Walking in Space, A & M.
The Birth of a Band, A & M.
The Great Wide World of Quincy Jones, Trip.
The Quintessential Charts, MCA.
Mode, ABC Records.
My Fair Lady Loves Jazz, Impulse.
This Is How I Feel about Jazz, ABC/Paramount.

Selected movie soundtracks

In the Heat of the Night, Liberty.
Bob & Carol & Ted & Alice, Bell.
Cactus Flower, Bell.
They Call Me Mr. Tibbs, Bell.
Dollars, Reprise.
For Love of Ivy, ABC.
The Wiz, MCA.
Roots, Warner Brothers.

Selected productions for others

Michael Jackson

Off the Wall, Epic, 1981.
Thriller, Epic, 1983.

The Brothers Johnson

Blam, A & M.
Light Up the Night, A & M.
Right on Time, A & M.
Look Out for #1, A & M.

George Benson

Give Me the Night, Warner Brothers.

Frank Sinatra

L.A. Is My Lady, Qwest.

Patti Austin

Every Home Should Have One, Qwest.

Donna Summer

Donna Summer, Geffen.

Leslie Gore

Leslie Gore's Golden Hits, Mercury.

Sources

down beat, April, 1985.
Life, December, 1984.
People, September 8, 1986.
Rolling Stone, April 12, 1984.
U.S. News and World Report, February 8, 1988.

—Anne Janette Johnson

The Judds

Mother-daughter country group

Virtually unknown in 1984, the Judds—a mother-daughter duo—have become one of the biggest acts in country music. Theirs is a Cinderella story of long years of hardship, of singing around kitchen tables and crisscrossing the country in search of work before landing a major recording contract and some of Nashville's most prestigious awards. As Alanna Nash puts it in *Stereo Review,* the two Kentucky natives have given "staid, lifeless country radio a direct and well-positioned kick in the pants by introducing a fresh, new direction for progressive country fare." Indeed, the two performers seem to have much in their favor: daughter Wynonna Judd is said to possess the most significant voice to enter country music in the last twenty years, and mother, Naomi, brings a daredevil spirit, uncommon verve, and astute songwriting to the team. Drawing on an inventive collage of sources, from folk to bebop to early rock and roll, the Judds have molded a personal style that animates lyrics "like a spring breeze blowing a window curtain," to quote Jay Cocks in *Time* magazine. Cocks adds that the Judds "will cross any musical boundaries, but . . . their real strength comes

For the Record. . .

Naomi Judd, given name Diana Judd, name legally changed to Naomi Judd; born c. 1946 in Ashland, Kentucky; daughter of Glen (a filling-station owner) and Polly Judd; married Michael Ciminella, c. 1963 (divorced, 1970); children: Wynonna, Ashley.

Wynonna Judd, given name Christina Ciminella, name legally changed to Wynonna Judd; born c. 1964 in Ashland, Kentucky; daughter of Naomi Judd and Michael Ciminella. *Education:* High-school graduate.

Formed country singing duo, the Judds, 1982; signed with RCA Records, 1983; released first album, 1984, and had first hit singles, "Had a Dream (for the Heart)" and "Mama, He's Crazy," 1984. Have made numerous tours of United States and Europe, 1984—, appearing at Caesar's Palace, Las Vegas, Nev., 1985, and Lincoln Center, New York, N.Y., 1987.

Awards: Three Grammy Awards for best country vocal duet; four Country Music Association awards for best vocal duet; named country duo of the year by the Academy of Country Music, 1985, 1986, 1987, 1988, and 1989; two platinum albums, *Why Not Me* and *Rockin' with the Rhythm.*

Addresses: *Other*— P.O. Box 17087, Nashville, Tenn. 37217.

from staying close to the roots"—the traditional roots of the country sound.

Both Naomi and Wynonna Judd were born in Ashland, Kentucky. Naomi, who was christened Diana, was the daughter of a comfortably well-off filling-station attendant. Her formative years in Ashland were very traditional until her younger brother, Brian, developed Hodgkin's disease. Not only did the cancer kill Brian, it caused the Judd family to splinter—Naomi, who married at seventeen and had daughter Wynonna at eighteen, embarked on a new life in Los Angeles in 1968. It was there that Wynonna—born Christina Ciminella—grew up, "a typical Hollywood kid, eating Ding-Dongs and watching *The Brady Bunch* on TV," to quote her mother in *Life* magazine. Naomi drifted through a series of jobs as a model and secretary, eventually deciding that the West Coast did not provide a suitable environment for her two daughters. In 1976 the family of three (Naomi had left her husband in 1970) returned to Kentucky to live in a rustic cottage on a mountaintop near Morrill.

Some early publicity exaggerated the primitive condi-

tions of the Judds' home in Morrill, but the cottage did lack a telephone and a television, forcing Wynonna and her sister, Ashley, to find their own amusements. Wynonna discovered the guitar, and singing and picking became an obsession with her. Meanwhile, Naomi struggled to pay the bills, and the family sometimes went without heat and electricity for days at a time. Finally the three Judds moved back to California, this time to Marin County, where Naomi enrolled in nursing school and worked the night shift as a waitress. Naomi remembers those California years as the hardest of all. In *Behind Closed Doors: Talking with the Legends of Country Music,* she said that she, Wynonna, and Ashley shared a tiny, one-bedroom apartment above a real-estate office. "We're talking serious poverty," she said. "There were times when I didn't know how we were gonna eat, or how I was even gonna pay the small rent that I paid. . . . It still amazes me how I did it."

Growing up under these conditions, Wynonna found herself drawn to music to the exclusion of all else. She often skipped school to listen to her Joni Mitchell and

> *"Despite their dizzying ride to the top of the C&W heap, the Judds are still as unpretentious as fried catfish and hush puppies."*

Bonnie Raitt albums, and her share of the chores never seemed to get done. "Wynonna was a very difficult teenager," Naomi told *Teen* magazine. "She was so obsessed with music that she never helped out around the house. She'd even take grocery money to buy new guitar strings." Mother and daughter seemed to fight constantly, only coming to an accord on the occasions when they found time to make music together. In these rare moments, they discovered that they could harmonize almost by telepathy, and soon the enterprising Naomi was fantasizing about a singing career for herself and her daughters.

The Judds moved to Nashville in 1979, after Naomi had completed nursing school. While the family's finances improved, Wynonna's enthusiasm for school and household duties continued to slide. She did attend high school in Nashville, however, and there, during a talent show, she impressed the daughter of record producer Brent Maher, who had several prominent country-music clients. In 1982 Maher's daughter was injured in an automobile accident, and quite by chance, Naomi

Judd was assigned to nurse her. After the girl's recovery, Maher was so grateful for Naomi's skillful nursing that he agreed to listen to a homemade demo tape that the Judds had cut themselves. It was a full month before he got to the tape, finally putting it in his car stereo on the way to work. "It takes me thirty minutes to get from the house to the studio," he told Alanna Nash, "and by the time I got there, I was on the phone calling them up." On the spot, Maher agreed to produce the Judds.

Maher called in two associates to help him with the Judds—guitarist-songwriter Don Potter and Ken Stilts, a wealthy businessman who agreed to manage the duo. Potter and Maher worked with the women for six months before they put anything on tape; most of that time was spent defining a style and building the distinctive country-jazz framework that has become the Judds' trademark. In 1983 the Judds won a contract with RCA with a live audition—a highly unusual way for an unknown group to proceed in Nashville. Stilts provided the financial resources to keep the family afloat and to begin a hectic round of national concert appearances, everywhere from Caesar's Palace in Las Vegas to tiny Arkansas community halls. By 1984 the Judds had released a mini-album of eight songs. Their first single, "Had a Dream (for the Heart)" made the country Top 20, and the second and third singles, "Mama, He's Crazy" and "Why Not Me," both topped the country charts. By 1986 they had two platinum albums, *Why Not Me* and *Rockin' with the Rhythm.* "I never thought it would happen this fast," Wynonna told *Life,* "—from the supper table to RCA to a couple of $200,000 tour buses."

Wide-ranging though their musical tastes may be, the Judds have one constant in their recordings: a sense of home and heart. Joe Galante, vice president of RCA Nashville told *Rolling Stone* that when he first heard the duo "it was just guitar and vocals and that absolute *emotion* in Wynonna's voice." Galante added: "I grew up in New York, I'm an old rock and roller. . . . I knew this was authentic country music, but I also intuitively knew that there was something hip about it, how tight their harmonies were. You could feel sensitivity, how they look at each other when they share a musical moment. Their message is open communication in most of their songs." *Life* correspondent Jamie James expresses a similar opinion: "Not for the Judds the mournful laments or 'cheatin-on-satin-sheets' sexy stuff," writes James. "They sing about family love and solid rural values—without ever lapsing into cornball. Their harmonies are smooth as Karo syrup and solidly supported by twangy acoustic rhythms in old-timey ballads. . . . Despite their dizzying ride to the top of the C&W heap, the Judds are still as unpretentious as fried catfish and hush puppies."

The Judds' "dizzying ride to the top" has caused some jealousy among industry hard-liners, some of whom feel that the pair failed to "pay their dues." Wynonna bristles at the charge. "So many people say, 'You made it so quickly and you haven't paid your dues. You haven't played in the honky-tonks for ten years,'" she said in *Behind Closed Doors.* "And I want to get up and go over and shake 'em. Because you have to realize that my mother had to work two jobs to put food on the table. We *have* worked, but it was working to survive. And in my heart, what has happened [for us] musically is something that is completely a miracle." In the same interview, Naomi also expressed gratitude for the change in her family's fortunes. "Wynonna and I consider that we aren't just one in a million," she said. "I mean, we're one in *millions,* to have been blessed with what's happened to us. . ... What is goin' on in our lives right now is so far beyond our control. I mean, it's absolutely in the Lord's will. We are doin' things that not even in my wildest imagination—which is pretty out there—I would have thought possible."

Selected discography

The Judds, RCA, 1984.
Why Not Me, RCA, 1985.
Rockin' with the Rhythm, RCA, 1985.
Heart Land, RCA, 1987.
Christmas Time with the Judds, RCA, 1987.
The Judds' Greatest Hits, RCA, 1988.
River of Time, RCA, 1989.

Sources

Books

Nash, Alanna, *Behind Closed Doors: Talking with the Legends of Country Music,* Knopf, 1988.

Periodicals

Life, February, 1986.
Rolling Stone, July 2, 1987.
Stereo Review, February, 1986; December, 1986.
Teen, December, 1987.
Time, January 13, 1986.

—Anne Janette Johnson

Albert King

Singer, songwriter, guitarist

"Albert King is a legend," stated guitarist Joe Walsh in *Guitar World*. "I can't think of anybody who would go out onstage with Albert on a good night and not be absolutely terrified to play the blues next to him. That guy'll run over you like Amtrak." Many guitarists (Rory Gallagher and Louisiana Red, to name two) have had the unfortunate experience of trying to take on Mr. Albert King, a.k.a. "the velvet bulldozer." Of the four blues Kings, Freddie, B.B., Earl and Albert, the latter certainly has the most recognizable and unorthodox style. To start with, he is left-handed but plays a right-handed guitar upside down (bass strings on the bottom) and tuned to an E-minor chord with a low C on the bottom. But it's not so much the equipment and setup; it's what he does with it. Instead of bending up as a right-hander would, King *pulls* the strings down with so much force that the notes sound like they're falling off a cliff and bouncing back up. "He's the best bender in the business," former Roomful of Blues guitarist Ronnie Earl told *Guitar Player*. "He's got three of the five best blues licks in the world. Three of the best notes in the history of music."

King was born in 1923 (or 1924, sources vary) in Indianola, Mississippi, and raised in Osceola, Arkansas. After being exposed to the blues while working in the fields, King made his first instrument, a one-string diddley bow, fashioned after the washtub bass. The six-year-old soon progressed to a guitar with a cigar box for a body but it would take another twelve years before he would purchase his first real six-string from a friend for $1.25. King learned from locals like Elmore James, Howlin' Wolf and Robert Nighthawk, but because he played backwards, he was forced to make adjustments. "I knew I was going to have to create my own style," King informed Dan Forte of *Guitar Player*, "because I couldn't make the changes and the chords the same as a right-handed man could. I play a few chords, but not many. I always concentrated on my singing guitar sound—more of a sustained note." King tried to imitate the sound of truck motors roaring by his window as a youth.

Once he felt his chops were up to par, King began sitting in with the group Yancey's Band while still maintaining his daytime gig as a bulldozer driver. King was trying to emulate the T-Bone walker guitar style when he left his next group, the In The Groove Boys, and moved to South Bend, Indiana. He sang with a gospel vocal group, the Harmony Boys, before moving onto Chicago. During his stay in the Windy City, King worked as a drummer, providing the backbeat for Jimmy Reed as well as for Brook Benton and Jackie Wilson.

In 1953, King got his first taste of the recording industry when he entered the studios of disc jockey and record

For the Record. . .

Born Albert Nelson, April 25, 1923 (some sources say 1924), in Indianola, Miss.; son of Mary Blevins (a church singer); stepson of Will Nelson (an itinerant preacher).

Worked as a bulldozer driver while learning to play guitar; played guitar with Yancy's Band and the In the Groove Boys during the 1940s; singer in gospel group, the Harmony Boys; worked as a drummer for Jimmy Reed, Brook Benton, and Jackie Wilson; recording artist (as guitarist), 1953—.

Awards: Inducted into W.C. Handy International Blues Awards Hall of Fame, 1983.

Addresses: *Home*—Lovejoy, Ill.

company (Parrot) owner Al Benson. "And that's when I recorded the very first tunes I ever recorded in my life— 'Walking From Door To Door' and 'Lonesome In My Bed.' Them two tunes sold better than 350,000 for his label. All I got out of it was fourteen dollars," he told *Guitar World.* "Bad Luck Blues" also did very well for King's reputation but little for his pocketbook. It would take another six years before King would again record. From 1959 until 1962, over a dozen singles were released on the Bobbin and King labels, the most notable being "Don't Throw Your Love On Me So Strong," a Top Twenty rhythm and blues hit from 1961. Once again, however, King was enormously underpaid, this time receiving only $800 for his efforts.

After a couple of tunes on Tennessee's Count-Tree label, King signed with Stax Records out of Memphis in 1966. His debut album, *Born Under a Bad Sign,* was a collection of his top singles from the previous two years, including "Crosscut Saw," "Oh, Pretty Woman," "As The Years Go Passing By," "Personal Manager," "The Hunter," and the title track. It would prove to be one of King's most popular albums and perhaps his most influential. Backed by Booker T and the MG's (Steve Cropper, Duck Dunn, Al Jackson, and the Mar-Keys horn section), it was a perfect blend of blues and funk with arrangements that satisfied both the black and white markets. Guitarists, including Eric Clapton, Peter Green, and the late Mike Bloomfield, were soon busy trying to figure out the secret to King's uniquely economical licks. "He can take four notes and write a volume," Bloomfield told *Guitar Player.*

Although King's recordings for Stax were incredible, his business dealings with them were just as one-sided as his Parrot days thirteen years earlier. "Al Bell talked

me into signing an eight-year contract, and during all the rest of it, for eight years, I got cheated and beat out of money," King told *Guitar World* of his Stax days. In 1968, concert promoter Bill Graham offered King $16,000 for a three-night stand at San Francisco's Fillmore West. Opening for John Mayall and Jimi Hendrix, King stole the show and became a favorite among rock fans. His *Live Wire/Blues Power* album gives testament to King's subtle, yet powerful, style that wins over audiences. "He wasn't just a good guitar player; he had a wonderful stage presence," Graham told *Guitar Player,* "he never became a shuck-and-jiver." King performed so well and enjoyed the Bay Area so much that he would later record another live album there.

King's sound was placed in many different settings while at Stax, which normally would cause an artist to alter their style to fit the music. But King has always been able to adapt to the settings and still retain his signature sound. Nearly a half-dozen different produc-

> *"Albert King is a legend. I can't think of anybody who would go out onstage with Albert on a good night and not be absolutely terrified to play the blues next to him."*
> *—Joe Walsh*

ers have tried everything from string sections and disco arrangements to female back-up singers and soul songs in their attempts to keep King sounding "modern." Sometimes it worked, but, even when it didn't, King's guitar work remained respectable. As Robert Palmer wrote in the liner notes to *Masterwords,* "[King's] mature playing and singing and the definitive soul rhythm section of the sixties clicked together to produce music that would fundamentally alter the mainstream of white rock as well as the sound of commercial blues within a few years' time."

In 1969 King became the first blues guitarist to perform with a symphony and at one point he even took night classes in music theory. But some critics have suggested that his style is too simple and repetitive. "The blues is like that anyway," King countered in *Guitar World.* "We know them changes, expect their arrival and aren't caught up in suspense as to where the blues is going." King uses his thumb instead of a pick, and although he cannot sing and play simultaneously, what separates him from the rest of the pack is his ability to keep his listeners on the edge until just the right moment, when the 6-foot-4, 260-pounder pulls the rug out from under with one of his patented blues bends.

After leaving Stax, King signed with Utopia Records, where Bert de Couteaux overproduced both *Truckload Of Lovin'* and *Albert*. Similarly, Allen Toussaint's production of *New Orleans Heat* for Tomato did its best to hide King's sound in the arrangements. Luckily, in 1983 King signed to the Fantasy label and released two blues classics: the Grammy-nominated *San Francisco '83* and *I'm In A Phone Booth, Baby* from 1984. Both albums offer some of King's best guitar work to date.

Although it's been over five years since King's last album, his sound has been kept alive through constant touring and by other artists like Stevie Ray Vaughan, whose "Texas Flood" is homage to the master. "I do owe a lot to that man," Vaughan confessed to *Guitar World*. "I don't know of anybody who can play sassier than Albert." Vaughan's work on David Bowie's *Let's Dance* LP introduced the King sound to a younger audience. "I kind of wanted to see how many places Albert King's stuff would fit," Vaughan said in *Guitar Player*. "It *always* does." The two squared off on the Cinemax session, *B.B. King and Friends,* and there is talk of Vaughan producing an Albert King album in the future if and when he signs with a new label. Joe Walsh has also been doing some recording with King as the deal shopping continues.

Selected discography

Solo LPs

The Big Blues, King, 1962.
Travelling to California, King, 1967.
Born Under a Bad Sign, Stax, 1967.
King of the Blues Guitar, Atco, 1968.
Live Wire/Blues Power, Stax, 1968.
Albert King Does the King Thing, Stax, 1968.
I'll Play the Blues for You, Stax, 1972.
Truckload of Lovin', Utopia, 1976.
Albert, Utopia, 1977.
New Orleans Heat, Tomato, 1978.
The Pinch, Stax, 1978.
Masterworks, Atlantic, 1982.

Blues for Elvis, Stax, 1983.
San Francisco '83, Fantasy, 1983.
I'm In a Phone Booth, Baby, Fantasy, 1984.
The Lost Session, Fantasy, 1986.
I Wanna Get Funky, Stax, 1987.
Blues At Sunrise, Stax, 1988.
Door to Door, Chess.
Laundromat Blues, Edsel.
WattStax, Stax.
Years Gone By, Stax.

With Steve Cropper and Pop Staples

Jammed Together, Stax, 1988.

With Little Milton

Chronicle, Stax.

With Little Milton and Chico Hamilton

Montreux Festival, Stax.

Sources

Books

Guralnick, Peter, *Lost Highway*, Vintage Books, 1982.
Guralnick, *The Listener's Guide to the Blues*, Facts on File, 1982.
Harris, Sheldon, *Blues Who's Who*, Da Capo, 1979.
The Illustrated Encyclopedia of Rock, compiled by Nick Logan and Bob Woffinden, Harmony, 1977.
Kozinn, Allan, Pete Welding, Dan Forte, and Gene Santoro, *The Guitar: The History, The Music, The Players*, Quill, 1984.
The Rolling Stone Record Guide, edited by Dave Marsh with John Swenson, Random House/Rolling Stone Press, 1979.

Periodicals

down beat, November, 1976; March, 1984; November, 1984.
Guitar Player, August, 1977; September, 1977; July, 1981; November, 1983; October, 1984; January, 1986; January, 1987.
Guitar World, March, 1984; November, 1985; September, 1988; December, 1988.
Living Blues, January/February, 1988.

Other

Masterworks (album liner notes by Robert Palmer), Atlantic, 1982.

—Calen D. Stone

Julian Lennon

Singer, songwriter, guitarist

When Julian Lennon released *Valotte,* his first album, he took "an important step toward establishing . . . musical credibility," according to Barbara Graustark in *People.* The oldest son of ex-Beatle and late rock legend John Lennon, Julian has satisfied most critics that he has a legitimate talent and is not merely exploiting his father's fame. *Valotte* sent two hit singles onto the charts, the title track and "Too Late for Goodbyes," and the album's sales put it into the platinum category. Lennon has followed up his successful debut with two other albums, *The Secret Value of Daydreaming* and *Mr. Jordan.*

Born John Charles Julian Lennon on April 8, 1963, in Liverpool, England, Julian was named first for his famous father, second for his maternal grandfather, and third for his paternal grandmother, Julia. Of course, it was the third name, or its shortened version, Jules, that his family and friends used. Because Julian was born when his father's group was beginning its successful rise to superstar status, he rarely saw the elder Lennon, who was often away on concert tours. Yet his father had a huge influence on him: "I learned a lot from him, looking at what he's done and what I've got to go through," the young singer told Brant Mewborn in *Rolling Stone.* In turn, Julian had some influence on John Lennon's career as well, from an early age. Though critics and fans alike have often interpreted the Beatles' "Lucy in the Sky with Diamonds" as a paean to LSD, Julian, like his father before him, maintains that the song came from a childhood picture he had drawn of one of his schoolmates, Lucy. "You better believe it!" he told Mewborn. And the group's "Hey, Jude" began as "Hey, Jules"—a song that Paul McCartney wrote to comfort Julian when his parents divorced in 1968.

Though Julian Lennon saw his father even more infrequently after the latter's marriage to Yoko Ono and subsequent move to New York City, by the time he was ten he had begun to develop musical interests. He played the drums and the guitar, and when he was eleven served as the drummer on "Ya Ya," a track on his father's album *Walls and Bridges.* When the younger Lennon was in his early teens, he began to teach himself how to play the piano.

As Julian grew older, he visited his father in New York more frequently, and the two began to repair their somewhat neglected relationship. But before they reached the degree of closeness that both desired, John Lennon was killed by an assassin in December, 1980. Julian was affected deeply by his father's death. He had been living with his mother, Cynthia, in Wales; afterwards he moved to London and aimlessly haunted the city's nightclubs. Julian wanted to work on his own

For the Record. . .

Full name John Charles Julian Lennon; born April 8, 1963, in Liverpool, England; son of John (a singer, songwriter, and musician) and Cynthia (a textile designer and television host; maiden name, Powell) Lennon.

Recording artist and concert performer, 1984—.

Addresses: *Other*— 200 W. 57th St. #1403, New York, N.Y., 10019.

musical projects and write songs, but was daunted by grief and the shadow of his father's immense talent. As Elizabeth Kaye summed it up in *Rolling Stone,* "when he was small, he worried that he could never write songs or sing them the way his father did. When he was older, he worried that anything he wrote or sang would sound too much like his father."

Julian stumbled into a record deal designed to exploit John's memory by having the son sing an unreleased song stolen from his father's estate. He was rescued from the situation by his stepmother, Yoko Ono, who bought him out of the contract, and Julian finally signed with Atlantic Records. He and his associates traveled to a quiet French château called Valotte to work on his debut album in peaceful privacy—hence the title of the 1984 album, *Valotte.* As Julian recorded *Valotte,* he gained confidence, and his feelings about his musical resemblance to John Lennon began to resolve themselves. *Valotte*'s producer, Phil Ramone, helped him; Lennon confided to Graustark: "He just said, 'Sing naturally, wherever the feeling takes you.'" As for the notes on which his voice sounds like his father's, Julian said, "I'm proud of them," and answers criticisms thus: "If my dad had been a world-famous carpenter and I did what he did, I would have been praised. People would have said, 'You're doing a good job.'"

Valotte, of course, met with favorable reception from reviewers and fans alike, and so did Julian Lennon's first string of concert performances. Carolyn Kitch in *McCall's* analyzed one of his U.S. shows: "His voice is polished and pure, and as he does songs from his debut album . . . he is self-confident, definitely his own performer. But when Julian launches into his encore— one of the Beatles' classics, 'Day Tripper'—the memories come back. When he sings the same lyrics and notes, Julian can't hide his inheritance. He is, after all, John Lennon's son." Lennon's second album, *The Secret Value of Daydreaming,* was not as successful as *Valotte. Secret Value* "doesn't carry [Julian] any nearer to self-discovery or self-revelation," lamented reviewer Anthony DeCurtis of *Rolling Stone.* DeCurtis did, however, praise some of the album's songs, such as "Let Me Tell You" and "Coward till the End?" and cited Lennon's "potential to do important work." *Mr. Jordan,* Lennon's 1989 release, has fared better with the critics.

Selected discography

Valotte (includes "Valotte," "Too Late for Goodbyes," "Well I Don't Know," "Jesse," and "O.K. for You"), Atlantic, 1984.
The Secret Value of Daydreaming (includes "Let Me Tell You," "Coward till the End?" "Stick Around," "This Is My Day," "You Don't Have to Tell Me," and "Want Your Body"), Atlantic, 1986.
Mr. Jordan (includes "Now That You're in Heaven"), Atlantic, 1989.

Sources

McCall's, February, 1986.
People, January 7, 1985.
Rolling Stone, December 6, 1984; June 6, 1985; May 8, 1986.

—*Elizabeth Thomas*

Jerry Lee Lewis

Singer, songwriter, pianist

Jerry Lee Lewis burst onto the emerging rock scene in 1957 with "Whole Lotta Shakin' Goin' On." A quick follow-up hit, "Great Balls of Fire," soon put him in a position to rival Elvis Presley for the title of "King of Rock and Roll." Famed for his antics at the piano, known to bang the instrument with fists, feet, head, and buttocks during concerts—he even once doused his piano with gasoline and set it on fire—Lewis drew huge audiences wherever he performed until public disapproval of his marriage to a thirteen-year-old third cousin sent his career into decline. He continued performing in small clubs for little money until 1968, when he decided to switch to country music. Hits like "What Made Milwaukee Famous" and "Middle Age Crazy" have brought Lewis back as one of country's biggest stars, though he still makes appearances in rock revue shows and likes to end his concerts with "Great Balls of Fire."

Born into a Pentecostal family in Ferriday, Louisiana, that includes cousins television evangelist Jimmy Swaggart and fellow country star Mickey Gilley, Lewis was formed by varied musical influences during his childhood. He and his cousins gathered around the piano to sing and play hymns while their parents were present, but would sneak off to hear the forbidden, rousing music of black rhythm and blues players in juke joints. Lewis also heard country artists such as Jimmy Rodgers and Hank Williams from his father's record collection, but he cites Al Jolson as the artist who made the biggest impression on him. He explains in an interview in Arnold Shaw's *The Rockin' 50s:* "When I was about twelve, I walked into a theatre. . . . Before the picture went on, they played a record. I never stayed for the picture. That record hit me so hard I rushed out, ran all the way home, sat down at the piano, and tried to sing 'Down Among the Sheltering Pines' exactly as Al Jolson had done it. . . . Although I heard the song just once, I knew every word. The way Jolson did it, each word stood out like an electrified stop sign. I've never forgotten those words—and I've never stopped admiring Al Jolson."

Lewis had two brief teenage marriages; the second, to Jane Mitcham, produced a son, Jerry Lee, Jr., who died at the age of nineteen in a car accident. While married to Mitcham, Lewis's strong Pentecostal upbringing led him to enter the Bible Institute in Wauxhatchie, Texas, in hopes of becoming a preacher. He was expelled within a year, however, when he was caught playing a hymn with an improvised rhythm and blues beat. By his own admission, Lewis has always been torn between the righteousness of Pentecostalism and the wild life—replete with women, drugs, and alcohol—of a rock and country superstar. He has difficulty reconciling one with the other, and told Jim Jerome in *People:* "Salvation

For the Record. . .

Born September 29, 1935, in Ferriday, La.; son of Elmo (a carpenter and contractor) and Mary Ethel (a preacher); married Dorothy Barton, c. 1951 (marriage ended); married Jane Mitcham, c. 1952 (marriage ended); married Myra Gale Brown, December, 1957 (divorced, c. 1970); married Jaren Gunn, 1971 (deceased, June 8, 1982); married Shawn Michelle Stephens (a cocktail waitress), June, 1983 (deceased, August 24, 1983); married Kerrie Lee McCarver Mann (a country singer), 1984; children: (second marriage) Jerry Lee, Jr. (deceased); (third marriage) Steve Allen (deceased), Phoebe Allen; (fourth marriage) Lori. *Education:* Attended Bible Institute (Wauxhatchie, Texas), c. 1953.

Solo vocalist and pianist, 1956—(rock performer, 1956-68; country performer, 1968—). Has appeared in several motion pictures, including *High School Confidential, American Hot Wax,* and *Disc Jockey Jamboree,* and as Iago in a rock version of Shakespeare's *Othello,* 1968, at the Los Angeles Music Center.

Awards: Inducted into Rock and Roll Hall of Fame, 1986.

Addresses: *Home*—Lewis Farms, Nesbit, MS 38651. *Office*—c/o In Concert International Inc., PO Box 22149, 117 16th Ave. S, Nashville, TN 37203.

was not only thirteen but his third cousin, and that he had married her before his divorce from Mitcham was final. Though in the South women often married young, and marriage between distant cousins was not uncommon, the British papers cried scandal, and there was talk of deporting Lewis. He returned from England early to find many of his concert bookings in the United States cancelled as well. With the exception of one more hit, the movie theme "High School Confidential," Lewis's career plummeted.

Lewis's marriage to Myra Gale lasted for thirteen years, seeing him through years in small clubs and his return as a popular country performer. They had two children, daughter Phoebe and son Steve Allen—named for the comedian who granted Lewis a television appearance early in his career—but the boy drowned in a swimming pool accident at the age of three. Lewis has seen a lot of personal tragedy; after Myra Gale divorced him, he married his fourth wife, Jaren Gunn, in 1971. After

> *Lewis heard country artists such as Jimmy Rodgers and Hank Williams from his father's record collection, but he cites Al Jolson as the artist who made the biggest impression on him.*

bears down on me. I don't wanna die and go to Hell. But I don't think I'm headin' in the right direction. . . . I should've been a Christian, but I was too weak for the Gospel. I'm a rock 'n' roll cat. We all have to answer to God on Judgment Day."

Lewis was playing in nightclubs in Natchez, Mississippi, when he was discovered by Sam Phillips of Sun Records, the same company that launched Elvis Presley's career. His debut tune, the 1956 "Crazy Arms," was a moderate country success, but it was "Whole Lotta Shakin' Goin' On," a song Lewis wrote and happened to perform on a studio recording break, that made him a rock and roll star. He almost didn't record "Great Balls of Fire," a song sent to Sun by black artist and songwriter Otis Blackwell that garnered Lewis a gold record, because he felt it was too sinful. The collective sales of the two hit singles, however, were over eleven million copies, as reported by Mark Humphrey in *Esquire.*

By 1958, Lewis had had another moderate hit with "Breathless," and he went off to tour Great Britain. In England reporters noticed the young wife who accompanied him; though Lewis claimed the former Myra Gale Brown was fifteen, investigation revealed that she

Lewis himself nearly died from a stomach ailment in 1981, Gunn, then estranged from him and seeking divorce, was found drowned in a swimming pool in June, 1982. In June, 1983, Lewis married Shawn Stephens; approximately two and a half months later she was found dead in their home of a drug overdose. Though Lewis, long nicknamed "The Killer," has been exonerated of any wrongdoing in the deaths of Gunn and Stephens, some reporters, including Richard Ben Cramer in *Rolling Stone,* have noted that Gunn's death was a "mysterious accident," and pointed out suspicious circumstances surrounding Stephens's. *People* magazine cited "inconsistent reports about the condition of Shawn's body when it was found," and in another *People* article Jane Sanderson added that Stephen's family asked the FBI to investigate her death. Lewis married his sixth wife, Kerrie McCarver Mann, in 1984.

Despite all of the upsets in his personal life, Lewis keeps performing. Jim Jerome described one of his dinner theater shows in a 1978 *People* article: "The voice is plaintive. It cuts like a laser of grief through the haze. [Lewis] is enveloped by his own feelings; he seems to perform only for himself." He commented on Lewis's finale, "Great Balls of Fire": "It's the moment the diners had hoped for, the confirmation that primordial rock 'n' roll lives—in them, like Lewis, ageless and vital." In his 1982 *Esquire* article, Mark Humphrey concluded: "If you think a redneck can't sing the blues, just listen to [Lewis] belt out 'Big-Legged Woman' or 'Sick and Tired.' If you think he's always a snide bastard without a redeeming trace of sincerity, listen to his moving rendition of the gospel standard 'Will the Circle Be Unbroken.' And if you think anything about the man can be neatly pigeonholed, think again."

Selected discography

Major single releases

"Crazy Arms," Sun, 1956.
"Whole Lotta Shakin' Goin' On," Sun, 1957.
"Great Balls of Fire," Sun, 1957.
"You Win Again," Sun, 1958.
"Breathless," Sun, 1958.
"High School Confidential," Sun, 1958.
"I'll Make It All Up to You," Sun, 1958.
"Break-Up," Sun, 1958.
"I'll Sail My Ship Alone," Sun, 1959.
"What'd I Say," Sun, 1961.
"Sweet Little Sixteen," Sun, 1962.

LPs

Golden Hits, Smash, 1964.
Greatest Live Show On Earth, Smash, 1964.
Country Songs for City Folks, Smash, 1965.
Return of Rock, Smash, 1967.
By Request, Smash, 1967.
Another Place, Another Time, Smash, 1968.
She Still Comes Around, Smash, 1969.
Country Hits, Smash, 1969.
She Even Woke Me Up to Say Goodbye, Smash, 1970.

Best of Jerry Lee Lewis, Smash, 1970.
Original Golden Hits, Sun, 1970.
Original Golden Hits Volume 2, Sun, 1970.
There Must Be More to Love, Mercury, 1971.
In Loving Memories, Mercury, 1971.
Original Golden Hits Volume 3, Sun, 1972.
The Killer Rocks On, Mercury, 1972.
Would You Take Another Chance, Mercury, 1972.
Who's Gonna Play This Old Piano, Mercury, 1973.
Sometimes A Memory Ain't Enough, Mercury, 1973.
London Session, Mercury, 1973.
Touching Home, Mercury, 1973.
Southern Roots, Mercury, 1974.
Boogie Woogie Country Man, Mercury, 1975.
Country Class, Mercury, 1976.
Country Memories, Mercury, 1977.
Best of Jerry Lee Lewis Volume 2, Mercury, 1978.
Keeps On Rockin', Mercury, 1978.
Jerry Lee Lewis, Elektra, 1979.
When Two Worlds Collide, Elektra, 1980.
Killer Country, Elektra, 1980.
Live at the Star Club Hamburg, Mercury, 1983.

Sources

Books

Cain, Robert, *Whole Lotta Shakin' Goin' On: Jerry Lee Lewis,* Dial Press, 1981.
Shaw, Arnold, *The Rockin' 50s,* Hawthorn, 1974.
Tosches, Nick, *Hellfire: The Jerry Lee Lewis Story,* Dell, 1982.

Periodicals

Esquire, June, 1982.
People, April 24, 1978; September 12, 1983; May 14, 1984; October 27, 1986.
Rolling Stone, March 1, 1984; November 21, 1985.
Time, March 14, 1983.

—Elizabeth Thomas

David Lindley

Guitarist

With his curly black hair flowing well below his shoulders, a wardrobe dedicated to color-clashing polyesters and an arsenal of mutant-pawnshop instruments, David Lindley has become probably the most anti-fashionable guitar hero ever. But looks can be deceiving; once he plugs in, Lindley can hold his own against *any* of the six-string slingers who rule the MTV airwaves. "He may not look it, but David Lindley is the picture of good taste," stated Dan Forte in *Guitar Player.* "He doesn't play what's expected; he plays what's needed." His playing has graced countless albums, going way beyond the standard cliches of rock guitar and entering a category of its own.

Lindley's first instrument was a baritone ukelele that he picked up at age fourteen. Although he was exposed to various Mediterranean and Middle Eastern records through his father's collection, the youngster's first interest was in flamenco guitar. Like his cohort, Ry Cooder, Lindley spent many hours absorbing the folk music at the Ash Grove, a popular Los Angeles club during the 1960s. He became extremely proficient, drawing from the styles of Sandy Bull, Dick Rosmini, the Pioneers, and especially Stu Jameson. By the time he was just eighteen, he had won his first Topanga Canyon Bluegrass Banjo and Fiddle Contest. After taking the trophy home five years in a row, contest officials graciously asked Lindley to become a judge and give others a chance to win.

His first group was the Mad Mountain Ramblers, an acoustic ensemble that played at the Disneyland amusement park in Anaheim, California. He played bluegrass with the Scat Band before forming Kaleidoscope in 1966. "It was an experiment to see what he could come up with, to see what would fit into what, and to eventually come up with original things," Lindley told *Guitar Player.* The group released four albums as Lindley began incorporating various instruments into his repetoire. He moved to England three years later, collaborating with singer/guitarist Terry Reid. It was during this period that Lindley was introduced to the sounds of reggae and ska, styles that dominate his current solo work.

Upon his return to the States in 1971, Lindley teamed up with songwriter Jackson Browne, beginning a nine-year association. "When David plays, it really means a lot to me—just pure meaning," Browne told *Guitar Player.* "It always has, from the first time he ever played music on one of my songs. He's my hero." Appearing on five LPs together, Lindley added stinging lap steel licks to Browne's finest efforts, including "That Girl Could Sing," "Redneck Friend," and "Running On Empty." Primarily a country music instrument previously,

For the Record. . .

Born in San Marino, Calif. Lived in England, 1969-71. Won Topanga Canyon Bluegrass Banjo and Fiddle Contest at age 18; played at Disneyland with the Mad Mountain Ramblers and the Scat Band during early 1960s; formed Kaleidoscope, 1966; studio and tour guitarist for Jackson Browne, 1971-80; studio and tour guitarist for numerous performers, including Leonard Cohen, Linda Ronstadt, Warren Zevon, James Taylor, David Crosby, Graham Nash, Maria Muldaur, America, Ry Cooder, Rod Stewart, Eddie Money, Karla Bonoff, Lonnie Mack, Jesse Colin Young, Joe Walsh, Duane Eddy, and Andreas Vollenweider, 1971—; has done guitar work for television, including "The Rockford Files Theme."

Awards: Won Topanga Canyon Bluegrass Banjo and Fiddle Contest five years in a row.

Addresses: *Record company*—Elektra/Asylum/Nonesuch Records, 962 N. La Cienega Blvd., Los Angeles, CA 90069.

Lindley began to master the sound in a rock setting after hearing the great Freddy Roulette perform one night in a San Francisco nightclub. "That's what I want to do," Lindley told *Guitar Player.* "I want to sound like *that* guy!"

When he was on break from his duties with Browne, others began to call on Lindley for their own sessions. Artists like Leonard Cohen, Linda Ronstadt, Warren Zevon, and John Hiatt are just a few who have relied on Lindley's sound to transform their songs into something special. His ability to move from one genre to another (Andreas Vollenweider to "The Rockford Files" theme) is truly amazing. "I do stuff like an ant—combination of taste and feel and sight and hearing. Like this all-encompassing feeler," Lindley stated in *Guitar Player.* "You don't play everything you know; you play whatever's appropriate to the song."

Part of what makes Lindley's sound so unique is his use of off-brand guitars and exotic instruments like the bouzouki, kora, slack-key guitar and the more conventional mandolin and violin. He is not locked in by the standard conception of each instrument either, using such radical techniques as bowing a banjo to obtain unheard of sounds. "I approach them as *one* instrument," *Guitar Player* reported Lindley as saying, "which I call the 'resident noise' in the head, and a feeling from way down deep." In reaction to the exorbitant prices for vintage instruments, Lindley has also made a career out of utilizing cheaper guitars, including Danelectros, Nationals, Teiscos, Goyas, and Supros (he has over 70 of these off-brand instruments). Lindley has also worked closely with inventor/designer Doc Kauffman in trying to achieve different sounds and studying the sustaining properties of musical equipment set-ups.

A year after his departure from Browne, Lindley released his first solo album, 1981's *El Rayo-X* ". . . a rare and tasty treat that is offbeat, fun, and instructive," according to Gene Santoro in *The Guitar.* With roaring slide guitar on "Mercury Blues" and "Your Old Lady," and an overall reggae flavor, Lindley made the transition from sideman to leader look simple. On his next two LPs, *Win This Record* and *Mr. Dave,* he continued to transpose most of the tunes into a reggae tempo which may have appeared, falsely, as if he were jumping on the Third World bandwagon as the style became popular in the mainstream. "Lindley hasn't changed very much," wrote Richard Grula in *Guitar World,* "it's just a classic case of the world finally catching up."

Lindley continued to do session work, literally redefining the role. He enjoyed a remarkable musical exchange with Ry Cooder on *Bop Til You Drop* and on various soundtrack LPs. The similarity between the two guitarists is astonishing and often very eerie. Of their joint tour of Japan, Cooder told Steve Fishell in *Guitar Player,* "he plays, and the thing gets sadder and sadder and more and more depressing in the most poetic way, and the audience recedes to some nether place." On *The Long Riders* and *Alamo Bay* it is nearly impossible to tell Cooder and Lindley apart.

In the mid-1980s, record companies, including the label Lindley was on, Asylum, began to trim down their rosters and Lindley found himself without a recording contract during one of his most popular phases. "It was a very strange period," he told *Guitar World.* "I didn't have a record, but I was going out on the road with El Rayo-X (also the group's name) and the audiences were getting bigger and bigger." Lindley had played on *Trio* with Dolly Parton, Emmylou Harris, and Linda Ronstadt when the latter heard about his problem. Ronstadt secured Lindley a deal with Elektra in exchange for the opportunity to produce his LP, *Very Greasy.* Her vision of Lindley's sound was perfectly suited to the guitarist as he breathed new life into Bobby Freeman's "Do Ya' Wanna Dance," the Temptations' "Papa Was A Rolling Stone," and Warren Zevon's "Werewolves of London." The album, as Richard Grula observed in *Guitar World,* "demonstrates how the world's various musical styles are irrevocably intertwined." And David Lindley knows exactly how to interpret them.

Selected discography

El Rayo-X, Asylum, 1981.
Win This Record, Asylum, 1982.
Mr. Dave, WEA International, 1985.
Very Greasy, Elektra, 1988.

With Jackson Browne

For Everyman, Asylum, 1973.
Late For The Sky, Asylum, 1974.
The Pretender, Asylum, 1976.
Running On Empty, Asylum, 1978.
Hold Out, Asylum, 1980.

With Linda Ronstadt

Heart Like A Wheel, Capitol, 1974.
Prisoner in Disguise, Asylum, 1975.

With Warren Zevon

Warren Zevon, Asylum, 1976.
Bad Luck Streak in Dancing School, Asylum, 1980.

With Ry Cooder

Jazz, Warner Bros., 1978.
Bop Till You Drop, Warner Bros., 1979.
The Long Riders, Warner Bros., 1980.
Alamo Bay, Slash, 1985.
Paris, Warner Bros., 1985.

With Graham Nash

Songs For Beginners, Atlantic, 1971.
Wild Tales, Atlantic, 1973.

With [David] Crosby and Nash

Wind On The Water, ABC, 1975.
Whistle Down the Wire, ABC, 1976.
Live, ABC, 1977.

With Maria Muldaur

Maria Muldaur, Reprise, 1974.
Waitress In A Donutshop, Reprise, 1974.

With Danny O'Keefe

So Long Harry Truman, Atlantic, 1975.
American Roulette, Warner Bros., 1977.

With Terry Reid

River, Atlantic, 1973.
Seed Of Memory, ABC, 1976.
Rogues Waves, Capitol, 1979.

With Kaleidoscope

Side Trips, Epic, 1967.
A Beacon From Mars, Epic, 1968.
Kaleidoscope, Epic, 1969.
Bernice, Epic, 1970.
When Scopes Collide, Pacific Arts Recording Co., 1976.

With America

America, Warner Bros., 1971.

With Karla Bonoff

Restless Nights, CBS, 1979.

With Lonnie Mack

Lonnie Mack And Pismo, Capitol, 1977.
Road Houses and Dance Halls, Epic, 1988.

With Eddie Money

Life Is For The Taking, CBS, 1978.

With Jesse Colin Young

American Dreams, Elektra, 1978.

With Rod Stewart

Atlantic Crossing, Warner Bros., 1975.

With James Taylor

In The Pocket, Warner Bros., 1976.

With Joe Walsh

There Goes The Neighborhood, Asylum, 1981.

With Duane Eddy

Duane Eddy, Capitol, 1987.

Sources

Books

Kozinn, Allan, Pete Welding, Dan Forte, and Gene Santoro, *The Guitar: The History, The Music, The Players*, Quill, 1984.

Periodicals

Guitar Player, July, 1977; March, 1980; August, 1981; April, 1982; October, 1988; March, 1989.
Guitar World, December, 1988.

—Calen D. Stone

Los Lobos

Mexican-American roots/rock band

When the roots-rock revival of the early 1980s appeared, Los Lobos would probably have been picked as the least likely to succeed. While bands like the Stray Cats and the Fabulous Thunderbirds stuck mainly to one genre, Los Lobos took on a bigger challenge by combining country swing, rock & roll, Mexican nortena, rhythm and blues, and the blues. It may sound like an impossible repetoire to pull off, but the five-piece unit from East Los Angeles shifts between their various influences effortlessly. As their producer T-Bone Burnette pointed out in *Musician,* in order to survive and retain their uniqueness, the band must maintain a certain musical balance. "There's a danger, because Los Lobos began by playing nortena music, of turning into a novelty . . . or of going so far away that it becomes just another hard rock band."

The four original members, David Hidalgo, Cesar Rosas, Louie Perez, and Conrad Lozano (Steve Berlin joined around 1983), had known each other since their high school days and grew up in basically the same neighborhood. Up until 1973, they had all played in various

Top 40 bands. Realizing that just regurgitating current popular songs was not what any of them wanted to do, they decided to explore their Mexican roots and learn the folk songs they were raised on but had never paid much attention to. "We were just rock and roll musicians, and we discovered this stuff," Perez told *Guitar Player*. "All of a sudden it was like we lifted a rock and there was this incredible life that was teeming under it."

They began by collecting as many of the old recordings as they could find and then dissecting each one in order to play it properly. Their skills were tested on many instruments that they had never even played before as they gathered in backyards to learn tunes by artists like Miguel Aveces Mejia from the late 1950s. They started playing at parties, weddings and other small events before landing their first full-time gig in 1978 at an Orange County Mexican restaurant. "It wasn't even a real Mexican restaurant," Rosas said in *Guitar World*. "One of those tourist joints. We were working there because we had come to a point where we had to either make more money from music or find other jobs; some of us had gotten married, and we weren't kids anymore."

For their first eight years, Los Lobos was an all-acoustic group playing only traditional music. They had accumulated over thirty different instruments but it took a UCLA student, Art Gerst, who was a fanatic for Mexican music, to set them straight on the proper and authentic techniques to use. "He told us he liked the spirit we had in our playing," Hidalgo told Harold Steinblatt in *Guitar World*. "Unfortunately, he also said that we were playing completely incorrectly." After that was straightened out, the band began to incorporate some Tex-Mex instruments, like the accordion, and songs from Flaco Jimenez, Jacito Gartito, Los Piuquenes del Norte, and Los Alegres de Tiran. As their influences broadened, so did their arsenal of equipment and before long they were pulling out their electirc guitars and amplifiers. Their two-year stint at the restaurant ended when the owner complained about their loudness. That incident was repeated shortly after at another restaurant when they played Cream's version of the old blues number, "Crossroads."

They had earlier recorded an album, *Just Another Band From East L.A.,* on a very limited budget, but it got them nowhere. With so many different influences between them, they decided to try and put together some originals. "We started writing songs to satisfy our need to play something in between, something that belonged to us," Perez stated in *down beat*. They sent a tape of songs to Phil Alvin, leader of another roots band that was gaining noteriety in L.A., the Blasters. Alvin was impressed enough to have Los Lobos open for them at the Whiskey nightclub in Hollywood and convinced his own label, Slash, to sign them. Suddenly, with a record contract under their belts, what had started out as a hobby and a labor of love was now much more serious. "We never thought that we might get gigs out of this, we just enjoyed what we were doing," Lozano told *Musician*. "But then we started getting TV coverage, and Chicano awareness began happening, and suddenly it turned out we had a lot of input, a lot of influence over people because of this music."

They released a seven-song EP, . . . *And A Time To Dance,* in 1983 to critical raves. Produced by Burnette and Blasters' saxman Steve Berlin, the record was just the beginning of Los Lobos' muscle-flexing. Dan Forte wrote in *Guitar Player* that the group "displayed almost an overabundance of confidence." Their Grammy Award for Best Mexican-American song for "Anselma" convinced anyone who doubted their authenticity.

Their range of musicianship was astonishing. Instead of hiring additional musicians for the different instruments, the four members split the chores among themselves. Perez, who along with Hidalgo is the group's chief songwriter, had begun playing drums only years after he joined the group. He was originally a guitarist, picking up the instrument when he was twelve and continuing to play throughout various rock bands. In his mid-twenties he was elected band drummer when Los Lobos began to go electric. "We couldn't see bringing anybody new into the band. And when we got into the Tex-Mex format, which had drums, I just sort of fell into that," he explained to *Guitar Player*. He continues, however, to add acoustic guitar for their recordings and in concert.

Bassist Lozano began playing British Invasion rock & roll when he was sixteen. Before joining Los Lobos, he played in another L.A. band, Tierra, who had a hit single with "Together." After juggling his time between the two bands, Lozano decided to become a full-time member of Los Lobos in 1973, about six weeks after the group had formed. He plays both the electric and acoustic bass in addition to the guitarron and vocal chores.

Rosas is from Sonora, Mexico and emigrated to L.A. with his family when he was seven. Although he had dabbled with the guitar previously, it wasn't until high school that he began to get serious. Basically self-taught, Rosas took some lessons early on in order to learn a bit about theory and chord work. With influences like Jimi Hendrix, Eric Clapton, and the blues Kings (Albert, B.B., and Freddie), Rosas provides the crunch for Los Lobos. In addition to guitar, he also plays the bajo sexto, mandolin, and the vihuela, and his vocals offer a distinctly rough contrast to Hidalgos.

"You have to understand, the band does work and evolve around David," Lozano said of Hidalgo in *Musician.* "His playing is so strong; his talent is still being tapped." A musician's musician, Hidalgo began his musical career as a drummer in the early 1970s, playing in a Christian rock band. He had already been playing guitar since he was 11, growing up on the standard rock influences like Chuck Berry and the Ventures. However, Hidalgo expanded into more sophisticated areas and began to absorb the work of guitarists like Les Paul, Charlie Christian, Django Reinhardt, Merle Travis and others like Hank Williams and the Hawaiian lap-steel players. His capabilities extend from guitar and violin to accordion and drums. "There are certain things you can only do on certain instruments," he told *Guitar Player.* "It's just that I wanted to hear those sounds, and nobody in the group played them, so I figured I'd try." In addition, Hidalgo's vocals provide the central figure to Los Lobos' sound and create great depth along with Rosas's. "I don't think it's an overstatement to say that their voices are as important to the impact of this music as Lennon's and McCartney's were to the Beatles," declared Jim Roberts in *down beat.*

Steve Berlin joined the group after working on their EP. His full tenor and baritone saxes add another dimension to Los Lobos' sound, as on the 1950s-styled party tune "I Got Loaded." "It got silly trying to do both the Blasters and Los Lobos, and since I got to play so much more with Los Lobos, it was more fulfilling," he told *down beat.*

Berlin also co-produced their first LP, *How Will The Wolf Survive?,* which featured blistering guitar on "Don't Worry Baby," courtesy of Rosas and lush chords on "A Matter of Time" by Hidalgo. Every song covered different territory, from Tex-Mex polkas to New Orleans rhythm and blues, and as Perez pointed out in *Guitar Player,* the group defied categorization. "As far as this band is concerned, coming from a diverse background and diverse musicianship, I think it would be unfair to stick us under one label." Not only unfair; impossible.

Their follow-up LP, *By The Light of the Moon,* showed them expanding even more. Not only was the musicianship superb, but the songwriting also belonged in a class of its own, moving beyond mere lyrics to social commentary. "The portraits that merge . . . are arresting as much for their diversity as for the appalling waste of human potential they illustrate time and again," wrote Gene Santoro in *down beat.* "Los Lobos have brought their rich musical hybrid . . . into the mainstream—with a vengeance."

In 1987 Los Lobos was the centerpiece of the soundtrack to the movie *La Bamba.* They were able to recreate, and sometimes outdo, the original recordings of the late Richie Valens. Their version of the title track reached

> "Los Lobos have brought their rich musical hybrid . . . into the mainstream—with a vengeance."

the American Top 10 and helped to secure an even larger audience for the group. With record sales beyond the wildest expectations of both Los Lobos and Slash, the band now had the clout to do what only a few artists (such as Bruce Springsteen with *Nebraska*) are capable of accomplishing.

In 1989 they released *La Pistola y El Corazon,* an album consisting solely of the type of folk songs that they began with some fifteen years earlier. "We talked about doing someting like this since the day we signed a deal with the company, to take this music and record it properly," said Hidalgo in *Guitar World.* As Harold Steinblatt stated in the same issue, "The record is no gimmick . . . it is a stunning personal statement of musical faith by a band at the height of its creative powers." Powers which have not gone unnoticed by other artists either, like Ry Cooder and Paul Simon, who have tapped Los Lobos' talents for various projects of their own.

Selected discography

Just Another Band from East L.A., Vista.
. . . And A Time to Dance (seven-song EP), Slash/Warner Bros., 1983.
How Will the Wolf Survive?, Slash/Warner Bros., 1984.
By the Light of the Moon, Slash/Warner Bros., 1987.
La Pistola y El Corazon, Slash/Warner Bros., 1988.

Los Lobos has also appeared on the *La Bamba* motion picture soundtrack and as guest performers on numerous albums, including Ry Cooder's *Alamo Bay,* Paul Simon's *Graceland* (1986), Elvis Costello's *King of America* (1986), the Fabulous Thunderbirds' *Tuff Enuff (1986),* and Roomful of Blues' *Live at Lupo's Heartbreak Hotel* (1986).

Sources

down beat, May, 1984; February, 1985; April, 1985; April, 1987.
Guitar Player, March, 1984; May, 1984; January, 1985; February, 1987; October, 1987; December, 1988.
Guitar World, September, 1986; February, 1989.
Musician, April, 1987.

—Calen D. Stone

Loretta Lynn

Singer, songwriter

The term "living legend" is bandied about quite freely in the music business, especially in Nashville. Few performers deserve that label more than Loretta Lynn, the country singer-songwriter from Butcher Hollow, Kentucky. Almost continuously since 1960 Lynn has been recording albums and touring the country in her custom-made bus, entertaining enthusiastic audiences often at the expense of her own health. In *Behind Closed Doors: Talking with the Legends of Country Music,* Alanna Nash calls Lynn "a woman whose name is synonymous with rural sensibility for millions of country and non-country fans alike." Nash adds that the performer "is one of the most important stylists—and arguably the most successful traditional female star—in the history of country music."

George Vecsey analyzes Lynn's appeal in a *Reader's Digest* profile. "Why is this woman with the attractive figure, blue Irish eyes and dark Cherokee hair so popular?" Vecsey writes. "Partly because she embodies every woman's desire to be respected and treated equally. . . . She doesn't tell women to 'stand by your man,' as one popular country song puts it. She tells them to 'stand *up* to your man.'. . . But most of all she touches so many women because there is something about her that convinces them that 'she knows our life,' that she is 'just like us.' And indeed she is." Describing Lynn's particular style of singing, Nash concludes: "No matter what trends come to dominate country music, . . . there will probably always be a market for Loretta Lynn. Her voice is . . . quirky, graceful, and enormously expressive, an instrument worthy of national treasure status."

Lynn's singular life story has been well documented, both in an autobiography, *Coal Miner's Daughter,* and in a movie of the same title. She was born and raised in a cabin in Butcher Hollow (pronounced "holler"), "way back up in the hills where nobody ever went to the hospital or saw a car," to quote Roy Blount, Jr., in *Esquire.* Lynn was the second of eight children born to Ted and Clara Webb, whose isolated home had neither running water nor electricity. Ted Webb worked in a coal mine at night and farmed his property by day; the highlight of the week for the whole family was listening to the Grand Ole Opry on the battery-powered radio each Saturday night. Loretta was only thirteen when she met Oliver "Mooney" Lynn, a war veteran seven years her senior. After a courtship of one month, the two married, and the naive, sheltered Loretta found herself facing a host of adult responsibilities.

Soon after her marriage, Lynn left Kentucky for Washington state, where her husband had found work in the timber industry. At fourteen she was pregnant with the first of four children she would have by the age of

Born Loretta Webb, April 14, 1935, in Butcher Hollow, Ky.; daughter of Ted (a coal miner) and Clara (Butcher) Webb; married Oliver V. Lynn, Jr., January 10, 1948; children: Betty Sue, Jack Benny (deceased), Clara, Ernest Ray, Peggy and Patsy (twins).

Country singer/songwriter, 1960—. Had first country hit, "Now I'm a Honky Tonk Girl," 1960; signed with Decca label (a division of MCA), 1961. First woman to be named entertainer of the year by the Country Music Association, 1972; named entertainer of the decade by the Academy of Country Music, 1980. Has performed as a duo with Ernest Tubb and Conway Twitty. Earned fifty-three top ten country singles and sixteen number one country albums, including the first country album by a female artist to be a certified gold record.

Awards: Grammy Award, 1971; named female vocalist of the year by the Country Music Association, 1967, 1972, and 1973; with Twitty, named top duet by the Country Music Association, 1972, 1973, 1974, and 1975; American Music Award, 1978.

Addresses: *Office*— United Talent, Inc., P.O. Box 23470, Nashville, Tenn., 37202. *Other*— 7 Music Circle N., Nashville, Tenn., 37203.

dance halls. For a time she opened for another country favorite, Patsy Cline, and Nash suggests that after Cline's death in 1963, Lynn "picked up the torch" and became "a link between traditional and contemporary country thought." At any rate, by 1965 Loretta Lynn was the most popular female country singer in America, with numerous number one hits and best-selling albums.

Traditionally, female fans of country music tend to like male performers. However, Lynn broke through to a female audience largely with songs she wrote herself, such as "Don't Come Home A-Drinkin' (With Lovin' on Your Mind)," "You Ain't Woman Enough (To Take My Man)," "Your Squaw Is on the Warpath," and "The Pill." Based not so loosely on her own experiences, her songs explored the problems of modern rural women—those in traditional marriages who still felt the need to assert some rights. Blount notes that Lynn has always been at her best celebrating "with neither self-pity nor a rolling pin but with vigorous indignation, those moments when the husband staggers home late." Vecsey like-

> *"She doesn't tell women to 'stand by your man'—she tells them to 'stand up to your man.'"*

wise finds Lynn's works "honest songs, funny songs, sad songs. Songs of hard times, sickness, children, shaky marriages, unrequited love. And they have built a special bond between Loretta and the women of middle America. No other country singer today touches them the way Loretta does."

Both as a solo act and in a duo with Conway Twitty, Lynn headlined on the country circuit for twenty years. By the mid-1970s, the punishing pace she kept—two shows per night as many as three hundred nights per year—began to take a toll on her health. She suffered from insomnia, depression, migraine headaches, bleeding ulcers, seizures, and exhaustion; more than once she collapsed onstage in the middle of a performance. Still Lynn persisted, driven by a strong feeling of obligation to her fans. Many observers thought that she had been struck a final blow in 1984, when her favorite son, Jack Benny, was drowned while horseback riding. Already in frail health when she received the news of Jack's death, Lynn dropped out of sight. She did not record or perform for two years, and since returning to

seventeen—"just a baby with babies," as she told Nash. In *Newsweek,* Pete Axthelm remarks that Lynn survived the hard times in Washington "by washing other people's clothes and picking strawberries with migrant workers." While her children were still young, her husband gave her a present—a twenty-dollar guitar to accompany the singing she did around the house. Lynn taught herself to pick and began to imitate her idol, country star Kitty Wells. Largely at her husband's insistence, Lynn then began performing at the local honky tonks and grange halls. At first the shy young woman found singing to strangers painful, but she warmed to it—and audiences warmed to her.

In 1960 Lynn cut her first single, "Now I'm a Honky Tonk Girl," on a small Vancouver recording label. Then she and her husband took to the road in their 1955 Ford to promote the song by word of mouth. "We drove 80,000 miles to sell 50,000 copies of 'I'm a Honky Tonk Girl,'" Lynn told *Newsweek.* The exhausting effort paid off when, against all odds, the song made the national country charts and peaked at number ten. Soon Lynn was performing regularly on the Grand Ole Opry and travelling through the South for live concerts at fairs and

the stage she has set a somewhat slower schedule for herself.

Lynn has returned, however, and after a long hiatus she is writing her own songs again. One pet project is a family album she hopes to cut with her sister, recording star Crystal Gayle, and several of her children. She also plans to release more solo material, work that bears her own style and does not pander to the pop-rock tastes so popular amongst some modern country performers. *McCall's* contributor Wanda Urbanska concludes that, whatever the fate of her forthcoming albums, Loretta Lynn "is one of those rarities: a star whose name and reputation are so immutable, so cherished by fans all over the country that she hasn't had to stay on the charts to fill the concert halls." Lynn herself commented on her remarkable career in the *McCall's* profile. "You either have to be first, best or different," she said. "I was just first to say what I thought. The rest of [country music's women stars] didn't write. I wrote it like it was."

Selected discography

Alone with You, MCA.
Back to the Country, MCA.
Before I'm Over You, MCA.
Blue Kentucky Girl, MCA.
Christmas Without Daddy, MCA.
Coal Miner's Daughter, MCA.
Don't Come Home A-Drinkin', MCA.
Here I Am Again, MCA.
Home, MCA.
Hymns, MCA.
I Like 'Em Country, MCA.
I Remember Patsy Cline, MCA.
Just a Woman, MCA.
Lookin' Good, MCA.
Loretta Lynn's Greatest Hits, MCA.
Loretta Lynn's Twenty Greatest Hits, MCA.
Loretta Lynn On Stage at the Grand Ole Opry, MCA.
Lyin', Cheatin', Woman Chasin', Honky Tonkin' You, MCA.

Making Love from Memory, MCA.
Out of My Head and Back in Bed, MCA.
Saturday Night, MCA.
Singin' with Feelin', MCA.
Somebody Somewhere, MCA.
Songs from My Heart, MCA.
Success, MCA.
They Don't Make 'Em Like Daddy, MCA.
When the Tingle Becomes a Chill, MCA.
Wings upon Your Horns, MCA.
Who Says God Is Dead?, MCA.
Woman of the World, MCA.
You Ain't Woman Enough, MCA.

With Ernest Tubb

Singin' Again.
Used to Be.

With Conway Twitty

We Only Make Believe.

Sources

Books

Lynn, Loretta, and George Vecsey, *Coal Miner's Daughter*, Regnery, 1976.
Nash, Alanna, *Behind Closed Doors: Talking with the Legends of Country Music*, Knopf, 1988.

Periodicals

Esquire, March, 1977.
McCall's, June, 1988.
Newsweek, December 4, 1972; June 18, 1973; March 17, 1975.
New York Times, October 25, 1972.
People, August 13, 1984.
Readers' Digest, January, 1977.

—Anne Janette Johnson

Yo-Yo Ma

Cellist

Yo-Yo Ma is a world-famous cellist whose performances draw sell-out crowds. Since his early childhood, Ma had an affinity for the cello that earned him prodigy status, and he matured into the talented interpreter of solo and ensemble works for cello. He has appeared with major orchestras throughout the world and recorded most of the solo cello repertoire. Ma's popularity rests not only on his technical mastery of the cello and superb musicianship, but his ability to communicate to the audience his love of the music he performs.

Born into an upper-class Chinese family living in Paris, Yo-Yo was the youngest of two musically talented children. Ma's affinity for music came as no surprise as his mother, Marina, was a mezzo-soprano and his father, Hiao-Tsiun, was a violinist, composer, and musicologist who specialized in the education of gifted children. The Ma children were schooled at home in the traditional Chinese fashion, with lessons in the Chinese language, literature, and calligraphy. Ma's first musical training was on the violin, but because his sister Yeou-Cheng also played that instrument, Ma wanted to in his words "play something bigger." Ma began to study the cello at age four with his father, who, when he could not find a small enough cello, gave his son a viola to which he had attached an end pin. Ma's father taught using a method that involved practicing for only a half hour each day and memorizing several bars of a Bach suite for unaccompanied cello. In this way, the young cellist learned three such suites by the time he was five years old and performed one of them at his first public recital at the Institute of Art and Archeology at the University of Paris. Despite his astounding ability, Ma was not pressured by his parents to go on tour as a child prodigy.

When Ma was seven years old his family moved to New York City, where his father taught at a school for musically gifted children, including the children of the virtuoso violinist Isaac Stern. One day Stern heard the young Ma play and recommended that he study with Leonard Rose at the Julliard School of Music. Ma auditioned for Rose and as a student in the college prepatory division became the youngest pupil ever of the distinguished cellist. Ma credits Rose with much of his success for, as he told Stephen Wigler of the *Baltimore Sun,* Rose taught him "everything I know about the cello." Remembering those lessons, Ma told Thor Eckert, Jr., a *Christian Science Monitor* reporter, "It was quite intense, and from the start Rose taught me that to play the cello you must have an absolute physical relationship with your instrument. When you play you must feel as though the instrument is a part of your body, the strings are your voice, and the cello is your lungs." For his part, Rose described the student's technical and interpretative ability: "He was very small and already quite ex-

For the Record. . .

Born October 7, 1955, in Paris, France; son of Hiao-Tsiun (a musicologist, violinist, and composer) and Marina Ma; married Jill Horner (a professor of German), May 20, 1978; children: Nicholas (born 1983), Emily (born 1985). *Education:* Received high school diploma from Professional Children's School, 1970; attended Julliard School, 1964-71; Harvard University, B.A. in Humanities, 1976.

Has performed as a soloist with numerous orchestras and chamber groups since age 15; also performs with his own chamber ensembles.

Awards: Awarded the Avery Fisher Prize, 1978; Grammy Award for recording of Elgar Cello Concerts, 1985.

Addresses: *Manager*—ICM Artists Ltd., 40 West 57th St., New York, NY 10019.

form with major orchestras, and Ma benefitted directly through performances with the New York Philharmonic and other ensembles. After being forced into a one-year hiatus from performing because of surgery to correct an unnaturally curved spine, Ma resumed a busy schedule of appearances that range to 125 per year.

When Ma plays the cello, the tone he produces is not as powerful as those of other famous cellists, but it is silky

---

At age fifteen Ma made his New York debut at Carnegie Hall and was asked by the famous composer-conductor Leonard Bernstein to perform on national television

---

traordinary. . . . When he was about seventeen, he gave a performance of Schubert's *Arpeggione,* which is a holy terror for cellists, and it was so gorgeous I was moved to tears," he told a writer for *Time.*

As a teenager, Ma attended New York City's Professional Children's School. He skipped two grades and graduated at age fifteen. That same year he made his New York debut at Carnegie Hall and was asked by the famous conductor/composer Leonard Bernstein to perform on national television for a fund-raising event for the Kennedy Center for the Performing Arts in Washington, D.C. Ma then entered Julliard's college division for a year and the following summer attended the Meadowmount music camp, where, freed from the discipline of his home, he rebelled with irresponsible behavoir. At the end of the summer, his rebellion against the narrowly defined focus of conservatory courses continued in his decision to attend Columbia University instead. Yet after a semester, Ma was also dissatisfied with the academic life at Columbia, and in 1972 he transferred to Harvard University, from which he graduated with a Bachelor of Arts degree in humanities in 1976. While at Harvard, Ma took courses in music history, theory, and appreciation and he played in student ensembles. He also began his professional music career by performing on weekends at local venues.

Ma began his full-time performance career in 1976 and in 1978 it was launched when Ma won the prestigious Avery Fisher Prize. The purpose of this award is to give talented young instrumentalists opportunities to per-

and he is undoubtedly a master of technique and expressivity. Ma performs and has recorded works from many eras and styles, ranging from Bach concerti to the Britten *Symphony for Cello.* Since he likes to learn several new pieces each year, early in his career Ma nearly exhausted the somewhat limited repertoire of works for solo cello and began to commission new works from such composers as Leon Kirchner, one of his teachers at Harvard, and Oliver Knussen. Not only does Ma perform as a soloist, but since he is committed to chamber music, he appears and records with his own piano trio, string quartet, and string trio.

Selected discography

Bach: *Complete Suites for Cello (No. 1 - 6),* CBS.
Barber: *Concerto for Cello,* CBS, 1988.
Beethoven: *Complete Sonatas (No. 1 - 5); Twelve Variations in F Major for Cello and Piano based on "Ein Madchen oder Weibchen" from Mozart's The Enchanted Flute; Twelve Variations in G Major for Cello and Piano based on "See the Conqu'ring Hero Comes" from Handel's Judas Macchabee; Seven Variations in E Flat for Cello and Piano based on "Bei Mannern, welche liebe fuhlen" from Mozart's The Enchanted Flute,* CBS.
Beethoven: *Concerto for Piano, Violin, Cello, and Orchestra in C Major, op. 56,* DG.
Boccherini: *Concerto for Cello and Orchestra No. 9 in B Flat,* CBS.
Bolling: *Suite for Cello and Jazz Piano,* CBS.
Brahms: *Sonatas for Piano and Cello, No. 1 and 2,* RCA, 1985.
Brahms: *String Quartet and Piano No. 3 in C Minor, op. 60,* CBS.

Brahms: *Double Concerto for Violin, Cello, and Orchestra in A Major, op. 102*, CBS.

Britten: *Cello Symphony*, CBS, 1988.

Dvorak: *Concerto for Cello and Orchestra in B Minor, op. 104; Rondo for Cello and Orchestra in G minor, op. 94; The Bohemian Forest, op. 68 (extract); Silence*, transcribed for cello and orchestra; CBS.

Dvorak: *Trios No. 3 and 4 for Piano, Violin, and Cello*, CBS.

Elgar: *Concerto for Cello and Orchestra in E Minor, op. 85;* Walton: *Concerto for Cello and Orchestra*, CBS, 1985.

Haydn: *Concerti for Cello and Orchestra, No. 1 and 2, op. 101*, CBS.

Japanese Melodies, CBS.

Kabalevski: *Concerto for Cello and Orchestra in G Minor, op. 49*, CBS.

Kreisler: *Transcriptions for Cello and Piano: Songs that the Sea Taught Me*, CBS.

Lalo: *Concerto for Cello and Orchestra in D Minor*, CBS, 1984.

Mozart: *Sonata in B Flat Major for Cello and Bassoon*, Malboro Recording Society.

Mozart: *Adagio and Fugue in C Minor*, CBS.

Mozart: *Divertissement for Violin, Viola, and Cello in E Flat Major*, CBS.

Paganini: *Transcriptions for Cello and Piano, No. 9, 13, 14, 17, 24, op. 1; Transcriptions for Cello and Piano*, CBS.

Saint-Sans: *Concerto for Cello and Orchestra No. 1 in A Minor, op. 33*, CBS.

Schoenberg: *Concerto for Cello and Orchestra in D Major, based on a concerto for harpischord by Matthias Georg Monn*, CBS.

Schubert: *String Quartet in G Major, op. 151*, CBS.

Schubert: *Quintet for Two Violins, Viola, and Two Cellos in C Major, op. 163*, CBS.

Shostakovitch: *Concerto for Cello and Orchestra in E Flat Major, op. 107*, CBS.

Strauss: *Don Quichotte*, CBS.

Sources

Baltimore Sun, May 25, 1986; March 21, 1988.

Christian Science Monitor, May 26, 1978.

Diapason-Harmonie, June 1988.

Kansas City Star, September 15, 1985.

New York Daily News, March 24, 1987.

Time, January 19, 1981.

Tuscon Citizen, March 16, 1988.

—Jeanne M. Lesinski

Barry Manilow

Singer, songwriter, pianist

"Barry Manilow has spent . . . years at the top of the heap, no matter where the critics would wish him," declared David Van Biema in *People* magazine. Though frequently denigrated by music reviewers as bland and lacking talent, Manilow has had a string of hit singles, including "Mandy," "Could It Be Magic," "This One's For You," "Weekend in New England," and "Copacabana," and has watched at least ten of his albums go platinum. Extremely popular with fans of the soft ballad genre, Manilow won several awards for his musical performance in the late 1970s, including a special Antoinette Perry (Tony) Award for two weeks of sold-out concerts on Broadway. In the 1980s he made successful forays into a jazz reminiscent of the 1930s and 1940s, and wrote his autobiography, *Sweet Life: Adventures on the Way to Paradise.*

Manilow was born June 17, 1946, in Brooklyn, New York. Two years later his father deserted the family, and Manilow was raised by his mother and grandparents. They were poor and lived in a slum area of Brooklyn that has since deteriorated further. "Ask a cabdriver to take you there now," Manilow told Stephen E. Rubin in *Ladies' Home Journal,* "and he'll run away." As the singer explained further, "I was really ugly, the ugliest kid in school. . . . I didn't have a lot of friends," and his shyness intensified his interest in music. He learned the accordion at an early age and later progressed to the piano. After his mother remarried in the late 1950s, Manilow's stepfather, a jazz enthusiast, took him to hear saxophonist Gerry Mulligan. This broadened the young musician's interests, and he began buying jazz and Broadway musical albums, but unlike most of his peers, Manilow held no affection for the rock and roll that was sweeping the country during his adolescence. He told Gerrit Henry in *After Dark:* "I really did not *like* [Bill Haley and the Comets'] 'Rock Around the Clock.' I think the Beatles finally convinced me there was something going on in rock."

After Manilow graduated from high school he entered the City College of New York to study advertising, but, quickly bored by marketing courses, he left for the New York College of Music. Due to lack of funds he never graduated, but he continued his studies at Juilliard while supporting himself with a job in the mail room of CBS's New York City headquarters. Eventually Manilow worked his way up to film editor for the local affiliate, WCBS-TV; his primary task was inserting commercials into the programming, but he also created new theme music for the station's late show. Meanwhile, in his spare time, Manilow was arranging music for others who tried out in Broadway auditions and playing piano in lounges and bars.

Roughly concurrent with an early marriage to a high

strongest suit. . . . I'm only a fair singer, I write nice songs, but I'm a great arranger." With the money he was earning in this position, Manilow felt secure enough to invest in making demonstration tapes of his own material, and he submitted them to Bell Records, which later became Arista. The result was a contract for a solo album, which, when finished, was *Manilow I.* Though one cut in particular from this effort, "Could It Be Magic," a richly emotional love song based on a prelude by classical composer Frederic Chopin, received favorable criticism and frequent FM airplay, Manilow did not have a major hit until his second album, *Manilow II,* in 1974. The featured single, "Mandy," a haunting song of regret for a formerly spurned lover, was a runaway success and put Manilow into the limelight and on his way to becoming one of the most popular singers of the 1970s.

Manilow followed "Mandy" with the upbeat "It's a Miracle," but for the most part he has scored his biggest successes with sad love ballads like "Trying to Get the Feeling," in 1975, "Weekend in New England," and "Looks Like We Made It," in 1976, "Even Now," in 1978,

---

"I was really ugly, the ugliest kid in school. . . . I didn't have a lot of friends."

---

his 1982 rendition of "Memory" from the Broadway musical "Cats," and 1983's "Read 'Em and Weep." In addition, Manilow wrote and performed the theme song for television's "American Bandstand" and sang "Ready to Take a Chance," which served as the theme of the film, "Foul Play."

Though chided by critics as amateurish in his singing style, Manilow feels this is the very trait that makes him so popular. He told Dennis Hunt in a *Los Angeles Times* interview: "You can hear me spitting, you can hear me making mistakes. . . . There's a more human element in a song if my voice cracks or if you can hear me sighing. It's emotional, it's realistic." Despite this attitude, enormous record sales, and myriad sold-out concert appearances, however, Manilow is upset by negative critical response. "All the things they say—'marshmallow,' 'syrupy,' 'ugly,' 'talentless,' 'can't sing,' 'wimp,' 'fag'—hurt so badly because I call myself all those things before they do," he confided to Van Biema. He deals with it, according to Van Biema, by working "even harder." Manilow also has attempted to change his image, while simultaneously indulging his own musical

school sweetheart that ended in divorce after a year, Manilow was named musical director of WCBS-TV's "Callback," a showcase for young musical talent. He won an Emmy in this capacity for his work writing many different kinds of musical arrangements—from opera to rock and roll. In the 1970s, Manilow began to supplement his income by writing and performing commercial jingles. His composing endeavors in this field include advertisements for Bowlene Toilet Cleaner, Band-Aid bandages, Chevrolet automobiles, and State Farm Insurance; in addition, he sang the famous "You Deserve a Break Today" theme for McDonald's fast food restaurants.

At around the same time, Manilow served as a substitute pianist for singer Bette Midler. Midler liked his work, and he became the musical director for her 1972 tour, fashioning the arrangements that helped Midler become a major star. As Manilow explained to Robert Windeler in another *People* article, "Arranging is my

taste, by writing and recording songs in the style of 1930s and 1940s jazz. He got together with jazz musicians, including his early influence Gerry Mulligan, to record the 1984 release, *2:00 A.M., Paradise Cafe*, which was viewed with greater kindness than his ballad albums by many critics. Manilow released a similar effort, *Swing Street,* in 1987.

Selected discography

Manilow I (contains "Sing It," "Sweetwater Jones," "Cloudburst," "One of These Days," "Oh; My Lady," "I Am Your Child," "Could It Be Magic," "Seven More Years," "Flashy Lady," "Friends," and "Sweet Life"), Bell, 1973.

Manilow II (contains "I Want to Be Somebody's Baby," "Early Morning Strangers," "Mandy," "The Two of Us," "Something's Comin' Up," "It's a Miracle," "Avenue C," "My Baby Loves Me," "Sandra," and "Home Again"), Bell, 1974.

Tryin' to Get the Feeling (contains "New York City Rhythm," "Trying to Get the Feeling," "Why Don't We Live Together," "Bandstand Boogie," "You're Leavin' Too Soon," "She's a Star," "I Write the Songs," "As Sure as I'm Standing Here," "A Nice Boy Like Me," "Lay Me Down," and "Beautiful Music"), Arista, 1975.

This One's For You (contains "This One's For You," "Daybreak," "You Oughta Be Home With Me," "Jump Shout Boogie," "Weekend in New England," "Riders to the Stars," "Let Me Go," "Looks Like We Made It," "Say the Words," "All the Time," and "See the Show Again"), Arista, 1976.

Barry "Live" (double album; includes "A Very Strange Medley," "Jump Shout Boogie Medley," and "It's Just Another New Year's Eve"), Arista, 1977.

Even Now (contains "Copacabana," "Somewhere in the Night," "A Linda Song," "Can't Smile Without You," "Leavin' in the Morning," "Where Do I Go From Here," "Even Now," "I Was a Fool," "Losing Touch," "I Just Want to Be the One in Your Life," "Starting Again," and "Sunrise"), Arista, 1978.

Greatest Hits, Volume I, Arista, 1978.

One Voice (contains "One Voice," "A Slow Dance," "Rain," "Ships," "You Could Show Me," "I Don't Want to Walk Without You," "Who's Been Sleeping in My Bed?," "Where Are They Now?," "Bobbie Lee," "When I Wanted You," and "Sunday Father"), Arista, 1979.

Barry (contains "Lonely Together," "Bermuda Triangle," "I Made It Through the Rain," "24 Hours a Day," "Dance Away," "Life Will Go On," "Only in Chicago," "The Last Duet," "London," and "We Still Have Time"), Arista, 1980.

If I Should Love Again (contains "The Old Songs," "Let's Hang On," "If I Should Love Again," "Don't Fall in Love With Me," "Break Down the Door," "Somewhere Down the Road," "No Other Love," "Fools Get Lucky," "I Haven't Changed the Room," and "Let's Take All Night"), Arista, 1981.

Live in Britain (includes "The Old Songs Medley," and "London/We'll Meet Again"), Arista, 1982.

Here Comes the Night (contains "I Wanna Do It With You," "Here Comes the Night," "Memory," "Let's Get On With It," "Some Girls," "Some Kind of Friend," "I'm Gonna Sit Right Down and Write Myself a Letter," "Getting Over Losing You," "Heart of Steel," and "Stay"), Arista, 1982.

Greatest Hits, Volume II (includes "Read 'Em and Weep," "Put a Quarter in the Juke Box," and "You're Looking Hot Tonight"), Arista, 1983.

2:00 A.M., Paradise Cafe (contains "Paradise Cafe," "Where Have You Gone," "Say No More," "Blue," "When October Goes," "What Am I Doin' Here," "Goodbye, My Love," "Big City Blues," "When Love Is Gone," "I've Never Been So Low on Love," and "Night Song"), Arista, 1984.

The Manilow Collection/Twenty Greatest Hits, Arista, 1985.

Manilow (contains "I'm Your Man," "It's All Behind Us Now," "In Search of Love," "He Doesn't Care," "Some Sweet Day," "At the Dance," "If You Were Here With Me Tonight," "Sweet Heaven," "Ain't Nothing Like the Real Thing," and "It's a Long Way Up"), RCA, 1985.

Swing Street, Arista, 1987.

Sources

Books

Manilow, Barry, *Sweet Life: Adventures on the Way to Paradise,* McGraw-Hill, 1987.

Periodicals

Ladies' Home Journal, April, 1979.
Los Angeles Times, December 4, 1976.
People, August 8, 1977; February 8, 1982; October 22, 1984; November 9, 1987.

—Elizabeth Thomas

Johnny Mathis

Singer

Johnny Mathis is one of the most successful singers of ballads in the American music world. His recordings have been represented on the music charts for longer than any except those of famous crooner Frank Sinatra, and he has earned at least eight gold albums. Rising to the peak of his reputation during the late 1950s and early 1960s, Mathis resisted the rock and roll phenomenon that swept the nation in those years and established a unique popularity for himself in the musical genre of easy listening. Perhaps because of the fact that much of his music celebrates the ideals of romantic love, Mathis is especially well-received by female listeners, but he has garnered critical acclaim as well. As reviewer Sidney Fields put it in the New York *Mirror:* "His voice has incredible range; he improvises on a theme in any tempo and mood with great originality; and he can move from a tender ballad to swing, to rhythm and blues, and even vehemence." Despite Mathis's longevity on the charts, however, he did not have a number one single until his 1978 duet with Deniece Williams, "Too Much, Too Little, Too Late."

Though he was born September 30, 1935, into a poor black family in San Francisco, California, Mathis's childhood and adolescence predicted his later success. His father, Clem, a former Texas vaudeville performer who Mathis calls "my biggest hero, the reason I started to sing," according to R. Windeler of *People* magazine, was quick to recognize and encourage his fourth child's talent. Clem bought Johnny a second-hand piano when he was eight, and taught him vaudeville routines for performance within the family. The young Mathis also sang in church, and won a local amateur talent contest when he was fourteen. The year before, he had impressed Oakland, California, music teacher Connie Cox so much that she offered him free voice lessons. The gesture was a helpful one because the Mathis family could not afford to pay for them; the lessons, primarily in classical and opera singing, continued for six years.

But music was not Mathis's only option for success. He was a good student with leadership quality. Mathis was the first black child ever elected student body president of San Francisco's Roosevelt Junior High School, and when he graduated to George Washington High School he served as the treasurer of his class. He also excelled in athletics, winning six letters for his participation in various sports, including basketball, hurdling, and high jumping. Mathis entered San Francisco State College with the intention of becoming an English teacher, but his continued athletic achievements led him to contemplate teaching physical education or coaching track. He set a college record for the high jump, and was invited to try out for the 1956 Olympic

Games, but he turned this down to concentrate on his musical career.

While attending San Francisco State, Mathis became interested in jazz, and began singing in local nightclubs with a sextet led by one of his fellow students, Virgil Gonsalves. Performing at San Francisco's Black Hawk club one night in 1955, Mathis attracted the attention of the club's co-owner, Helen Noga. Noga was determined to make him a star, and became his manager. She helped Mathis obtain more nightclub bookings, during one of which, at a gay bar that also featured female impersonators, he was discovered by George Avakian, head album producer for Columbia Records.

Though somewhat regretful of leaving his college education unfinished, Mathis went to New York City to record for Columbia. While in New York, he also performed in some of the better clubs there, including the Village Vanguard and the Blue Angel. The first album Mathis made was flavored with jazz arrangements, and did not sell well. But Avakian had faith in his latest discovery, and sent him to work with the head of Columbia's singles department, Mitch Miller. Miller realized that the young singer's talent had been misdirected, and steered him away from jazz to the soft ballad style that became Mathis's trademark. "Wonderful! Wonderful!," released in 1957, became Mathis's first big hit. He soon followed this up with "It's Not for Me to Say," and, perhaps his best-known recording, the romantic "Chances Are."

Mathis also became involved in films, singing the title song for the 1957 film "Lizzie," and making an appearance in the picture as a nightclub singer. He had a

slightly larger role, also as a nightclub singer, in "A Certain Smile," released in 1958. Most sources assert that Mathis's presence in "Smile" was the only thing that saved it from box office failure; he did, however, score a hit with the title song. More recently, Mathis and singer Jane Olivor had a popular success with "The Last Time I Felt Like This," the theme from the film version of playwright Neil Simon's "Same Time Next Year."

Mathis continued to have many successes throughout the late 1950s and early 1960s, including "Small World," "Misty," and "What Will Mary Say," but then his popularity as a recording artist waned. He became dissatis-

> *Despite Mathis's longevity on the charts, he did not have a number one single until 1978.*

fied with Noga's handling of his career in 1964, and established his own company, Rojon Productions, in order not only to become his own manager but to promote new talent.

Mathis has remained in demand as a concert performer, however, and his 1978 return to the charts—his duet with Deniece Williams, "Too Much, Too Little, Too Late"—was a milestone for him. It was his first number one record, and, because of Williams's following, made Mathis popular with black audiences for the first time; his previous Columbia hits had been aimed primarily at whites.

Selected discography

Major single releases; on Columbia, except as noted

"Wonderful! Wonderful!," 1957.
"It's Not for Me to Say," 1957.
"Chances Are," 1957.
"The Twelfth of Never," 1957.
"Wild is the Wind," 1957.
"No Love (But Your Love)," 1957.
"Come to Me," 1958.
"All the Time," 1958.
"Teacher, Teacher," 1958.
"A Certain Smile," 1958.
"Call Me," 1958.
"You Are Beautiful," 1959.
"Let's Love," 1959.
"Someone," 1959.

"Small World," 1959.
"Misty," 1959.
"The Best of Everything," 1959.
"Starbright," 1960.
"Maria," 1960.
"My Love for You," 1960.
"How to Handle a Woman," 1961.
"Wasn't the Summer Short?" 1961.
"Sweet Thursday," 1962.
"Marianna," 1962.
"Gina," 1962.
"What Will Mary Say," 1963.
"Every Step of the Way," 1963.
"Sooner or Later," 1963.
"I'll Search My Heart," 1963.
"Your Teen-Age Dreams," Mercury, 1963.
"Come Back," Mercury, 1963.
"Bye, Bye, Barbara," Mercury, 1964.

"Taste of Tears," Mercury, 1964.
"Listen, Lonely Girl," Mercury, 1964.
"On a Clear Day You Can See Forever," Mercury, 1965.
"I'm Coming Home," 1973.
"Life is a Song Worth Singing," 1973.
(With Deniece Williams) "Too Much, Too Little, Too Late," 1978.
(With Williams) "You're All I Need to Get By," 1978.
(With Jane Olivor) "The Last Time I Felt Like This," 1979.

Sources

Mirror (New York), August 26, 1962.
People, October 23, 1978.

—*Elizabeth Thomas*

John "Cougar" Mellencamp

Singer, songwriter, guitarist

John "Cougar" Mellencamp is rock music's poet of the American heartland, a strident artist whose original songs mirror the rebellion and hopelessness of a generation of blue-collar youths. Himself a lifelong inhabitant of a small town—Seymour, Indiana, population 15,000—Mellencamp writes and sings about both the joys and frustrations of small-town life; stylistically, his music harks back to the rough-and-tumble acoustic rock of the 1960s. As Jim Miller notes in *Newsweek,* by "hymning the virtues of the rural Midwest," Mellencamp "has brought to life a moral universe previously unsung in the rock tradition. And in an era when almost every other rock act seems like a state-of-the-art commercial ploy or a cartoon for a new video, Mellencamp has pulled off an almost impossible feat: he has taken some of the most elementary facets of old-fashioned rock—its romance, its implicit promise that any kid can make his mark, its youthful air of adventure—and made them seem brand new."

Between 1982 and 1987 Mellencamp cut four albums, each of which generated two top-ten singles. Combined, the albums have sold an estimated fourteen million copies worldwide, ranking the Indiana rocker among the industry's most successful performers. This popularity has come to Mellencamp despite a fumbling debut that saw him cast as "Johnny Cougar" and a subsequent period of mutual animosity between the singer and his reviewers. "Cursed with a corny stage name," writes David Fricke in *Rolling Stone,* "he was a man who loved to hate—his record company, the critics who dismissed him as a minor-league [Bruce] Springsteen, even his own songs." Mellencamp's ascendancy in the 1980s has brought respect from critics and musical peers as well as a more mellow attitude on the performer's part. "I looked at other artists who had been in the music industry and I thought, I don't want to be like them," Mellencamp told *Newsweek.* "They were just hateful to everybody—cynical, unhappy, eventually drunk. So what else was left for me to do, except really *care* about the people who were buying my records? You know, there's some poor guy making $2.50 an hour nailing wood for some boss who abuses him, and he buys my records, he comes to my concerts. I *owe* him something."

Mellencamp was born in Seymour, Indiana, in 1951, the newest member of a fiercely proud family that had long been scorned by Seymour's elite. At birth the youngster had a crippling deformity of the spine, meningocele, that required dangerous surgery and a lengthy hospital stay. Mellencamp survived, but his mother tended to overcompensate for his rocky start by spoiling him and worrying about his personality. His father, on the other hand, pushed John to excel in school and athletics, only managing to instill in the child a rebelliousness and

For the Record. . .

Born October 7, 1951, in Seymour, Ind.; son of Richard (vice-president of an electronics firm) and Marilyn (Lowe) Mellencamp; married Priscilla Esterline, 1969 (divorced, 1981); married Vicky Granucci, May 23, 1981; children: (first marriage) Michelle; (second marriage) Teddi Jo, Justice Renee. *Education:* Vincennes University, A.A., 1973. *Politics:* Left-wing populist.

Rock singer-songwriter, 1975—. Cut first album, *Chestnut Street Revisited,* for MCA, 1976; moved to Riva Records, 1977, and Mercury Records, 1979. Had first two number-one hits, "Hurts So Good" and "Jack and Diane," 1982. With Willie Nelson, organized "Farm Aid" concerts, 1985 and 1986; testified before a congressional subcommittee on the family farm crisis, 1987. Has made numerous concert appearances in the United States and abroad.

Addresses: *Office*—c/o PolyGram Records, 810 Seventh Ave., New York, N.Y. 10019. *Other*— Rt. # 1, Box 361, Nashville, Ind. 47448.

hostility that became chronic by his high-school years. Growing up in Seymour in the late 1960s, Mellencamp was one of the first teens to grow his hair long, drink and take drugs, and protest the Vietnam War. At seventeen he eloped with Priscilla Esterline, his pregnant sweetheart.

Marriage and fatherhood did little to increase Mellencamp's sense of responsibility, although he did stop abusing alcohol and drugs in the early 1970s. He attended Vincennes University, a community college near Seymour, majoring in communications, and after two years there he drifted through a series of odd jobs, including telephone installation and construction work. Mellencamp had played in rock bands since his early teens, and as he entered his twenties he began to compose music and accompany himself on an acoustic guitar. In 1974 he began to travel to New York City in search of a recording contract, and after a few false starts he met Tony DeFries, a flamboyant manager whose clients included David Bowie.

Promising to make him a "big star in a year's time," DeFries signed Mellencamp to a five-year contract and got MCA to produce Mellencamp's first album. Unfortunately, DeFries's idea of stardom and Mellencamp's were quite different. The performer was stunned to see his debut album, *Chestnut Street Revisited,* released under the name "Johnny Cougar," and DeFries's other marketing techniques—including an embarrassing

parade in Seymour—were equally disconcerting. According to Andrew Slater, the effect of DeFries's management was to make Mellencamp seem like a "cartoon character from the Midwest [come] to life." Slater adds that *Chestnut Street Revisited* "suffered not only its unabashed 'Springsteen influence,' but the ton of hype that served to promote such a trivial debut." The album failed to sell, "Johnny Cougar" failed to hit, and MCA refused to release any more Mellencamp work. Mellencamp and DeFries dissolved their partnership.

The aspiring rocker quickly discovered that, as much as he disliked it, he would have to retain the Johnny Cougar stage name if he hoped to engage another manager. In 1977 he signed with Billy Gaff, a Los Angeles agent, and went to record in London for Riva Records, Gaff's personal label. *A Biography,* his 1978 album, sold moderately well in England and very well in Australia, where his single "I Need a Lover" went to number one. Still Mellencamp faced disdain among critics and fans for his slickly marketed image and derivative music, so he returned to the United States determined to reshape his career to suit himself. Meanwhile, "I Need a Lover" peaked on the American charts at number twenty, literally earning him a second chance.

In 1980 Mellencamp released *Nothin' Matters and What If It Did,* a modestly successful album that was particularly popular on FM rock radio. On this album and the subsequent million-selling *American Fool,* Mellencamp became "streetwise and tough," with "a viselike grip on his blue-collar background," to quote Slater. The critic also observed that Mellencamp was "an assaultive performer with a rough-and-tumble voice [who] writes of women, cars and his own restless youth . . . fashioning a longing for teenage freedom and first-love euphoria into chart-topping rock hits." With *American Fool* and its cynical hits "Jack and Diane" and "Hurts So Good," Mellencamp finally began to earn the grudging respect of rock critics. However, he was not ready to make peace with them or with the music moguls who had burdened him with a phony image.

Christopher Connelly described Mellencamp's attitude in a 1982 *Rolling Stone* profile: "Cougar's battle for individuality isn't a battle to impose his thinking on anyone, it's a fight to get out from under all the philosophies that everyone—from his family to the record industry to music critics—have imposed on him. He's rejected all interpretations of his music, just as he's tried to reject all forms of authority. Rather than offering himself up as a storyteller from the neglected Midwest, Cougar is adamant that his music is meaningless. His songs are . . . 'insignificant'. . . He hates being taken seriously. And he goes far beyond that:. . . Life is boring, but hey, you can deal with it." Only when

Mellencamp reclaimed his full name, with the 1983 album *Uh-Huh,* did he adopt a more conciliatory attitude toward press and public.

Uh-Huh, with its chart-topping singles "Authority Song," "Pink Houses," and "Crumblin' Down," revealed a more introspective, if no less rebellious, Mellencamp. Subsequent albums such as *Scarecrow* and *The Lonesome Jubilee* have seen an expanded use of the artist's personal experiences in songs such as "Paper in Fire" and "Small Town," as well as an ever-intensifying political commitment to family farmers and factory workers—a contingent Mellencamp feels has been ignored by the so-called "Reagan Revolution." In 1985 Mellencamp joined forces with Willie Nelson and other populist singers to create "Farm Aid," a live concert benefitting farmers who faced foreclosure. *New York Times Magazine* correspondent Timothy White writes: "It is this new self-discipline and focused fire that have enabled Mellencamp to reclaim rock—which has in recent years become largely frivolous—as a vehicle for social commentary. Rock-and-roll is a billion-dollar industry, so such a move by a singer of Mellencamp's status is nothing if not provocative."

Throughout his career Mellencamp has been compared to Bruce Springsteen—so often, in fact, that the two performers have made good-natured jokes about it. White finds Mellencamp and Springsteen distinctly different, however. Springsteen, notes the critic, "is a melodramatist whose personality is deliberately disguised by his theatrics. He carefully restricts contact with the public and is rarely seen offstage. Mellencamp, on the other hand, is an open book, with no larger-than-life bravura—even though the deeply personal side to his music has been little known. Springsteen's flamboyant sound is all flesh, but Mellencamp's more accessible rock is all bone." In two respects the performers are almost identical: neither will allow his songs to be used as product endorsements—Mellencamp will not even let beer or cigarette companies sponsor his tours—and both give long, exhausting live concerts, laced with political commentary and raucous, old-style rock and roll.

Mellencamp's 1989 album *Big Daddy* "proves that there is still room for irony in popular music," according to *Philadelphia Inquirer* reviewer Tom Moon. Moon notes that on *Big Daddy,* Mellencamp "has fashioned a style of music that prizes honesty above all. The emotional manipulation employed by any number of songwriters has no place in his current ruminations, which are based on blues-riff statements, folk songform and the regional quirks he has combined into an instantly iden-

tifiable sound." Those "regional quirks" will continue to be a significant force in Mellencamp's work, since he has made rural Indiana his permanent home. The artist spoke about his influences in the *New York Times Magazine,* saying: "See, a lot of the time I write in the third person, but I'm mostly describing my own ordeals. When those unsettled struggles prey on your mind, you become haunted. To get free, you must defeat your ghosts." Most of Mellencamp's ghosts are hidden in his restless past, waiting to find their way into his earthy rock and roll. "My best stuff," Mellencamp said, "is about me and my family tree grappling against both the world and our own inner goddamned whirlwind."

Selected discography

Chestnut Street Revisited, MCA, 1976.
A Biography, Riva, 1978.
John Cougar, Mercury, 1979.
Nothin' Matters and What If It Did, PolyGram, 1980.
American Fool, PolyGram, 1982.
Uh-Huh, PolyGram, 1983.
Scarecrow, PolyGram, 1985.
The Kid Inside, Rhino, 1986.
The Lonesome Jubilee, PolyGram, 1987.
Big Daddy, PolyGram, 1989.

Sources

Books

Torgoff, Martin, *American Fool: The Roots and Improbable Rise of John Cougar Mellencamp,* 1986.

Periodicals

Chicago Tribune, August 15, 1982.
Life, October, 1987.
Newsweek, January 6, 1986.
New York Times, August 30, 1987.
New York Times Magazine, September 27, 1987.
People, October 11, 1982.
Philadelphia Inquirer, May 14, 1989.
Rolling Stone, September 16, 1982; December 9, 1982; January 30, 1986; October 8, 1987.
Washington Post, October 3, 1985; December 9, 1985.

—Anne Janette Johnson

Pat Metheny

Guitarist, composer

"If it's not jazz, and maybe it's not, then I don't know what to call it. My music is based on the principle of playing bebop: it's chord changes and improvisation on the changes," Pat Metheny told *New Republic.* Perhaps jazz fusion, or jazz/rock, are better categories, but Metheny isn't interested in categories, only in playing his music—which he does to packed venues ten months out of the year. He is a hard-working and unassuming musician, happiest when he's on the road performing in tee-shirt and high-top sneakers to appreciative audiences.

Metheny comes from a musical family. His grandfather, father, mother, and older brother all played the trumpet. Marching band music was their favorite style, and country music was also pervasive around Lee's Summit, Missouri, where Metheny was born and grew up. But he enjoyed all kinds of music, from the Beatles to the Beach Boys to Miles Davis. At age 12 he discovered Ornette Coleman when he found an album of his for fifty cents in a record store cut-out bin: "I thought it was the greatest thing I ever heard in my life," he told *down beat.*

Following the family tradition, Metheny learned to play the trumpet first and then took up guitar at age 14. By the end of his high school years he was balancing his time between jazz gigs with small bands in nearby Kansas City and playing French Horn in half-time shows in order to earn the music credits he needed to graduate from high school. He briefly attended Miami University but then moved to Boston to take a teaching assistantship with jazz vibraphonist Gary Burton, who was teaching at the Berklee College of Music. In 1974 he was asked to join Burton's band and stayed with the group for about three years, recording on three albums. After leaving Burton he organized and toured with his own bands; toured with singer/songwriter Joni Mitchell; scored the film soundtrack for *The Falcon and the Snowman;* and by the late 1980s had garnered four Grammys from more than a dozen albums.

Because he began listening to jazz as a child, Metheny has developed a great respect for tradition. As he told *down beat,* "if you're 15 and you want to be a jazz musician, you've still got to go back to 1900 and start checking it all out. . . . And I'm more convinced of that each year—you have to have a thorough understanding of the tradition in order to consider going one step further." And his career has focused not on traditional jazz, but on extending the tradition by evolving his own personal style, which, while rooted in jazz, incorporates elements from other traditions as well as new technology.

A *down beat* review of an 1984 concert provides a good overview of the complexity of the artist's diverse

For the Record. . .

Full name, Patrick Bruce Metheny; born August 12, 1954, in Lee's Summit, Mo. *Education:* Attended Miami University.

Began playing guitar at age 14; member of local jazz bands in Kansas City, Mo., while in high school; guitarist with the Gary Burton Quintet, 1974-77; musical director and guitarist for the Pat Metheny Group, 1978—. Composer of film scores, including *Under Fire*, 1983; (with David Bowie) *The Falcom and the Snowman,* 1984; and *Twice in a Lifetime,* 1985.

Awards: Winner of four Grammy Awards, 1982, 1983, 1984, and 1987; received award for best jazz album, Boston Music Awards, 1986; named best jazz musician in *Jazziz* magazine's readers' poll, 1986; named best jazz guitarist, Boston Music Awards, 1986; Pat Metheny Group selected outstanding jazz fusion group, Boston Music Awards, 1986.

Addresses: *Offices*—c/o Ted Kurland Associates, Inc., 173 Brighton Ave., Boston, MA 02134.

told interviewer Tim Schneckloth, "they're 10,000 years away from being able to approach the power and the beauty of an acoustic instrument."

In 1986 Metheny found the opportunity to perform with the idol of his youth when he and Ornette Coleman went on tour to support their first joint album, *Song X.* A review of the concert in Coleman's hometown, Fort Worth, Texas, stated: "The audience was a mixed collection of mainstream fusion Metheny fans and hardcore harmonic partisans, all of whom were curious—and if the truth be told, a trifle skeptical—of what would happen when the guitarist's rounded tones and melodic sensibilities collided with Ornette's hard-edged angular logic." The *down beat* review concluded: "They shouldn't have worried."

During the early 1980s Metheny was using a home computer as a composing tool and experimenting with guitar synthesizers. But it was the Synclavier, an instrument with a built-in 32-track digital memory and the ability to create practically any sound for an instrument, that totally changed his way of working. He uses it in the studio for nearly all his composing and in performance

style: "Metheny balances three separate aspects in his music—the first being his own irrepressible Midwestern lyricism, the second a penchant for Brazilian rhythms, and the third the wild card of Ornette Coleman's jagged, insular logic." His work with keyboardist Lyel Mays and Brazilian percussionist Nana Vasconcelos on the albums *As Falls Wichita, So Falls Wichita Falls* and *Offramp* illustrate the first two of these aspects, emphasizing his flowing, melodic style and appreciation for exotic rhythms. And his lyricism is particularly emphasized in his straight-ahead jazz performances with Ornette Coleman on the album *Song X,* and with Coleman alumni Charlie Hayden and Dewey Redman on *80/81* and *Rejoicing.*

As Falls Wichita, So Falls Wichita Falls established Metheny as a unique new voice in jazz. In a *down beat* interview he stated: "With that record we wanted to do a piece of music that was somehow away from the song form. So much of what we were doing were songs in which the improvisation was based on the harmonies in the song—in the jazz tradition. We wanted to try something where the improvisation happened not so much in the linear sense as in the *textural* sense." On the album, Mays, a multi-keyboardist and composer with his own album releases, moves easily from stunning solos to creating lush musical environments for Metheny's guitar work. Vasconcelos's drums and simple acoustic instruments offer an earthy rhythm with a grounding effect on the otherwise predominantly electronic sound. "As hip as synthesizers are," Metheny

---

Pat Metheny stands to be one of the great innovators in the jazz tradition.

---

to create a wide range of sounds for his guitar. On many of his recordings his guitar takes on tones which hearken back to his youth: trumpet and other horns.

But he cautions those eager to leap on the high-technology bandwagon: "I'm convinced more and more that the guitar synthesizer is bringing along a situation where *everything* is possible as an improviser," he told interviewer Art Lange. "This technology is not only making it possible, but it's so much more *fun* to have this range to choose from as opposed to just having one sound; now you've got *any* sound, and you can apply everything you've learned to that particular sound—if what you've got to play is strong enough to support that sound. That's where it gets sticky."

In a review of Metheny's 1985 release *First Circle,* jazz reviewer Jim Roberts observed: "There is a tendency, I think, to take Pat Metheny's accomplishments for granted, maybe because he still looks like a shaggy kid in a t-shirt and doesn't make pronouncements about his 'art.' But the fact is that the range of his music, on record and in concert, is unmatched by any of his contemporaries (and few of his elders)." Pat Metheny stands to be one of the great innovators in the jazz tradition.

Selected discography

Released by ECM, except as noted

Bright Size Life, 1975.
Watercolors, 1977.
Pat Metheny Group, 1978.
American Garage, 1979.
80/81, 1980.
As Falls Wichita, So Falls Wichita Falls, 1981.
Offramp, 1982.
New Chautauqua.
Rejoicing, 1983.
First Circle, 1985.

Song X (with Ornette Coleman), Geffen, 1986.
Still Life (Talking), Geffen, 1987.
Travels, 1987.

Sources

Audio, October, 1986.
down beat, October, 1982; November, 1982; May, 1984; January, 1985; April, 1986; June, 1986; August, 1986.
High Fidelity, September, 1981; January, 1985.
New Republic, May 30, 1983.
Newsweek, April 14, 1986.
Rolling Stone, May 9, 1985.
Stereo Review, November, 1981; September, 1982.

—*Tim LaBorie*

Steve Miller

Singer, songwriter, guitarist

Steve Miller, along with the Grateful Dead and the Jefferson Airplane/Starship, is one of the few artists whose career skyrocketed out of the music scene in San Francisco during the 1960s. "Miller has ascended with the confidence that comes from thinking that you've always belonged there," wrote John Milward in the *Rolling Stone Record Guide*. Miller found his fame and fortune in the Bay Area by way of Chicago via Texas and Wisconsin. Born and raised in Milwaukee til age five, he began playing guitar just one year before the family moved to Dallas. Miller's first lessons came from friends and patients of his father, a proctologist. Les Paul and Mary Ford, T-Bone Walker, Tal Farlow, Charles Mingus, and Red Norvo frequented their household and Miller's father often recorded the artists in various nightclub settings.

With such a remarkable foundation to start with, Miller formed his first band, the Marksmen, at just twelve years of age. Schoolmate Boz Scaggs joined the group after Miller taught the ninth-grader some basics on the guitar. Together they played fraternity dances and parties throughout their high school days until it was time to start college. Miller enrolled at the University of Wisconsin aiming for a degree in English. He played with four or five bands before settling with the Ardells, who played during the school term, and the Fabulous Knight Trains, his summertime band. Scaggs came up from Texas to join Miller and their collaboration lasted three years.

Miller told Dan Forte in *Guitar Player* that "the Beatles came out, and it just blew my mind that they could get a record contract and people thought they were so different. It was like what we were doing, but nobody ever thought we would make records." Miller took a year off to go to Europe to absorb a different musical culture before heading back to Wisconsin. During summer break, he went to Chicago to check out the clubs and ended up staying for two years. Along with Barry Goldberg he formed the Goldberg-Miller Blues Band and began performing amongst the seasoned veterans of the Windy City. "You had to be good," Miller said in *Guitar Player,* "it was a very competitive situation, and you either had it or you didn't. When we were in Chicago, we knew we were playing better music than anybody on either coast."

In 1966 Miller went back to Texas with the intention of finishing school, but, after hearing so much about the California music explosion, he decided to go west. Within four days of his arrival, Miller had formed a band and was playing at the Avalon Ballroom, combining, as Gene Santoro wrote in *Guitar World,* "polished ballads with polished blues with polished psychedelic musical clouds of sound." He soon summoned Scaggs to return from Sweden (where the singer had become somewhat of a star in his own right) and the Steve Miller Band became headliners. Having played for money for well over a decade by now, Miller was disappointed with the lack of professionalism displayed by the "hippie" bands. "I wasn't into the real heavy-duty drug experience, the continually ongoing trip," he told *Rolling Stone*'s Charles Perry. "I was more into getting a record contract, making music, traveling around the world and stuff."

He achieved that goal after nearly ten months of negotiating with thirteen different record companies. In 1967 Capitol Records signed Miller to a landmark contract that virutally set the standard for future bands. "They weren't ready for middle-class, educated people," Miller told *Guitar Player,* "What they were expecting was dummies." His shrewd business sense paid off with an offer that included a $50,000 advance, a $10,000 bonus for one year, four one-year options which would total $750,000 if taken, complete artistic control over the product and an unprecedented 32 cents an album (12 cents was the norm). "We were in a perfect position. The record companies, typically not understanding anything about the music, were given instructions to go to San Francisco and sign those acts," he said in *Rolling Stone.* "They knew that we were one of the four popular groups. . . . They wanted to sign the phenomena."

After the Monterey Pop Festival in August of 1967, Miller was fed up with the drug culture and broke loose from the West Coast. Cream had just released their *Fresh Cream* LP and Miller was obsessed with Eric Clapton's guitar work. "He totally captured my mind, soul, and spirit," Miller confessed to *Guitar Player.* "I couldn't do it. I didn't have the will to practice that way." Wanting a sound similar to Clapton's, and not being

able to get it from American engineers, he headed to London to record his first album, *Children of the Future.* With the single "Living in the USA," the LP sold an impressive 150,000 copies.

Also in 1968, Miller rèleased *Sailor,* which, according to Bruce Malamut in *Guitar World,* is "without question one of the Great Five rock albums of all time." These two LPs, in addition to his third (*Brave New World,* containing the single "Space Cowboy") constitute the best of Miller's early work. Produced by Glyn Johns, they have a definite British sound and, as John Milward wrote in the *Rolling Stone Record Guide,* follow a formula of "well-produced bunches of songs that ran together like rock and roll suites."

It would take five more albums before Miller would reign again. *The Joker* (1973) went gold, as did the title track, which also was a number one single in the States. For the next ten years Miller would have a string of hits: "Fly Like An Eagle," "Take the Money and Run," "Rock 'n' Me" (from *Books of Dreams*), another gold album with *Circle of Love,* and the platinum-selling *Abracadabra*

Steve Miller has tried to let his music speak for itself and to avoid the superstar label.

(with the title track being his third number one single). Miller seemed to have found a formula for creating catchy songs that relied on keyboards, multi-tracked vocals, and special effects more than on the standard guitar solo. "It's like a game, like a crossword puzzle," Miller explained in *Guitar Player.* "And as long as you get some tunes that've got feeling and soul and substance to them, there you go."

He may have overdid the studio tricks, however, on his 1984 album *Italian X-Rays.* Recorded on a prototype Sony multitrack "digital domain" recording system, it was too bogged down with electronics to really go anywhere. He toned down considerably for *Living in the 20th Century* with side one consisting of standard Miller fare ("I Want to Make The World Turn Around") and side two featuring all blues selections. The album was dedicated to the late Jimmy Reed, whom Miller had the honor of backing up in Dallas when he was only fourteen. Miller's blues playing is tasty and seemingly effortless, having picked it up naturally from artists like Reed and T-Bone Walker instead of studying it like so many other guitarists have done. "Blues is the well, the inspiration for me," he told Matt Resnicoff in *Guitar World.* "It's just part of me. I hear it, I feel it, I know it."

Miller took even more of commercial chance on his next LP, *Born 2 B Blue.* After doing some work on jazzman Ben Sidran's live album (*On The Live Side*), Miller decided to record a disc of standards, including "Zip-a-dee-doo-day," "God Bless the Child," and "Ya Ya." "It's better to have this to do than to go back and do "Jungle Love" one more time," he told *Guitar World* of the music, calling it a "real challenge, and a good one, and that's what saved my career. I was getting real tired of making rock 'n' roll albums." Sidran, who helped Miller with the project's jazz arrangements, had previously worked with Miller and cowrote "Space Cowboy".

Throughout his career, Steve Miller had tried to let his music speak for itself and to avoid the superstar label. His album covers contain blurry photos of himself and he often uses different personalities both in and out of music, including the Gangster of Love, the Space Cowboy, and Maurice. "The problem with images is that once you take a solid image as an entertainer, it's hard to back out," he told Tim Cahill in *Rolling Stone.* "I like to slip in and out of characters. . . . I would rather not be recognizable on the street." His sound, on the other hand, is very identifiable.

Selected discography

Released by Capitol

Children of the Future, 1968.
Sailor, 1969.
Brave New World, 1969.
Your Saving Grace, 1969.
Number Five, 1970.
Rock Love, 1971.
Recall the Beginning . . . A Journey From Eden, 1972.
Anthology, 1972.

The Joker, 1973.
Fly Like an Eagle, 1976.
Book of Dreams, 1977.
Greatest Hits, '74 - '78, 1978.
Circle of Love, 1982.
Abracadabra, 1982.
Steve Miller Live, 1983.
Italian X-Rays, 1984.
Living in the 20th Century, 1984.
Born 2 B Blue, 1988.

With Chuck Berry

Chuck Berry Live at the Fillmore Auditorium, Mercury, 1967.

Sources

Books

Christgau, Robert, *Christgau's Record Guide,* Ticknor & Fields, 1981.
Logan, Nick, and Bob Woffinden, *The Illustrated Encyclopedia of Rock,* Harmony, 1977.
The Rolling Stone Illustrated History of Rock and Roll, edited by Jim Miller, Random House/Rolling Stone Press, 1976.
The Rolling Stone Record Guide, edited by Dave Marsh with John Swenson, Random House/Rolling Stone Press, 1979.

Periodicals

Guitar Player, January, 1978; February, 1987.
Guitar World, September, 1983; March, 1985; November, 1985; February, 1989.
Rolling Stone, February 26, 1976; June 17, 1976; July 15, 1976; February 10, 1977; July 14, 1977.

—*Calen D. Stone*

Ronnie Milsap

Singer, songwriter, pianist

Ronnie Milsap is a perennial favorite among the country stars centered in Nashville. Born blind and poor in the Smoky Mountain region, Milsap learned to make music as a youngster. He decided in 1973 to concentrate on country tunes after having played rhythm and blues, classical, and even rock and roll. Since then, to quote *Los Angeles Times* contributor Thomas K. Arnold, Milsap has been "to country music what Stevie Wonder is to pop. They're both prodigious hit-makers, they're both considered legends in their respective genres and they're both blind." Arnold adds that "virtually everything [Milsap has] recorded has turned to gold."

Milsap's blindness is a result of congenital glaucoma, a condition that rendered him sightless at birth. The performer has candidly admitted that had he not been blind, he might never have become a musician at all. He told *People:* "I was sent to a special school where my training was excellent. If I hadn't been blind, I would probably still be in the backwoods of North Carolina working in a sawmill." Milsap was indeed born in the "backwoods"—in Robinsville, a tiny farming community near the Tennessee border. He was turned over to his grandparents to raise, and they in turn sent him, at age five, to the State School for the Blind in Raleigh.

The school was four hundred miles from his home, but rather than languishing in homesickness, Milsap prospered in the educational environment. He learned to play the violin from a sensitive teacher whom Milsap described as "a consummate musician and a philosopher who could communicate with a bewildered child." Milsap was given a thorough grounding in classical music, and, in addition to the violin, he learned to play keyboards, woodwinds, and the guitar. He also experimented with a number of different musical styles, forming a rock band with several other blind students and playing rhythm and blues and jazz.

Milsap attended Young-Harris Junior College in Atlanta, studying pre-law and earning honor-roll grades. He was offered a full scholarship to Emory University, but he decided to pursue professional musicianship instead. In 1965 he formed his own band and supported himself by doing sideman work for blues artist J. J. Cale. By 1969 his band had a regular gig at T.J.'s, a Memphis club. They played all sorts of music—country, rock, jazz, blues, and pop—and in 1970 they recorded a hit single, "Loving You Is a Natural Thing." Gradually Milsap realized that his talent lay primarily in country music. In 1973 he moved his family to Nashville, signed with RCA Records, and quickly became a celebrity with the chart-topping singles "I Hate You," "Pure Love," and "Please Don't Tell Me How the Story Ends."

Born in Robinsville, N.C.; son of James Lee and Grace (Calhoun) Milsap; married Frances Joyce Reeves, October 30, 1965; children: Ronald Todd. *Education:* Young-Harris Junior College, A.A., 1964.

Singer, pianist, bandleader, 1965—. Signed with Scepter Records, c. 1967; cut first single, "Never Had It So Good." Worked as opening act for rhythm and blues artists J. J. Cale, Bobby Bland, and the Miracles. Moved to Nashville, 1973; signed with RCA Records; had first number one single, "I Hate You," 1973.

Awards: Named male vocalist of the year by the Country Music Association, 1974, 1976, and 1977; album of the year awards from Country Music Association, 1975, 1977, and 1978; named entertainer of the year by the Country Music Association, 1977; Grammy Awards 1986, for *Lost in the Fifties Tonight*, and 1987 (with Kenny Rogers) for best country vocal duet.

Addresses: *Office*—12 Music Circle S., Nashville, Tenn. 37203.

According to Melvin Shestack in *The Country Music Encyclopedia*, Milsap was considered "Nashville's 'own' performer" after he began a regular engagement at Roger Miller's King of the Road motel. Milsap's albums sold well, and his personal appearances were met with enthusiastic ovations. In 1974 he earned the first of many awards from the prestigious Country Music Association—"best male vocalist of the year." He was named "entertainer of the year," the CMA's highest honor, in 1977. *People* magazine correspondent Dolly Carlisle suggests that determination opened doors for Milsap, but his talent and his memorable songs kept the door open. Milsap's "rich emotive tenor and mellow lyrics" have suggested "a Smoky Mountain Manilow," Carlisle writes.

Many country artists seek the elusive "crossover" hit—the song that will top the pop *and* country charts. Milsap scored on this front with "Smoky Mountain Rain," a dramatic heartbreak song released in 1981. He has also made the pop charts with the singles "(There's) No Gettin' Over Me" and "Any Day Now." Milsap does not strive for the pop sound, however. He told Shestack

that he remains true to the genre of his region. "The only music I heard for the first six years of my life was country," he said. "It's hard to get away from those early influences. I have played, and can play, any kind of music, but you must do what your heart feels is right, and to me that's country."

Selected discography

(All Together Now) Let's Fall Apart, RCA, 1973.
Pure Love, RCA, 1974.
A Legend in My Time, RCA, 1975.
20/20 Vision, RCA.
Where My Heart Is, RCA.
A Rose by Any Other, Warner Bros.
Night Things, RCA.
Ronnie Milsap Live, RCA.
Vocalist of the Year, Crazy Cajun.
Mr. Mailman, DJM.
Inside Ronnie Milsap, RCA.
It Was Almost Like a Song, RCA.
One More Try for Love, RCA.
There's No Gettin' Over Me, RCA.
Ronnie Milsap's Greatest Hits, RCA.
Keyed Up, RCA, 1985.
Ronnie Milsap's Greatest Hits, Volume 2, RCA, 1985.
Back on My Mind Again, RCA, 1986.
Believe It!, RCA, 1986.
Christmas with Ronnie Milsap, RCA, 1986.
Collector's Series, RCA, 1986.
Lost in the Fifties Tonight, RCA, 1986.
Heart and Soul, RCA, 1987.

Sources

Books

The Illustrated Encyclopedia of Country Music, Harmony Books, 1977.
Shestack, Melvin, *The Country Music Encyclopedia*, Crowell, 1974.

Periodicals

Los Angeles Times, March 8, 1989.
People, April 28, 1980.

—*Anne Janette Johnson*

Joni Mitchell

Singer, songwriter, guitarist, and pianist

"**B**y taking risks, [Joni] Mitchell has survived into the late 1980s with her art still blazing," declared Nicholas Jennings in *Maclean's* magazine. Mitchell, who started out as a folksinger in the 1960s, is respected as an innovative contributor to various musical genres. In addition to folk, she has made successful forays into rock, country, and jazz. Though perhaps best known for her folk compositions "Both Sides, Now" and "The Circle Game," Mitchell also had hits with "Big Yellow Taxi," "Help Me," "Raised on Robbery," and "Turn Me On (I'm a Radio)." Most of her albums have become gold records, and she won a Grammy Award for the best folk performance in 1970 for her album *Clouds*. Mitchell is also a talented painter; she adorns her album covers with her own brushwork, and in 1988 exhibited her paintings in Tokyo, Japan.

Mitchell was born Roberta Joan Anderson in 1943 in Fort MacLeod, Alberta, Canada. The only child of a grocery store manager and a former schoolteacher, Mitchell grew up listening to her mother quote the works of poet and playwright William Shakespeare. She was also encouraged early in her musical abilities; after the family moved to Saskatoon, Saskatchewan, her father bought her a secondhand piano. Mitchell told Michael Small in *People* that the piano lessons lasted a few years, but "they conflicted with listening to Wild Bill Hickock on the radio, so I quit." Instead, she taught herself how to play guitar with a Pete Seeger instruction book. Receiving her primary and secondary education in the time before art and music were a part of the curriculum, Mitchell found little to interest her academically, and thus was a mediocre student. She centered her efforts in school, however, on extracurricular activities. Mitchell explained to Small: "I was always the school artist. . . . I did the backdrops for plays, [and] illustrated the yearbook and the school newspaper."

After graduating from high school, Mitchell enrolled in the Alberta College of Art in Calgary with the aim of studying commercial art. Bored with her classes, she began to concentrate more on her musical talent, and after about a year, left to try her luck as a folksinger in Toronto, Ontario. When Mitchell arrived there, she did not have a musician's union card, so she worked in a department store to earn the union dues. Eventually, however, Mitchell became well known in Toronto's folk circles, playing at clubs like the Riverboat. At this time she met Chuck Mitchell, a folk singer from Detroit, Michigan. They married shortly after they met—one account claims it was only thirty-six hours—and moved to Detroit. Though Mitchell took her stage name from a derivative of her middle name and her husband's surname, the marriage did not last long, and after about a year she left him and moved to New York City.

Spark. On *Spark,* Mitchell recorded a version of the jazz classic made famous by singer Annie Ross, "Twisted," and the rock-influenced "Raised on Robbery." Also, that album marked the first project on which she used her longtime jazz backup group, the L.A. Express. She continued her jazz experimentation with 1975's *The Hissing of Summer Lawns,* which, though rated the worst album of the year by *Rolling Stone* magazine, according to Small, became a gold record and has been reassessed in the light of praise from others in the musical field. In 1979, Mitchell released *Mingus,* a collaboration with jazz artist Charles Mingus that she worked on with him just before he died of Lou Gehrig's disease. Featuring lyrics Mitchell wrote to Mingus's music, the album was not a critical or popular success. As Mitchell told Small: "It cost me plenty. It put me in a no-man's land where radio stations couldn't pin me down. But," she asserted, "if I had to do it over again, I would."

During the earlier years of her career, Mitchell had been the subject of much press gossip concerning

> *Joni Mitchell is also a talented painter; she adorns her album covers with her own brushwork, and in 1988 exhibited her paintings in Tokyo, Japan.*

her affairs with fellow musicians, including Jackson Browne, James Taylor, and Graham Nash and David Crosby of the group Crosby, Stills, and Nash. The press "portrayed me as this heartbreaker," Mitchell revealed to Small. She put an end to this kind of speculation, however, in 1982, when she married her second husband, bass player Larry Klein. Klein has played for Mitchell on some of her albums, including *Dog Eat Dog.* Released on Geffen records in 1985, *Dog Eat Dog* was yet another turning point for Mitchell. Widely considered her most political album, it is rock-oriented and features protest songs which "rail against greed, TV evangelism and the far right," according to Nicholas Jennings in *Maclean's.* Jennings, however, preferred Mitchell's 1988 *Chalk Mark in a Rain Storm,* which he labeled "her best album in years. . . . Although Mitchell's anger [displayed in *Dog Eat Dog*] is muted on *Chalk Mark in a Rain Storm,* her resolve remains strong."

Mitchell struggled for about a year and a half in a New York folk scene clogged with acts until she was discovered by Reprise records. In 1968, she put out *Joni Mitchell,* her first album, later retitled *Song to a Seagull.* The work garnered mixed reviews, but Mitchell's next album, *Clouds,* released in 1969, featured her unique chording style and the song "Both Sides, Now." Though the single was a much bigger hit for fellow folk songstress Judy Collins, who released a cover version, it won Mitchell a reputation as a songwriter, and the album it came from won Mitchell a Grammy.

Tiring of city life, Mitchell moved to California and settled in Laurel Canyon, near Los Angeles. There she was inspired to write the material for her third album, 1970's *Ladies of the Canyon,* which included "Big Yellow Taxi." *Canyon* also included "Woodstock," celebrating the 1969 rock music festival of the same name, and was well-received by music critics. Hailed for her major effort in *Canyon,* Mitchell was lauded by Don Heckman in the *New York Times:* "Her crystal clear imagery is as shining bright as ever, and her melodies, if anything, seem to be improving."

After Mitchell followed up *Canyon* with 1971's *Blue,* she moved to Asylum records to record *For the Roses,* which featured "Turn Me On (I'm a Radio)." The song has a country sound, and Mitchell continued her branching into different musical fields on 1974's *Court and*

Selected discography

LPs

Joni Mitchell (includes "I Had a King," "Michael From the Mountains," "Nathan La Freneer," and "Cactus Tree"), later retitled *Song to a Seagull,* Reprise, 1968.

Clouds (includes "Both Sides, Now," "Chelsea Morning," and "The Fiddle and the Drum"), Reprise, 1969.

Ladies of the Canyon (includes "Big Yellow Taxi," "The Circle Game," and "Woodstock"), Reprise, 1970.

Blue (includes "The Last Time I Saw Richard" and "A Case of You"), Reprise, 1971.

For the Roses (includes "Turn Me On (I'm a Radio)," "Woman of Heart and Fire," "See You Sometime," and "Lesson in Survival"), Asylum, 1972.

Court and Spark (includes "Twisted," "Help Me," "Raised on Robbery," "The Same Situation," "Car on a Hill," and "Free Man in Paris"), Asylum, 1974.

Miles of Aisles (live; includes "The Last Time I Saw Richard," "Carey," and "Big Yellow Taxi"), Asylum, 1975.

The Hissing of Summer Lawns (includes "Harry's House" and "The Jungle Line"), Asylum, 1975.

Hejira, Asylum, 1976.

Don Juan's Reckless Daughter, Asylum, 1977.

Mingus, Asylum, 1979.

Shadows and Light (live), Asylum, 1980.

Dog Eat Dog, Geffen, 1985.

Chalk Mark in a Rain Storm (includes "My Secret Place," "Dancin' Clown," "Snakes and Ladders," "Cool Water," "Number One," and "Lakota"), Geffen, 1988.

Sources

down beat, September 6, 1979.

Maclean's, April 4, 1988.

Newsweek, November 4, 1985.

New York Times, April 15, 1970.

People, December 16, 1985.

—*Elizabeth Thomas*

Rick Nelson

Singer, songwriter, guitarist

Rick Nelson was the singer and actor for whom the phrase "teen idol" was coined, according to Kent Demaret in *People* magazine. Using his family's television show, "The Adventures of Ozzie and Harriet" as a launching pad for his musical career, Nelson had many hit records, including "Poor Little Fool," "Travelin' Man," and "Hello, Mary Lou," throughout the late 1950s and early 1960s. But despite his wholesome good looks and television star status, most music critics agree that Nelson was more than a manufactured pretty face to be lumped with the likes of Fabian and Frankie Avalon. Demaret quoted rock critic David Hinkley as saying that "'the deceptively clean-cut kid named Ricky Nelson' helped 'smuggle rock and roll into American living rooms,'" and rock historian Greg Shaw as declaring, "Of all the Hollywood teen idols, only one can be said to have any claim to lasting importance—Ricky Nelson." On the occasion of Nelson's 1985 death in a plane crash, fellow rock musician John Fogerty (formerly of Creedence Clearwater Revival) offered to David Fricke in *Rolling Stone* the following tribute: "He was Hollywood, but the records he made were totally legitimate rockabilly, as good as any of the best stuff from [early country-rock recording company] Sun Records."

Born Eric Hilliard Nelson on May 8, 1940, in Teaneck, New Jersey, Rick got his start in the entertainment field when he first appeared on his parents' radio program in 1948. His father and mother, Ozzie and Harriet Nelson, had had a family show on the radio previous to that, but until 1949 other children had played the parts of Rick and his older brother, David. When "The Adventures of Ozzie and Harriet" moved to television in 1952, the youngest Nelson helped make the program one of the most popular early sitcoms. To the American television audience, "Ricky was the darling gnome next door, wolfing down chocolate malts and diligently minding his p's and q's," according to Fricke. But as Rick grew older, he became interested in the rockabilly music being produced on the Sun Records label by artists like Carl Perkins and Jerry Lee Lewis. Legend has it that a girlfriend's enthusiasm for the swivel-hipped rocker Elvis Presley led Nelson to boast that he, too, was going to make a record; at any rate, that was the way the situation was presented on the 1957 "Ozzie and Harriet" episode on which the aspiring singer made his musical debut.

After Nelson performed on national television the first song he recorded—a cover version of rock pioneer Fats Domino's "I'm Walkin'"—the single sold a million copies in one week. Following a couple more releases on the Verve label, Nelson signed with Imperial—Domino's label—and proceeded to turn out hit after hit. Ozzie Nelson, closely involved in his son's new career, made a point of showcasing most of Rick's records on

Full name, Eric Hilliard Nelson; born May 8, 1940, in Teaneck, N.J.; died in an airplane crash, December 31, 1985, near De Kalb, Tex.; son of Oswald "Ozzie" George (a musician, screenwriter, director, producer, and actor) and Harriet (a singer and actress; maiden name, Hilliard) Nelson; married Kristin Harmon (an actress), April 20, 1963 (divorced, 1982); children: Tracy Kristine, Gunnar Eric and Matthew Gray (twins), Sam Hilliard.

Actor on parents' radio program, "The Adventures of Ozzie and Harriet," 1948-52, and on television version of the show, 1952-66; recording artist and concert performer, 1957-85; actor in feature films, including *The Story of Three Lovers*, *The Wackiest Ship in the Army*, and *Rio Bravo*.

the television series. In effect, as Demaret pointed out, the promotion tactic made Rick Nelson "the first rock-video star." "The Adventures of Ozzie and Harriet" ran until 1966; by the time it went off the air Nelson had earned at least nine gold records and sold over thirty-five million copies of his hits. Some of the most memorable of these are 1957's "Be-Bop Baby" and "Stood Up," 1958's "Lonesome Town," 1959's "Never Be Anyone Else But You" and "It's Late," 1962's "It's Up to You" and the autobiographical "Teenage Idol," and 1963's "Fools Rush In."

By the end of his family's television show, Nelson, like many other American rock and roll artists who began their careers in the 1950s, found his popularity being eclipsed by British acts like the Beatles. No longer making hit records and out of an acting job, he decided to pursue his longtime interest in country music. Nelson made a few country albums and scored a minor chart hit with the song "You Just Can't Quit." Then he heard folk singer Bob Dylan's album excursion into country, *Nashville Skyline,* and was inspired to form a country-rock group, the Stone Canyon Band. With them, Nelson released *Rudy the Fifth* in 1969 and scored another minor hit with a remake of Dylan's "She Belongs to Me." Though Nelson himself did not make a major impact with the music he played during this period, the work was a major influence on later rock groups such as the Eagles and Fleetwood Mac.

Nelson's last and best-selling hit record was the result of an unpleasant experience for him. In 1971 he was invited to play an oldies concert in New York City's Madison Square Garden. In this period of his life Nelson usually scorned nostalgic celebrations of the early rock and roll that brought him success, but the prestige attached to a Madison Square Garden performance overcame his reluctance. Though he played a few old favorites, he interspersed new material among them, and was booed by the audience. Deeply hurt, Nelson protested his treatment in his 1972 single, "Garden Party." As quoted by Fricke, the song contained the disdainful lines: "If you gotta play at garden parties/ I wish you a lotta luck/ But if memories were all I sang/ I'd rather drive a truck." Ironically, the promoter of the Madison Square Garden concert, Richard Nader, told Fricke that Nelson had misinterpreted the crowd's re-

> *"The deceptively clean-cut kid named Ricky Nelson helped smuggle rock and roll into American living rooms."*

action: "Coincidentally . . . in the top tier there were some rowdies. The cops were moving them out, and the people were booing the cops. . . . Rick thought the booing was for him."

"Nelson had apparently come to terms with his past," according to Michael Goldberg in *Rolling Stone,* and was performing in rock and roll revival concerts prior to his death. His last performance was at a friend's night club in Guntersville, Alabama, and he was en route to another concert in Dallas, Texas, when his private plane crashed near De Kalb, Texas, due to a heater fire.

Selected discography

Major single releases

"I'm Walkin'," Verve, 1957.
"A Teenager's Romance," Verve, 1957.
"You're My One and Only Love," Verve, 1957.
"Be-Bop Baby," Imperial, 1957.
"Have I told You Lately That I Love You?" Imperial, 1957.
"Stood Up," Imperial, 1957.
"Waitin' In School," Imperial, 1957.
"My Bucket's Got a Hole in It," Imperial, 1958.
"Believe What You Say," Imperial, 1958.
"Poor Little Fool," Imperial, 1958.
"I Got a Feeling," Imperial, 1958.
"Lonesome Town," Imperial, 1958.
"Never Be Anyone Else But You," Imperial, 1959.
"It's Late," Imperial, 1959.
"Just a Little Too Much," Imperial, 1959.

"Sweeter Than You," Imperial, 1959.
"I Wanna Be Loved," Imperial, 1959.
"Mighty Good," Imperial, 1959.
"Young Emotions," Imperial, 1960.
"I'm Not Afraid," Imperial, 1960.
"Yes, Sir, That's My Baby," Imperial, 1960.
"You Are the Only One," Imperial, 1961.
"Travelin' Man," Imperial, 1961.
"Hello, Mary Lou," Imperial, 1961.
"A Wonder Like You," Imperial, 1961.
"Everlovin'," Imperial, 1961.
"Young World," Imperial, 1962.
"Teenage Idol," Imperial, 1962.
"It's Up to You," Imperial, 1962.
"That's All," Imperial, 1963.
"Old Enough to Love," Imperial, 1963.
"Today's Teardrops," Imperial, 1963.
"You Don't Love Me Any More," Decca, 1963.
"I Got a Woman," Decca, 1963.
"String Along," Decca, 1963.
"Fools Rush In," Decca, 1963.
"For You," Decca, 1963.
"Congratulations," Imperial, 1964.
"The Very Thought of You," Decca, 1964.
"There's Nothing I Can Say," Decca, 1964.
"A Happy Guy," Decca, 1964.
"Mean Old World," Decca, 1965.
"You Just Can't Quit," Decca, 1967.

"She Belongs to Me," Decca, 1969.
"Easy to Be Free," Decca, 1970.
"Garden Party," MCA, 1972.
"Palace Guard," MCA, 1973.

LPs

For You, Decca, 1963.
Every Thought of You, Decca, 1964.
Spotlight on Rick, Decca, 1965.
Best Always, Decca, 1965.
Love and Kisses, Decca, 1966.
Bright Lights, Decca, 1966.
Country Fever, Decca, 1967.
Another Side of Rick, Decca, 1968.
Rudy the Fifth, Decca, 1969.
Garden Party, MCA, 1972.
All My Best, 1985.

Sources

Newsweek, January 13, 1986.
People, January 20, 1986.
Rolling Stone, February 13, 1986.
Time, January 13, 1986.

—*Elizabeth Thomas*

Wayne Newton

Singer

"Pound for pound, day for day, Wayne Newton is the highest-paid cabaret entertainer ever," writes Robert Windeler in *People* magazine. Newton has graced the stages of Las Vegas resort casinos for more than twenty years, performing two high-energy shows per night, seven nights a week, as many as forty weeks per year. His popularity in the nightclub setting is unprecedented; not even Johnny Carson or Frank Sinatra can command the high fees and lengthy engagement contracts that have become commonplace for him. "Nostalgia fans remember Newton as a pudgy, baby-faced, adenoidal tenor with three big hits: 'Heart,' 'Danke Schoen,' and 'Red Roses for a Blue Lady,'" notes Betsy Carter in *Newsweek*. "Today, Newton has . . . cultivated a silky baritone and outfitted himself in sequined cowboy suits—an image that has earned him the Las Vegas billing of 'The Midnight Idol.'. . . His mellow blend of pop, rhythm-and-blues, country and rock wins no fewer than five ovations each night from the predominantly middle-aged, Middle American audience." *Esquire* contributor Ron Rosenbaum observes that Newton "has built an entertainment empire out of what was once a lounge act, transformed himself into a Tom Jones-type sex symbol, [and] become the highest-grossing entertainer in Las Vegas history" because he "has somehow captured and concentrated, become an emblem of, the essence of *Vegasness*."

Wayne Newton was born in 1942 in the Virginia seaport town of Norfolk. Both of his parents were half American Indian—his father Powhatan, his mother Cherokee. When Newton was still young his family moved to the Shenandoah Valley, just west of Norfolk. There, in the town of Roanoke, he began a singing career at the age of five. "By the time I was 6 I knew exactly what I wanted to do with my life," Newton told *People*. Sometimes alone and sometimes with his brother Jerry, Newton performed on the local radio stations, quickly becoming a minor celebrity.

When Newton was ten, his family moved again, this time to Phoenix, Arizona. His parents thought the desert climate would help his bronchial asthma, and they were proven correct. Newton had his own radio show in Phoenix as a teenager, and at sixteen he dropped out of high school to perform in lounges with his older brother. They began at the Fremont Hotel. According to Windeler, "Wayne was too young to go through the Fremont's front door, much less into the casino. In the lounge, however, the Newtons were an instant hit. Their two-week contract stretched to 51. They abandoned their Spartan digs in a fleabag motel for an apartment, then a house."

The brothers realized that lounge singing could be-

For the Record. . .

Born April 3, 1942, in Norfolk, Va.; son of Patrick (an automobile mechanic) and Evelyn (Smith) Newton; married Elaine Okamura (a flight attendant), 1966; children: Erin.

Singer, 1947—. With brother Jerry, singer for radio stations in Roanoke, Va. and Phoenix, Ariz., 1947-58; lounge singer in Las Vegas, Nev., and New York, N.Y., 1958-71; solo performer, principally in Las Vegas, 1971—. Has staged shows at the Sands, Caesar's Palace, Desert Inn, Flamingo, Frontier Hotel, Harrah's, the Aladdin, and Tamiment International Resort. Earned first number one hit, "Danke Schoen," 1963.

Has entertained in numerous nightclubs in the United States and abroad; sang for U.S. troops in Vietnam, 1966, and for troops in Beirut, Lebanon. Television appearances include "Red, White & Wow," "A Christmas Card," and "North and South: Book II," 1986.

Addresses: *Office*—Flying Eagle, Inc., 3180 S. Highland Dr., Suite 1, Las Vegas, Nev. 89109-1042. *Other*— 6629 S. Pecos, Las Vegas, Nev. 89120.

come a dead-end street, so in 1963 they took their show on the road, opening for Sophie Tucker and Jayne Mansfield. While they were performing at the prestigious Copacabana Lounge in New York City, the Newtons met Bobby Darin, who offered to produce some records with Wayne. Newton scored a million-selling hit with "Danke Schoen" and propelled that success into top bookings in New York and Las Vegas. Both "Danke Schoen" and his other big single, "Red Roses for a Blue Lady," were performed in "an eerie, post-pubescent soprano," to quote Windeler, marking Newton as an adolescent singer even after he reached twenty-one.

Two factors helped to change Newton's image from that of a pleasant teen to that of a stage idol. First, he disbanded his partnership with his brother and began to perform solo. Second, he became a favorite of the aging Howard Hughes, who saw to it that Newton always had the best Las Vegas bookings. "For Wayne," writes Windeler, "the split with his brother was a kind of watershed, a declaration of professional independence that coincided with a hard-won sense of personal freedom. . . . With Jerry gone, Wayne was his own man at last and anxious to prove it. Having already sweated off his baby fat, he scaled his voice down to a plausible tenor . . . clipped off his ducktail and pompadour and laid in a flamboyant new wardrobe." He also settled into the Las Vegas showrooms like no one had ever done

before, selling out night after night and eventually earning one million dollars per month.

Although Newton denies that he is dependent upon Las Vegas for his fame, the fact remains that town and performer are inextricably entwined. Rosenbaum has analyzed the element that contributes to Newton's domination of the nightclub stage. "At the heart of Wayne's mesmeric mastery over his audience is the notion of Suspending the Rules," Rosenbaum writes. ". . .From the very opening minutes of his act Wayne begins playing on the expectation of something special happening, the dream that tonight some magic suspension of the rules is in the offing—the ultimate unpurchasable Vegas experience. . . . Having established the illusion that there's something extremely special going on tonight, some magical show-biz chemistry between himself and his audience, unique to this evening, unique perhaps to his three decades in show business, something so great that he's ready to keep singing till dawn or till his throat gives out, he then proceeds to Step

---

Wayne Newton "has somehow captured and concentrated, become an emblem of, the essence of Vegasness."

Three: creating the illusion that the rules have *already* been violated. . . . Everyone leaves The Show feeling totally satisfied, thinking how hip, how simpatico, how special the whole evening was; how they've been present at one of those rare moments when the rules went by the board; how Wayne drove himself past his own limits, knocking himself out for them. . . . It take a shrewd and talented showman to pull off an illusion of this sort night after night, show after show."

This is not to suggest, however, that Newton's show is founded solely on deception and hype. Newton is not only extremely sensitive to his audience, he is also an able musician who can play eleven instruments—all by ear—and who is equally at home singing pop, country, folk, and big band standards in his three-octave range. In addition, he takes full responsibility for song selection, costumes, lighting, and staging. "There isn't anything up there onstage that I wasn't totally involved in," Newton told *People*. "I have to take all of the blame and some of the credit. People may dislike Wayne Newton, but they're never gonna be able to say Wayne Newton didn't work hard."

In his spare time, Newton raises Arabian horses and flies light airplanes. He lives outside Las Vegas on a fifty-two acre ranch called Casa De Shenandoah with his daughter, Erin. For a time he owned the Aladdin Casino, but he sold his interest when adverse—and unproven—publicity linked him to organized crime. Finding his reputation sullied by the unsubstantiated charges, Newton sued NBC Television in 1986 and eventually won a settlement. He has since concentrated on performing, and his is still the most coveted ticket in Las Vegas. "I have to entertain," Newton told *People*. "If nobody paid me, I'd do it on a street corner."

Selected discography

Best of Wayne Newton, Capitol.

Sources

Esquire, August, 1982.
Newsweek, January 12, 1976; June 2, 1980.
People, April 30, 1979; November 17, 1986.

—Anne Janette Johnson

Stevie Nicks

Singer, songwriter

S tevie Nicks first came to the attention of rock and pop audiences when she and Lindsey Buckingham joined the already established band Fleetwood Mac in 1975. Her singing and songwriting were responsible for many of the hit singles that brought Fleetwood Mac supergroup status in the late 1970s, including "Rhiannon" and "Dreams." Though Nicks has continued as a productive member of the band, she has also released several successful solo albums, from 1981's *Bella Donna* to 1989's *The Other Side of the Mirror.* She has had smash duets such as "Whenever I Call You Friend" with Kenny Loggins and "Stop Dragging My Heart Around" with Tom Petty, and popular solo hits, including "Stand Back," "Talk to Me," and "Rooms on Fire."

Nicks was born May 26, 1948, in Phoenix, Arizona. Her father's stints as an executive with various corporations decreed that she move many times in her childhood and adolescence, living in the states of New Mexico, Texas, Utah, and California. According to Timothy White in his 1984 book *Rock Stars,* Nicks obtained her introduction to music from her eccentric grandfather, Aaron Jess Nicks, a failed country singer. He taught Stevie the female parts in some old call-and-response country standards well before her fifth birthday, and took her with him to perform in gin mills. Later, in her sophomore year at a Los Angeles, California, high school, Nicks sang with a vocal group modeled on the Mamas and Papas, called Changing Times. But another one of her father's moves took her to California's San Francisco Bay area to complete her secondary education.

One of Nicks's fellow students in her new high school was Lindsey Buckingham. Like Nicks, he was a singer and musician and had already begun to write songs; the two were drawn to one another. Around 1968, after Nicks left San Jose State College without earning a degree, she and Buckingham joined a San Francisco acid rock group named Fritz. By that time the pair was living together, as well as collaborating musically. Nicks told interviewer Jon Pareles in *Mademoiselle* that Buckingham's musical arrangements gave her compositions an extra boost: "I need somebody to help me change what I write from a little classical minuet, for piano and lady singer, into a song—I need somebody to put the power into it. Lindsey spoiled me. . . . I didn't have to explain much to him—I'd just have to play a song once, and I'd never have to play it again."

Fritz broke up around 1971, after having first relocated to Los Angeles. Nicks and Buckingham remained there and continued their creative efforts as a duo. They landed a recording contract with Polydor Records, and released one album in 1972, appropriately titled *Buckingham-Nicks.* The disc did not do well, and Nicks had to work—as a dental assistant for one day, as a waitress for longer stints—to support herself and Buckingham. As she recalled for Pareles, "Lindsey wasn't quite so willing to go out and work anywhere. So I figured it was better for him to stay home and practice, because he plays so beautifully, and I'd go out and make the money."

Meanwhile, Fleetwood Mac underwent yet another major membership change, and were looking for new musicians. The group was also looking for a new recording studio, and they happened upon the one where Nicks and Buckingham had recorded their album. The studio played *Buckingham-Nicks* for Fleetwood Mac as an example of their finished work, and the band's remaining members, Mick Fleetwood, and Christine and John McVie, were as much impressed with the artists as with the production. Nicks and Buckingham were contacted, and the duo agreed to become a part of Fleetwood Mac.

Nicks's first hit with the group, "Rhiannon," which White lauded as "a surging, mesmerizing song about a Welsh witch," is exemplary of the other-worldly, supernatural quality of many of her compositions. As Pareles reported, "she believes she has a guardian angel; she believes her soul has been around for three million years. And she is fascinated by all sorts of mystical ideas and . . . wondrous coincidences." Banks concurred: "Most of us would like a temporary respite from life's serrated edges, and a few of us have secret gardens of the imagination into which we occasionally steal. The dif-

ference between Stevie Nicks and the rest of the world is that, given the choice, she usually opts for never-never land—and she brings along a lunch pail and a pup tent." Nicks has been criticized, however, for her music's mysticism; for instance, Mark Coleman in his *Rolling Stone* review of *Rock a Little,* Nicks's third solo album, judged that "when she starts setting her secrets free, weaving apocryphal situations and creating moony, enigmatic characters, the going gets a bit thick." But he conceded: "Nicks can still take an unassuming little rock song and polish it into a gem."

The combination of Nicks, Buckingham, Fleetwood, and the McVies proved the catalyst for Fleetwood Mac to quickly achieve the popularity that had heretofore eluded the band. But success brought problems for Nicks. The strain of constant touring broke up her longtime relationship with Buckingham, along with the marriage of the McVies, and also pushed Nicks's throat past the breaking point. She occasionally lost her voice

> "The difference between Stevie Nicks and the rest of the world is that, given the choice, she usually opts for never-never land—and she brings along a lunch pail and a pup tent."

onstage, causing the group's concerts to receive bad press reviews.

With the help of a specialist, however, Nicks resolved her vocal problems, and despite the death of two love relationships, Fleetwood Mac remained intact and turned its turbulent emotions into the best-selling album, *Rumours.* Many of the record's hits, including Nicks's "Dreams," were autobiographical accounts of the breakups. The group's follow-up album, *Tusk,* was not as successful, but Nicks scored a hit on it with the melodic "Sara"—a hit that later embroiled her in controversy when a woman from Grand Rapids, Michigan, claimed that she herself had written it and sent it to Warner Brothers, Fleetwood Mac's recording company. The suit was eventually withdrawn by the woman's lawyers, who came to believe Nicks had indeed written it herself—demo tapes of the song, dated months previous to the time the woman said she had sent her lyrics to Warner Brothers, confirmed the fact.

Though Nicks was not inclined to leave Fleetwood Mac,

which Pareles compared to "a loving extended family," she did turn her attention to solo projects with *Bella Donna* in 1981. Nicks explained to Pareles: "I had to learn to stand up and lead. I had to learn to do this alone." Her decision proved a good one; not only did *Bella Donna* bring forth her first solo hit, "Edge of Seventeen," but her three other solo albums have brought her even more acclaim and popularity with listeners. And Nicks is grateful to her fans. "When I see people singing along to one of my songs," she confided to Pareles, "I want to go out and hug them. I have trouble remembering the words myself—and they know them all!"

Selected discography

With Lindsey Buckingham

Buckingham-Nicks, Polydor, 1972.

With Fleetwood Mac; on Warner Bros. Records

Fleetwood Mac (includes "Rhiannon" and "Landslide"), 1975.

Rumours (includes "Dreams" and "Gold Dust Woman"), 1977.
Tusk (includes "Sara"), 1979.
Mirage (includes "Gypsy"), 1982.

Solo LPs; on Modern Records

Bella Donna (includes "Edge of Seventeen," "Stop Dragging My Heart Around," and "Leather and Lace"), 1981.
Wild Heart (includes "Stand Back" and "If Anyone Falls"), 1983.
Rock a Little (includes "Talk to Me" and "I Can't Wait"), 1985.
The Other Side of the Mirror (includes "Rooms on Fire"), 1989.

Sources

Books

White, Timothy, *Rock Stars,* Stewart, Tabori & Chang, 1984.

Periodicals

Mademoiselle, August, 1982.
Rolling Stone, January 30, 1986.

—Elizabeth Thomas

Ted Nugent

Guitarist, songwriter, singer

Ted Nugent was born just outside of Detroit, Michigan, in 1949. He received his first musical instrument at the age of nine after his aunt, an airline stewardess, sent him an acoustic guitar that had been left on a flight unclaimed. He took formal lessons for a few years to learn theory and proper technique and by the time he was just thirteen years old his first band, the Lourds, had opened for the Supremes and the Beau Brummels at Cobo Hall. "The Lourds played unbefore-heard-of kick-ass rock and roll," Nugent told Tom Vickers of *Rolling Stone.* "If you weren't into it it might send you to nausea city."

Unfortunately the band lasted only until Nugent's family moved to Chicago when he was sixteen. With a former Army staff sargeant for a father, Nugent was raised in a very strict family structure and wasted little time in forming his next group (The Amboy Dukes, in 1965) and hitting the road after high school. "I went after my success with a vengeance," he told *Rolling Stone.* In 1967 Nugent moved the group back to Detroit, where they recorded a minor midwest hit, "Baby Please Don't Go."

That same year they broke the national charts with their psychedelic onslaught, "Journey to the Center of the Mind," which reached number 8. Amazingly, Nugent received no money from the song and the group spent their entire ten years bouncing between labels (Polydor, Discreet, and Mainstream) and dealing with poor management. They released nearly a dozen albums of pioneering heavy metal: "Listening to Amboy Dukes' albums was like going into hand-to-hand combat with your speakers," wrote Billy Altman in *Rolling Stone.*

The group was fueled by Nugent's high-powered licks that spewed forth from his Gibson Byrdland guitar. Normally used as a jazz instrument, Nugent cranked the hollowbody to maximum volume, which caused a tremendous amount of feedback. Although he uses other guitars today (Les Pauls and Paul Reed Smith solidbodies), he first discovered the Byrdland's potential when he heard Jim McCarty using one with Mitch Ryder and the Detroit Wheels in 1964. "[McCarty] was so sensational that I was bent on playing it," Nugent told Steve Rosen in *Guitar Player.* "I was also bent on playing loud. To do that you either have to elimate the feedback characteristics—by buying a different guitar—or learn to control it. I started putting the feedback to good use."

Initially influenced by Wayne Cochran, Duane Eddy, Lonnie Mack, Keith Richards, and Jimi Hendrix, he was soon creating his own unique voice on the guitar by manipulating the toggle switch and volume knobs for effects, playing with his teeth, bending the strings behind the bridge to create vibrato and playing with more speed and volume (he's 85% deaf in his left ear) than anyone before him. "[Nugent's] as fast, raunchy, and unrelentless as any heavy metallic glitterite around," stated Don Menn in *Guitar Player.* "Some of his blues-rock riffs could have melted a bazooka."

Nugent not only pushed his guitar playing, but his onstage antics as well, to the limit. His outrageous wardrobe and attitude soon earned him the title of "Motor City Madman." An avid hunter (he's a staunch member of the NRA) and outdoorsman, his stage apparel consists of a loincloth, deerskin, feathers, necklasses made out of animal teeth, headbands, and fringe boots. With his wild hair looking like a lion's mane, Nugent has been known to jump off huge stacks of amplifiers with bow and arrow in hand, daring anyone to challenge his presence. Another theatric featured excrutiatingly high volumes aimed at breaking glass balls; it sometimes failed and the balls had to be shot out by a roadie with a BB gun.

Nugent labels this entire persona "gonzo," and it embodies just about every aspect of his life. "My philosophy is two eyes for an eye," he declared to Charles M. Young in *Rolling Stone.* He has abhored drugs ever since he saw what happened to the late Jimi Hendrix (the two used to jam together) and he has even fired band members for drug use. Nugent's ego has also earned him noteriety in the past for statements like "Sometimes I ask myself—have I the right to be this good?," to *Guitar Player*'s Tom Wheeler. His obsessions with himself, hunting, and sex have pretty much dominated his song themes and clever titles.

Just prior to the Dukes' break-up Nugent began stag-

ing guitar duels with veteran metalheads like Frank Marino of Mahogany Rush, Wayne Kramer from the MC5, and Mike Pinera of Iron Butterfly and Blues Image. These six-string wars helped further Nugent's macho image as he usually outplayed or outstaged those who tried to steal the spotlight from him. In 1975 he decided to go solo, signing with Epic and releasing his self-titled debut. *Ted Nugent* hit its listeners with hard-driving selections, including "Motor City Madhouse," "Just What the Doctor Ordered," and "Stranglehold." Nugent's live shows were just as merciless, leaving audiences with a serious case of shell shock "roughly akin to pressing a stethoscope to the roaring engine of a trail bike," reported Young in *Rolling Stone.*

Nugent's next two albums, *Free For All* and *Cat Scratch Fever* (note Jeff Beck's influence on the bolero "Homebound"), featured more of the same obnoxious lyrics and blazing fretwork. An in-concert performance was captured on 1977's *Double Live Gonzo* and by the next year Nugent fronted the top-grossing band in North

> *"[Nugent's] as fast, raunchy, and unrelentless as any heavy metallic glitterite around. Some of his bluesrock riffs could have melted a bazooka."*

America. In March of 1978 he headlined the California Jam II gig at the Ontario Motor Speedway in front of 250,000 screaming fans. With the addition of *Weekend Warriors,* Nugent's first five Epic LPs had gone platinum. His formula was simple, according to Wheeler in *Guitar Player:* "Less chord changes than Alice Cooper; more chord changes than Black Sabbath; sounds best loud."

For the next six years though, Nugent's popularity began to dwindle. He continued to release four more albums, but the generation that had grown up on his style had done just that; grown up. And the younger crowd was now into a sound, introduced by Eddie Van Halen, that utilized fingerboard tapping and extreme wang-bar tactics to create dive-bombing crashes. But Nugent explained his slump to Steve Gett in *Guitar For The Practicing Musician:* "Because I've got a big mouth; because I'm so exuberant and so easy-going, and I'm having so much fun that it intimidates them."

By 1984, however, Nugent had gotten the hint (and a

new label) and joined the club with *Penetrator* and 1986's *Little Miss Dangerous,* which showed he could compete with his contemporaries. He had previously employed singers to cover the vocals while occassionally belting out a song or two himself. But on his 1988 release, *If You Can't Lick 'Em . . . Lick 'Em,* Nugent handled all the lead vocals. Although he has not regained his former position in the heavy metal hierarchy, he is still indeed a dedicated guitarist to be reckoned with. "All I can say is that if I didn't have the ulterior diversions, with my hunting, my outdoor activities and my family, I would stay on the road 360 days a year," he told Gett. I've never felt anything less than outrageous enthusiasm for my music."

Selected discography

Solo LPs

Ted Nugent, Epic, 1975.
Free For All, Epic, 1976.
Cat Scratch Fever, Epic, 1977.
Double Live Gonzo, Epic, 1977.
Weekend Warriors, Epic, 1978.
State of Shock, Epic, 1979
Scream Dream, Epic, 1980.
Great Gonzos/The Best of Ted Nugent, Epic, 1981.
Intensities in Ten Cities, 1981, CBS.
Penetrator, Atlantic, 1984.
Little Miss Dangerous, Atlantic, 1986.
If You Can't Lick 'Em . . . Lick 'Em, Atlantic, 1988.

With the Amboy Dukes

Ted Nugent and the Amboy Dukes, Mainstream, 1968.

Journey to the Center of the Mind, Mainstream, 1968.
Marriage on the Rocks—Rock Bottom, Polydor, 1970.
Survival of the Fittest, Polydor, 1974.
Call of the Wild, Discreet, 1974.
Tooth, Fang, and Claw, Discreet, 1975.
Journeys and Migrations (double reissue), Mainstream, 1975.
Dr. Slingshot (compilation), Mainstream, 1975.

Sources

Books

Christgau, Robert, *Christgau's Record Guide,* Ticknor & Fields, 1981.
The Illustrated Encyclopedia of Rock, compiled by Nick Logan and Bob Woffinden, Harmony, 1977.
The Rolling Stone Record Guide, edited by Dave Marsh and John Swenson, Random House/Rolling Stone Press, 1979.

Periodicals

Guitar for the Practicing Musician, January, 1986.
Guitar Player, December, 1975; November, 1976; March, 1977; December, 1977; August, 1979; September, 1980; May, 1984; June, 1988.
Guitar World, March, 1987; July, 1988.
Rolling Stone, April 8, 1976; November 18, 1976; July 28, 1977; August 25, 1977; March 23, 1978; January 11, 1979; March 8, 1979; March 19, 1981.

—Calen D. Stone

Roy Orbison

Singer, songwriter

Roy Orbison's "was a voice like no other ever heard in rock—silky, soaring, tender, gritty, haunted with pain. And durable," eulogized Jim Jerome of *People* magazine. Orbison, the singer and songwriter responsible for rock and roll classics such as "Only the Lonely," "Crying," "In Dreams," and "Oh, Pretty Woman," began his career with Sun Records of Memphis, Tennessee, along with other rock greats Elvis Presley and Jerry Lee Lewis. He had a string of hit singles that lasted from the late 1950s to the early 1960s before the combined effects of the British rock invasion and a series of personal tragedies brought about a decline in his career. Orbison kept performing on stage, however, and in the late 1970s and early 1980s his music began resurfacing in remakes by artists as varied as Linda Ronstadt, Don McLean, and Van Halen. In 1980 he had a country hit with duet partner Emmylou Harris, "That Loving You Feeling Again"; the performance won the pair a Grammy Award. In 1986, the use of Orbison's eerily passionate "In Dreams" in the film "Blue Velvet" refocused attention on his music. At the time of his death from a heart attack at the age of fifty-two, Orbison was again on the charts as a member of the Traveling Wilburys, and had an album of his own, *Mystery Girl,* ready for release.

Orbison was born April 23, 1936, in Vernon, Texas. His family soon moved to Wink, Texas, where he spent most of his youth. Like many of the South's rock pioneers, Orbison's earliest musical influences came from the sounds of country and gospel music; his intent was to become a country music performer. His father, who worked on oil rigs, taught him to play guitar when he was six years old. By the time Orbison was attending high school, he was the leader of the Wink Westerners, his own country group, and had his own show on a local radio station.

While attending North Texas State University, Orbison became acquainted with another fledgling singer, Pat Boone, who was also a student there. Boone encouraged him to continue with his musical efforts, and Orbison formed another band, with which he soon landed a television show in Midland, Texas. Through his television work and other musical activities, Orbison came into contact with country-rock artist Johnny Cash, who urged him to send a demonstration tape of his music to Sam Phillips, the head of Sun Records. Despite his primary interest in the mainstream country genre, Orbison sent Phillips the rock-oriented "Oooby Dooby," because he thought it meshed better with the kind of songs Sun was producing at the time. Phillips liked what he heard, and in 1956, "Oooby Dooby" became Orbison's first hit.

But Orbison did not stay with Sun for long. Wesley Rose

For the Record. . .

Born April 23, 1936, in vernon, Tex.; died of a massive heart attack, December 6, 1988, in Hendersonville, Tenn.; father was an oil field worker; mother's name, Nadine; married first wife, Claudette (died, 1966); married second wife, Barbara, 1969; children: (first marriage) Wesley, Roy Dwayne (died, 1968), Anthony (died, 1968); (second marriage) Roy Kelton, Alex. *Education:* Attended North Texas State University.

Worked on oil rigs as youth; had own radio show and was leader of the Wink Westerners (country group), in Wink, Texas, as teenager; recording artist and concert performer, 1956—; also recorded and performed (with Bob Dylan, Jeff Lynne, George Harrison, and Tom Petty) with group The Traveling Wilburys, 1988; hosted local television show in Midland, Texas, 1955; actor in motion pictures, including *The Fastest Guitar Alive,* 1965.

Awards: Grammy Award (with Emmylou Harris) for best country vocal performance by a duo or group, 1980, for "That Loving You Feeling Again"; member of Rock and Roll Hall of Fame; member of Nashville Songwriters Association Hall of Fame.

---

of Acuff-Rose, a music publishing company, hired him as a staff writer in 1957. In this capacity Orbison wrote a major hit for the Everly Brothers, "Claudette," which was inspired by his first wife, and a lesser success for Jerry Lee Lewis, "Down the Line." His own ambitions as a singer had not diminished, however, and Rose arranged a recording contract for Orbison at Monument Records. On the Monument label he scored hits with 1960's "Only the Lonely," 1961's "Running Scared," 1962's "Dream Baby," and many other songs. Orbison made concert tours throughout the United States and Europe; he was even more popular in England than he was in his own country. In 1963, he was the headliner for rock and roll shows that also featured a group whose members Orbison became friendly with, the Beatles, who were already a phenomenon in England but as yet unknown in America. It was for one of these shows that Orbison began wearing his trademark dark glasses while performing on stage. Suffering from poor eyesight, when the singer left his glasses on a plane, he had to wear his prescription sunglasses in order to see well. This new prop unfortunately led to a rumor among some of Orbison's fans that he was blind.

In 1965, after selling over seven million copies of his 1964 hit "Oh, Pretty Woman," Orbison switched recording companies. He chose MGM because it would give

him motion picture exposure as well as musical, and soon after he joined the company he made the film, "Fastest Guitar Alive." Though his release of the single "Ride Away" was only a moderate success, there was nothing to indicate that Orbison would not continue to be a major part of the American popular music scene. In 1966, however, his wife Claudette was killed in a motorcycle accident while crossing an intersection moments after Orbison himself. To cope with his grief, Orbison buried himself in concert engagements, but did not do much in the way of writing or recording new material. He had no sooner begun to recover and to start new recording efforts when, in 1968, a house fire killed two of his sons while he was away on tour. By the time Orbison was ready to release records again, he had been so long away from the charts that his audience had dwindled.

Undaunted, Orbison continued to tour, especially in England and Europe, where his popularity had never waned. He remarried in 1969, to a German-born woman named Barbara who eventually became his

---

Roy Orbison's "was a voice like no other ever heard in rock—silky, soaring, tender, gritty, haunted with pain."

---

manager. Orbison suffered another personal setback in 1978, however, when, after he collapsed from running up some stadium bleachers, it was discovered he needed coronary bypass surgery. He was determined to continue performing, though, and according to Jerome in another *People* article, told the woman who did the surgery, "Make sure it's a clean, pretty incision. I perform with my shirts open pretty far down."

Though the comeback album he made in 1979 following his operation was not particularly successful, Orbison did see success again in 1980, when his duet with Emmylou Harris won a Grammy Award. Recordings of his songs by other artists, and re-releases of his own recordings brought him back into demand as a concert performer in the United States—two nights before his death Orbison played to an appreciative audience in Akron, Ohio. Orbison had also achieved new success as a member of the Traveling Wilburys, a group that was filled out by ex-Beatle George Harrison, Tom Petty of the Heartbreakers, former Electric Light Orchestra member Jeff Lynne, and Bob Dylan. The Wilburys had a hit single, "Handle With Care," and the album it came from, *Volume One,* reached number eight on the U.S. record charts. Orbison was in Tennessee visiting his mother when he died.

Selected discography

Major single releases

"Oooby Dooby," Sun, 1956.
"Uptown," Monument, 1960.
"Only the Lonely," Monument, 1960.
"Blue Angel," Monument, 1960.
"I'm Hurtin'," Monument, 1960.
"Running Scared," Monument, 1961.
"Crying," Monument, 1961.
"Candy Man," Monument, 1961.
"Dream Baby," Monument, 1962.
"The Crowd," Monument, 1962.
"Workin' For the Man," Monument, 1962.
"Leah," Monument, 1962.
"In Dreams," Monument, 1963.
"Falling," Monument, 1963.
"Mean Woman Blues," Monument, 1963.
"Blue Bayou," Monument, 1963.
"Pretty Paper," Monument, 1963.
"It's Over," Monument, 1964.
"Oh, Pretty Woman," Monument, 1964.
"Goodnight," Monument, 1965.
"Say You're My Girl," Monument, 1965.
"Let the Good Times Roll," Monument, 1965.
"Ride Away," MGM, 1965.
"Crawling Back," MGM, 1965.
"Breakin' Up Is Breakin' My Heart," MGM, 1966.
"Twinkle Toes," MGM, 1966.
"Too Soon to Know," MGM, 1966.
"Communication Breakdown," MGM, 1966.
"Cry Softly, Lonely One," MGM, 1968.
(With Emmylou Harris) "That Loving You Feeling Again," Warner Bros., 1980.
(With the Traveling Wilburys) "Handle With Care," Warner Bros., 1988.

LPs

There Is Only One, MGM, 1965.
The Orbison Way, MGM, 1966.
The Classic, MGM, 1966.
Roy Orbison Sings Don Gibson, MGM, 1967.
Cry Softly, Lonely One, MGM, 1968.
Many Moods of Roy Orbison, MGM, 1969.
The Original Sound, Sun, 1970.
Memphis, MGM, 1973.
All Time Greatest Hits, Monument, 1973.
Laminar Flow, Elektra, 1979.
(With the Traveling Wilburys) *Volume One,* Warner Bros., 1988.
Mystery Girl, Elektra, 1989.

Sources

Periodicals

People, June 18, 1979.
Rolling Stone, January 26, 1989.

Obituaries

People, December 19, 1988.
San Jose Mercury News, December 7, 1988.

—*Elizabeth Thomas*

David
Ott

Composer

David Lee Ott is rapidly becoming one of the most prominent American composers of the post-World War II generation. His works have been performed by orchestras in Cleveland, Detroit, Kansas City, Pittsburgh, and New York and as part of major music festivals throughout the Western Hemisphere. Ott has been the recipient of many grants and awards, and he has been nominated three times for the Pulitzer Prize in Music.

Ott was born in Crystal Falls, Michigan, on July 5, 1947, to homemaker Marian Shivy Ott and George Lawrence Ott, a car carrier for General Motors. Both were self-taught recreational pianists, and inspired by his mother, Ott began piano lessons at age six. Later he learned to play the clarinet and trombone, and as a high school student he accompanied the school choir and used his musical talent in church activities as well. Ott aspired to a career in music education—to become a band director like the man who had sparked his interest in music.

The first person in his family to attend college, Ott studied at the University of Wisconsin—Platteville, from which he graduated with honors in 1969 with a bachelor of science in music education. While working toward his B.S., Ott's teaching goals had shifted from high school to college teaching, and he continued his studies as a piano major at Indiana University under Alfonso Montecino. Upon earning his master of music degree in 1971, Ott taught piano and music theory at Houghton College in Houghton, New York. From 1975 to 1977 he completed doctoral course work in composition and theory, with a minor in art history at the University of Kentucky, where he then taught for a year before accepting a position at Catawba College in Salisbury, North Carolina, where he taught piano, theory, and jazz-related studies. He earned his doctorate in musical arts in 1982.

Until Ott began his doctoral work, he had done only limited composing, mostly arranging popular works for jazz ensemble, but he gradually focussed on composing. Part-time work as music director of a local church brought Ott to the attention of an employee at Kentucky Public Broadcasting, and he was asked to score music for educational films, which he did from 1976 to 1981. While an assistant professor at Pfeiffer College in Misenheimer, North Carolina, from 1978 to 1982, Ott began to teach composition and hear his original works performed, including his first commissions—*Welcome, All Wonders* and *Genesis II.*

The eighties proved to be productive for Ott. Since

For the Record. . .

Full name, David Lee Ott; born July 5, 1947, in Crystal Falls, Mich.; son of George Lawrence (a car carrier for General Motors) and Marian (Shivy) Ott; married Susan Tonne (a music copyist), September 5, 1970; children: Andrea, Matthew, Marian. *Education:* University of Wisconsin—Platteville, B.S. in music education, 1969; Indiana University, M.M. in piano performance; University of Kentucky, D.M.A. in theory and composition, 1982. *Religion:* Lutheran.

Houghton College, Houghton, N.Y., assistant professor of piano, 1972-75; University of Kentucky, Lexington, lecturer in music, 1976-77; Catawba College, Salisbury, N.C., assistant professor of music, 1977-78; Pfeiffer College, Misenheimer, N.C., assistant professor of music, 1978-82; DePauw University, Greencastle, Ind., associate professor of music, 1982—, composer-in-residence. Active in numerous local and state-wide musical organizations; church organist and choir director.

Awards: Named outstanding professor at Houghton College, 1975, and Depauw University, 1985; arts grants from North Carolina Arts Council, 1982, Wisconsin, 1983, and Indiana, 1984; nominated for Pulitzer Prize in music, 1983, 1986, and 1988; Fisher fellowship, 1987; named distinguished alumnus, University of Wisconsin—Platteville, 1987.

Addresses: *Office*—DePauw University School of Music, Greencastle, IN 46135.

ear for his work-in-progress and labors over copying scores and parts.

In 1988 Ott completed what he considers to be two pivotal works: *Concerto for Two Cellos* and *DodecaCelli*. The double cello concerto was commissioned by the District of Columbia's National Symphony Orchestra (NSO) and first performed by soloists David Teie and Steve Honigberg. Working with Teie reinforced what Ott had already been making an integral part of his compositions—engaging melodies. The double concerto was warmly approved by the NSO's music director, the world renowned cellist and conductor Mstislav Rostropovich, who hailed it as "a finely crafted composition" and "an exciting work by a rising young American composer." The enthusiasm generated by this piece led to the commissioning of *DodecaCelli* by the cello section of the NSO for the 1988 World Cello Congress at the University of Maryland. In this piece Ott again demonstrated his ability to compose enthralling melodies, and he thoroughly explored the textural possibilities of the instrument. At the conclusion of its world premier performance by the cello section of the NSO, the audience of mostly cellists responded with a standing ovation.

Ott has composed many different kinds of works, including orchestral and choral pieces and the score for the the ballet *Visions; The Isle of Patmos* for the Indianapolis Ballet Theatre. This work is based on Saint John's visions while on the Isle of Patmos. While working with choreographer Daci Dindonis, Ott not only learned about the technical aspects of ballet production but the importance of melody to dance; without the rhythmic drive of melody, dancers would be left motionless on stage.

As a composer-in-residence at DePauw University in Greencastle, Indiana, Ott has, like many composers today, the resources of academia to support him financially, giving him greater freedom to compose. Throughout his teaching career, Ott has received awards for excellence and is popular with his students, undoubtedly because of his dedication and enthusiasm. Ott believes that music schools today should make students more aware of post-1940s music and that of other cultures, as well as the cultural basis of the music currently in the curricula. Ott himself is fascinated by architecture, and his tone poem *Water Garden* is based on his impressions of Philip Johnson's architectural work of the same name.

Ott is also active outside the academic sphere. Believing that in order to run successful arts programs busi-

1983 he has published over a dozen orchestral works, many of them for a solo instrument with orchestral accompaniment: piano, cello, viola, brass ensemble, alto flute. Stylistically Ott's works reflect the trend of the late 1970s and 1980s loosely defined as "New Romanticism," which emphasizes melody and expressiveness instead of the abstract and often strident sounds of serialism and other experimental genres. As a collegiate music student, Ott had been unmoved by much of the twentieth-century music studied in history classes. When he seriously began to compose, he realized that his work was not in sync with then current experimental trends, but he has never allowed this difference in styles to change his approach to composition. Ott frequently composes at the piano, using piano improvisations for inspiration. His training as a music educator has also served him well, for he had to learn the capabilities and difficulties of all instruments in the standard orchestra, and when working on a solo piece Ott will often consult the soloist for whom the work was commissioned concerning technical matters. Ott's wife, Susan, frequently provides a sympathetic and critical

ness people and artists must work together, Ott is a member of a number of arts organizations: Board of Directors of the Indianapolis Chamber Orchestra, Advisory Committee for Arts Midwest, Advisory Panel of the Indiana Arts Commission. In addition, Ott generously shares his talents with his church as organist and choir director. Religion plays an important role in Ott's life, and throughout his career he has composed choral pieces based on biblical texts.

David Ott's future as a composer appears bright. With commissions for the 1990s rapidly accumulating, he will certainly have ample opportunities to express himself through his music and further define the stature of his talent.

Compositions

Welcome, All Wonders, 1979.
Genesis II, 1980.
Commemoration & Celebration, 1983.
Piano Concerto in B Flat, 1983.
Essay for Tenor Saxophone, 1983.
Cornerstone of Loveliness, 1983.
Short Symphony, 1984.
Concerto for Percussion and Orchestra, 1984.
From Darkness Shines, 1984.
Concerto for Cello and Orchestra, 1985.
Lucinda Hero: An Opera, 1985.
Judgement and Infernal Dance, 1985.
Fantasy for Cello and Piano, 1985.
Water Garden, 1986.
Lord of All Being, 1986.
Sonata for Trombone, 1986.
The Mystic Trumpeter, 1987.
Celebration at Vanderburgh, 1987.
Concerto for Saxophone and Orchestra, 1987.
He Hath Put All Things Under His Feet, 1987.
Concerto for Viola and Orchestra, 1988.
Viola Sonata, 1988.
Concerto for Two Cellos, 1988.
Visions; The Isle of Patmos, A Ballet, 1988.
DodecaCelli, 1988.
Vertical Shrines, 1989.

Selected discography

Sonata for Trombone and Piano, Coronet Records, 1987.
Three Movements for Brass Quintet, Carolina Brass, 1985.

Sources

Washington Post, February 6, 1988.
Washington Times, February 8, 1988.

—Jeanne M. Lesinski

Buck Owens

Singer, songwriter, guitarist

One of the biggest country-music stars of the 1960s, Buck Owens was languishing in semi-retirement until he was "rediscovered" in 1987. Owens's rowdy honky-tonk music—better known as "The Bakersfield Sound"—had fallen out of vogue in the late 1970s; its revival by "country purists" has meant a welcome resurgence of interest in Owens and his band, the Buckaroos. *Guitar Player* magazine contributor Dan Forte notes that, from his base in Bakersfield, California, Owens "went against the country-pop grain, recording with his own road band, spotlighting a driving drum beat and hot guitar solos while eschewing string sections and studio background singers. In doing so, he was a major influence on the late-'60s country-rock movement that was spearheaded by the Byrds and the Flying Burrito Brothers and spawned the current legion of back-to-basics country stars such as Dwight Yoakam, George Strait, Randy Travis, and the Desert Rose Band." Owens may inspire others, but he does not lack fans himself—after eight years of almost complete anonymity, he booked more than one hundred live appearances in 1989.

Owens was born Alvis Edgar Owens, Jr., in Sherman, Texas, a small town near the Oklahoma border. His father was a farmer, and the family was very poor. As soon as he was able, "Buck" began to pull his own weight by picking cotton and doing farm work before and after school. He continued this practice when his family moved to Tempe, Arizona, in search of better fortunes. Owens dropped out of high school quite young and worked as a truck driver, ditch digger, hay baler, and fruit swamper. In his free time he began to experiment with musical instruments—first the mandolin and piano, then an electric guitar he bought himself. He listened to country music on the radio and imitated the guitar riffs of the professionals. By the age of sixteen he had mastered the guitar and was performing in Arizona's rough-and-tumble honky-tonks. He married at seventeen and quickly fathered two sons.

In 1951, when he turned twenty-one, Owens packed up his family and moved to Bakersfield, California. He had heard that Bakersfield provided opportunities for country musicians, and the rumor proved to be true. There he was able to find regular gigs in dance clubs as well as lucrative studio work in nearby Los Angeles. Owens played session music for a number of Capitol Records stars, including Tennessee Ernie Ford, Kay Starr, Sonny James, Gene Vincent, and Tommy Collins. His own solo contract with Capitol came in the late 1950s, after he had begun writing songs for himself and others.

Owens had his first hit, "Under Your Spell Again," in 1959. By then he was busy forming his own band, the

For the Record. . .

Given name Alvis Edgar Owens, Jr.; born August 12, 1929, in Sherman, Tex.; son of Alvis Edgar (a laborer) and Maicie W. Owens; married Bonnie Owens (a singer), 1947 (divorced, 1955); married Phyllis Owens (divorced, 1972); children: (first marriage) Buddy, Mike; (second marriage) John.

Singer, songwriter, guitarist, 1950—. Signed with Capitol Records, 1956 (some sources say 1957 or 1958); had first number one hit, "Under Your Spell Again," 1959. Formed band Buck Owens and the Buckaroos, 1960. Moved to Warner Brothers label, 1976; returned to Capitol, 1988.

Star of syndicated television shows "Hee Haw," 1969-85, and "The Buck Owens Ranch Show." Owner of Blue Book Music Company, Thunderbird Broadcasting Company, Buck Owens Broadcasting, Inc., Aztec Radio, Inc., and radio stations KUZZ, KKXX, and KNIX.

Awards: Instrumental group of the year award from Country Music Association, 1968; named artist of the decade by Capitol Records, 1969; recipient of Pioneer Award from Country Music Association, 1989.

Addresses: *Office*—1225 N. Chester Ave., Bakersfield, Calif. 93308.

Buckaroos, who would play behind him both on the road and in the studio. Chief among the band members was a young fiddler, Don Rich. Owens taught Rich to play guitar—eventually the pupil surpassed the teacher—and the pair became inseparable partners. "From that time on," writes Irwin Stambler in the *Encyclopedia of Folk, Country, and Western Music,* "the only direction was up." Owens produced a phenomenal thirty-one chart-topping country hits, putting Bakersfield on the music map with his spirited, drum-laden dance tunes. His number one songs include "Act Naturally," "My Heart Skips a Beat," "Together Again," "I've Got a Tiger by the Tail," "Waitin' in Your Welfare Line," and the instrumental "Buckaroo." By 1969 Owens was well established as a top country star.

Television offered an enticement to Owens in the late 1960s, and it almost proved his undoing. He became the cohost of "Hee Haw," an enormously popular comedy-variety series, and he hosted his own syndicated show, "The Buck Owens Ranch Show." Of the two, "Hee Haw" offered Owens far more exposure—so much exposure, in fact, that his record sales, once numbering a million a year, dropped off precipitously. "Television lays you bare; there's nothing left," Owens told *Guitar Player.* "If there's any mysterious part about

you, television tells it all." Not only was Owens on the air at least once a week, the format of "Hee Haw" forced him to play the role of country bumpkin. Even a weekly solo with the Buckaroos did little to counteract the prevailing "Hee Haw" image. Owens's musical career was dealt a further blow in 1974, when Don Rich died in a motorcycle accident. "The death of his 'compadre' signaled Owens' decline," writes Forte. "The albums Buck made after Don Rich's passing were admittedly half-hearted, and in 1979 Owens hung up his performing shoes to concentrate on his considerable business affairs."

Owens's decision to quit performing was made in part because he did not like the direction country music was taking. He has said that the music coming out of Nashville in the mid- to late-1970s was dull and uniform, because many country artists were using the same backup musicians and producers, and most country artists were striving for crossover pop hits. "If everyone who makes an album uses virtually the same studio and engineers, and picks from the same pool of musicians that all hang out together, the records are all

> *"I like real music. If it's country, I want it honky-tonk. I'm a honky-tonker."*

going to sound alike," he told *Guitar Player.* "I just kind of dropped out. I couldn't compete. . . . I just felt like, 'Why keep beating these people up if they don't want to hear this stuff?'" The "stuff" to which Owens referred was his honky-tonk "Bakersfield Sound." In the 1980s a new generation of country musicians, some based in Los Angeles, have revived Owens's style with great success.

Dwight Yoakam was the first country singer to persuade Owens to perform again. After eight years of busy "retirement"—he still taped "Hee Haw" and ran several lucrative businesses—Owens agreed to sing some of his old hits with Yoakam. In 1987 the two appeared together at about a dozen concerts; then they recorded "The Streets of Bakersfield," a top ten country single that was nominated for a Country Music Association award. Owens made two discoveries: he was in demand as a musician again, and he still loved music enough to want to perform. He has returned to the stage on a regular basis and has released two albums, *Hot Dog!* and a reissue of his live 1966 appearance at New York's Carnegie Hall. Owens, who once tried to compromise with Nashville's slick standards, claims he is glad to be back making the kind of music he wants to make—the high-energy, rhythmic, steel-guitar sound associated primarily with him. "I like *real* music," he told *Guitar Player*. "If it's country, I want it honky-tonk. I'm a honky-tonker."

Selected discography

Buck Owens on the Bandstand, Capitol, 1963.
Buck Owens Sings Tommy Collins, Capitol, 1963.
I've Got a Tiger by the Tail, Capitol, 1963.
Best of Buck Owens, Capitol, 1964.
I Don't Care, Capitol, 1964.
Together Again, Capitol, 1964.
Before You Go, Capitol, 1966.
Carnegie Hall Concert, Capitol, 1966.
Roll Out the Red Carpet for Buck Owens and His Buckaroos, Capitol, 1966.
America's Most Wanted Band, Capitol, 1967.
Buck Owens and His Buckaroos in Japan, Capitol, 1967.
Open Up Your Heart, Capitol, 1967.
It's a Monster's Holiday, Capitol, 1974.
Buck 'Em!, Warner Brothers, 1976.
(Contributor) Dwight Yoakam, *Buenas Noches from a Lonely Room,* Reprise, 1987.

Hot Dog!, Capitol, 1988.

Also recorded *The Instrumental Hits of Buck Owens and His Buckaroos, Live at the White House, Dust on Mother's Bible,* and *Guitar Player.*

Sources

Books

The Illustrated Encyclopedia of Country Music, Harmony Books, 1977.
Shestack, Melvin, *The Country Music Encyclopedia,* Crowell, 1974.
Stambler, Irwin and Grelun Landon, *The Encyclopedia of Folk, Country, and Western Music,* St. Martin's, 1969.

Periodicals

Chicago Tribune, October 30, 1988.
Guitar Player, February, 1989.
Los Angeles Times, July 30, 1988.
Newsweek, January 9, 1989.

—*Anne Janette Johnson*

Robert Palmer

Singer, songwriter

Robert Palmer hovered on the brink of superstardom for more than a dozen years until a spirited rock and roll single, "Addicted to Love," pushed him to the top in 1986. Since then the handsome and well-groomed Palmer has become a favorite with rock's maturing audience. In *Gentleman's Quarterly,* Greg Collins observes that even though Palmer's biggest hits are hard-rocking numbers like "Bad Case of Lovin' You (Doctor, Doctor)" and "Simply Irresistible," a "more restrained sensibility is what Robert Palmer has to offer rock music. . . . [He is] not your basic mainstream material."

Known for his elegant designer suits and his preference for fine food and wines, Palmer is also an experimental musician who has been among the first to experiment with reggae, electronic sound, and international folk music motifs. Still, the singer told *People* magazine, he is savoring his first real taste of the pop music spotlight. "I'm not somebody who started in a garage six months ago and MTV put me up there," he said, referring to his decade-long British solo career. "This is much more delicious. It almost feels like I'm getting away with something. It's all fallen into place perfectly, a nice accident."

The son of a British naval officer, Palmer moved frequently in his youth, spending time in such exotic locales as Malta, Naples, and Cyprus. He described himself in *Gentleman's Quarterly* as a lonely child who "hung out mostly with adults" and who never saw a movie or a television until he was twelve. In *Rolling Stone,* he claimed that he received his only musical training—in guitar—from a "little old lady who burned a paraffin stove." Most of his musical influences came from American records, especially the rhythm and blues work of Lena Horne and Nat King Cole. At fifteen Palmer joined his first band, providing guitar and vocals, but it was many years before he decided to be a professional musician. In the meantime he studied graphic design and immersed himself in the many exotic forms of music that would someday enter into his songwriting work.

During his early twenties, Palmer drifted through a number of locally renowned British rock groups, including Dada, Vinegar Joe, and the Alan Bown Band. In those days, writes Collins, Palmer would "open for Jimi Hendrix and the Who and whoever else was big and touring England at the time. Palmer, however, did not approve even then of the rock life-style." Palmer admitted as much. "I loved the music, but the excesses of rock and roll never really appealed to me at all," he said. "I couldn't see the point of getting up in front of a lot of people when you weren't in control of your wits." Even then Palmer dressed well and performed with a certain restraint. "I'm not concerned that my stuff isn't extreme," he told *Rolling Stone.* "I don't want to be heavy. I can't think of another attitude to have toward an audience than a hopeful and a positive one. And if that includes such unfashionable things as sentimentality, well, I can afford it."

Palmer signed a solo contract with Island Records, a British company, in the mid-1970s. He then cut a string of albums that were "critically celebrated but commercially lackluster," to quote Steven Dougherty in *People.* His 1974 record, *Sneakin' Sally through the Alley,* was a modest success, as was his 1978 effort, *Every Kinda People.* The small Island label gave Palmer great experimental leeway, and, according to Collins, "he taught himself to play different instruments and built an electronically sophisticated home studio. Palmer was into synthesizers before anyone else in the pop field." David Fricke notes in *Rolling Stone,* however, that Palmer's albums cast him "as a lesser white soul brother to Boz Scaggs and Hall and Oates—slick urban R&B in one more three piece suit."

Palmer had slipped into relative obscurity by 1984, and he was working on a new album when he was contacted by John Taylor and Andy Taylor of the group Duran Duran. They asked Palmer to write and perform a few songs for an ad hoc group called Power Station—a sort of project-between-projects. Everyone involved was surprised when Power Station placed three songs in the American top ten and produced an album that

sold better than had any of Palmer's solo efforts. Palmer was never tempted to make Power Station his permanent band, however. In a brave leap of faith, he went back to work on his solo album, *Riptide,* releasing it in 1986.

The gamble paid off. *Riptide* became Palmer's first number one-selling album, and "Addicted to Love," with its sexually charged music video, topped the charts for several weeks. Then Palmer decided to challenge his success even further. His next album, *Heavy Nova,* joined an incongruous variety of influences, from hard rock to 1940s torch songs to a bossa nova instrumental. *Heavy Nova* was another platinum success, and its best-known single, "Simply Irresistible," was one of the biggest hits of the summer of 1988.

Having finally tapped into the American market, Palmer signed with EMI Records in 1988 and appeared in a popular Pepsi Cola commercial singing "Simply Irresistible" in 1989. Collins suggests, though, that the limelight may not change Palmer's desire to experiment, as it has not changed his drug-free, retiring lifestyle. "A baritone who can also sing tenor and falsetto, [Palmer] has incredible range, allowing him to sing in almost any style he chooses," writes Collins. "He knows full well that his rock and roll does well in America. But then there's all this new stuff running around in his head that he really likes." Collins concludes: "But the star machine is revving up. Robert Palmer's days of quietude may be numbered."

Selected discography

Sneakin' Sally through the Alley, Island, 1974.
Pressure Drop, Island, 1975.
Some People Can Do What They Like, Island, 1976.
Double Fun, Island, 1978.
Secrets, Island, 1979.
Pride, Island, 1983.
Riptide, Island, 1986.
Heavy Nova, EMI, 1988.

Sources

Gentleman's Quarterly, July, 1988.
Glamour, July, 1988.
People, June 9, 1986.
Rolling Stone, October 18, 1979; June 5, 1986.

—Anne Janette Johnson

Dolly Parton

Singer and songwriter

No country singer has had greater success in the pop market than Dolly Parton, the curvaceous blonde from Tennessee's Smoky Mountains. "As much as anyone," writes Gene Busnar in *Superstars of Country Music,* "Dolly has extended the connections between folk traditions and contemporary styles." Much attention has been lavished on Parton's gaudy attire, cascading wigs, and outgoing, chatty personality, but beneath the surface glitter lurks a genuine musician determined to enjoy her life and art. As Margo Jefferson observes in *Ms.* magazine, Parton "is making no effort to hide or disguise her origins. She is indelibly country. The vibrato and light twang of her voice evoke the Anglo-Saxon ballads of the Southern mountains, and the jigs and reels of the early string bands. Her rhythmic fluidity suggests the affinity for black blues and church singing that always lies beneath the surface of so much country music. And she has been experimenting with assorted styles since her first recordings." Concerning Parton's association with the stereotypical "dumb blonde," those who know her characterize her as an astute businesswoman with unrelenting ambitions. Busnar states, "Dolly makes it crystal clear that she is the brains behind all those . . . wigs." The performer herself puts it more succinctly in *Ms.:* "If people think I'm a dumb blonde because of the way I look, then they're dumber than they think I am. If people think I'm not very deep because of my wigs and outfits, then they're not very deep. . . . If I was trying to really impress men or be totally sexy, I would dress differently."

Parton's affinity for fancy hairstyles and jewel-studded dresses stems in large part from her impoverished upbringing in Sevier County, Tennessee. She was born near the Smoky Mountains in 1946, the fourth of eleven children of Robert Lee and Avie Lee Parton. According to Busnar, "the pain of growing up poor and hungry weighed heavily on the young girl and, like Cinderella in the fairy tale, Dolly dreamed that someone would magically turn her shack into a palace and her raggedy clothes into magnificent gowns." Parton's romantic visions of wealth soon gave birth to an iron determination to succeed. If she wanted to get rich and give her farmer parents an easier life, she realized she would have to make a name for herself. "I knew I'd be the first member of my family in generations to leave the mountains and actually *go* out in the world," she said in Busnar's account. "I never doubted I'd make it." Parton began writing songs and singing at the age of seven. She made her professional debut on a Knoxville radio show at ten and had secured a guest appearance at the Grand Ole Opry at twelve. Parton told *Ms.,* "I got so much applause, it just confirmed what I believed. I thought: Well, this is for me. I am definitely destined to be a star. I'm going to make a lot of money. I'm going to

For the Record. . .

Full name Dolly Rebecca Parton; born January 19, 1946, in Sevier County, Tenn.; daughter of Robert Lee (a farmer) and Avie Lee (Owens) Parton; married Carl Dean (a contractor) May 30, 1966. *Education:* Graduated from high school in Sevier County, Tenn.

Singer/songwriter, 1956—. Singer on the "Cass Walker Program," Knoxville, Tenn., 1956; appeared at the Grand Ole Opry, 1958; co-star of "The Porter Wagoner Show," 1967-74; solo artist, 1974—. Formed and headed "Dolly Parton and the Traveling Family Band," c. 1970-77; star of the musical variety show "Dolly," 1987, ABC-TV. Feature films include *Nine to Five,* 1980, *The Best Little Whorehouse in Texas,* 1982, and *Rhinestone,* 1984 (also wrote songs for the soundtracks). Owner of the theme park Dollywood, in Sevier County, Tenn.

Awards: Grammy Award, 1978, for *Here You Come Again;* recipient of People's Choice awards, 1980 and 1988; named female vocalist of the year by the Academy of Country Music, 1980; Academy Award nomination, 1981, for song "Nine to Five"; (with Emmylou Harris and Linda Ronstadt) Album of the Year award from the Academy of Country Music, 1987, for *Trio;* Grammy Award, 1988, for *Trio.*

Addresses: *Home*—P.O. Box 1976, Nolensville, TN 37135. *Agent*—Creative Artists Agency, Inc., 1888 Century Park East, Suite 1400, Los Angeles, CA 90067.

buy Mama and Daddy a house. We're going to have clothes, cars. . ."

First, however, Parton graduated from high school. Intuitively she felt that she would need an education to help her manage the fantastic career she had planned. Immediately after graduation, she packed a cardboard suitcase and moved to Nashville to begin her career. On her first night in town she met a handsome contractor, Carl Dean, in a Nashville laundromat. They married and pursued their separate interests—Parton a singing career, Dean a small business buying and selling farm equipment. Within a year, in 1967, Parton had landed a starring role on the popular "Porter Wagoner Show." She began recording duets with Wagoner, himself a country-music superstar, and both their careers were strengthened by the association. Busnar writes, "With the addition of Dolly, Wagoner was able to successfully combine traditional folk elements with rock and pop influences to put on a show rivaled only by Johnny Cash and his troupe. However, Dolly was already looking not only beyond Porter Wagoner, but also beyond the confines of the entire Nashville scene."

In the mid-1970s several female artists began crossing over from country to pop. Parton, who had never sold more than two hundred thousand copies of an album, decided to gamble on her marketability in the pop-music business. It was an audacious move for a performer so strongly identified with country—she not only ran the risk of alienating her country fans, she also ran the risk of being too eccentric a personality to attract pop listeners. She was fond of saying, "I'm not leavin' country, I'm just takin' it with me," as she fired her backup band and signed on with a Los Angeles-based management company. For Parton, the move to Hollywood was a smart one. Her subsequent songs "Here You Come Again," "Islands in the Stream," and "Nine to Five" were million-sellers that appealed as much to her old fans as to her new ones. She also landed film work in the movies *Nine to Five, The Best Little Whorehouse in Texas,* and *Rhinestone,* and only the latter failed to show a hefty profit. By 1981 Parton was an international

> "If people think I'm a dumb blonde because of the way I look, then they're dumber than they think I am."

star. Women especially liked her earthy humor and—surprisingly—her figure-enhancing gowns. Jefferson notes, "Isn't it pleasant to be reminded that ruffles, pleats, drapes, sequins, curls, lashes, hoops, spangles, powders and paints can be simply toys—entertainment and sports for women quite apart from their value in the game of sexual barter and exchange?" Parton, Jefferson says, returned the joy to femininity.

Like many performers, Parton finally succumbed to the stress of her profession. In 1982 she fainted during a performance and was hospitalized for exhaustion and a host of internal problems. According the Scot Haller in *People,* the crowds "were faced by a different Dolly: hoarse, overweight, unhealthy and unhappy." After a long recuperation at her home in Nashville, Parton began working again, but she has never quite regained the pinnacle of success that she had reached before her illness. In 1987 she was given a prime-time television variety show, *Dolly,* that failed in the ratings. The movie *Rhinestone* served as proof that she was not a guaranteed draw at the box office. Still, Parton has continued to enjoy a healthy career between her music and her pet project, a theme park called Dollywood that she built near her mountain home in Tennessee. Busnar analyzes Parton's musical talents: "In her typical fashion, Dolly often jokes about not being a particularly good singer. But, in fact, she is one of our best and most important contemporary female vocalists. Although she is often imitated, Dolly has an unmistakable quality in her voice that somehow combines elements of traditional American folk music, the strength and power of religious music, and her own unique brand of fun." Busnar adds, most importantly, that Parton's "songwriting skills have helped her become an awesome force in the music business."

Alanna Nash praises Parton for another aspect of her career in *Ms.*, namely her astute (and independently made) career decisions and her preservation of family and marital ties. "Dolly Parton has realized the American dream on her own terms," writes Nash. "Throughout her . . . career, Parton has followed the classic female paradigm of using the access that comes with personal achievement to create opportunities for those we love. . . . [She] has come to symbolize the Smoky Mountains heritage. For Parton, this heritage has not only meant preserving the old ways, but also making the most out of what you have, and then showing others how to do it too." Parton, who is said to be looking forward to performing until she turns a hundred, told *People* that the way she looks and dresses is the way she *chooses* to look and dress. "The personality is for real," she said. "I don't have to put on makeup to feel like Dolly. I *am* Dolly."

Selected discography

Just Because I'm a Woman, RCA, 1968.
In the Good Old Days, RCA, 1969.
My Blue Ridge Mountain Boy, RCA, 1969.
Fairest of Them All, RCA, 1970.
A Real Live Dolly, RCA, 1970.
Hello, I'm Dolly, Monument, 1970.
Best of Dolly Parton, RCA, 1970.
Golden Streets of Glory, RCA, 1971.
Joshua, RCA, 1971.
As Long As I Have Love, Monument, 1971.
Coat of Many Colors, RCA, 1971.
Touch Your Woman, RCA, 1972.
My Favorite Songwriter: Porter Wagoner, RCA, 1972.

Just the Way I Am, Camden, 1973, rereleased, 1986.
My Tennessee Mountain Home, RCA, 1973.
Mine, RCA, 1973.
Real Live Bubbling Over, RCA, 1974.
Love Is like a Butterfly, RCA, 1974.
Best of Dolly Parton, RCA, 1975.
All I Can Do, RCA, 1976.
New Harvest . . . First Gathering, RCA, 1977.
Here You Come Again, RCA, 1977.
Heartbreaker, RCA, 1978.
Great Balls of Fire, RCA, 1979.
Dolly Dolly Dolly, RCA, 1980.
9 to 5 and Odd Jobs, RCA, 1980.
Heartbreak Express, RCA, 1982.
The Best Little Whorehouse in Texas, RCA, 1982.
(With Kris Kristofferson, Willie Nelson, and Brenda Lee) *Kris, Willie, Dolly, and Brenda: The Winning Hand*, Monument, 1982.
Burlap and Satin, RCA, 1983.
Collector's Series, RCA, 1985.
Portrait, RCA, 1986.
Think about Love, RCA, 1986.
The Best of Dolly Parton, Volume 3, RCA, 1987.
The Best There Is, RCA, 1987.
(With Emmylou Harris and Linda Ronstadt) *Trio*, Warner Brothers, 1987.
Rainbow, Columbia, 1988.

Also recorded *The Great Pretender*, RCA, and *Jolene*, RCA.

Sources

Books

Busnar, Gene, *Superstars of Country Music*, J. Messner, 1984.
Nash, Alanna, *Dolly Parton*, Reed Books, 1978.
Simon, George T., *The Best of the Music Makers*, Doubleday, 1971.

Periodicals

Life, March, 1987.
Ms., June, 1979; July, 1986.
New York Times Magazine, May 9, 1976.
People, August 2, 1982; July 9, 1984; May 5, 1986.
Rolling Stone, October 23, 1975; August 15, 1977.

—Anne Janette Johnson

Les Paul

Guitarist, songwriter, inventor

Besides being a phenomenal guitarist, Les Paul can be credited with pioneering most of the major breakthroughs in musical technology that are today considered industry standards (although in the 1940's they must have been mind-boggling): phase shifting, overdubbing, reverb, delay, and sound-on-sound recording. He is also the inventor of the eight-track recorder and perhaps the most popular electric guitar today, the Gibson Les Paul. In addition, his recordings made with his former wife, Mary Ford, in the 1950s have sold well over the ten million mark. Even today, in his seventies, Paul is still working on new inventions and creating magical music. "Les Paul is more of a hell-raiser than some of the burnt-out cases who play the guitar with his name on it," reported *Guitar World*. Anybody who plugs a six-stringer in, whether they know it or not, has been influenced by the man. From Wes Montgomery to James Burton to Jimi Hendrix, Les Paul has been a major inspiration.

Paul began his musical education about the same time he discovered electronics. By age nine he had built his first crystal radio set and was beginning to blow on the harmonica. The first sound he heard on his new radio was a guitar and soon he was plucking on one of his own. Shortly afterwards, Paul was playing for small organizations, like the Lions Club, as Rhubarb Red and making $30-35 per week. Many of the dates were outside and he needed to be loud enough to be heard. He solved that by sticking a phonograph needle inside an acoustic guitar and plugging it into his radio for amplification. At thirteen he had built his own broadcasting station and a recording machine.

Paul began singing in a country band with guitarist Joe Wolverton and a year later the two formed their own acoustic duet, Sunny Joe and Rhubarb Red, playing together until 1933. After the Chicago World's Fair, Paul stayed in the Windy City working two jobs: one as Rhubarb Red on WJJD's morning show playing western music; the other playing Eddie Lang- and Djago Reinhardt-styled jazz at night on WIND as Les Paul. He began toying with the idea of a solidbody guitar to increase sustain (the theory being that the pickups and the body should remain still, allowing the strings to vibrate longer) and in 1934 he commissioned the Larsen Brothers to build him such an instrument. Two years later he retired his Rhubarb Red character and formed a jazz trio with Jim Atkins (Chet's brother) and Ernie Newton.

The three headed to New York and landed a job with Fred Waring and His Pennsylvanians, playing nationally on NBC radio, five nights a week, for the next three years. With such a huge audience, some listeners weren't quite ready for the sound of an electric guitar

Name originally Lester William Polfuss; born June 9, 1916, in Waukesha, Wis.; son of George and Evelyn (Stutz) Polfuss; married Mary Ford (real name, Colleen Summers; a singer), December 1949 (divorced, 1964); children: Lester, Gene, Colleen, Robert, Mary.

Played guitar and harmonica under pseudonym Rhubarb Red while a teenager; performed on-air at Chicago radio stations WIND and WJJD during early 1930s; formed Les Paul Trio, 1936; played with Fred Waring and His Pennsylvanians, 1937-40; worked as musical director for WIND and WJJD, 1940-43; drafted into Armed Forces Radio Service as an entertainer for the troops, 1943-46; opened own recording studio, c. 1947; began recording career (with wife, Mary Ford), 1949—; inventor of synchronous multi-track tape recorder, c. 1949, and of sound-on-sound recording technique; co-host, with wife, Mary Ford, of television show, "Les Paul and Mary Ford At Home," during 1950s; design consultant to Gibson Guitar Corp.; inventor of numerous electronic and musical devices; served as musicial director of television show "Happy Days," beginning in 1974.

Awards: Grammy Award (with Chet Atkins) for best country instrumental, 1976, for album *Chester & Lester*; named (with Mary Ford) to Grammy Hall of Fame, 1977; received Grammy Achievement Award for contributions to recording and musical instruments industry, 1983; named to Rock and Roll Hall of Fame, 1988; the Smithsonian Institution dedicated a wing of their American Music Exhibit to Les Paul.

Addresses: *Home*—Mahwah, New Jersey.

and sent letters to Paul demanding that he unplug. After flipping a coin, Paul decided to stick by his idea, which over the years has caused him both grief and satisfaction. "In spite of all the opposition you just go in and you battle," he told Steve Rosen of *Guitar World,* "because you know you're right and it's a great feeling to know you're right. And that's determination."

After the Waring gig ended in 1940, Paul headed back to Chicago to play with the Ben Bernie band while working as the musical director for WJJD and WIND. He continued to experiment with the solidbody and in 1941 assembled "The Log," a hunk of four-inch-thick lumber with two pickups and an Epiphone neck attached to it (two sides were bolted on for cosmetic purposes). "You could go out and eat and come back and the note would still be sounding," he told Tom Evans in *Guitars.* "It didn't sound like a banjo or a mandolin, but like a

guitar, an electric guitar. That was the sound I was after."

When Paul moved to California in 1943, two neighbors who were also pioneers of the electric guitar, Paul Bigsby and Leo Fender, used to come over and check out his radical concept. Paul tried to get his instrument marketed, but nobody was interested. "When I took it to Gibson around 1945 or 1946, they politely ushered me out the door," he told *Guitar Player*'s Jon Sievert. "They called it a broomstick with a pickup on it." Seven years after Paul's invention, Fender introduced the Broadcaster, the first production solidbody electric guitar. Gibson began to frantically search for that guy with the crazy broomstick.

Once in Los Angeles Paul was drafted by the Armed Forces Radio Service as an entertainer for troops. Stationed in Hollywood, he backed artists like Dinah Shore and the Andrew Sisters and even cut an album as Paul Leslie entitled *Jazz At The Philharmonic.* After recording "It's Been A Long, Long Time" with Bing Crosby in 1946, the singer convinced Paul to build his own sound studio. With a precision flywheel from a Cadillac automobile as a recording lathe and utilizing his own garage, Paul began to record other artists as well as his own songs, including "Lover" and "Brazil," in which he played all the parts himself. Paul had seven number-one hits using multiple *disc* recording, including "Nola," "Goofus," and "Little Rock Getaway," which mark the beginning of the Les Paul sound. "In 1948, the door was open, and there was a hole sitting there, and I came along with the idea of the Les Paul sound," he explained to *Guitar Player.* "It was wide open for me to come in and clean up and sell millions of records, because there was nobody in that bag."

That same year, Paul's right arm was severely crushed in an auto accident. Nearly amputated, doctors permanently set the arm in a position which allowed Paul to continue to play guitar. A year later he met and married Gene Autry's singer, Colleen Summer. She changed her name to Mary Ford and the pair began an illustrious career which included their own seven-year television show, "Les Paul and Mary Ford At Home." Their first multi-track *tape* hit, "How High The Moon," was released in March of 1951 and, after reaching number one, went on to sell 1.5 million copies. The duo peaked in 1953 with "Vaya Con Dios," which was number one for nine weeks.

In 1952 Ampex began marketing the first multi-track (8) tape recorder ever, which Paul had designed a few years earlier. By then Gibson had found Paul, and after working with him on the designs, released the first Les Paul model guitars. He decided on a gold finish to make them look richer and shaped the guitar like a violin so it would be associated with the prestigious Stradivarius instruments. There were four additional models to choose from (the Custom, Junior, TV and Special) and in 1961 Gibson came up with the thinner, double-cutaway model, the SG. Unhappy with that product, Paul asked that his name be removed from the headstock. In 1968, Gibson reintroduced the single cutaway and eventually ended up with seven variations of the Les Paul guitar.

Paul and Ford were divorced in 1964 and he veered away from music to concentrate on inventing. One of his most unique ideas, but as yet unavailable to the public, is the Paulverizer: a remote control box for a tape recorder that plugs into the guitar and lets the player control any number of sounds right from the instrument. In 1974 he started playing professionally again while working as the musical director for the "Happy Days" television show. He recorded an album (in one day!) with the great Chet Atkins in 1977, *Chester and Lester*. Of Atkins and the record, Paul told *Guitar*

> *Les Paul can be credited with pioneering most of the major breakthroughs in musical technology that are today considered industry standards.*

Player, "He's so rhythmically tight and colorful and distinctive that it leaves me wide open to tear off way out in the field somewhere and fly my kite. In show business, there are guys who can wing it, and you're talking to a winger."

After a coronary bypass operation in 1979, Paul took a five-year break before beginning his steady Monday night gig at Fat Tuesdays, a Manhattan nightclub. Even though he suffered a broken eardrum and contracted arthritis in his left hand (limiting him to the use of only his index and middle fingers), Paul is still in league all his own. "I've had to make a new way of playing, but in some ways it's proved to be advantageous," he told Jas Obrecht of *Guitar Player*. It stretches your head out, makes you think more." In 1988 Cinemax filmed a show at New York's Majestic Theater honoring Paul with special guests Van Halen, Steve Miller, B.B. King, and Stanley Jordan paying tribute. When an earlier hit, "Nola," recently reached number 1 in China, Paul decided to start releasing his older work on video and

compact disc. And as usual, he continues to work with Gibson inventing new products. Les Paul virtually wrote the book on music electronics, and after 22 gold records, "The Wizard of Waukesha" remains one of the true innovative geniuses of 20th-century music.

Selected discography

10-inch format

New Sound, Capitol, 195?
New Sound, Volume 2, Capitol, 195?
Bye Bye Blues, Capitol, 195?

LPs

Hit Makers, Capitol.
Les & Mary, Capitol.
Time To Dream, Capitol.
Lover, Capitol.
Hits of Les & Mary, Capitol.
Les Paul & Mary Ford, Harmony, 1965.
Les Paul Now, London, 1968.
Very Best of Les Paul, Capitol, 1974.
Tiger Rag, Pickwick.
Les Paul Story, Volume 1, Capitol, 1974.
Les Paul Story, Volume 2, Capitol, 1974.
The World Is Waiting For the Sunrise, Capitol, 1974.
Guitar Tapestry, Project 3.
Chester and Lester, RCA, 1976.
Guitar Monsters, RCA, 1978.
The Genius of Les Paul—Multi Trackin, London, 1979.
Early Les Paul Trio (transcriptions of 1947 radio broadcasts), Capitol.
The World Is Still Waiting for the Sunrise, Capitol.
The Fabulous Les Paul and Mary Ford, Columbia, 1988.

Sources

Books

Evans, Tom, and Mary Anne Evans, *Guitars: From the Renaissance to Rock*, Facts on File, 1977.
The Rolling Stone Record Guide, edited by Dave Marsh with John Swenson, Random House/Rolling Stone Press, 1979.

Periodicals

down beat, May, 1988.
Guitar Player, May, 1976; December, 1977; June, 1979; February, 1982; June, 1983; August, 1984.
Guitar World, September, 1984; November, 1986; November, 1987; December, 1988.
Rolling Stone, May 6, 1976.

—Calen D. Stone

Itzhak Perlman

Violinist

Itzhak Perlman is one of the most famous and sought-after international violin virtuosos of the latter twentieth century. His warm, lyrical sound, formidable technique and musicianship, and rapport with audiences have led to his superstar status. Perlman has performed with orchestras and in recitals throughout the world, earning record sums. His albums of classical violin pieces consistently top the best-seller charts, and he is widely known to the public from televised performances and talk show appearances. "His talent is utterly limitless," violinist and friend Isaac Stern told *Newsweek*'s Annalyn Swan. "No one comes anywhere near him in what he can physically do with the violin."

Perlman's parents, Chaim and Shoshana, met and married in Israel, to which they had separately emigrated in the 1930s. Shortly after Itzhak was born his talent became evident. The two and a half-year-old could sing on key opera arias that he heard on the radio, and at age three and a half the toddler asked for a violin, which his parents bought for him at a local thrift store.

Tragedy struck Perlman at age four when he contracted polio myelitis, which permanently paralyzed his legs and necessitated his wearing heavy braces and walking with the aid of crutches. During his lengthly convalescence, Perlman continued to pratice the violin, and he later studied with Rivka Goldgart at Schulamit Academy in Tel Aviv. The young boy with perfect pitch made such progress that he was considered a child prodigy. In 1958 he was discovered during a talent search and chosen to represent Israel on the *Ed Sullivan Caravan of the Stars* during its tour of the United States.

After the tour, Itzhak and his mother moved into an apartment in New York, a difficult move. "It wasn't easy: not speaking the language, leaving childhood friends behind, leaving my father—who joined us a year later. It took six months to get myself attuned and it was depressing in the beginning, but when you are a kid you get used to things very quicky," he related to a reporter for the *New York Daily News*. The young violinist received his secondary education at home with tutors and enrolled in the preparatory division of New York's Juilliard School of Music. For five years he studied under the renowned teachers Dorothy DeLay and Ivan Galamian and eventually earned a diploma. Remembering that time, DeLay told Swan, "What set Itzhak apart from the beginning was his sheer talent and enormous imagination. Itzhak was on a kind of creative high that has never let up."

Perlman also spent several summers at Meadowmount School of Music in upstate New York, where he met violinist Toby Friedlander, whom he married in 1967. During those years Perlman also helped support his family by playing for Jewish fund-raising dinners. A more auspicious performance, his Carnegie Hall debut, took place on March 5, 1963, with his rendition of Wieniawski's *Violin Concerto No. 1.* The need to perform as a soloist from a sitting position instead of standing—as is customary—necessitated that Perlman hold the violin in a somewhat unorthodox position, but this has not adversely affected his ability. In fact, his solo career was launched when he won the prestigious Leventritt Competition, with its $1000 cash award and bookings for solo appearances with the New York Philharmonic and other major symphony orchestras.

Since that time Perlman has become one of the most popular instrumentalists in the realm of classical music. His technical command of the violin, superb musicianship and lyrical tone, and showmanship have endeared him to audiences worldwide. Perlman's celebrity status has given him much freedom—financial and artistic. He performs on any of a number of Stradivarius or Guarnieri violins, extremely expensive eighteenth-century violins renowned for their distinctive tonal quality. He also enjoys limiting his concert schedule to approximately one hundred performances per year. He schedules concert dates around family events, with ample time to rest between appearances as traveling is especially rigorous when transportation and logding are often not easily accessible.

Perlman likes to add several new works to his repertoire each year—exclusively pieces that appeal to him—and spend a long but leisurely time preparing them. He delights in searching out unusual works of considerable musical value and has also commissioned new works for the violin. Perlman's enormous discography includes most of the classical repertoire for violin, for which he has garnered numerous Grammy Awards, as well as forays into folk songs and jazz. When not performing or recording, Perlman finds time to share his talents in other ways, such as teaching masters classes at the music camp in Aspen, Colorado.

Believing that media exposure will attract wider audiences to classical music, Perlman has appeared many times on television—talk shows, news magazines, children's shows—during which he dispells with his sense of humor the image of classical music as elitist or "stuffy." He also uses such appearances to speak out on behalf of the handicapped for improved access to public buildings and transporatation, and he has supported aid to the handicapped through several hospi-

> *Itzhak Perlman is one of the most famous and sought-after international violin virtuosos of the latter twentieth century.*

tals, foundations, and educational programs, even funding a scholarship for musically talented disabled children.

Perlman is very much the family man and lives unostentatiously in his New York City apartment, once the home of Babe Ruth. He prefers to commute home as often as possible rather than spend nights in a hotel and often calls home three or four times a day.

He enjoys many hobbies: cooking, swimming, playing table tennis, and rooting for the Yankees and Knicks.

Selected discography

Bach: *Violin Concertos in D Minor and G Minor,* EMI/Angel.
Bach: *Sonatas and Partitas for Solo Violin,* EMI/Angel.
Beethoven: *Piano Trios No. 6 and 7,* EMI/Angel.
Beethoven: *Sonatas No. 1 - 7,* London.
Beethoven: *Violin Concerto,* EMI/Angel.
Berlioz: *Reverie et Caprice;* Lalo: *Symphonie Espanole,* Deutsche Grammaphon.

Brahms: *Violin Concerto*, EMI/Angel.

Chausson: *Pome;* Ravel: *Tzigane;* Saint-Sans: *Havanaise; Introduction and Rondo Capricioso,* EMI/Angel.

Dvorak: *Violin Concerto*, EMI/Angel.

Elgar: *Violin Concerto*, DG.

Encores—Kreisler, Sarasate, Novcek, Ben Haim, Wieniawski,
Debussy, Tartini, Valle, Rachmaninov, Schumann, Paganini,
EMI/Angel.

Goldmark: *Violin Concerto No. 1;* Korngold: *Violin Concerto in D
Major,* EMI/Angel.

Joplin: *Easy Winners*, EMI/Angel.

Khachaturian: *Violin Concerto;* Tchaikovsky: *Meditation*, EMI/
Angel.

Kreisler: *My Favourite Kreisler*, EMI/Angel.

Mendelssohn-Bartholdy: *Violin Concerto in E Minor;* Bruch:
Violin Concerto No. 1 in G Minor, EMI/Angel.

Mozart: *Violin Concerto No. 1*, DG.

Paganini: *Violin Concert No. 1;* Sarasate: *Carmen Fantasy*, EMI/
Angel.

Prokofiev: *Violin Concertos No. 1 and 2*, RCA.

Sibelius: *Violin Concerto;* Sinding: *Suite for Violin and Orchestra,
op. 10*, EMI/Angel.

Salut d'amour—Virtuoso Pieces by Albniz, Brahms, Dvorak,
Elgar, Falla, Kreisler, Phillips.

Starer: *Violin Concerto;* Kim: *Violin Concerto*, EMI/Angel.

Stravinsky: *Divertimento; Suite Italienne; Duo Concertante*, EMI/
Angel.

Tchaikovsky: *Piano Trio*, EMI/Angel.

Tchaikovsky: *Violin Concerto*, EMI/Angel.

Vieuxtemps: *Violin Concertos No. 4 and 5*, EMI/Angel.

Vivaldi: *The Four Seasons*, EMI/Angel.

Wieniawski: *Violin Concertos No. 1 and 2*, EMI/Angel.

Sources

Books

Schwarz, Boris, *Great Masters of the Violin*, Simon and Schuster,
1983.

Periodicals

Atlanta Journal, October 20, 1985; October 4, 1988.
Greensboro News and Record, January 19, 1986.
Hartford Courant, April 4, 1987.
Houston Post, January 9, 1989.
Indianapolis Star, May 15, 1988.
Kansas City Star, November 25, 1984; May 20, 1987.
Lansing State Journal, October 31, 1988.
Newsweek, April 14, 1980.
New York Daily News, June 29, 1986.
Seattle Times, October 21, 1988.
The Strad, February 1986.

—*Jeanne M. Lesinski*

Pink Floyd

Rock group

Rock band Pink Floyd holds one of the most impressive records in the music industry—its 1973 album *Dark Side of the Moon* has been on *Billboard* magazine's top two hundred chart longer than any other. Additional distinctions include being known as Great Britain's first psychedelic rock band and the first British band to use a light show in concert performance. Indeed, Pink Floyd is as much renowned for its elaborate stage shows, with lights, films, and inflatable balloons, as for its songs, such as "Money," "Time," and "Another Brick in the Wall." Considered serious musicians by most rock critics, Pink Floyd is "doing art for art's sake, and you don't have to be high to get it," declared disc jockey Tom Morrera in an interview with *Time*'s Jay Cocks. "They'll take you on a trip anyway."

Pink Floyd was founded in or around 1964 by Roger "Syd" Barrett in London, England. Barrett named the group for two of his favorite blues musicians, Pink Anderson and Floyd Council, and the band was initially blues-influenced. But Barrett, serving as the primary songwriter and playing lead guitar, quickly shaped

For the Record. . .

Band formed c. 1964 by **Syd Barrett** in London, England; original members included Syd Barrett (real name, Roger Barrett; born January 6, 1946, in Cambridge, England) lead guitar, vocals; acted as primary songwriter in early years (left group, 1968); **Roger Waters** (born September 6, 1944, in Great Bookham, England) bass, piano, vocals; became primary songwriter after Barrett left (left group c. 1985); **Rick Wright** (born July 28, 1945, in London) keyboards, vocals (left group, 1980; rejoined c. 1987); and **Nick Mason** (born January 27, 1945, in Birmingham, England) drums. Current lead guitarist and songwriter **David Gilmour** (born March 6, 1944, in Cambridge, England) joined group in 1968. Performed in clubs in London, 1964-67; signed with EMI Records, 1966; recording artists and concert performers, 1967—.

Awards: 1973 album, *Dark Side of the Moon*, remained on *Billboard*'s charts longer than any other in history.

Addresses: *Office*—c/o 43 Portland Rd., London W11, England.

Pink Floyd's uniquely mystic, psychedelic sound; he was abetted in this effort by bass player Roger Waters, keyboardist Rick Wright, and drummer Nick Mason. In the early years the band had another member, Bob Close, but he only played with them briefly. Pink Floyd began by playing clubs in the London area; their first regular job was at the Marquee in early 1966, and they soon attracted a small, loyal following. Later in the year the band had moved to the Sound/Light Workshop in London, where they included a light show in their act—a first in Great Britain. By the end of 1966, they had not only become the house band at the UFO Club, but had signed a deal with EMI Records (who released their music in the United States on the Tower label). Pink Floyd's first single, written by Barrett, was "Arnold Layne." The song, about a transvestite, was considered controversial—even underground station Radio London banned it—yet it enjoyed a fair amount of success in England. Another of Barrett's musical creations, "See Emily Play," did even better with British audiences, but their critically acclaimed first album, *The Piper at the Gates of Dawn,* was not as popular with American audiences.

Early in 1968 Pink Floyd recruited another guitarist, David Gilmour, to supplement Barrett. The founder's behavior had become erratic, allegedly as a result of his experimentation with psychedelic drugs such as LSD, and he left the band two months after Gilmour

joined. Barrett's subsequent life has become the subject of rumor and speculation. He apparently recorded a few albums in the 1970s with Gilmour and Waters, but, according to David Fricke of *Rolling Stone*, Barrett "withdrew into a debilitating madness" from which "he never recovered."

After Barrett's departure from Pink Floyd, Gilmour played lead guitar for the band and Waters shouldered most of the songwriting responsibility. The group's eclectic, mystic flavor, begun by Barrett, was preserved under the leadership of Waters. Albums like *Saucerful of Secrets* (1968) and *Ummagumma* (1969) helped build Pink Floyd's reputation as a cult band, and they began to receive offers to write and perform music for films. Motion pictures that feature the sounds of Pink Floyd include *More, Let's All Make Love in London, The Committee,* and *Zabriskie Point.* They continued to garner critical acclaim into the early 1970s with the albums *Atom Heart Mother, Meddle,* and *Obscured by Clouds,* the soundtrack from the film *Le Vallee.* At the same time, by rarely granting interviews and keeping

> *"Pink Floyd is doing art for art's sake, and you don't have to be high to get it. They'll take you on a trip anyway."*

low personal profiles, the band members created an aura of darkness and mystery about themselves. Gilmour explained to Chet Flippo in *People* that he and his fellow musicians did not want Pink Floyd's strange image destroyed by the knowledge that its members were somewhat ordinary: if they had made themselves more visible, "the fans might have gotten too much information about us sitting at home watching television and drinking beer."

Pink Floyd's status as a cult band changed radically, however, with the release of *Dark Side of the Moon,* about the alienation and mental illness stemming from societal pressures. "Money," a single from the album, gave the group its first major American hit. As Flippo put it, "*Dark Side,* bleak and gothic, reached out and tapped some previously unreached citizens of our planet." Although it has stayed on *Billboard*'s charts longer than any other album, Gilmour told Flippo that *Dark Side*'s success has "always baffled me, still baffles me. I mean, when we made it, we knew it was the best we'd done. But we hadn't even gone *gold* before then."

Though they sold well, the follow-up albums to *Dark Side, Wish You Were Here* (1976) and *Animals* (1977), were considered inferior to their predecessor. *Animals,* however, became Pink Floyd's first platinum album. The effort portrayed society as divided into three different kinds of animals—dogs, pigs, and sheep—and the concert tour to promote *Animals* was graced by props such as a giant inflatable flying pig. But Pink Floyd's 1979 product, *The Wall,* brought both higher critical acclaim and greater popular success. Including the hit "Another Brick in the Wall," the album, reported Cocks, "is a lavish, four-sided dredge job on the angst of the successful rocker, his flirtations with suicide and losing bouts with self-pity, his assorted betrayals by parents, teachers and wives and his uneasy relationship with his audience, which is alternately exhorted, cajoled and mocked." The concert tour that followed *The Wall's* release featured such a complicated stage show, including props like a thirty-foot-tall inflatable woman and a huge wall composed of cardboard boxes that collapsed during the performance's climax, that it only went to four cities: New York, Los Angeles, London, and Cologne, West Germany.

After the *Wall* tour, Rick Wright left Pink Floyd due to artistic tensions between its members. The band put out another album, *The Final Cut,* in 1983, but the tensions continued until Waters separated from the group in or around 1985. Amid legal battles between Waters and the other members over who had the right to use the Pink Floyd name, Gilmour and Mason, later rejoined by Wright, released an album, *Momentary Lapse of Reason,* and went on tour as Pink Floyd in 1987.

Selected discography

Piper at the Gates of Dawn (includes "Arnold Layne" and "See Emily Play"), Tower, 1967.
Saucerful of Secrets (includes "Let There Be More Light" and "Set the Controls for the Heart of the Sun"), Tower, 1968.
More, Harvest, 1969.
Ummagumma, Harvest, 1969.
Atom Heart Mother, Harvest, 1970.
Meddle (includes "Echoes"), Harvest, 1971.
Relics, Harvest, 1971.
Obscured by Clouds, Harvest, 1972.
Dark Side of the Moon (includes "Money" and "Time"), Harvest, 1973.
Wish You Were Here, CBS, 1976.
Animals, CBS, 1977.
The Wall (includes "Another Brick in the Wall"), CBS, 1979.
The Final Cut, CBS, 1983.
Momentary Lapse of Reason, CBS, 1987.

Sources

People, March 12, 1984.
Rolling Stone, January 15, 1987; June 4, 1987; October 22, 1987; November 19, 1987.
Time, February 25, 1980.

—*Elizabeth Thomas*

Robert Plant

Singer, songwriter

With the 1988 release of *Now And Zen,* Robert Plant celebrated his twentieth anniversary as a reigning vocalist of hard rock. Plant has been at rock music's forefront since he joined Led Zeppelin in 1968. His best-known songs, including "Stairway to Heaven" and "Whole Lotta Love," are classics that remain the definitive expressions of early 1970s rock. Since the 1980 demise of Led Zeppelin, Plant has undertaken a solo career that reflects his mature but ongoing interest in his chosen genre; *Now and Zen* has received better reviews than any of his Led Zeppelin work and heralds new directions for the thoughtful rocker. Plant told *People* magazine that when his group disbanded, after many well-publicized disasters, he still had the ambition to make good music. "My intention was to go in the complete reverse direction from sliding into obscurity," he said. "After the end of Zeppelin, I didn't really see anything. But as time went on, I started to pick up the pieces." Now, touring on his own to sellout crowds, Plant has proven himself an artist "with deep roots in the music's past but a lively interest in its present—and future—as well," to quote *Rolling Stone* reviewer Kurt Loder.

In early 1968 Plant was an obscure singer with a band called Hobbstweedle, based in England's Midlands region. *Rolling Stone* contributor Stephen Davis describes the British teenager as "a great tall blond geezer who looked like a fairy prince and possessed a caterwauling voice. They called him the Wild Man of Blues from the Black Country." Plant's name came to the attention of Jimmy Page of the Yardbirds; Page was trying to start a new band and needed a charismatic lead singer. Page and some friends travelled to Birmingham to hear Plant perform at an obscure teacher's college. Plant amazed them with his keening soprano, so out of context with his tall, rugged physique. "It unnerved me just to listen," Davis quotes Page as saying. "It still does, like a primeval wail." Davis notes that before too long Page was convinced that Plant had the very voice he needed, one with a "distinctive, highly charged, sexual quality." Plant accepted the opportunity to work with Page and convinced his friend John Bonham to join the group, too. In October of 1968 Led Zeppelin was founded, with Plant, Page, Bonham, and John Paul Jones.

People correspondent Jim Jerome writes: "From its launch in 1968, Led Zeppelin figured to be testing the dubious proposition that heavy metal could be lighter than air. Yet through the mellower-than-thou '70s, rock's fiercest foursome was more than buoyant: Led Zep sold some 40 million LPs worldwide [and] set concert attendance records all over the planet." Plant hit his stride as a lyricist while in the group, composing songs such as "Kashmir," "Black Dog," "Misty Mountain Hop," and the winsome "Stairway to Heaven," based on ancient Celtic legends. Davis claims: "With its starkly pagan imagery of trees and brooks, pipers and the May Queen, shining white light and the forest echoing with laughter, ["Stairway to Heaven"] seemed to be an invitation to abandon the new traditions and follow the old gods. It expressed a yearning for spiritual transformation deep in the hearts of a new generation. In time, it became Led Zeppelin's anthem."

Unfortunately, in a tradition they helped to spawn, the members of Zeppelin conducted themselves with reckless hedonism while on tour, abusing alcohol and drugs and indulging their sexual appetites with ever-willing female fans. Plant told *Rolling Stone* that he recalls few details from those days. "I can remember a stream of carpenters walking into a room as we were checking out," he said. "We'd be going out one way, and they'd be going in the other way, with a sign, CLOSED FOR REMODELING, being put on the door. It's kind of embarrassing. But without being too facetious, that's what people *wanted*. Once the seed was sown, it would be terrible if it was just once a week. It had to be all the time."

Dire predictions followed such excessive behavior, and indeed the group began to be plagued with extreme bad luck. As Davis puts it, by 1975 "the old Zeppelin carnival atmosphere had dissipated. There were strange portents in the air." In that year Plant and his family were involved in an automobile accident; two years later, Plant's young son died suddenly of a severe respiratory infection. A certain rivalry had always existed in Led Zeppelin—especially between Plant and Page—and this too escalated. The group finally split up in 1980 following the alcohol-induced death of Bonham, a blow that hit Plant particularly hard. Plant told *People* that Bonham's death "was one of the most flattening, heartbreaking parts of my life. . . . It was so final. I never even thought about the future of the band or music." When he began to recover, however, Plant returned to the stage with one determination—he would not be content to rehash the Zeppelin classics for the rest of his career. "I went out and stifled whatever cries there were—not the least of them from myself—for Zeppelin material," he said. "People don't want to let go of something they loved so much. It's a shame to say goodbye."

"Scorned by the punks and embarrassed by cheap Zeppelin imitators, Plant spent his first three solo albums roaming the shifting terrain of Eighties rock in search of an identity that had nothing to do with lemon squeezing or 'Stairway to Heaven,'" notes David Fri in *Rolling Stone.* "He never found it. He had a couple of

> *Robert Plant has been at rock music's forefront since he joined Led Zeppelin in 1968."*

hits along the trail, like 'Big Log,' from his 1983 album *The Principle of Moments.* But for all of their adventuresome drive and hip future-rock angularity, Plant's solo records in general lacked the unbridled passion and risky spontaneity of Zeppelin in full flight." Undaunted by the new critical indifference to his work, Plant continued to experiment. One such lark, a five-track EP called *The Honeydrippers, Volume One,* went platinum in 1985. In that short set of songs, culled from vintage rhythm and blues tunes, Plant was joined by Page, Jeff Beck, and pianist Paul Shaffer, among others. All were surprised by the success of *The Honeydrippers,* but, courageously, all decided not to proceed exclusively in that direction.

Plant returned to his solo career, forming his own backup band and trying his best not to load his concerts with Zeppelin songs. His fourth solo album, *Now and Zen,* was a critical and commercial hit. "This record is some kind of stylistic event: a seamless pop fusion of hard guitar rock, gorgeous computerization and sharp, startling songcraft," writes Loder. "[It] is so rich in conceptual invention that you barely notice that Plant sings better on it—with more tone, control and rhythmic acuity—than he has in the seven years since Led Zeppelin imploded. Better, in some ways, than ever."

With the success of *Now and Zen,* Plant has softened toward his Zeppelin music and has added a substantial amount of it to his concert sets. "I wanted to establish an identity that was far removed from the howling and the mud sharks of the Seventies," he told *Rolling Stone.* "So if I go onstage now and sing 'Misty Mountain Hop,' it's cool because I've given it the time in between. I can come out and do it without having traded on it all the way down the line." Asked if he is pleased about the enduring popularity of Led Zeppelin music, Plant concluded: "When I look back, I don't get any sense of great achievement out of the fact that people still like [the music] a lot. I get achievement out of the fact that it was good."

Selected discography

With Led Zeppelin

Led Zeppelin, Atlantic, 1969.
Led Zeppelin II, Atlantic, 1969.
Led Zeppelin III, Atlantic, 1970.
Houses of the Holy, Atlantic, 1973.
Physical Graffiti, Swan Song, 1975.

The Presence, Swan Song, 1976.
The Song Remains the Same, Swan Song, 1976.
In Through the Out Door, Swan Song, 1979.
Coda, Swan Song, 1982.

With the Honeydrippers

The Honeydrippers, Volume One, Atlantic, 1985.

Solo LPs

Pictures at Eleven, Swan Song, 1982.
The Principle of Moments, Atlantic, 1983.
Shaken 'n' Stirred, Es Paranza, 1985.
Now and Zen, Atlantic, 1988.

Sources

Books

Davis, Stephen, *Hammer of the Gods: The Led Zeppelin Saga,* Morrow, 1985.
The Rolling Stone Record Guide, Random House, 1979.

Periodicals

People, August 27, 1979; August 9, 1982.
Rolling Stone, January 31, 1985; July 4, 1985; March 10, 1988; March 24, 1988; July 14-28, 1988.

—Anne Janette Johnson

Vernon Reid

Guitarist, songwriter

The art world has always been populated by two factions: those who create "art for art's sake" and those who fashion their creations into some kind of political or social statement. Among the latter group is guitarist/composer Vernon Reid. Through his band Living Colour, an all-black rock quartet that blasted into stardom between 1988 and '89, he is seeking to improve opportunities for black musicians. "I've been trying to raise people's consciousness," the England-born New Yorker told the *Los Angeles Times*. "I want them to find a new way to think about rock musicians. It doesn't have to be some blue-eyed guy with long, blond hair playing it. It can be somebody who looks like me."

Reid's crusade is directed against the paradox that under lies rock history: Even though rock and roll evolved from the Afro-American tradition of the blues, it has always been the territory of white musicians. Blacks, meanwhile, have been cast by the music industry into their own "urban contemporary" genre. "The career prospects are grim for a black musician who falls outside the rigid stylistic confines of the 'urban contemporary' sound," Joe Gore observed in a *Guitar Player* cover story on Reid. "Black musicians who don't rap, croon romantic ballads, or make good-timey party records usually find themselves locked out of both black and white markets."

In September, 1985, Reid responded to this predicament. Along with *Village Voice* writer Greg Tate, he formed the Black Rock Coalition, an organization that provides networks of support and education for black musicians. "Basically what we try to do is . . . demystify the business," Reid explained to the *Chicago Tribune*. "If you're trying to break in [to the business], it's like walking up to a building that's completely smooth glass and there's no doorway." Yet getting more blacks into the industry is only part of the BRC's agenda. At the same time, it is trying to chip away at the barriers that make it difficult for blacks to enter in the first place. In a founding manifesto, Reid and Tate spelled out the BRC's intentions: "The Black Rock Coalition opposes the racist and reactionary forces in the American music industry which deny black artists the expressive freedom and economic rewards that our Caucasian counterparts enjoy as a matter of course. We too claim the right of creative freedom and total access to American and international airwaves, audiences, and markets. . . ." As Reid explained more succinctly to the *New York Times,* "The Black Rock Coalition says rock-and-roll is the music of our forefathers, and we are the heirs to that music.

The embodiment of that philosophy is Living Colour. By demonstrating that they can rock in any "color" they choose, the New York-based group—composed of Reid, lead singer Corey Glover, bass player Muzz Skillings, and drummer/percussionist William Calhoun—have begun an erosion of the stylistic—and thus racial—divisions erected by the music industry. "[T]he basic underpinning of our music is freedom of choice," Reid told the *New York Times,* "freedom from people's expectations about what you should and shouldn't do." Accordingly, their 1988 debut album *Vivid* displayed a multiple musical personality, encompassing heavy metal, avant-garde jazz, soul, punk, calypso, funk, and rap. At the same time, the lyrics broke with the entertainment-oriented subjects that have come to be expected from black songwriters, dealing instead with issues confronting the black urban community—from prejudice ("Funny Vibe") to urban renewal ("Open Letter [to a Landlord]") to the failure of the media to depict the realities of lower-class life ("Which Way to America?"). That the public was ready for such boldness was proved by *Vivid*'s remarkable success. Early in 1989, less than a year after its release, the record cracked the Top Ten for both albums and singles ("Cult of Personality"); soon afterward, with sales topping one million, it passed the platinum mark.

Born c. 1959 in England to West Indian parents; during childhood, moved with family to Brooklyn, New York. *Education:* Brooklyn Technical High School, art studies major.

During teens, studied with jazz guitarists Ted Dunbar and Rodney Jones; in the early 1980s, after a brief stint with rhythm and blues singer Kashif, joined the Decoding Society, a jazz ensemble led by drummer Ronald Shannon Jackson; c. 1983, formed precursor to Living Colour; during early and mid-80s, collaborated with a variety of New York artists, including the art/dance band Defunkt, the avant-funk groups M-Base and the Contortions, progressive percussionist Daniel Ponce, jazz guitarist Bill Frisell, rappers Public Enemy, avant-garde composer John Zorn, experimental guitarist Arto Lindsay; in 1985, with music critic Greg Tate, formed the Black Rock Coalition; in 1986, formed current lineup of Living Colour; played on Mick Jagger's *Primitive Cool* LP, 1987.

Addresses: Home—Brooklyn, NY. *Band*—Living Colour, Box 407, Bushwick Finance Station, Brooklyn, NY 11221. *Record company (press/public information)*—Epic Records, 1801 Century Park West, Los Angeles, CA 90067; (213) 556-4870. *Black Rock Coalition*—Box 1054 Cooper St., New York, NY 10276.

On *Vivid,* Reid is showcased not only as a composer and lyricist—he wrote or co-wrote ten out of the LP's eleven cuts—but also as one of rock's brilliant new guitarists, inspiring several critics to rhapsodize about his solo style. "Reid . . . generates all the heat and light you could ask for with nothing but flying fingers and synaptic lightning-flashes," wrote Robert Palmer in *Spin.* "[He] textures his playing, giving every chord precise and proper weight, imparting a distinctive timbre, a certain eccentric spin to every note, at the most furious tempos. His riffing sizzles like oxidizing metal; his solos are brilliant databursts. . . . Even the likes of Eddie Van Halen might lose some sleep over this stuff." But as Reid revealed to *Guitar Player,* he is not content to roam solely within the boundaries of rock. "I've always been fascinated by ragtime guitar playing. I really want to do that—it's *killing* me. I want to have a richer chord vocabulary. I want to go back into jazz and really learn standards."

Reid's stylistic versatility is not surprising, considering the tastes he has cultivated as a listener. Born around 1959, he was weaned on diverse samplings from his parents' record collection—the calypso of Lord Kitchener and the Mighty Sparrow, the pop-rhythm and blues blend of Dionne Warwick and the Temptations, the British rock of the Dave Clark 5, and the funk of James Brown. As a teenager he tuned in to the guitar styles of jazz-rock pioneer, John McLaughlin and rockers Jimi Hendrix, Jeff Beck, Eric Clapton, and especially Carlos Santana, whose Latin-flavored style inspired him to bring his own ethnic roots to rock. At the same time he explored other genres, from the ground-breaking jazz of Charlie Parker, John Coltrane, and Eric Dolphy to the modern classical music of Bela Bartok and Edgar Varese.

Reid took up guitar at the age of 15 and began studying with top jazz guitarists Ted Dunbar and Rodney Jones. Within a few years he was playing professionally. "I had this vision of playing the powerful, rock-oriented music," he told the *Los Angeles Times,* "of being this strong, solid musician who could play whatever he wanted—even this kind of music that black musicians hardly ever played. I knew what I wanted and I went after it." Appropriately, his career began with a baptism of fire: He joined the highly acclaimed Decoding Society, a hard-edged jazz-rock experimental group led by drummer Ronald Shannon Jackson. After touring extensively and recording six albums with Jackson, he collaborated with a variety of artists, all of whom, like Jackson, represented the cutting edge of New York's multi-faceted music scene—the art/dance band Defunkt, the avant-funk Contortions and M-Base, progressive percussionist Daniel Ponce, jazz guitarist Bill Frisell, avant-garde composer John Zorn, experimental guitarist Arto Lindsay, militant rappers Public Enemy, and others.

Meanwhile, about 1983 Reid formed his own band, a prototype of Living Colour. The band underwent several personnel changes until 1986, when they settled into their current lineup and began attracting attention at the New York clubs. Around that time, Mick Jagger was preparing to record *Primitive Cool,* his second solo LP, and had been advised by colleagues to enlist Reid as a guest guitarist. After seeing Living Colour perform, the legendary Rolling Stone not only gave Reid the job but also offered to help produce the demonstration tape for *Vivid.* "We were a band like any other band playing at CBGBs," Reid told *Rolling Stone,* referring to a hard-rock club in Manhattan. "One night Mick Jagger comes in, checks us out, and the ball starts to roll from there." Jagger produced two tracks—the Carribean-flavored "Glamour Boys" and the rap-tinged hard-rocker "Which Way to America?"—through which the band caught the attention of Epic Records. "But getting a deal wasn't an automatic thing, even with Mick Jagger's name as producer on those tracks," Reid explained to the *Los Angeles Times.* "It helped that we're a good band. But we had to be *real* good—better than a white rock band has to be—to convince them to gamble on us." After cutting the demo, Living Colour hit the road for 18 months, promoting the record along the Northeast club and college circuit. The tour generated a lot of positive press—and Epic, convinced, signed them.

Though he is obviously pleased by the success of Living Colour, Reid has been quick to point out that they are the exception to the rule; in several interviews he has stressed the many talented black rock acts compared to the few who have record contracts. "It's not about 'Now we got through the door, close the door behind us,'" Reid told *Rolling Stone* early in 1989. "What I hope our success is doing is encouraging other black rock bands to stick with it, because this is the result of six years of hard work. Other bands have told me our success is giving them the feeling that it's possible." Remaining optimistic, however, is often a challenge for him. "If you're black you have some rage in you," he told the *Los Angeles Times*. "It may be buried deep in some people but it's there. Playing music has helped me deal with my anger at the position of blacks in this country and the position of black rock musicians in the music business."

As a composer, Reid draws from not only the black American experience but also his African roots. Among his works-in-progress is a multi-media theater piece called *Afrerica,* which he is creating in collaboration with a writer named Sekow Sundiata. "It's based on the idea of the Africa that black Americans have in their heads," he explained to *Guitar Player.* "There's the physical Africa, and then there's the African construct that we've put together to help us survive. Black nationalists have seized on Africa as this golden Valhalla or Asgard, this incredibly magical and good place. It's like an amalgam of what they would like to see happen here and the bit of African history that they know. There are so many Africas, and so many societies in Africa, each

with its own morals. We've taken what we like about all these things. *Afrerica* is about this fantastical concept. It's one of my life projects; it will change as my compositional abilities improve."

Selected discography

With Ronald Shannon Jackson and the Decoding Society

Eye On You, About Time.
Mandance, Antilles.
Barbeque Dog, Antilles.
Decode Yourself, Island.

With others

Defunkt, *Thermonuclear Sweat,* Hannibal.
Bill Frisell & Vernon Reid, *Smash and Scatteration,* Minor Music, 1985.
John Zorn, *The Big Gundown,* Nonesuch, 1986.
Mick Jagger, *Primitive Cool,* Columbia, 1987.
Public Enemy, *Yo! Bum Rush the Show,* Def Jam Columbia, 1987.
Ambitious Lovers (Arto Lindsay, Peter Scherer), *Greed,* Virgin, 1988.

With Living Colour

Vivid, Epic, 1988.

Sources

Guitar Player, October, 1988.
Los Angeles Times, January 22, 1989; February 25, 1989.
New York Times, April 24, 1989; May 21, 1989.
Rolling Stone, March 23, 1989.
Spin, May, 1988.

—*Kyle Kevorkian*

Lionel Richie

Pop singer, songwriter

Lionel Richie "now stands at the pinnacle of pop music, recognized around the world as the most successful singer/songwriter working today," Charles Whitaker announced in a 1987 *Ebony* article. "His string of nine No. 1 hits," Whitaker continued, "in nine consecutive years, is a music business record." Richie began as a lead singer with the Commodores, a funk/pop group that came to the attention of music fans in the early 1970s, and started forging his distinguished solo career in 1982. Since that time he has garnered many awards, including three Grammys, several American Music Awards, and a 1986 Oscar for Best Original Song with his hit theme to the film *White Knights,* "Say You, Say Me."

Richie was born in Tuskegee, Alabama. His mother and father, a school principal and a systems analyst for the U.S. Army, respectively, lived on the campus of Tuskegee Institute (now Tuskegee University), where his grandfather had worked with the college's founder, black leader Booker T. Washington. As a child, Richie was exposed to many different kinds of music, particularly by his maternal grandmother, Adlaide Foster, who taught him piano and preferred classical composers such as Johann Sebastian Bach and Ludwig van Beethoven. Even then, Richie showed signs of the talent he would later become, though his grandmother did not then appreciate this fact: "During my lessons," Richie recalled for Todd Gold in *People,* "I kept trying to make up my own songs, and it annoyed her." The fledgling artist was also influenced by the ballets and symphonies he attended at Tuskegee, but he preferred listening to gospel, rhythm and blues, and country.

Richie eventually enrolled in Tuskegee Institute; his initial goal was to become an Episcopal priest. He brought with him a saxophone that an uncle had given him as a child, though he did not know how to play it—according to Gold, "he thought it would help him meet girls." Regardless, it helped Richie to meet five other Tuskegee freshmen who were forming a musical group and sought him out because they heard he had a saxophone. Apparently, Richie's lack of prowess on the instrument proved no obstacle—he told Robert E. Johnson in *Ebony* that the men who would later become the Commodores "took . . . two years to find out that I'd had no training on the sax." While Richie and the group practiced, aspiring to, as he put it for interviewer Lynn Van Matre of the *Chicago Tribune,* "revolutionize the music business," or "come out with a new sound, you know, and kill them," he also gave up his clerical ambitions in favor of an economics major and an accounting minor, which helped both the Commodores and himself in later business dealings.

For the Record. . .

Full name, Lionel B. Richie, Jr.; born c. 1949, in Tuskegee, Ala.; son of Lionel, Sr. (a systems analyst) and Alberta (a school principal) Richie; married Brenda Harvey (a musical production assistant), 1975. *Education:* Graduated from Tuskegee Institute (now Tuskegee University), 1974.

Joined musical group the Commodores while in college; left group to become solo recording artist and concert performer, 1982. Has written songs and produced records for other performers, including Kenny Rogers.

Awards: Winner of three Grammy Awards; six American Music Awards; two American Black Achievement Awards from *Ebony* magazine and one People's Choice Award; Academy Award for best original song in a motion picture (White Knights), 1986, for "Say You, Say Me."

Addresses: *Residence*—Beverly Hills, Calif.; and Tuskegee, Ala. *Office*—1112 N. Sherbourne Dr., Los Angeles, CA 90069.

The Commodores first began to gather a following when they won the opportunity to open for the Jackson Five's concerts in the early 1970s. Around the same time, they signed a contract with Motown Records, and after a two-year period of searching for the right producer and arranger, began to put out albums. At first the Commodores gained a reputation for party and dance music with disco-oriented hits like the instrumental "Machine Gun," and the song responsible for the dance craze of the same name, "Bump." Another of their most popular singles was "Brickhouse."

But by the mid-1970s, most of the Commodores, including Richie, started to feel that funky dance tunes were too ephemeral. They wanted to move towards writing and recording ballads, which they thought more likely to become timeless standards. In the same period, Richie worked more intensely on his songwriting skills than previously. The Commodores' 1975 album *Caught in the Act* contained their first ballad hits, "Sweet Love," and "Just to Be Close to You." They followed these up with more slow songs, which gained popularity in large measure due to Richie's romantic lyrics and smooth singing voice. "Easy," "Three Times a Lady," "Sail On," and "Still" confirmed Richie and the Commodores' change of style.

Richie was already working on other projects in 1980, including producing an album and writing the song "Lady" for country artist Kenny Rogers. In 1982 Richie decided to leave the Commodores to pursue a solo career, though his decision was not due to conflicts within the group. His first album on his own, *Lionel Richie,* gained him a hit with "Truly," which also won him his first Grammy, as Best Male Vocalist, in 1983. His string of hits, some of which helped Richie earn his music business record, includes 1983's "All Night Long," "Penny Lover," and "Hello"; and 1987's "Dancing on the Ceiling." Richie has also had great success with film themes such as "Endless Love" and the Oscar-winning "Say You, Say Me." Perhaps his most far-reaching and influential musical project, however, was the song "We Are the World," which Richie co-wrote with pop superstar Michael Jackson. The disc was recorded by U.S.A. for Africa, and its profits were donated to the cause of famine relief in Ethiopia.

Richie believes his success as a songwriter comes from God, whom he told Johnson was his "co-composer." He explained further: "I give credit to my co-writer because all I did was write down what He told me to

> "Lionel Richie now stands at the pinnacle of pop music, recognized around the world as the most successful singer/songwriter working today."

write down." Richie also revealed to Johnson that he prefers to collaborate during the night. "In other words," he said, "from about eleven to about seven in the morning is a very wonderful time because . . . God ain't worried with too many other folks . . . I know He is very busy during the day, so I wait for late night, and it works for me."

Regardless of the authorship of Richie's songs, along with the phenomenal mainstream popularity that he enjoys come accusations from some critics that he has abandoned his black musical roots, especially after the hit he recorded with the country group Alabama, "Deep River Woman." Richie responded to this issue for Whitaker in *Ebony:* "I'm trying through my music to break the stereotype that says to satisfy Black people you have to play something funky. I'm broadening the base, trying to show that Black artists are capable of playing all kinds of music."

Selected discography

With the Commodores; on Motown

Machine Gun (includes "Machine Gun" and "Bump"), 1974.
Caught in the Act (includes "Zoom," "Sweet Love," and "Just to Be Close to You"), 1975.
Commodores (includes "Easy" and "Three Times a Lady"), 1977.
Midnight Magic (includes "Sail On" and "Still"), 1979.
Heroes (includes "Jesus is Love," "Got to Be Together," and "An Old-Fashioned Love"), 1980.

Also recorded the song "Brickhouse."

Solo LPs; on Motown

Lionel Richie (includes "Truly," "You Are," and "My Love"), 1982.
Can't Slow Down (includes "All Night Long" and "Penny Lover"), 1983.

Say You, Say Me (includes "Say You, Say Me"), 1986.
Dancing on the Ceiling (includes "Dancing on the Ceiling"), 1987.

Also recorded the song "Deep River Woman" with Alabama; also co-wrote "We Are the World."

Sources

Periodicals

Chicago Tribune, December 12, 1982.
Ebony, January, 1985; February 1987.
Jet, April 21, 1986; August 15, 1988.
People, April 14, 1986.

—*Elizabeth Thomas*

Robbie Robertson

Singer, songwriter, composer, guitarist, producer

Robbie Robertson has been a professional musician since 1959, when he began playing guitar with Ronnie Hawkins and the Hawks in juke joints and dives all across North America. Six years later, before thousands of fans, he was backing Bob Dylan as the folkie was making his transition to electric. By then the Hawks were known simply as the Band and were soon creating their own powerful originals. After another tour with Dylan, the Band decided to call it quits in 1976 and Robertson began working in movies, both acting and scoring soundtracks, while remaining relatively behind the scenes for nearly a decade. In 1987 he released his first solo LP, proving that his songwriting and guitar abilities were stronger than ever.

Robertson began playing guitar at age ten after his cousins introduced him to country music. After a brief period of Hawaiian lap steel lessons, the fifteen-year-old knew his life was in music and started writing songs. He developed a trademark guitar sound that can be traced back to blues masters like Muddy Waters. "I didn't realize that they were using slides, so for years I worked on developing a vibrato technique equivalent to a slide," he told Steve Caraway in *Guitar Player*. "It all made me develop a certain style." At sixteen Robertson quit school to join Hawkins as a bass player until the guitarist, Fred Carter, quit a few months later. For the next two years he practiced endlessly as the band toured Canada and the rural sections of the States. As the teenager was viewing the richness of Americana, he also became one of the most unique players around. "Robbie was the first guy to get into white funk, in Canada or anywhere," Hawkins told Ben Fong-Torres in *Rolling Stone*. "They were always two years ahead of their time."

Robertson fingerpicked as a youth to alleviate boredom and to accompany himself, but now he was beginning to explore the ringing tone offered by harmonics (picking a string and then grazing it with a finger to bring out a bell-like overtone). "Within a year (of joining the Hawks) I was actually onto something," he said in *Guitar Player*. "I was the only one playing a certain way in a big area; up north it just wasn't happening for that kind of guitar playing." In fact, besides Roy Buchannan on the east coast, it wasn't happening anywhere else. Robertson's guitar exploded on Hawkins's biggest hit, "Who Do You Love," in 1963, which would be their last year backing up the wild singer.

For the next two years drummer Levon Helm fronted the group as Levon and the Hawks toured Canada. After hearing them in Toronto, John Hammond, Jr., brought the members to New York, where Robertson played on some of the bluesman's recordings. While working in

New Jersey the Hawks received a call from Dylan asking them to play with him at a Hollywood Bowl gig. They accepted and in the summer of 1965 they hit the road as Dylan's support band, playing America and Europe sans Helms—the only U.S. citizen in the group—who had headed back home to Arkansas, as Mickey Jones replaced him until the tour was over.

Helm rejoined Robertson and the rest of the Band (Garth Hudson, Richard Manuel, and Rick Danko) in West Saugerties, New York, where they retreated to write and record songs for their 1968 debut LP, *music From Big Pink.* The album reflected Dylan's lyrical influence as they worked closely with the singer while he recovered from a motorcycle accident. The Band's mountain-music sound also rubbed off on Dylan, as evidenced on his songs from the same period later released as *The Basement Tapes.* In Robertson, Dylan found not only an exceptional writer but also an excellent guitarist. He was, according to Dylan in *Rolling Stone,* "the only mathematical guitar genius I've ever run into who does not offend my intestinal nervousness with his rear guard sound."

As solid as their first LP was, their second release, *The Band,* would be remembered as the album that helped listeners bring life after the 1960s into focus. The Band moved to Los Angeles to record the LP as Roberstson took over as chief songwriter. As a Canadian giving his view of America, Robertson created "one of the greatest and most profound rock and roll albums ever made," stated Dave Marsh in *The Rolling Stone Record Guide,* "as close to a perfect statement of purpose as any rock group has ever come." Songs like "Across the Great Divide" and "The Night They Drove Old Dixie Down"

established Robertson as a premier tale-teller. "In my mind there's this mythical place in America where *the storyteller* lives. And he tells stories based on this place and people who've come through, and his experiences," he later told *Musician.*

In 1970, Robertson, at age twenty-six, appeared alongside his Bandmates on the cover of *Time* magazine with the release of *Stage Fright,* their third LP. With such an incredible album to follow, *Stage Fright* was a fine effort but not nearly as overwhelming. Their follow-up, *Cahoots,* was even weaker yet as Robertson's lyrics lacked his visionary punch. A live album, *Rock of Ages,* was recorded on New Year's Eve, 1971, at New York's Academy of music with the addition of Allen Toussaint's beefed-up New Orleans-style horn section. Robert Christgau, in his *Record Guide,* called it "the testament of artists who are looking backwards because the future presents itself as a vacuum—a problem that has afflicted even their best work." Although the record helped bring the Band back into the mainstream, it was followed by *Moondog Matinee,* a disappointing oldies album from a group known for their marvelous originals ("Life is a Carnival," "Chest Fever," "The Weight," "Up on Cripple Creek," and "The Shape I'm In").

After playing to 600,000 fans at the Watkins Glen, New York, festival, the Band hooked up with Dylan again for his 1974 tour. The live show, released as *Before the Flood,* was a huge success netting nearly $2.5 million. "No way do we feel we deserve it," Robertson told *Rolling Stone.* "But I don't think a gallon of gas is worth a dollar, either." After the tour and live album, Dylan went back into the studios with the Band to record his *Planet Waves* LP.

The Band took a few years off before hitting the road for an American tour in 1976. But, after just two months, they decided the group had run its course and announced their farewell concert for Thanksgiving Eve in San Francisco. "I've been playing in the band for sixteen years and I'm thirty-two," Robertson said to Patrick Snyder in *Rolling Stone.* "It's been eight years in the back streets and eight years uptown. We're going to conclude this chapter of our life. . . . We have to bring it to a head." They did it with style, too, putting on a star-studded finale that included some of music's most famous names: Neil Young, Joni Mitchell, Dr. John, Neil Diamond, Paul Butterfield, Muddy Waters, Eric Clapton, Van Morrison, Ringo Starr, Emmylou Harris, and, of course, Ronnie Hawkins and Bob Dylan. The $25-per-seat concert at Bill Graham's Winterland, site of their debut some seven years earlier, featured the Band playing their hits and backing up their friends with the fire and passion that made them one of rock and roll's classiest acts. Director Martin Scorcese filmed the show, entitled *The Last Waltz* ("so far no one has even tried to match it," wrote Greil Marcus in *The Rolling Stone Illustrated History of Rock and Roll*) and a subsequent triple live album of the same name was released in 1978.

With such a natural screen presence in the movie, the next step for Robertson was acting. He appeared as Patch, a carnival hustler, in the movie *Carny* and also worked on the soundtrack for the film. "It's not a matter of me shifting from rock and roll into movies," he told Chet Flippo in *Rolling Stone*. "It's a natural course, a gradual thing. It's all storytelling, if it's music or movies or books." Robertson teamed up with Scorcese to score three more films: *Raging Bull, King of Comedy,* and *The Color of Money*. For the latter, Robertson did a last-minute rush job for the lyrics to Eric Clapton's hit "It's in the Way That You Use It."

Robertson had laid low for the most part while members of the Band had reunited without him shortly after their

---

The Band *would be remembered as the album that helped listeners bring life after the 1960s into focus.*

---

breakup (he did join them onstage once in 1989). In 1986 keyboardist Manuel died from the very reasons that Robertson had decided to quit life on the road. "We're talking about living a dangerous life. One thing equals another whether it's drinking or drugs or driving as fast as you can or staying up for as long as you can," he told Bill Flanagan in *Musician*. "That way of life seemed very fitting. At a certain age you don't think, 'this is insane!'"

Robertson signed a recording contract with EMI, which was later bought by Geffen Records, and in June of 1986 he began working on his first solo LP while finishing up *The Color of Money* with Gil Evans. *Robbie Robertson* was produced by Daniel Lanois with a bevy of friends lending their support: Peter Gabriel, Maria McKee, Tony Levin, the BoDeans, Garth Hudson, and Bill Dillon. Among the songs, "Broken Arrow," "Hell's Half Acre," "Showdown at Big Sky," and "Somewhere Down the Crazy River" once again display Robertson's talent for writing musical mini-novels. "Sweet Fire of Love" was a special treat with U2's The Edge trading

blistering guitar licks with Robertson. The big question was why did he wait so long? "I never said I'm not going to write songs for a while; I just didn't have the *lure* to get in there, sit down and suffer. I wasn't so sure I had something to say," he told *Musician*. "I just didn't want to make mediocre moves."

Selected discography:

Solo LPs

Robbie Robertson, Geffen, 1987.

With the Band

Music From Big Pink, Capitol, 1968.
The Band, Capitol, 1969.
Stage Fright, Capitol, 1970.
Cahoots, Capitol, 1971.
Rock of Ages, Capitol, 1972.
Moondog Matinee, Capitol, 1973.
Northern Lights - Southern Cross, Captol, 1975.
Islands, Capitol, 1977.
The Last Waltz, Warner Brothers, 1978.
The Best of The Band, Capitol, 1976.
Anthology, Capitol, 1978.

With Bob Dylan

Planet Waves, Asylum, 1974.
Before the Flood, Asylum, 1974.
The Basement Tapes, Columbia, 1975.

With Eric Clapton

So Many Roads, Vanguard.
I Can Tell, Atlantic.
The Best of John Hammond, Jr., Vanguard.

Composer of soundtracks for motion pictures, including *Raging Bull, King of Comedy, Carny,* and *The Color of Money*. Producer of records, including (for Jesse Winchester) *Jesse Winchester,* Ampex, 1970; (for Neil Diamond) *Beautiful Noise,* Columbia/CBS, 1976, and *Love at the Greek,* Columbia/CBS, 1977; and (for Hirth Marinez) *Hirth from Earth*.

Sources

Books

Christgau, Robert, *Christgau's Record Guide,* Ticknor & Fields, 1981.
Dalton, David, and Lenny Kaye, *Rock 100,* Grosset & Dunlap, 1977.

The Illustrated Encyclopedia of Rock, compiled by Nick Logan
and Bob Woffinden, Harmony, 1977.
The Rolling Stone Illustrated History of Rock and Roll, edited by
Jim Miller, Random House/Rolling Stone Press, 1979.
The Rolling Stone Record Guide, edited by Dave Marsh with
John Swenson, Random House/Rolling Stone Press, 1979.
What's That Sound?, edited by Ben Fong-Torres, Anchor Books,
1976.

Periodicals

Guitar Player, December, 1976; January, 1988.
Musician, September, 1987.
Rolling Stone, January 29, 1976; December 16, 1976; December
30, 1976; May 19, 1977; June 26, 1980.

—*Calen D. Stone*

Duke
Robillard

Guitarist, singer, songwriter

In a special "Who's Who of the Blues" section in *Guitar World,* writer Dave Rubin described Duke Robillard as "the most awesome of younger blues guitarists. . . . His solos sting and soar, his rhythm always swings, and when he jumps on a slow blues he has creativity and chops in abundance. Whether he's playing a chunky shuffle or a swinging jazz standard, every note rings with authority, conviction and true blues feel."

Like most of his contemporaries, Robillard was first influenced by the early rock and rollers like Chuck Berry, Buddy Holly, and Duane Eddy, whom he heard through the record collection of his older brother, also a guitarist. Wanting a guitar of his own, Robillard told his father he needed to build one for a school project. The two fashioned a crude instrument modeled after the Telecaster of James Burton, Ricky Nelson's guitarist on the "Ozzie and Harriet" television show. When the British Invasion hit the States he began to check out artists like Muddy Waters, Howlin Wolf, and Elmore James, who had influenced the popular English groups. The seventeen-year-old decided it was time to form a band of his own. "I was playing blues, y'know, learning

it and playing it. I got *real* serious about it right after I got out of high school and started the first Roomful Of Blues with bass, drums, guitar, piano, and harp," he told Bog Angell of *down beat.*

With Fran Christina (now of the Fabulous Thunderbirds) on drums and sixteen-year-old Al Copley on piano, the group styled themselves after the Chicago sound of the Paul Butterfield Blues Band. They broke up briefly in 1969 and Robillard formed Black Cat, another blues band, which survived for only a short period. After reforming Roomful, Robillard's musical tastes took a sharp turn. "I really came upon rhythm and blues by mistake," he told Mark von Lehmden of *Rolling Stone.* "Somebody gave me a few 78s by Joe Turner, Ruth Brown, people like that. And then I heard Buddy Johnson." The Johnson album that so affected Robillard is called *Rock and Roll Stage Party,* of which he says, "there's not one bad note on it."

Saxophonist Scott Hamilton turned Robillard on to some of the early horn players in jazz and also the stylish outfits of the 1930s bands. Soon Roomful began dressing in vintage clothing and playing songs that emulated the jump bands that had long since faded away. Another reason Robillard felt more comfortable with the older swing style was the vocals. "My trying to sing like Muddy Waters was impossible. Amos Milburn or Louis Jordan was more feasible. So in 1970, Roomful added horns," he told Dan Forte in *Guitar World.* Robillard's vocals, according to von Lehmden, "modulate effortlessly from a Satchmo growl to a Joe Turner shout to a B.B. King plea."

Robillard's guitar voice also changed with the band's new sound. He began to absorb the sounds of the very first of the electric guitarists: Charlie Christian, Tiny Grimes, Oscar Moore, and perhaps the most influential blues guitarist, T-Bone Walker. "Got me [a Gibson] ES-5, just like he had, and started playing the guitar flat (held horizontally) like he did," Robillard told Dan Forte. "I mean, I *became* T-Bone. I got *too* into him." Fabulous Thunderbirds guitarist Jimmie Vaughan confirms Robillard's dedication in *Guitar Player.* "When I walked into the club where he was playing with Roomful, it was like hearing T-Bone Walker." That was no small feat, considering that artists like B.B. King have spent much of their career trying to duplicate T-Bone's sound exactly.

It would take another six or seven years before producer/songwriter Doc Pomus caught Roomful's act at a New York nightclub. He was able to convince Island Records to sign the band, and in 1978 they released their first LP, *Roomful of Blues.* Their music, which almost immediately caused live audiences to start jitterbugging, was now captured on vinyl. They decid-

For the Record. . .

Born 1949, in Burrillville, R.I. Formed original Roomful of Blues, 1967; formed Black Cat, 1969; reformed Roomful of Blues, c. 1969; group released its first LP, 1978; left Roomful of Blues, 1980, worked with Robert Gordon and with the Legendary Blues Band; formed band the Pleasure Kings during early 1980s.

Addresses: *Agent*—Tom Radai, 2613 South 51st St., Milwaukee, WI 52319.

Manager—Ronald Martinez, P.O. Box 11, Mansfield, MA 02048.

ed to stretch out from the east coast and began to tour the south, where the nine-piece unit got a taste of New Orleans-flavored rhythm and blues. Their second LP, *Let's Have a Party,* reflects that influence as well as Robillard's switch from the hollow-body Gibson to a Fender Stratocaster, via a recommendation from Jimmie Vaughan. "Before I met him, my playing was smoother. . . . Then I heard Jimmie play those Buddy [Guy] and Otis [Rush] things, and I thought 'Jeez, a white guy *can* do it,'" he told Dan Forte in *Guitar Player.* "Jimmie was instrumental in me coming out of my shell as far as going from a smoother player to doing some rough stuff also."

Roomful was doing quite well reproducing the songs of yesteryear, but Robillard wanted to introduce originals into their repetoire. "Roomful was a fake jazz band," he told *down beat*'s Bob Angell. "We improvised, but only in 12-bar, 16-bar [rhythm and blues] phrases." Unable to work out a compromise, he left the band in 1980 and joined with rockabilly singer Robert Gordon. His replacement in Roomful, Ronnie Earl, cites the pressure of having to fill Robillard's spot. "I was literally having nightmares of crowds chanting in unison, 'Where's Duke?'," Earl told *Guitar Player.* "He was really the only guy around here [New England area] who you could go see."

After three months, Gordon's band took a break and Robillard recorded two albums with the Legendary Blues Band while putting together a trio of his own, the Pleasure Kings (with Thomas Enright on bass and Tommy DeQuattro on drums). Gordon called Robillard back into service with the Pleasure Kings as his opening act, but the trio decided to go out on their own. "For the first time, I placed my guitar in a trio setting and began focusing on my original influences—the classic rock and roll guitarists—trying to synthesize everything

I learned into something new," Robillard told Frank Joseph in *Guitar Player.*

Despite a show-stopping performance at the 1983 San Francisco Blues Festival, their first album received a poor review by *down beat*'s Jim Roberts. "Duke's singing and playing is routine—everything is worked out just right, but most of it is pretty ho-hum and unispired. Maybe he tried too hard to be perfect and recorded too many takes." After having worked with a nine-piece band for nearly twelve years, Robillard was obviously very meticulous about recording procedures and the record was polished a little too much for some critics.

The trio loosened up on their next effort, *Too Hot to Handle,* with Robillard turning in stunning solos on "Duke's Mood" and "T-Bone Boogie." Once again though, Robillard changed directions in 1987 by reverting back to an almost pure jazz approach on *Swing.* With songs still based on blues progressions, upright bassist Scott Appelruth and drummer Doug Hinman were able to bring the mood down and help Robillard play *a la* Django Reinhardt. Scott Hamilton pitched in on tenor sax. Of the record, Robillard told *Guitar World,* "I think it lets people know that I'm into, and capable of, a lot of stuff, and I do it with conviction."

Robillard's 1988 release, *You Got Me,* included the

> Writer Dave Rubin described Duke Robillard as "the most awesome of the younger blues guitarists."

Pleasure Kings once again as well as Dr. John and Vaughan helping out on second guitar. Although it leans more toward rock, the album show how Robillard has managed to draw upon his mastery of so many guitar styles and form them into his own unique voice. "It took me a long time to be able to play the different techniques," he told Forte in *Guitar World,* "but now I feel really comfortable in all the different veins—like I'm three different people."

Selected discography

Duke Robillard and the Pleasure Kings, Rounder, 1983.
Too Hot to Handle, Rounder, 1985.
Swing, Rounder, 1987.
You Got Me, Rounder, 1988.

With Roomful of Blues

Roomful of Blues, Island, 1978.
Let's Have a Party, Antilles, 1979.

With the Legendary Blues Band

Life of Ease, Rounder.
Red, Hot, 'N Blue, Rounder, 1987.

With Johnny Adams

Room With a View of the Blues, Rounder, 1988.

Sources

down beat, February, 1984; March, 1984.
Guitar Player, September, 1984; January, 1986; July, 1986;
  August, 1987; June, 1988; August, 1988.
Guitar Wold, September, 1988; March, 1989.
Rolling Stone, March 9, 1978; May 18, 1978.

—*Calen D. Stone*

Linda Ronstadt

Singer

Few performers in any medium have proven more daring than Linda Ronstadt, a singer who has made her mark in such varied styles as rock, country, grand opera, and *mariachi.* In the 1970s Ronstadt churned out a veritable stream of pop hits and heart-rending ballads that delighted country and rock fans alike. Just when she seemed pegged as a pop idol, however, she turned her talents to opera—in *The Pirates of Penzance* and *La Bohème*—and to torch songs accompanied by the Nelson Riddle Orchestra. Almost every Ronstadt experiment has met with critical acclaim and, surprisingly, with fan approval and hefty record sales. *Newsweek* contributor Margo Jefferson attributes this success to Ronstadt's voice, which she describes as having "the richness and cutting edge of a muted trumpet." Jefferson concludes, "In a field where success is often based on no more than quick-study ventriloquism, Linda Ronstadt stands out. She is no fad's prisoner; her compelling voice wears no disguises."

Time reporter Jay Cocks calls Ronstadt "gutsy," "unorthodox," and a challenger of creeds. As the singer tells it, she developed a habit of rebellion early in life and stuck to it with singleminded determination. Ronstadt was born and raised in Tucson, Arizona, the daughter of a hardware-store owner who loved to sing and play Mexican music. Ronstadt herself enjoyed harmonizing with her sister and two brothers—she was proud when she was allowed to take the soprano notes. At the age of six she decided she wanted to be a singer, and she promptly lost all interest in formal schooling. Aaron Latham, a classmate at Tucson's Catalina High School, wrote in *Rolling Stone* that by her teens Ronstadt "was already a larger-than-life figure with an even larger voice. She didn't surprise anyone by becoming a singer. Not that anyone expected her fame to grow to the dimensions of that voice. But the voice itself was no secret."

Ronstadt attended the University of Arizona briefly, dropping out at eighteen to join her musician boyfriend, Bob Kimmel, in Los Angeles. With Kimmel and guitar player Kenny Edwards, Ronstadt formed a group called the Stone Poneys, a folk-rock ensemble reminiscent of the Mamas and the Papas and the Lovin' Spoonful. The Stone Poneys signed a contract with Capitol Records in 1964 and released a single, "Some of Shelley's Blues," in early 1965. Their only hit as a group came in 1967, when "Different Drum," a cut from their second album, made the charts. By that time, intense touring, drug abuse, and a series of disappointing concert appearances as openers for the Doors caused the Stone Poneys to disband. Ronstadt told *Rolling Stone* that her band was "rejected by the hippest element in New York

do," "You're No Good," "Blue Bayou," and "Poor, Poor Pitiful Me," the singer had established herself as rock's most popular female star. Stephen Holden describes Ronstadt's rock style in a *Vogue* magazine profile. Her singing, according to Holden, combined "a tearful country wail with a full-out rock declamation. But, at the same time, her purity of melodic line is strongly rooted in folk." A *Time* contributor elaborates: "She sings, oh Lord, with a rowdy spin of styles—country, rhythm and blues, rock, reggae, torchy ballad—fused by a rare and rambling voice that calls up visions of loss, then jiggles the glands of possibility. The gutty voice drives, lilts, licks slyly at decency, riffs off Ella [Fitzgerald], transmogrifies Dolly Parton, all the while wailing with the guitars, strong and solid as God's garage floor. A man listens and thinks 'Oh my, yes,' and a woman thinks, perhaps, 'Ah, well . . .'"

A leap from rock to operetta is monumental; few voices could make it successfully. In 1981 Ronstadt astonished the critics and her fans by trilling the demanding soprano part of Mabel in a Broadway production of *The*

> *"No one in contemporary rock or pop can sound more enamored, or winsome, or heartbroken, in a love song than Linda Ronstadt."*

Pirates of Penzance. Her performance led *Newsweek* correspondent Barbara Graustark to comment, "Those wet, marmot eyes turn audiences on like a light bulb, and when her smoky voice soars above the staff in a duet with a flute, she sends shivers down the spine." Ronstadt's appearance as Mimi in *La Bohème* off-Broadway in 1984 was received with less enthusiasm by the critics, but the singer herself expressed no regrets about her move away from rock. "When I perform rock 'n' roll," she told *Newsweek,* "it varies between antagonistic posturing and to-the-bones vulnerability. I wanted to allow another facet of my personality to emerge. . . . I've gained confidence in knowing that now . . . I can handle myself in three dimensions, and even if I never use my upper extension except in the bathtub, I've gained vocal finish."

That "vocal finish" was applied to yet another Ronstadt experiment—two albums of vintage torch songs, *What's New?* and *Lush Life,* featuring the Nelson Riddle Orchestra. Jay Cocks calls *What's New?* a "simple, almost reverent, rendering of nine great songs that time

as lame. We broke up right after that. We couldn't bear to look at each other."

Ronstadt fulfilled her Capitol recording contract as a solo performer, turning out some of the first albums to fuse country and rock styles. On *Hand Sown . . . Home Grown* (1969) and *Silk Purse* (1970), Ronstadt teamed with Nashville studio musicians for an ebullient, if jangly country sound. The latter album produced her first solo hit, the sorrowful "Long, Long Time." In retrospect, Ronstadt has called her debut period the "bleak years." She was plagued by the stresses of constant touring, difficult romantic entanglements, cocaine use, and critical indifference—and to make matters worse, she suffered from stage fright and had little rapport with her audiences. "I felt like a submarine with depth charges going off all around me," she told *Time.* Ronstadt eluded failure by moving to Asylum Records in 1973 and by engaging Peter Asher as her producer and manager. Asher collaborated with her on her first bestselling albums, *Don't Cry Now* and the platinum *Heart Like a Wheel.*

Heart Like a Wheel was the first in a succession of million-selling albums for Ronstadt. By the mid-1970s, with hits such as "When Will I Be Loved?," "Despera-

has not touched. . . . No one in contemporary rock or pop can sound more enamored, or winsome, or heart-broken, in a love song than Linda Ronstadt. Singing the tunes on *What's New,* or even just talking about them, she still sounds like a woman in love." Stephen Holden writes, "One of the charms of Ronstadt's torch singing is her almost girlish awe in the face of the songs' pent-up emotions. Instead of trying to re-create another era's erotic climate, she pays homage to it with lovely evenhanded line readings offered in a spirit of wistful nostalgia." Holden adds that *What's New* "revitalized Ronstadt's recording career by selling over two million copies, and, coincidentally, defined for her generation the spirit of a new 'eighties pop romanticism."

More recent Ronstadt projects have departed even further from the pop-rock vein. In 1987 the singer released *Canciones de mi padre,* an album of *mariachi* songs that her father used to sing. *Newsweek* critic David Gates calls the work "Ronstadt's best record to date," noting that "its flawless production is the only concession to Top 40 sensibilities. And Ronstadt . . . has found a voice that embodies not merely passion and heartache, but a womanly wit as well." Ronstadt also earned several prestigious awards for her 1986 album *Trio,* a joint country-music venture with Dolly Parton and Emmylou Harris. While Ronstadt will not rule out recording more rock, she seems far more fascinated by other forms and other, more remote, historical periods. Gates finds the raven-haired artist "the most adventurous figure in American popular music," concluding that, at the very least, Ronstadt is "commendable in her refusal to bore herself."

Selected discography

With the Stone Poneys

Evergreen, Capitol, 1967.
Evergreen, Volume II, Capitol, 1967.
Linda Ronstadt, the Stone Poneys, and Friends, Volume III, Capitol, 1968.
The Stone Poneys Featuring Linda Ronstadt, Capitol, 1976.

Solo LPs

Hand Sown . . . Home Grown, Capitol, 1969.
Silk Purse, Capitol, 1970.
Linda Ronstadt, Capitol, 1972.
Don't Cry Now, Asylum, 1973.

Heart Like a Wheel, Capitol, 1974.
Different Drum, Asylum, 1974.
Prisoner in Disguise, Asylum, 1975.
Hasten Down the Wind, Asylum, 1976.
Linda Ronstadt's Greatest Hits, Asylum, 1976.
Simple Dreams, Asylum, 1977.
Blue Bayou, Asylum, 1977.
Retrospective, Capitol, 1977.
Living in the U.S.A., Asylum, 1978.
Mad Love, Asylum, 1980.
Linda Ronstadt's Greatest Hits, Volume II, Asylum, 1980.
Get Closer, Asylum, 1982.
What's New?, Asylum, 1983.
Lush Life, Asylum, 1984.
For Sentimental Reasons, Asylum, 1986.
Prime of Life, Asylum, 1986.
Rockfile, Capitol, 1986.
'Round Midnight: The Nelson Riddle Sessions, Asylum, 1987.
Canciones de mi padre, Asylum, 1987.

With Dolly Parton and Emmylou Harris

Trio, Warner Bros., 1986.

Sources

Books

The Illustrated Encyclopedia of Country Music, Harmony Books, 1977.
Stambler, Irwin, *The Encyclopedia of Pop, Rock, and Soul,* St. Martin's, 1974.

Periodicals

down beat, July, 1985.
Esquire, October, 1985.
Newsweek, October 20, 1975; April 23, 1979; August 11, 1980; December 10, 1984; February 29, 1988.
People, October 24, 1977; April 30, 1979.
Rolling Stone, December 2, 1976; March 27, 1977; October 19, 1978; November 2, 1978; August 18, 1983.
Saturday Review, December, 1984.
Time, February 28, 1977; March 22, 1982; September 26, 1983.
Vogue, November, 1984.
Washington Post Magazine, October 9, 1977.

—Anne Janette Johnson

Sade

Singer, songwriter

"**S**ade's music . . . is so hot because it sounds so cool," declared critic Cathleen McGuigan in *Newsweek*. The Nigerian-born British singer has risen rapidly to prominence with her first two albums, *Diamond Life* and *Promise;* both went platinum. Her sound is "one that has definite jazz overtones but is mixed with a pop flavor and a hint of passion," according to Walter Leavy in *Ebony,* and it has captured the imagination of music fans and reviewers alike, particularly those in the young professional grouping. Sade is responsible for the huge hit singles "Smooth Operator" and "The Sweetest Taboo," and she won a Grammy in 1986 as the year's best new artist.

Sade was born Helen Folasade Adu in Ibadan, Nigeria, to a British mother and a Nigerian father. Her stage name, a shortened form of her middle name, was adopted almost immediately, because her Nigerian neighbors refused to call her by the English name Helen. Sade remained in Nigeria until she was four years old, when her parents separated and her mother took her and her older brother to England. The family stayed with Sade's grandparents in a small village in Essex, then moved to Holland-on-Sea when Sade's mother remarried. Despite the fact that the young girl and her brother were the only children of black descent in the area and Sade was sometimes the target of racial slurs, she had a comfortable circle of friends with whom she went dancing. As a teenager, however, she had no professional musical aspirations. She told a *Washington Post* interviewer: "Obviously I've stood in front of the mirror with a hairbrush just like anyone. But that was the extent of it." Sade and her friends enjoyed funk and soul music, and she particularly admired the work of Aretha Franklin, Smokey Robinson, and the late Marvin Gaye. She also liked singing along with her mother's record collection, which included the albums of Frank Sinatra and Dinah Washington.

By the time she was seventeen Sade had discovered a desire to become a fashion designer, and when she graduated from high school she enrolled in St. Martin's College of Art in London. She worked her way through school by waitressing and serving as a bicycle messenger, but she still found time to enjoy dancing in the London nightclubs. When Sade obtained her degree, she and another woman tried to keep a men's fashion designing business afloat, but it was difficult, as she explained to the *Washington Post:* "You can't make things at a reasonable cost. . . . Everything was economic. It stunted any creativity, and I ended up not enjoying it." Another thing Sade did not enjoy was the modeling work she did at that time to help support herself. Though since her emergence on the music scene she has been lauded almost as much for her sleek, slim, elegant look as for her songs, she confided to a reporter for the Toronto *Globe and Mail:* "I'm quite anti-fashion in a sense. I hate it when everyone starts wearing the same clothes simply because that's what's supposed to be in this year."

Sometime in the early 1980s, when Sade had given up on modeling in disgust, a friend persuaded her to try out as a backup singer for a group specializing in jazz and funk, Pride. Thinking that singing would be a pleasant hobby, she auditioned, and though she was rejected at first, she was called back when no one more suitable could be found. Pride never earned a recording contract, but did gain a following in the London nightclubs—a following that grew when Sade began to team up with fellow Pride member and saxophone player Stuart Matthewman to write songs. The two performed their creations in special sets aside from the rest of Pride, and these sets began to win Sade fans of her own. When Pride disbanded, the group's manager, Lee Barrett, became Sade's manager, and Sade and Matthewman recruited backup musicians.

Sade was signed by Epic Records in 1983. Her first album, *Diamond Life,* met with acclaim in England, and the first hit from it was "Your Love is King." But while a dance tune from *Diamond Life,* "Hang On to Your Love," received some play in New York City discos, CBS/Portrait Records, who held Sade's U.S. contract, did not release the album until 1985 because they feared it would not have the same popular appeal that it did in England. When *Diamond Life* was released in

America, it shot up the charts quickly, first propelled by "Smooth Operator," then by "Your Love is King." Sade's debut album also sold well in Europe, and with six million copies of *Diamond Life* sold worldwide, she had become an international star by the end of 1985.

It was at about this time that Sade released her second album, *Promise.* When *Diamond Life* was beginning to fade from the charts, *Promise* began to climb them. The biggest hit from the album was what Stephen Holden called a "delicately spicy love ballad," "The Sweetest Taboo," but other songs, such as "Maureen" and "Never as Good as the First Time," were successful as well. But while many critics were singing Sade's praises and lauding her cool, understated style, other reviewers were sounding notes of dissent. McGuigan pointed out that Sade's work is "very similar in feeling and pace. Perhaps too similar: for all the dark, lush glamour of the sound, Sade has yet to show a wide range in style or voice." And Leavy agreed that "questions about her musical ability do pop up from time to time." But Barry Walters argued in *Village Voice* that Sade's method of "never letting go, simmering but never boiling" when interpreting her songs is what makes her distinct from the other stars of popular music. Her style continues to attract fans: in 1988 Sade's third album, *Stronger Than Pride,* brought forth the hit single "Nothing Can Come Between Us."

Selected discography

Diamond Life (includes "Your Love Is King," "Smooth Operator," "Sally," "Why Can't We Live Together," and "Hang On to Your Love"), Portrait, 1985.

Promise (includes "Sweetest Taboo," "Maureen," "Never as Good as the First Time," "Tar Baby," "Fear," and "Mr. Wrong"), Portrait, 1985.

Stronger Than Pride (includes "Nothing Can Come Between Us" and "Love Is Stronger Than Pride"), Portrait, 1988.

Sources

down beat, August, 1985.
Ebony, May, 1986.
Newsweek, March 25, 1985.
New York Times, November 27, 1985.
People, February 3, 1986.
Rolling Stone, April 25, 1985, May 8, 1986.
Village Voice, December 31, 1985.
Washington Post, December 12, 1985.

—Elizabeth Thomas

Rod Stewart

Singer, songwriter

For nearly two decades Rod Stewart has been one of the most popular male vocalist in contemporary music. From his blues-drenched days with the Jeff Beck Group to the hard-rockin' boogie of the Faces and on to a middle-of-the-road solo career, Stewart's raspy vocals have graced over two dozen LPs.

Born into a blue-collar London family in 1945, he worked a number of odd jobs after this schooling, including a stint as a gravedigger and an apprenticeship with the Brentford soccer team, before embarking on a journey through Europe as a wandering minstrel. Shortly after learning to play the banjo from English folksinger Wizz Jones, Stewart was repatriated from Spain for being destitute. Once back in his homeland, Stewart landed a semi-pro singing gig with Jimmy Powell and His Five Dimensions. He recorded a version of "Good Morning Little Schoolgirl" for Decca in 1964 before teaming up with Long John Baldry in the Hoochie Coochie Men. After that he sang rhythm and blues with Brian Auger's Steampacket while building a reputation as Rod the Mod for his stylish outfits. Stewart also recorded a few singles for the Immediate and Columbia labels and sang briefly with Shotgun Express, a band that featured Peter Green and Mick Fleetwood, later of Fleetwood Mac.

Stewart's first major exposure came in 1968, when he and Ron Wood joined forces with guitarist Jeff Beck, who had quite a following on both sides of the Atlantic from his groundbreaking work in the Yardbirds band. Stewart recorded two albums with Beck, *Truth* and *Beck-Ola* (he also continued doing session work with the Python Lee Jackson group), but his undeveloped vocals were overshadowed by Beck's incredibly forceful playing. Bassist Wood told *Guitar Player* that "Rod had to play down his role a lot. He was still looking for a role at the time too. . . . He didn't quite know what he was trying to do about showmanship either. So whenever he was uncertain, he used to run behind an amplifier and hide."

In 1969 Beck fired Wood and drummer Mickey Waller. Wood hooked up with the Small Faces and when their singer, Steve Marriott, quit to join Humble Pie, he asked Stewart to take over the vocal chores. After shortening their name to the Faces (Kenny Jones—drums; Ian MacLagan—keyboards; Ronnie Lane—bass; and Wood—guitars), Stewart began recording with them on the Warner Bros. label while also signing a solo contract with Mercury Records. His debut LP, *An Old Raincoat Won't Ever Let You Down* (later retitled *The Rod Stewart Album*), featured acoustic folk songs, rockers, and self-penned originals. His sandpapery voice showed the heavy influence of Sam Cooke and Ramblin' Jack Elliott, especially on the ballads. The

Full name, Roderick David Stewart; born January 10, 1945, in North London, England; father owned a news agents shop in Holloway, England; married Alana Collins, April 6, 1979 (divorced, 1984); children: Alana, Sean; (with Kelly Emberg) Ruby Rachel.

Worked at a variety of jobs before musical career, including gravedigger and soccer player; sang with Jimmy Powell and His Five Dimensions, c. 1964; released first record, 1964; later sang with Long John Baldry's Hoochie Coochie Men, Brian Auger's Steampacket, and Shotgun Express; singer with the Jeff Beck Group, 1968-69; singer with the Faces, 1969-76; also appeared and recorded as solo performer, 1969—; songwriter.

Awards: Named rock star of the year by *Rolling Stone* magazine, 1971; "Tonight's the Night" selected single of the year in the *Rolling Stone* Critics' Poll, 1976.

Addresses: *Office*—c/o Bill Gaff Management, Hotel Navarro, Suite 705 112, New York, NY 10019. *Record company*—Warner Bros. Records, 3300 Warner Blvd., Burbank, CA 91510.

Faces' debut, on the other hand, gave Stewart a chance to cut loose on bluesy rock & roll.

At first, Stewart was more successful in the United States. His second LP, *Gasoline Alley,* featured "Cut Across Shorty" and "Country Comfort," which furthered his image as the Everyman who could display his emotions. It was 1971's *Every Picture Tells A Story,* however, that made him a superstar. With the beautiful, autobiographical single "Maggie May," he had both the number 1 album and number 1 single in the U.S. and the U.K., the first time ever in pop history. The LP also included "Mandolin Wind" and a smoking version of the Temptations' "I'm Losing You." Of the title cut, Greil Marcus wrote in *Rolling Stone,* "'Every Picture Tells A Story' . . . is the greatest rock & roll recording of the last ten years. . . . John Lennon once said he wanted to make a record as good as 'Whole Lot of Shakin' Going On'; Rod Stewart did it." "You Wear It Well," from his follow-up, *Never A Dull Moment,* reached number 13 as the LP went gold.

Meanwhile, the Faces were chugging along merrily in their Scottish tartans, gaining noteriety as a party band. Stewart yearned to just be one of the boys and despised it when they were billed as Rod Stewart and the Faces. Their concerts were sloppy good times that

earned them the title of "the poor man's Rolling Stones. Ronnie Lane was replaced by Free's bassist, Tetsu, in 1973 as Warner Bros. and Mercury battled in court over Stewart's contract. *Sing It Again Rod,* a compilation of previous releases, was issued just prior to his final Mercury outing, 1974's *Smiler,* which featured two Sam Cooke tunes; "Bring It On Home To Me" and "You Send Me."

By then Wood had begun a solo career of his own and the future of the Faces looked uncertain. Stewart had publicly slammed their last studio effort together, *Ooh La La,* while *Atlantic Crossing* was his first solo LP not to feature any of the Faces. Reports of Stewart "going Hollywood" and his stormy relationship with actress Britt Eklund furthered the distance between him and the group. Recorded in Muscle Shoals, Alabama, *Atlantic Crossing* went gold, containing one fast side and one slow side, which featured "Sailing," a number 1 hit in England (the country he began avoiding because of their high taxes). On December 18, 1976, Stewart announced that he would play solo exclusively and the

> *From his blues-drenched days with the Jeff Beck Group to the hard-rockin' boogie of the Faces and on to a middle-of-the-road solo career, Rod Stewart's raspy vocals have graced over two dozen LPs.*

breakup of the Faces quickly followed. Wood had been juggling his time between them and the Stones, performing with them on their 1975 tour and later becoming a permanent member.

Stewart's career continued to soar but critics and fans who knew his rock side were disappointed with his light-weight solo outings. "Rarely has a singer had as full and unique a talent as Rod Stewart," stated Marcus in *The Rolling Stone Illustrated History of Rock & Roll.* "Rarely has anyone betrayed his talent so completely." Regardless, his 1976 LP, *A Night On The Town,* gave Stewart another number 1 hit, "Tonight's The Night," staying on the U.S. charts for eight weeks. But syrupy ballads like the Cat Stevens composition "The First Cut Is The Deepest" and "The Killing Of Georgie" had no place in the world of punk rock, whose disciples denounced Stewart and his rich lifestyle.

Instead of turning around and showing the New Wavers how to burn, Stewart assembled a Face-less band that played less rock than his old mates. Besides that, they scored a number 1 *disco* hit with "Do Ya Think I'm Sexy" from the *Blondes Have More Fun* LP. Stewart continued in the mellow vein and scored more hits with "Passion" and "Young Turks" on the album *Tonight I'm Yours*. He employed Jeff Beck in 1984 for *Camouflage*, which supplied three more top ten tunes: "Infatuation," "Some Guys Have All The Luck," and "Love Touch." Beck was to have played on the tour to support the record but Stewart only wanted to give the guitarist fifteen minutes of stage time. He did return the favor by singing on Beck's album a year later, adding gut-wrenching vocals to "People Get Ready."

Selected discography

Solo LPs

An Old Raincoat Won't Ever Let You Down, Mercury, 1969 (later retitled *The Rod Stewart Album*).
Gasoline Alley, Mercury, 1970.
Every Picture Tells A Story, Mercury, 1971.
Never A Dull Moment, Mercury, 1972.
Sing It Again, Rod, Mercury, 1973.
Smiler, Mercury, 1974.
Atlantic Crossing, Warner Bros., 1975.
The Best of Rod Stewart, Mercury, 1976.
The Best of Rod Stewart, Vol. II, Mercury, 1976.
A Night on the Town, Warner Bros., 1976.
Foot Loose & Fancy Free, Warner Bros., 1976.
Blondes Have More Fun, Warner Bros., 1978.
Greatest Hits, Vol. I, Warner Bros., 1979.
Tonight I'm Yours, Warner Bros., 1981.
Absolutely Live, Warner Bros., 1981.
Camouflage, Warner Bros., 1984.
Out of Order, Warner Bros., 1988.

With Jeff Beck Group

Truth, Epic, 1968.

Beck-Ola, Epic, 1969.

With Jeff Beck

Get Workin', Epic, 1985.

With the Faces

The First Step, Warner Bros., 1970.
Long Player, Warner Bros., 1971.
A Nod Is As Good As A Wink . . . To A Blind Horse, Warner Bros., 1971.
Ooh La La, Warner Bros., 1973.
Coast to Coast/Overture & Beginners (live), Mercury, 1973.
Snakes and Ladders/The Best of Faces, Warner Bros., 1976.

Sources

Books

Christgau, Robert, *Christgau's Record Guide*, Ticknor & Fields, 1981.
Dalton, David, and Lenny Kaye, *Rock 100*, Grosset & Dunlap, 1977.
The Illustrated Encyclopedia of Rock, compiled by Nick Logan and Bob Woffinden, Harmony, 1977.
The Rolling Stone Illustrated History of Rock and Roll, edited by Jim Miller, Random House/Rolling Stone Press, 1976.
The Rolling Stone Interviews, by the editors of *Rolling Stone* magazine, Random House/Rolling Stone Press, 1981.
The Rolling Stone Record Guide, edited by Dave Marsh with John Swenson, Random House/Rolling Stone Press, 1979.

Periodicals

Guitar Player, December, 1975.
Guitar World, January, 1985.
Rolling Stone, November 6, 1975; January 29, 1976; April 22, 1976; August 26, 1976; January 13, 1977; February 10, 1977; December 15, 1977; December 29, 1977; April 6, 1978; February 8, 1979.

—*Calen D. Stone*

Sting

Singer, songwriter, composer, bassist, guitarist, and record company executive

Throughout the 1980s Sting has been one of the most diverse and influential entertainers working in both the music and film industries. His recordings with the Police created a new genre that combined new-wave punk with reggae rhythms and intelligent lyrics while his successive solo albums bridged the gap between rock and jazz. All the while he has been honing his acting skills by appearing in over half a dozen feature films.

Sting's career began as a semi-pro musician at the age of seventeen. In the traditional jazz clubs of his hometown of Newcastle, England, he learned to play the bass and read music while absorbing the somber dress and style associated with jazz. He performed in various bands at night while holding down a steady day job as a school-teacher. Sting pointed out in *Rolling Stone* that while most musicians were into the rebellious attitude, he decided to go along with the system instead of fighting it. "I used it to go the hilt. So much so that I became a part of the system . . . somehow, I knew my day would come. I would play this game and go along with it for awhile."

By age twenty he already had a wife and child but decided it was time to make a move and so went to London in hopes of becoming a full-time professional musician. He was soon discovered by Stewart Copeland, a drummer searching the clubs for prospective band members. The two teamed up with a guitarist, who was quickly replaced by Andy Summers, and formed the Police during the punk movement in late 1976. Desperate for work, the three dyed their hair blonde for a part in a Wrigley chewing gum commercial and decided to leave it that way afterwards. They recorded a thrashing single, "Fall Out," for Miles Copeland's (Stewart's brother and band manager) Illegal Records label, eventually selling around 10,000 copies. A & M signed the Police, the group gambling that they would become popular by insisting on higher royalties instead of a big advance.

Amazingly, they toured America before any record had even been released. It was strictly a low-budget affair with shoddy rented equipment and audiences that sometimes numbered less than ten. However, once their first single, "Roxanne," was released, the Police became bigger than any of their contemporaries. They were categorized as New Wavers mainly because of the time and place they emerged from. But in reality, with the exception of Elvis Costello, they were much more sophisticated as musicians than bands like the Clash or the Sex Pistols (who complained that the Police just used the punk movement and never really shared the same vision).

A & M rushed to release their debut LP, *Outlandos*

on "Spirits in the Material World" which reached number 11 on the charts.

In various interviews Sting pointed out that the group knew it could succeed if they followed a plan that avoided all the pitfalls of previous failed rock groups. A shrewd business sense, in addition to exceptional talent, helps to explain their enormous popularity. "We're ambitious," Sting told James Henke in *Rolling Stone*. "We want to have power. . . . The opportunities presented themselves and we took 'em." Unfortunately, the Police contained three enormous egos as well, which caused the group to collapse after their fifth album, *Synchronicity,* in 1983. They left on top, though, with a number 1 hit and Grammy award-winner, "Every Breath You Take." In the midst of a divorce, Sting produced some of his most moving work on the LP and created a masterpiece with "King of Pain."

Sting had been taking acting roles during the Police days, appearing as Ace Face in the Who's *Quadrophenia,* amongst others, and continued to develop his craft

> *While most musicians were into the rebellious attitude, Sting decided to go along with the system instead of fighting it.*

after the breakup of the Police. In 1985 Sting released his debut solo LP, *Dream of the Blue Turtles.* Employing musicians Branford Marsalis, Darryl Jones, Kenny Kirkland, and Omar Hakim, he formed a fresh new sound that was neither rock nor jazz. Four singles made the top twenty: "If You Love Somebody Set Them Free," "Love is the Seventh Wave," "Fortress Around Your Heart," and "Russians," in which Sting questioned the world power-struggle that threatens everyone's lives. The album's recording process and tour were both filmed and a double-live LP, *Bring on the Night,* was issued a year later. In its liner notes Sting stated that *Dream of the Blue Turtles,* "to my horror and embarassment, was nominated for a Grammy in the Jazz category . . . the first time I've ever been relieved *not* to receive an award."

. . . *Nothing Like the Sun* followed in 1987 with a similar formula. Sting scored again with his innovative rhythms and insightful lyrics on "History Will Teach Us Nothing," "We'll Be Together," "Englishman in New York," and a fine reworking of Jimi Hendrix's "Little Wing," featuring

d'Amour (recorded for only $6,000) as "Roxanne" reached number 32 on the charts in 1979 on the strength of Sting's high-pitched, pleading vocals. "Sting sounds like a guy who's just made sergeant and is looking to back up his new stripes," wrote Tom Carson in *Rolling Stone.* Within a year their second album, *Reggatta de Blanc,* was out and tunes like "Message in a Bottle" (number 1 in eleven countries) and "Walking on the Moon" displayed the unique Police sound of poly-rhythms and lush chordal work. *Zenyatta Mondatta,* their third LP, entered the British charts at number 1 and stayed there for eight weeks, spawning two top-ten hits, "De Do Do Do, De Da Da Da" and "Don't Stand So Close to Me."

In 1980 they embarked on a Third World tour that included untypical rock venues like Nairobi, Bombay, Athens, Hong Kong, and Cairo. Afterwards, Sting (who wrote the majority of their tunes) began to go beyond the typical adolescent lyrics on the ensuing LP, *Ghost in the Machine.* "I've developed my songwriting away from the subjects of love, alienation, and devotion to a more political, socially aware viewpoint," he stated in *Guitar Player.* The new outlook was evident especially

the late master, Gil Evans. Sting is one of a new breed of musicians who are trying to say and do something about world problems, like saving the tropical forests, while composing music that speaks strongly. "In the world . . . we have to say something, because it's the only power we have," he told David Fricke in *Rolling Stone*. "It's not whether we succeed or not. We just have to do it."

Selected discography

With the Police

Outlandos d' Amour, A & M, 1979.
Regatta de Blanc, A & M, 1979.
Zenyatta Mondatta, A & M, 1980.
Ghost in the Machine, A & M, 1982.
Synchronicity, A & M, 1983.
The Singles; Every Breath You Take, A & M, 1986.

Solo LPs

Dream of the Blue Turtles, A & M, 1985.
Bring on the Night, A & M, 1986 (import only).
. . . Nothing Like the Sun, A & M, 1987.

Sources

down beat, December, 1983; May, 1984; August, 1984; December, 1984; May, 1985; November, 1986; December, 1987; December, 1988.
Guitar Player, September, 1982.
Guitar World, April, 1988; October, 1988.
Musician, September, 1987.
Rolling Stone, June 14, 1979; December 13, 1979; November 16, 1980; December 25, 1980; February 19, 1981; September 1, 1983; September 25, 1986; November 5, 1987.

—Calen D. Stone

Liz Story

Pianist, composer

Although she was an accomplished pianist and had studied at Juilliard, Liz Story lost interest in a music career until she saw Bill Evans play one night at the Bottom Line in New York. That concert opened up performance possibilities that she had never considered. "What hit me was the improvisation. I had the impression that improvising music had died in the 18th century, that it was a musical feat people knew about in some other time," she told *down beat*. "All these lights went on. I had, for the first time, a clear idea of what I would do in music." She met Evans after the show and, at his suggestion, she began to study with Stanford Gold.

The timing of Story's entrance onto the music scene was fortuitous. She arrived when a new form of music, popularly dubbed New Age, was gaining wide acceptance. William Ackerman helped pioneer New Age music through his Windham Hill label, which he formed in 1976 to release his first album of guitar music. He began signing new artist and in less than ten years the label was grossing more than $20 million per year. A good introduction to the label is the album *An Evening With Windham Hill,* which features several artists including Story, who plays on the cut "Spare Change."

Story recorded her first solo album, *Solid Colors,* for Windham Hill in 1983. *High Fidelity* reviewed the album: "At this early stage in her career she is balancing between her limitations and her special skills. The pluses are self-evident—a virtually flawless technical capacity, a fine gift for melody, a great sense of creative passion . . . we are presented with a performer-composer with the melodic power to move an audience."

But *down beat* said her career was hurt when *Billboard* listed her Windham Hill LPs in their jazz charts and "critics, expecting her to tackle Ellington and Monk, panned her performances." Although Story's music may sound like jazz to some (she is listed in both the Jazz and New Age sections of the *Schwann Catalog*), her style departs from the standard organization of modern jazz. *High Fidelity* saw this: "Unlike such commercially prominent piano soloists as Chick Corea and Keith Jarrett, she makes little or no use of the traditional jazz resources of gospel and blues music." Instead, her music is a unique, personal, improvisational style which incorporates modern jazz, classical, and pop music elements.

A review in *People* discussing "Forgiveness," from her album *Speechless,* gives a visual description of her playing style: "At first the piece carries a solid, brown-

For the Record. . .

Born October 28, 1956, in San Diego, Calif.; married Mark Duke (a record producer). *Education:* Studied music at Hunter College and at Juilliard, New York, N.Y.; later studied music with Stanford Gold; and at the Dick Grove Music Workshops, Los Angeles.

Began playing piano at age 11; gave improvisational performances for the lunch crowd at a restaurant while attending the Dick Groves Music Workshops; signed with Windham Hill Records, 1982; released first album, 1982.

Addresses: *Agent*—Jeff Laramie, SRO Artists Inc., P.O. Box 9532, Madison, WI 53715. *Manager*—Alan Oken, Klugman & Oken, 11500 W. Olympic Blvd., Suite 400, West Los Angeles, CA 90064.

hued dignity that would make it an excellent sound track for a painting by one of the Flemish masters. While making only minor changes in the musical theme, Story gradually lightens the tone by degrees until, by the end, she is playing in almost a watercolor effect. Every listener could paint a different word picture of each of the seven pieces contained here, since Story's music is likely to evoke different mental images and feelings in different people."

Story arrived on the music scene at a time of transition, when new musicians were evolving a music that is a blend of different styles and does not fit easily into traditional categories. It is too early to judge whether New Age will last another ten years, but for now Story's contributions are widely accepted and well-appreciated.

Selected discography

An Evening With Windham Hill (on "Spare Change"), Windham Hill, 1983.
Solid Colors, Windham Hill, 1983.
Unaccountable Effect, Windham Hill, 1985.
Part of Fortune, Novus, 1986.
Speechless, Novus, 1988.

Sources

Audio, December, 1985.
down beat, September, 1985; October, 1988.
High Fidelity, July, 1983; January, 1984.
Ms., May, 1986.
People, October 10, 1988.

—*Tim LaBorie*

Barbra Streisand

Singer, songwriter

The multitalented Barbra Streisand has made her mark as an actress, a singer, and a comedienne in a career spanning three decades. Streisand landed her first job as a nightclub singer in 1961 and just four years later was headlining on Broadway in the award-winning musical *Funny Girl.* Since then she has cut numerous albums, starred in motion pictures, and even directed and produced her own films. *Harper's Bazaar* contributor J. Curtis Sanburn claims that Streisand has that special "star quality" that eludes all but the best entertainers. In her case, writes Sanburn, "star quality makes for a driven, creative dynamo; the biggest, most powerful performer in Hollywood. She's big because she keeps building on her talent, and we respond with surprise and recognition each time she gives us something new, yet distinctly Barbra."

Streisand has admitted that she never wanted to be a singer—she preferred serious roles in straight drama. It was as a singer that she first attracted attention, however, and she remains one of the best-selling recording artists on the Columbia label. Her untrained but spectacular voice is instantly recognizable in a wide variety of musical styles, from old Broadway standards to pop and disco, to plaintive ballads like "Evergreen." According to Burt Korall in the *Saturday Review,* it is Streisand's manner—not her vocal prowess—that has distinguished her from other female singers. Korall claims that Streisand is not "musically motivated" or "inspired by the melodic line," but rather an artist who "shapes songs by heeding the guidelines established in the lyrics. She works as an actress would." Korall continues: "If anything, Miss Streisand brings to material an overabundance of emotion, a tendency to overstatement. . . . Fortunately, however, Miss Streisand often allows songs and experiences to speak to her. In turn she responds naturally to the emotions and thoughts elicited. Moving inward, alone with her feelings, she unfolds them in a touching, well-shaded, progressive way, as if savoring close contact with them. The show business flashiness recedes and the sensitive, warm person emerges."

Barbara Joan Streisand was born in Brooklyn, New York, in 1942. By any standards, her childhood was unhappy—her father, a high-school literature teacher, died of an epileptic seizure when she was less than two, leaving the family without any income. Streisand grew up in her grandparents' home, a lonely, resentful child, whose only doll was a hot-water bottle with a sweater wrapped around it. At fourteen she determined that she wanted to be an actress, and she began to cultivate a bohemian appearance and eccentric mannerisms to enhance her individuality. Streisand's mother begged her to take typing classes, "just in case" acting would not support her, but the youngster refused to consider

For the Record. . .

Given name, Barbara Joan Streisand; born April 24, 1942, in Brooklyn, N.Y.; daughter of Emanuel (a literature teacher) and Diana (Rosen) Streisand; married Elliott Gould (an actor), March, 1963 (divorced); children: Jason. *Education:* Graduated from Erasmus Hall High School (with honors), 1959; attended Yeshiva of Brooklyn.

Worked as nightclub singer at the Bon Soir, New York, N.Y., 1960-61; had professional theatrical debut in *An Evening with Henry Stoones,* off-Broadway, 1961; made Broadway debut in musical *I Can Get It for You Wholesale,* 1962; recording artist with Columbia Records, 1962—; star of numerous television specials, including "My Name Is Barbra," 1964. Film actress, producer, and director, 1968—, movies include *Funny Girl,* 1968, *Hello, Dolly,* 1969, *The Owl and the Pussycat,* 1970, *What's Up, Doc?* 1972, *Up the Sandbox,* 1972, *The Way We Were,* 1973, *For Pete's Sake,* 1974, *Funny Lady,* 1975, *A Star Is Born* (also producer), 1976, *The Main Event,* 1979, *All Night Long,* 1981, *Yentl* (also director and producer), 1983, *Nuts,* 1987.

Awards: Academy Award for best actress, 1969, for *Funny Girl,* Academy Award for best song of the year (with Paul Williams), 1976, for "Evergreen"; Grammy Awards for best female pop vocalist, 1963, 1964, 1965, 1967, 1977, and 1986; recipient of special Tony Award, 1970.

Addresses: 5775 Ramirez Canyon Rd., Malibu, CA 90265.

Columbia Records, and her first release, *The Barbra Streisand Album,* became 1963's top-selling album by a female performer. She followed that success with *The Second Barbra Streisand Album* and *The Third Barbra Streisand Album,* both of which sold very well.

The lead role in the musical comedy *Funny Girl* assured Streisand's ascent to superstardom. The Broadway show, produced in 1964, profiled the life of vaudeville comedienne Fanny Brice. In many respects it was the perfect vehicle for Streisand, combining comedy, drama, and several melodic songs. Streisand also appeared in the film version of *Funny Girl,* earning her first Academy Award for her work. A *Newsweek* reviewer calls Streisand's portrayal of Brice "the most accomplished, original and enjoyable musical comedy performance ever put on film." Capitol Records released the *Funny Girl* album in 1964; it was one of the few Broadway albums to be recorded live rather than in a studio.

As the 1970s progressed, Streisand moved more and more into film work and recording. Eventually, the

> *Streisand has admitted that she never wanted to be a singer—she preferred serious roles in straight drama.*

the possibility of failure in her chosen profession. After graduating with honors from Erasmus Hall High School in Brooklyn, Streisand moved to Manhattan, where she bunked with friends and literally sang for her supper in nightclubs and bistros. When someone suggested that her last name sounded "too Jewish," she changed the spelling of her first name instead.

In 1961 Streisand won a talent contest at a Greenwich Village bar. That exposure led to her first regular engagement—at the Bon Soir, another Village club. There her innovative performances of "Who's Afraid of the Big Bad Wolf?" and "Happy Days Are Here Again" gained the attention of discriminating New York audiences. Soon she was appearing on local television shows and within a year she had a substantial part in a Broadway musical, "I Can Get It for You Wholesale." The show ran nine months with Streisand as an unattractive secretary named Miss Marmelstein, and when it closed, the twenty-one-year-old singer found herself in great demand. She signed a recording contract with

encroachments on her privacy and a growing stage fright caused her to quit performing live shows. She managed to retain her superstar status, however, because many of her films did well at the box office, and her records continued to make the charts. In 1971 she had her first pop hit, "Stoney End," a rousing song that marked a departure from her classic Broadway and torch-song repertory. Two years later she had her first hit-movie-hit-song combination with "The Way We Were," a wistful ballad about parted lovers. The dual success was repeated in 1976 when she earned an Academy Award for the song "Evergreen," (which she co-wrote with lyricist Paul Williams) from the film *A Star Is Born,* in which she played the lead. Both "Evergreen" and "The Way We Were" revealed a softer and more winsome Streisand sound, with an appeal that crossed generational lines.

Streisand was one of the few mainstream stars to have a hit disco song, "The Main Event," released in 1979. In that case, the song fared better than the film of the same title, starring Streisand and Ryan O'Neal. By the late 1970s, when "The Main Event" made the charts, Streisand was a near-recluse, protected by attack dogs and bodyguards from the many prying fans who annoyed her. She was beginning her research for *Yentl*, a film project that consumed her for a number of years. Before she began work on *Yentl* in earnest, she recorded an album with artist Barry Gibb of the Bee Gees. That record, *Guilty*, was one of her biggest sellers, and the title song reached number one on the Top 40 charts.

Yentl (1983) tells the story of a young Jewish girl who disguises herself as a boy in order to study the Talmud in a school. Not only did Streisand play the lead in the musical film, she also produced and directed the work. After spending so much time on the project—and after being rewarded with a good box-office draw—Streisand was greatly disappointed to be passed over for Academy Award nominations. In *People* magazine, Jeff Jarvis contends that a reputation for temperamental behavior on Streisand's part has alienated the Hollywood establishment, while her accomplishments spark jealousy. Streisand answered her critics in a *Ladies' Home Journal* profile. "I used to apologize for being a perfectionist," she said. "Now I don't. I *do* care about every detail. That's the way I operate. . . . People who like working for me want to be pushed, want to be stretched. And people who don't like working for me, I guess, don't."

As Streisand continues her dual acting and singing careers, she still refuses to perform live. She hardly needs to—*Nuts*, her 1987 film with Richard Dreyfuss, was a critical and commercial success, and her 1986 Columbia release, *The Broadway Album*, brought a poignant *West Side Story* song to the charts. Now in her forties, Streisand is reported to be one of the highest-paid women performers in history, with lifetime earnings in excess of $100 million. The entertainer prides herself on her artistic integrity, her perfectionism, and her constant quest for innovation. "As you get older, you realize your mortality," she told *Ladies' Home Journal*. "So I'd like to do everything I can to avoid being an old person who says, Why didn't I do that? Why didn't I take that chance?"

Selected discography

The Barbra Streisand Album, Columbia, 1963.
The Second Barbra Streisand Album, Columbia, 1963.
The Third Barbra Streisand Album, Columbia, 1964.
Funny Girl, Capitol, 1964.
People, Columbia, 1965.
My Name Is Barbra, Columbia, 1965.
Je m'appelle Barbra, Columbia, 1966.
Color Me Barbra, Columbia, 1966.
Simply Streisand, Columbia, 1967.
Stoney End, Columbia, 1971.
Barbra Joan Streisand, Columbia, 1972.
Live Concert at the Forum, Columbia, 1972.
The Way We Were, Columbia, 1974.
A Star Is Born, Columbia, 1976.
Streisand Superman, Columbia, 1977.
Wet, Columbia, 1979.
(With Barry Gibb) *Guilty*, Columbia, 1980.
Yentl, Columbia, 1983.
Emotion, Columbia, 1984.
The Broadway Album, Columbia, 1986.

Also recorded *Butterfly*, *A Christmas Album*, *Classical Barbra*, *Happening in Central Park*, *Lazy Afternoon*, *Memories*, *Songbird*, and *What about Today?*

Sources

Books

Stambler, Irwin, *Encyclopedia of Pop, Rock and Soul*, St. Martin's, 1974.

Periodicals

Esquire, October, 1982; April, 1985.
Harper's Bazaar, November, 1983.
Ladies' Home Journal, August, 1979; January, 1988; June, 1988.
Newsweek, January 5, 1970.
People, January 3, 1983; December 12, 1983; March 12, 1984; March 10, 1986.
Saturday Review, January 11, 1969.
Working Woman, March, 1986.

—Anne Janette Johnson

Stryper

Christian rock band

"**W**e're gonna rock!" The cry rises up from a stage surrounded by screaming fans, augmented by the thunder of drums and the wail of heavy-metal guitar riffs. Not uncommon. What is uncommon is that the sentence isn't finished. "We're gonna rock—for the Rock, Jesus Christ." When it comes to Stryper—Michael Sweet, Robert Sweet, Oz Fox (Richard Martinez), and Timothy Gaines—initial impressions of yellow-and-black spandex and long flyaway hair may be deceiving. Nonetheless, the group is based not on deceit but on the Truth they use the vehicle of rock music to spread.

Before rocking for God, the band rocked for fun. The Sweet brothers were part of Roxx Regime, a band into which they first recruited lead guitarist Fox, and later Gaines as bassist. Though they considered themselves a Christian band even then, their lifestyles belied the fact. According to Michael Sweet in a *Rolling Stone* interview in 1987, "We thought we were [Christians], but then on the weekends we'd get together and be guzzling the beers and doing our own thing. We got caught up in

For the Record. . .

Group formed as heavy-metal Christian rock band, 1983; original members include **Robert Sweet** (born c. 1960), drums; **Michael Sweet** (born c. 1964; wife's name, Kyle Rae), guitar and vocals; **Oz Fox** (real name, Richard Martinez; born c. 1962; wife's name, Leslie), guitar; and **Timothy Gaines** (born c. 1963; wife's name, Valerie), bass. Band members originally performed together in rock band Roxx Regime before forming Stryper, 1983; released first record, 1984; released first album, 1985.

Addresses: *Record company*—Enigma Records, 1750 East Holly Ave., P.O. Box 2428, El Segundo, CA 90245-1528.

playing just regular music, and you don't think there's anything wrong with it. But there really is, you know." To Stryper, the wrongness of playing secular music is that they were ignoring what they felt they should have been playing. Said Robert Sweet in the same interview, "the wrong is if you know the truth and you don't tell people. See, we felt there was a much more deeper meaning to life than just sex and drugs and party, party." The band's commitment to change in 1983 was supported strongly by Michael and Robert's mother, Janice Sweet. "I always thought that the potential was there for somebody to do [Christian rock], and I thought it may as well be these guys."

Stryper, whose name is derived from the book of Isaiah in the Old Testament ("With His stripes we are healed") released their first mini-LP, *The Yellow and Black Attack,* in 1984. It was followed a year later with the album *Soldiers Under Command,* which, according to *People* magazine in April of 1986, sold 275,000 copies. Compared to heavy metal groups like Quiet Riot, the numbers were not significant. But in the world of contemporary Christian music, 275,000 was a respectable number. *To Hell With the Devil,* released in 1986, made an even bigger impact, moving quickly into the Top Forty and selling nearly half a million copies in a matter of months. *In God We Trust,* released by Enigma in 1988, was to fare even better.

For all their success, controversy about their sound and their intent have come from every direction. One *Los Angeles Times* critic seemed to indicate the band's lack of sincerity by pointing out Michael Sweet's claim that an audience could "glorify God" by requesting that MTV air Stryper's video "Calling on You." Disgruntled young evangelists picketed concerts, denouncing the "worship of idols" by Christian fans, while older Christians indicated the inappropriateness of Stryper's clothing and stage performance. Says Robert Sweet, "If you can't draw people's attention, you can't tell them what you're trying to say. God outlines what sin is. It's not clothing or length of hair. Sin is a wrong attitude."

During concerts, the group tosses miniature Bibles into the audience and occasionally employs the help of born-again motorcyclists—Bikers for God—to help with crowd control. Before performances they pray. When fans follow the group to the hotel, they have been known to sit in the lobby and read the Bible with them. Of their unusual combination of message and medium, drummer Robert Sweet commented in *People,* "I'm tired of people being turned off to God. They think God is boring, that if you get Jesus, you've ruined your good time. But that's not the case." Bassist Tim Gaines adds, "It's good for kids to have something positive to look forward to, rather than a let's-go-kill-ourselves attitude." One way or another, Stryper is delivering a message fans may or may not be picking up anywhere else. Says Janice Sweet of the band's popularity and success, "It's because of the source behind this band and what they stand for. They glorify God, and there's no doubt that God is doing a lot of miracles for this band."

Selected discography

The Yellow and Black Attack, Enigma, 1984.
Soldiers Under Command, Enigma, 1985.
To Hell With the Devil, Enigma, 1986.
In God We Trust, Enigma, 1988.

Sources

People, April 14, 1986.
Rolling Stone, February 26, 1987.

—Meg Mac Donald

James Taylor

Singer, songwriter, guitarist

James Taylor's poetic soft-rock ballads have been an American favorite for more than fifteen years. Taylor has been richly represented on the pop charts since 1970, with hits such as "Fire and Rain," "Carolina in My Mind," "You've Got a Friend," and "Handy Man," but his work transcends the banality of most pop music. As Burt Korall puts it in the *Saturday Review,* the songwriter-singer-guitarist "brings to bear a substantial gift and admirable artfulness in the creation and performance of songs. Endearingly musical, he pairs memorable melodic lines with words that fit their contours tightly and well and document a singularity of vision. . . . The songs are delightful and enriching." Taylor's work is touching because it reveals intensely personal yet universal yearnings—and does so with sweet, simple melodies that do not overshadow the sentiment. "A fund of feelings, buoyantly lyrical and light on the one hand and darkly reflective on the other, mingle in his monologues," Korall writes. "One cannot remain indifferent for long."

At the outset of his career, Taylor was called a "new troubadour," an artist who was leading rock music away from the frenzied pitch it had established. Although Taylor feels that others preceded him in this endeavor—Bob Dylan, the Mamas and the Papas—he was the first to reach mainstream superstardom with the sound. His "tunes," as he calls them, are fusions of blues and jazz, folk (especially the ballad form), and even country music; though he has gone back toward classic rock in his more recent albums, most of his work is still acoustic. Korall claims that what emerges from the pastiche of Taylor's influences "is simultaneously literate and formal and relaxed and unpretentious. The thrust is rather direct, yet each one of Taylor's stories of love, loneliness, anguish, and puzzlement is open to interpretation. He always leaves the listener that option." *New York Times Magazine* contributor Susan Braudy concludes simply that Taylor "sounds like a kid sitting by himself on his bed singing his lonely interior monologues."

Most musicians sing about heartache, despair, and confusion, but few have experienced those feelings more intensely than James Taylor. The son of an affluent medical-school dean with a spacious home in North Carolina, Taylor grew up with every privilege—private schooling, summer vacations in Martha's Vineyard, plenty of money, and the affection of his family. The privileges were accompanied by expectations, however, and Taylor found himself enrolled in the strict Milton Academy, a boys' school in Massachusetts. The lonely young man hated the rigors of the academy, and when he returned home he found himself alienated from his North Carolina cohorts as well. At seventeen he became severely depressed and voluntarily entered

For the Record. . .

Full name James Vernon Taylor; born March 12, 1948, in Boston, Mass.; son of Isaac M. (a medical doctor and former dean of the University of North Carolina Medical School) and Gertrude (a singer, maiden name Woodard) Taylor; married Carly Simon (a singer), 1972 (divorced); children: Sarah, Benjamin. *Education:* Graduated from high school.

Singer, songwriter, guitarist, 1968—. Signed with Apple Records, 1968, produced first album, *James Taylor,* 1969; moved to Warner Brothers Records, 1970, had first hit album, *Sweet Baby James,* 1970, and first number one single, "Fire and Rain," 1970; moved to Columbia Records, 1977. Appeared in the film "Two Lane Blacktop," 1971.

Awards: Include nine gold albums, four platinum albums, and a 1978 Grammy Award.

Addresses: *Office*—c/o Asher, 644 N. Doheny Dr., Los Angeles, CA 90069.

McLean Hospital, an exclusive private psychiatric institution. Taylor stayed at McLean for ten months, finishing his high-school studies and writing his first songs there. Then, in the summer of 1966, he left without formal discharge and joined some friends in New York City.

In New York Taylor and his friend Danny Kortchmar formed a band called the Flying Machine. The group found a regular gig at the Night Owl in Greenwich Village, but Taylor only earned about twelve dollars a night. Gradually Taylor's personal problems resurfaced, and to make matters worse he became dependent on heroin. In January of 1968 Taylor fled New York for a new start in London. He produced an unpolished demonstration tape at a London studio and began to submit it to producers. He got an enthusiastic response from Peter Asher, a former performer who was scouting talent for Apple Records, a company founded by the Beatles. Both Asher and Paul McCartney liked Taylor's sound, and they signed him to an Apple contract. Taylor's first album, *James Taylor,* was released by Apple in 1969. The work, which included backup playing by McCartney and a number of songs Taylor wrote himself, was a critical success, but it failed to sell well. Discouraged—and debilitated by his heroin use— Taylor returned to the United States for another long stay in a mental institution.

By midsummer 1969 Taylor's health was restored, and he began to tour. He broke his contract with Apple and signed with Warner Brothers in America, bringing Peter Asher along as his personal manager/producer. In 1970 Taylor released *Sweet Baby James* on the Warner label, a collection of simply orchestrated soft folk-rock songs that has since sold more than two million copies. From *Sweet Baby James* Taylor had his first number-one single, "Fire and Rain," a poignant work that explores the hopelessness of mental illness and the sadness of suicide. *Sweet Baby James* and subsequent Taylor albums have revealed a signature style, according to Rick Mitz in *Stereo Review,* a style characterized by "rich melodies and the careful melding of music and lyric. . . . But the distinguishing trademark of [Taylor's sound] is self-revelation through lyrics."

A *Rolling Stone* correspondent notes that Taylor achieved "instant prominence" and drew the praise of critics and fans "for the confessional boldness of his dark folk narratives—inky, anguish-racked songs that would

> *Taylor's work is touching because it reveals intensely personal yet universal yearnings—and does so with sweet, simple melodies that do not overshadow the sentiment.*

have made for unnerving listening had they not been structured around the bright resonances of his nasal North Carolina twang and the clipped, suspended chordings of his ringing acoustic guitar. He crooned about confinement in a mental institution, about nervous breakdowns and dungeon-deep depressions, and somehow he left such disquieting realities a little gentler on our minds." A *Time* magazine contributor elaborates: "What [Taylor] has endured and sings about, with much restraint and dignity, are mainly 'head' problems, those pains that a lavish quota of middle-class advantages . . . do not seem to prevent, and may in fact exacerbate. Drugs, underachievement, the failure of will, alienation, the doorway to suicide, the struggle back to life—James Taylor has been there himself."

Life improved for Taylor throughout the 1970s—he married singer Carly Simon and had two children—and many of his songs lost their anguished edge. He did not lack for hits, however. His tunes "Country Road," "Handy Man," "How Sweet It Is," and "Her Town Too" made the billboard charts, as did the cheerful song he wrote for his daughter, "Your Smiling Face." Gradually Taylor's music began to take on a harder rock edge too, especially in concert. To quote Mitz, Taylor "has survived and thrived in a business that eats up its musicians like popcorn."

Now in his forties, Taylor continues to cut albums and write his own music, but he admits that composing has become more difficult for him. "I want to write great songs," he told *Rolling Stone*, "but I don't want to suffer, you know. I'm not going to wear a couple of shoe sizes too small just because I might write a better song." The suffering has not gone out of Taylor's life completely, though. He still struggles with alcohol abuse and depression, combatting both by exercising and taking time to relax. His marriage to Carly Simon ended in divorce after several years of mutual bitterness, but *Newsweek* correspondent Harry F. Waters suggests that such setbacks have only caused Taylor to "grow up" musically. The singer himself seems to agree. "I spent a lot of time with a feeling of negative faith," he told *Newsweek*, "an assumption that the world had a nasty surprise just around each corner. But I'm comfortable now. I don't have any investment any longer in things turning out badly."

Selected discography

James Taylor, Apple, 1969.
Sweet Baby James, Warner Brothers, 1970.
James Taylor and the Original Flying Machine, Euphoria, 1971.
Mud Slide Slim and the Blue Horizon, Warner Brothers, 1971.
One Man Dog, Warner Brothers, 1972.
Walking Man, Warner Brothers, 1975.
Rainy Day Man, Trip, 1975.
Two Originals, Warner Brothers, 1975.
Gorilla, Warner Brothers, 1975.
In the Pocket, Warner Brothers, 1976.
The Best of James Taylor, Warner Brothers, 1976.
J. T., Columbia, 1977.
James Taylor's Greatest Hits, Warner Brothers, 1977.
Flag, Columbia, 1979.
Dad Loves His Work, Columbia, 1980.
That's Why I'm Here, Columbia, 1985.
Never Die Young, Columbia, 1988.

Sources

Newsweek, February 8, 1971; November 4, 1985.
New Yorker, November 25, 1972.
New York Times Magazine, February 21, 1971.
People, October 6, 1980.
Rolling Stone, September 6, 1979; June 11, 1981.
Saturday Review, September 12, 1970.
Stereo Review, January, 1978.
Time, March 1, 1971.

—Anne Janette Johnson

Kiri
Te Kanawa

Operatic soprano

Kiri Te Kanawa is an operatic soprano of international stature, particularly known for her artistic interpretations of roles in Mozart and Strauss operas. Te Kanawa radiates enormous confidence in her voice and joy in singing that, along with her beauty, appeal to audiences worldwide.

Born on March 6, 1944, in Grisbane, New Zealand to a mother of European origin and a Maori father, Kiri was adopted at five weeks old by Tom and Nell Te Kanawa. Tom Te Kanawa, a Maori—a people of Polynesian descent—ran a truck contracting business. Little did the Te Kanawas know when they named their daughter Kiri, the Maori word for bell, that someday commentators would be remarking on their daughter's bell-like voice. Nell came from a musical family—her great-uncle was English composer Sir Arthur Sullivan—and played the piano for gatherings with family and friends. By the time Kiri was eight years old her ability was recognized by a talent scout, who asked to her to sing for a local radio show.

Determined that their daugher's talent would not be wasted, in 1956 the Te Kanawas moved to Auckland, Australia, so that Kiri could study with Sister Mary Leo of St. Mary's College for Girls. Sister Leo, who had been a professional opera singer before joining a religious order, recognized her young pupil's talent and agreed to lessons twice a week. Unfortunately Kiri proved to be an undisciplined student and was forced to leave St. Mary's College after only two years due to poor academic performance. She nevertheless privately continued her studies with Leo while completing a business course and working as a receptionist. At this time Kiri also sang from a repetoire of light songs at weddings and clubs.

In 1960 the young singer participated in the Auckland Competition, one of several singing competitions that allowed winners to get some exposure via radio and a recording that might lead to further study abroad. Kiri was chosen as having the most promising voice. Still under the tutelege of Sister Mary Leo, Te Kanawa expanded her range beyond mezzo soprano and in 1965 she placed first in the Mobile Song Quest, sponsored by several Australian newspapers. During this time, Te Kanawa also gathered quite a following at clubs, made a number of popular recordings and appeared in several New Zealand films.

If she were to truly succeed in the world of classical music, Te Kanawa needed more formal training in Europe. In 1966, she entered the London Opera Centre. Kiri's first year at the Centre was very difficult for she was lonely and lacked the formal training of most of the students there. But she persevered and in the process learned that her voice truly lay in the soprano range.

For the Record. . .

Born March 6, 1944, in Grisbane, New Zealand; daughter of Thomas (a contractor) and Nell (a homemaker; maiden name Leeces) Te Kanawa; married Desmond Stephen Park (a mining engineer), August 30, 1967; children: Antonia (adopted), Thomas (adopted). *Education:* Attended St. Mary's College for Girls, Auckland, Australia; studied voice at London Opera Centre, London, England, beginning in 1966; studied voice with Vera Rozsa, beginning in 1969. *Religion:* Roman Catholic.

Winner of voice competitions in New Zealand, 1960, and in Australia, 1965, that led to concert and club bookings, recording contracts (for pop songs), and appearances in several films; made opera debut, as the Countess Almavira in Mozart's *The Marriage of Figaro,* at the Royal Opera House (Covent Garden), London, England, 1970.

Awards: Winner of Auckland (New Zealand) Competition, 1960; winner of Mobil Song Quest (Australia), 1965; Member of the Order of the British Empire (Civil Division), 1973; named New Zealander of the year, 1973; named Dame Commander of the Order of the British Empire, 1982.

Addresses: *Agent*—Jack Mastrianni, Columbia Artists, 165 W. 57th St., New York, N.Y. 10019.

On August 30, 1967, Kiri married Desmond Park, an Australian mining engineer whom she had met in London. The following year she began to sing some professional roles as well as in student productions at the Opera Centre. In 1969 Te Kanawa began a long and fruitful relationship with voice teacher Vera Rozsa, a former mezzo-soprano at the Vienna State Opera. Kiri credits much of her success to Rozsa, from whom she learned interpretation and acting as well as the technical aspects of singing. In 1970 Te Kanawa made her debut at London's Royal Opera House—also known as Covent Garden—in the role of the Countess Almavira in Mozart's *The Marriage of Figaro,* and was offered a three-year contract as a junior principal at that institution.

The early 1970s proved to be pioneering years for Te Kanawa, who appeared in a variety of roles: Donna Elvira in Mozart's *Don Giovanni,* Micaela in Bizet's *Carmen,* and Amelia in Verdi's *Simon Boccanegra.* In 1974 she made her debut at the Metropolitan Opera in New York as Desdemona in Verdi's *Otello.* Kiri was asked to appear unexpectedly early when the lead soprano fell ill and canceled only three hours before the performance, which was to be broadcast live na-

tionally. After this performance, Kiri, who was normally positively reviewed by critics, received raves and suddenly became an international star.

Though Te Kanawa has long admitted that she often procrastinates when learning roles, until 1975 she maintained a hectic schedule. She then contracted a serious illness, which taught her the importance of pacing herself. After three months of recuperation, Kiri was back at rehearsals. In 1976 she added Mim in Puccini's *La Bohme,* Tatyana in Tchaikovshy's *Eugene Onegin,* and Fiordiligi in Mozart's *Cos fan tutte* to her repertoire. The following year she appeared as Arabella in Strauss's opera of the same name, and in the late seventies appeared as Rosalinde in *Die Fledermaus* by Strauss and Violetta in *La Traviata* by Verdi.

Since early in her career, Te Kanawa has frequently been in the eyes of the media. In 1975 she became the subject of a television profile by the British Broadcasting Corporation, and she has made a number of televi-

> *Little did the Te Kanawas know when they named their daughter Kiri, the Maori word for bell, that someday commentators would be remarking on their daughter's bell-like voice.*

sion appearances: She portrayed Donna Elivra in Joseph Losey's film production of *Don Giovanni,* and in 1981 she was chosen by Prince Charles of Wales to sing at his marriage to Lady Diana Spencer, which drew a television audience of over 600 million viewers. In reaction to her status as a celebrity, Kiri guards her family's privacy—she and Desmond adopted a daughter Antonia in 1976 and son Thomas in 1979—and clearly separates her professional life from her personal life.

In the 1980s Te Kanawa's voice and interpretations continued to mature, largely in the repertoire she had already established, and she has made numerous recordings of operatic and popular works. Though Te Kanawa is in high demand worldwide, critics have not reached a consensus on her ability. Though commentators agree that she has a beautiful voice and enthralling stage presence, they have negatively criticized her acting. In 1985 Te Kanawa became dissatisfied with singing opera and took a nine-month sabbatical to perform only concerts and recitals. She returned to the operatic stage the following year but has limited her annual total appearances to between forty-five and fifty in an effort to maintain her voice in peak form and balance her career and private life.

Selected discography

Ave Maria, Philips.
Bach: *St. Matthew Passion*, London.
Beethoven: *Symphony No. 9*, EMI/Angel.
Berlioz: *Nuits d't*, Deutsche Grammaphon.
Bernstein: *West Side Story*, DG.
Bizet: *Carmen*, London.
Blue Skies, London.
Brahms: *German Requiem*, London.
Canteloube: *Songs of Auvergne, Vols. 1 and 2*, London.
Christmas with Kiri, London.
Come to the Fair, EMI/Angel.
Durufl: *Requiem*, CBS.
Gershwin: *Songs*, Angel.
Gounod: *Faust*, Philips.
Great Love Scenes, CBS.
Handel: *Messiah*, London.
Mahler: *Symphony No. 2*, Philips.
Mahler: *Symphony No. 4*, London.
Mozart: *Arias*, Philips.

Mozart: *Don Giovanni*, CBS.
Mozart: *Marriage of Figaro*, London.
Puccini Heroines, CBS.
Puccini: *La Rondine*, CBS.
Puccini: *Tosca*, London.
Ravel: *Sheherazade;* Duparc: *Seven Songs*, EMI/Angel.
Recital—Schubert, Schumann, Wolf, Faur, Duparc, CBS.
Strauss: *Arabella*, London. ˙
Strauss: *Four Last Songs*, CBS.
Verdi and Puccini: *Arias*, CBS.

Sources

Books

Fingleton, David, *Kiri: A Biography of Kiri Te Kanawa*, Atheneum, 1983.

Periodicals

Chicago Tribune, December 7, 1987.
Grammophon, February 1988.
High Fidelity/Musical America, June 1983.
Opera News, February 1983; December 20, 1986.
Ovation, September 1985.
Variety, April 30, 1986.

—*Jeanne M. Lesinski*

U2

Irish rock band

The message, if there is a message in our music, is the *hope* that it communicates," U2's lead singer, Bono, announced to Jim Miller in *Newsweek.* Something of a rarity among popular rock groups, U2 emphasizes spiritual values and social and political conscience in its songs, which "speak equally to the [civil rights protests in Selma, Alabama] of two decades ago and the Nicaragua of tomorrow," according to Jay Cocks of *Time.* Hailing from Dublin, Ireland, the group won some international attention with the release of its 1980 album, *Boy,* but it was not until 1983's *War*—which featured the protest songs "New Year's Day" and "Sunday, Bloody Sunday"—that U2 began to gain a large following of rock fans.

Though the foursome, consisting of Bono, guitarist Dave "The Edge" Evans, drummer Larry Mullen, Jr., and bassist Adam Clayton, is credited with bringing ideals back to a genre often primarily concerned with the celebration of worldly pleasures, Bono admitted to Cocks that he "would hate to think everybody was into U2 for 'deep' and 'meaningful' reasons. We're a noisy

rock-'n'-roll band. If we all got onstage, and instead of going 'Yeow!' the audience all went 'Ummmm' or started saying the rosary, it would be awful." In Miller's opinion, Bono and U2 need not worry: "Playing droning clusters of notes and using chiming, bell-like timbres, as well as abrasive, buzz-saw textures, the Edge creates an electronic wall of sound that has an elemental power. . . . For all the nervous jangle of the music, its sheer scale and Celtic overtones create a weird, primordial resonance." Whether it be the words they are singing or the sound of the music they play, in the words of Christopher Connelly in *Rolling Stone,* U2 "has become one of the handful of artists in rock [and] roll history . . . that people are eager to identify themselves with."

The group began in 1976 when Mullen was expelled from a Dublin high school marching band for having long hair. Frustrated at not having an outlet for his drum work, he posted a notice on the school's bulletin board asking for others who wanted to start a rock band. Of the several students who came to his house to audition, Mullen told Cocks: "I saw that some people could play. The Edge could play. Adam just *looked* great. Big bushy hair, long caftan coat, bass guitar and amp. He . . . used all the right words, like gig. I thought, this guy *must* know how to play. Then Bono arrived, and he meant to play the guitar, but he couldn't play very well, so he started to sing. He couldn't do that either. But he was such a charismatic character that he was in the band anyway, as soon as he arrived."

At first the boys saw the band as a recreational activity, practicing on Wednesday afternoons. Clayton was the most serious about making a success of it, and found a manager, Paul McGuinness, for them in 1978. After that, they struggled to obtain opening gigs for popular Dublin bands. "You see," Mullen confessed to Cocks, "we couldn't play. We were very, very, very bad." They steadily improved, however, and, after Bono had pushed the band's tapes upon several recording executives, U2 landed a recording contract with Island in 1980. *Boy,* their first album, gained them an appreciative audience in their native country and Great Britain, and one single from it, "I Will Follow," received air play in the United States. U2's second album, *October,* did not sell as well. The production was rushed, because Bono, who serves as the group's main lyricist, had his book of lyrics stolen from him—the group had to hurry to release the pilfered songs before the thief could. Also, as Bono revealed to Anthony DeCurtis of *Rolling Stone:* "We were, during *October,* interested in other things, really. We thought about giving up the band. . . . We wanted to make a record, and yet we didn't want to make a record, because we were going through a stage where we thought, 'Rock [and] roll is just *full of shit,* do we want to spend our lives doing it?'"

U2 came back big, however, in 1983 with *War,* which included the hits "New Year's Day" and "Sunday,

> Bono "would hate to think that everybody was into U2 for 'deep' and 'meaningful' reasons. We're a rock-'n'-roll band."

Bloody Sunday." "New Year's" concerns the domination of Poland by the Soviet Union; "Sunday, Bloody Sunday" takes its theme from the conflict between Protestants and Catholics in Northern Ireland, particularly from "a massacre of civilians by the British" in that troubled country, according to Connelly in *Rolling Stone.* *War* not only established U2 as a favorite of U.S. audiences, but as a rock group of social conscience. The band appropriately debuted "Sunday, Bloody Sunday" at a concert in Belfast, Northern Ireland, and Bono took to waving a white flag on stage during performances. He told Connelly it was supposed to be "a flag drained of all color"; Connelly interpreted: "as if to say that in war, surrender was the bravest course."

The Unforgettable Fire, U2's 1984 effort, continued in the idealistic vein of *War,* especially in its hit single "Pride (In the Name of Love)," a celebration of American civil rights leader Martin Luther King, Jr. Taking its name from a series of paintings by survivors of the atom bombings of Hiroshima and Nagasaki, Japan, it also included more eclectic selections such as "Elvis Presley and America," which Miller labeled "an all-too-effective evocation of Presley's catatonic stupor in his last days." Though, as Miller pointed out, "some critics have poked fun at the lyrics of the songs" on *Unforgettable,* it became U2's biggest selling album until it was usurped by 1987's *The Joshua Tree.*

The Joshua Tree, lauded as "U2's . . . best album" by Cocks, includes the hit singles "With or Without You" and "I Still Haven't Found What I'm Looking For." Also on the disc is "Bullet the Blue Sky," a protest song inspired by Bono's trip to El Salvador. According to Cocks, "you can still hear the ache of fear in his voice, the closeness of the memory." In 1988, the group released a film and corresponding soundtrack album, *Rattle and Hum,* chronicling their 1987 world tour. As Jeffrey Ressner reported in *Rolling Stone,* "the picture is neither a straightforward concert movie nor a traditional rock documentary," containing footage of U2's visit to Presley's mansion, Graceland, and of the band singing with a church choir in Harlem, New York. U2 has also taken an active roll in many rock benefits, including the Live Aid effort for Ethiopian famine relief, and shows to raise money and awareness for Amnesty International, an organization seeking to help political prisoners.

Selected discography

Boy (includes "I Will Follow," "Twilight," "Into the Heart," "Out of Control," and "Shadows and Tall Trees"), Island, 1980.

October (includes "Gloria," "I Fall Down," "Rejoice," "Fire," "Tomorrow," and "Scarlet"), Island, 1981.

War (includes "New Year's Day," "Two Hearts Beat as One," "Seconds," and "Sunday, Bloody Sunday"), Island, 1983.

Under a Blood Red Sky (live album), Island, 1983.

The Unforgettable Fire (includes "Pride," "MLK," "Bad," "A Sort of Homecoming," and "Elvis Presley and America"), Island, 1984.

The Joshua Tree (includes "With or Without You," "In God's Country," "I Still Haven't Found What I'm Looking For," "Where the Streets Have No Name," "Bullet the Blue Sky," and "One Tree Hill"), Island, 1987.

Rattle and Hum, Island, 1988.

Sources

Maclean's, November 2, 1987.
Newsweek, December 31, 1984.
People, April 1, 1985.
Rolling Stone, October 11, 1984; March 14, 1985; May 7, 1987; September 8, 1988.
Time, April 27, 1987.

—Elizabeth Thomas

Luthur Vandross

Singer, songwriter, producer, and arranger

Luthur Vandross was well-known and respected among professional musicians long before he debuted as a solo star in 1981 with the hit album *Never Too Much*. For several years, he had been contributing his talents as a backup singer, songwriter, and arranger to albums by the likes of Chaka Khan, Carly Simon, Quincy Jones, and Roberta Flack. His solo appeal is due in part to his rich tenor and superb stylings, which, Richard Harrington declared in the *Washington Post,* put Vandross "in the pantheon of classic soul singers that stretches from Ray Charles and Sam Cooke to Al Green." It is also attributable to his preference for unabashedly romantic love songs in an era of sexually explicit lyrics. "Some people are tired of letting it all hang out, and Vandross's lyrics speak to a special romantic need," wrote Orde Coombs in *New York.*

Vandross grew up in the Alfred E. Smith public housing project on New York City's lower East Side. He was surrounded by music from birth; his mother, a widow, sent her son to piano lessons when he was only three years old, and his eldest sister was a member of The Crests, a doo-wop group best remembered for the song "Sixteen Candles." "My sister was too young to go out to rehearsals, so the group would work out in our living room," Vandross recalled in *Ebony.* He immersed himself in the music of Dionne Warwick, Aretha Franklin, the Supremes and other black groups of the time, becoming so wrapped up in their world that when Ross left the Supremes his grade average dropped from a B+ to a C-.

The great black women singers, not the men, inspired him to sing, Vandross insists. "I acknowledge what Stevie Wonder, Donny Hathaway, Tony Bennett and all the fabulous male singers did, but that's not what aroused my artistic libido," he stated in *Jet.* A pivotal event in his young life was his 1963 attendance of a Dionne Warwick concert at the Brooklyn Fox Theatre. "She wiped me out. . . . She knocked me down with that tone quality. That's when I made the decision to sing. I wanted to do to somebody what she did to me." Yet Vandross, whose natural shyness was compounded by a serious weight problem, was so self-conscious that he could not bring himself to sing aloud around his family. By the age of sixteen, however, he had become confident enough to audition for and win a place in a sixteen-member vocal group, Listen My Brother, managed by the owners of the famous Apollo Theater. After graduating from Taft High School, Vandross enrolled at Western Michigan University, but after an unsuccessful year there he returned to New York to concentrate on a musical career. In 1972 a song he wrote, "Everybody Rejoice (Brand New Day)" was selected for use in the Broadway musical *The Wiz.* The royalties helped him pay the rent on his first apartment, but he continued to work a variety of non-musical jobs as well.

Nineteen seventy-four was the year Vandross really made his break into professional music. A childhood friend, Carlos Alomar, had become the guitarist for David Bowie. He took Vandross to the recording studio where Bowie's *Young Americans* was being made. While listening to the studio tape, Vandross began singing his ideas for the chorus to Alomar. Bowie, standing unnoticed nearby, was impressed with what he heard. He hired Vandross to sing and arrange backup vocals on *Young Americans*. He also used a Vandross composition, "Fascination," on the album, and took the singer along as part of his backup chorus when he went on tour. Through Bowie, Vandross met many influential figures in the music industry and was soon doing session work with top performers.

Encouraged by his success, Vandross and some other singers formed their own group, Luther. They made two albums for Atlantic in 1976, but neither was successful, and Luther soon disbanded. Its former members went on to become parts of the groups Kleer and Chic. Vandross sang lead vocals on several hit songs during the mid-1970s, including Bionic Boogies's "Hot Butterfly," Change's "Glow of Love" and "Searchin'," and Chic's "Dance Dance Dance" and "Everybody Dance," but his contributions were uncredited. His voice was heard by even more people after he met a producer of commerical jingles while working on Quincy Jones's *Sounds . . . And Stuff Like That.* Soon Vandross was a member of what he called in the *Washington Post* "a very small clique of people who do all the jingle work,"

singing the praises of everything from beer and soda to AT&T and the U.S. Army. He remarked that the difference between session work and jingle work was "amazing. . . . [In session work] you go in at 12 and come out at a quarter to midnight and you make $600. A jingle will book you from noon to 1 o'clock and you make $35,000."

Jingle work was lucrative, but Vandross was ready for the challenge of a solo career. In 1981 he put together a demo tape and made the rounds of the major record companies, but was repeatedly rejected because he insisted on producing himself. Epic finally gambled on his ability, and the company's risk paid off handsomely. His debut album, *Never Too Much,* sold over a million copies, and Vandross won Grammy Award nominations for best new artist and best male rhythm and blues singer. *Never Too Much*'s popularity was matched by 1982's followup release, *For Ever, For Always, For Love,* and by the 1983 album *Busy Body.* Vandross also found time to produce the album *How Many Times Can We Say Goodbye?* for Dionne Warwick and to revitalize Aretha Franklin's career by producing two of her best albums in years, *Jump to It!* and *Get It Right.*

> *Luthur Vandross is "in the pantheon of classic soul singers that streches from Ray Charles and Sam Cooke to Al Green."*

Vandross commented in the *Washington Post* that becoming a star was somewhat frightening: "After being a session singer—you come in with your hair nappy, in sneakers, your shirt hanging out. It doesn't matter what you look like, you've just got to *sound* good. Now all of a sudden to have everybody looking at you is a *deep* transition." His apprehensions about appearing in public were reflected in his early stage shows. Like his albums, they were lavishly produced. Elaborate sets, special effects, actors, and dancers all served to distract audiences from the star.

Vandross seemed to reach a personal turning point in 1985. The album he released that year, *The Night I Fell in Love,* was full of his trademark love songs, but featured a tough, spare sound. The accompanying tour was also stripped down to the bare essentials. With his band hidden offstage, Vandross, who had lost about 100 pounds, stood alone. A *Variety* reviewer was enthusiastic about the changes, writing of a concert in New York City, "With absolutely no props, gimmicks or vaudeville skits, a very streamlined Vandross enthralled

20,000 attendees with his fantastic voice and sense of humor." His popularity grew even greater with the albums *Give Me the Reason* and *Any Love,* which increased his appeal to white listeners. Summing up Vandross's appeal, Richard Harrington stated: "Few people have devoted themselves to love songs so completely and successfully. . . . He has dedicated himself to combining [a] big-hearted, big-voiced approach to the love song with the sharp, powerful rhythm tracks of the '80s. . . . When this approach clicks . . . it produces some of the most exhilarating love songs this side of Smokey Robinson."

Selected discography

LPs; all for Epic

Never Too Much, 1981.

Forever, For Always, For Love, 1982.
Busy Body, 1984.
The Night I Fell in Love, 1985.
Give Me the Reason, 1987.
Any Love, 1989.

Sources

Ebony, December 1985.
Jet, June 17, 1985.
New York, February 15, 1982.
New York Times, October 3, 1982; January 7, 1987.
People, November 10, 1983.
Variety, January 22, 1986; May 28, 1986; April 22, 1987.
Washington Post, January 29, 1984; April 6, 1986.

—Joan Goldsworthy

Sarah Vaughan

Singer

Sarah Vaughan's richly expressive voice has held the jazz world in thrall for more than four decades. Vaughan's recordings and live performances convey a physical delight in singing as well as an artist's sensitivity to the complicated harmonies and rhythms of modern jazz. As Louie Robinson notes in *Ebony,* however, the "delicious elegance" of Sarah Vaughan "has always been a little too rich for the masses to digest. You can sing along with Mitch Miller, but how in the world do you match the undulating flights of one of the most remarkable voices of the century?" Indeed, Vaughan long ago gave up trying to market herself to a pop audience, opting instead to create a body of work she could be proud to perform. She has thereby earned the highest critical regard, and the appreciation, to quote Robinson, of "those with the . . . taste and musical knowledge to appreciate the vocal miracles she performs night after night, year after year."

In a *down beat* magazine profile of Vaughan, composer Gunther Schuller deemed the singer the "greatest vocal artist of the century." Schuller claimed that Vaughan's "is a perfect instrument, attached to a musician of superb instincts, capable of expressing profound human experience, with a wholly original voice." *Saturday Review* contributor Martin Williams expresses a similar opinion. "Sarah Vaughan is in several respects the jazz singer par excellence," Williams contends, "and therefore she can do things with her voice that a trained singer knows simply must not be done. She can take a note at the top of her range and then bend it or squeeze it; she growls and rattles notes down at the bottom of her range; she can glide her voice over through several notes at mid-range while raising dynamics, or lowering, or simply squeezing." This vocal experimentation meshes perfectly with the improvisational freedom of bebop and jazz. "Only once in each generation come a voice like this," claims Dave Garroway in *The Jazz Titans,* "one artist who brings a new approach, a new way of communicating the emotions which stir every soul."

An only child, Sarah Lois Vaughan was born in Newark, New Jersey, in 1924. Both of her parents enjoyed making music in their spare time—her carpenter father as a guitarist and piano player, her mother as a singer with the local Baptist church choir. Sarah herself joined the choir as soon as she was able, and she took piano and organ lessons from the age of eight. Gospel music was not young Sarah's only passion, however. She has admitted to sneaking into neighborhood bars during her teens to hear jazz played by visiting performers. She also played piano in the jazz band at Newark's Arts High School, where, as she told *down beat,* she "learned to take music apart and analyze the notes and put it back together again."

Vaughan was only eighteen when, on a friend's dare, she entered an amateur contest at Harlem's Apollo Theatre. She won the contest—and a week's engagement at the Apollo—with a jazz rendition of "Body and Soul." Vaughan told *down beat* that she feels she became famous not because of rigorous training but because she was in the right place at the right time. "I was going to be a hairdresser before I got into show business," she said. "I always wanted to be in show business, and when I got in, I didn't try. I just went to the amateur hour, and in two weeks I was in show business. It shocked me to death and it took me a long time to get over that." Vaughan's week at the Apollo had not run its course before she was discovered by Billy Eckstine, a

young singer with the Earl Hines Orchestra. Eckstine persuaded Hines to hire Vaughan, and her career was launched. She had her professional debut April 23, 1943, as a singer and second pianist for Hines.

The following year, Billy Eckstine formed his own band, and Vaughan joined him. Eckstine's was one of the first major bebop groups, and through his aegis Vaughan met Dizzy Gillespie and Charlie Parker, two jazz pioneers who were to have great influence on her style. It was Gillespie, in fact, who landed Vaughan her first solo recording contracts with Continental and Musicraft Records. Together Vaughan and Gillespie cut "Lover Man," her first song to receive national attention. Subsequent Vaughan singles "Don't Blame Me" and "I Cover the Waterfront" also attracted favorable review.

Vaughan became a solo performer in 1945, and in 1947 she married trumpeter George Treadwell. Under Treadwell's management, Vaughan blossomed from a shy, gap-toothed, awkward young woman into a sophisticated and elegant performer. She began earning top billing at prestigious clubs in Chicago and New York, and by 1950 she was selling an estimated three million records annually. Still, Vaughan had to undergo the same sort of bigotry other black performers faced— inadequate or nonexistent dressing rooms in the white clubs, segregated restaurants, and occasional alley beatings by gangs of hoodlums. She was even pelted with tomatoes once during a performance at a Chicago theatre. Aware that only a small percentage of her audience was hostile, however, Vaughan persisted, constantly experimenting with her vocal range until, as Williams puts it, "fewer and fewer popular songs could contain her."

In 1953 Vaughan signed with Mercury Records and embarked on a short but successful pop career. By 1959 she had made the *Billboard* charts with songs like "C'est la Vie," "Mr. Wonderful," "The Banana Boat Song," "Smooth Operator," and the million-selling "Broken-Hearted Melody." Most singers struggle valiantly for chart-topping hits, but Vaughan did not like the direction her career was taking. "The record companies always wanted me to do something that I didn't want to do," she told *down beat.* "'Sarah, you don't sell many records,' they'd say, and so *Broken Hearted Melody* came up. God, I hated it. I did that in the '50s and everybody loves that tune. It's the corniest thing I ever did." Eventually Vaughan decided to follow her own instincts, and, as James Liska notes in *down beat,* the material to which she lent her talent emerged "with the inimitable Sarah Vaughan stamp clearly on it—a stamp which seems to just happen."

Doc Watson

Singer, guitarist, banjo player

Doc Watson, a native of the North Carolina mountains, has been belatedly recognized as one of the nation's best folk artists. Watson plays and sings traditional Appalachian string music—the sort of songs heard on rural front porches before radio began to homogenize American tastes. Blind since early childhood, Watson taught himself to pick guitar and banjo by listening to old recordings; his own award-winning albums contain numerous tunes he listened to on his mother's knee. *People* magazine contributor Roger Wolmuth suggests that for Watson, music "would become the means of passage from a life of darkness into one made rich and bright by his artistry." Wolmuth continues: "Watson's blizzard-quick flat picking and warm, mountain-clear baritone have . . . established the soft-spoken Blue Ridge Mountain native as one of America's premier acoustic musicians."

Watson was pulled from the obscurity of his Blue Ridge birthplace by a resurgent interest in traditional folk music. He was almost forty when a recording he made for the Smithsonian Institution led to invitations to such prestigious concert sites as the Newport Folk Festival, Carnegie Hall, and even the White House. Between 1960 and 1987 Watson undertook a full schedule of touring and studio work, often accompanied by his son Merle, who died in 1985. Wolmuth states that Watson's records "are often capsule courses in American music history. Hoedown dance tunes, gospel hymns, even '50s rockabilly hits seem part of a cultural continuum when translated through his guitar. . . . To a mostly Northern audience more familiar with such folkie pretenders as the Kingston Trio and the Brothers Four, [Watson and his family] represented old-time music at its authentic best. Homespun and unpretentious, they were the embodiment of the family string band that had been a Southern tradition for generations."

Born Arthel Lane Watson in Deep Gap, North Carolina, Doc grew up in a large farming family of very modest means. His parents and eight siblings were crowded into a three-room house that admitted snow and rain through cracks in the siding. Watson was not blind from birth; he lost his sight as a young child through an undiagnosed illness. Growing up disabled, Watson drew solace from music. Both of his parents loved to sing, and his father could play several instruments. When Watson was eleven his father made him a banjo, using the skin of a recently-deceased cat. Watson learned to play by listening to his father and to old recordings by the Carter Family and Gid Tanner and His Skillet Lickers. After briefly attending the Raleigh School for the Blind (he dropped out at fourteen); Watson went to work with his father, cutting wood with a cross-saw. He earned enough to buy his first commercially-made instrument, a Sears-Roebuck guitar.

Watson made his performing debut at a fiddlers' convention in Boone, North Carolina. He was seventeen. The following year he began to play regularly on a radio broadcast from Lenoir, North Carolina. With professional musicianship in mind, he gave up his acoustic guitar and old mountain songs for an electric guitar and a repertory of standard country hits; soon he was a local favorite as a member of the Jack Williams Band. Watson played with the Williams group throughout the 1950s, supplementing his income by tuning pianos. Thus he was more or less a fixture in his mountain community when Ralph Rinzler visited in 1960.

Rinzler, a folk and bluegrass enthusiast, was the assistant secretary at the Smithsonian Institution in Washington, D.C. He had travelled south to record banjo player Clarence Ashley. Ashley introduced Rinzler to Watson, who somewhat grudgingly picked up his old acoustic guitar and sang some traditional tunes. Rinzler made a recording of Watson and his family, brought it north, and released it the same year. "Within months," writes Wolmuth, "the guitarist would be on tour, a local secret no more." By 1963 Watson found himself performing before 13,000 fans at the Newport Folk Festival—he both benefitted by and contributed to the new wave of interest in folk among educated Northern audiences.

In 1964 Watson's son Merle joined him on the road and in the studio. The two were inseparable, and Merle's attentive care allowed Watson to travel to such exotic locales as Japan, Europe, and Africa. When Merle died in a tractor accident in 1985, the elder Watson—grief-stricken and bereft of an indispensable companion—began to restrict his concert appearances. Today Watson is in semi-retirement on his property in Deep Gap. He has never produced a so-called "hit" album, but his numerous recordings on folk labels have brought him relative prosperity. To quote a contributor to the *Illustrated Encyclopedia of Country Music*, Watson "is now a revered figure among old and young alike, drawing wild receptions quite out of keeping with his down-home musical style."

Although Watson has played at bluegrass festivals and even has opened for Bill Monroe, his music is not to be confused with bluegrass. Many of Watson's songs, and his picking style as well, predate the advent of bluegrass—his is the sound of the old country string band, his songs the ballads of the hill country. His best-known tunes such as "Tom Dooley," "Shady Grove," "Darlin' Cory," "Ground Hog," and "Willie Moore" date to far simpler times in the last century. Watson's resurrection of these earthy folk works form "an antidote to a pop

business . . . backsliding into blandness," according to the reviewer in the *Illustrated Encyclopedia of Country Music*. Watson told *People* that, had he kept his sight, he might have become a carpenter or an electrician. "I sure wouldn't have gone on the road with the guitar," he said. "But a man's got to do what he can do. When they

> Doc Watson's records "are often capsule courses in American music history."

let you in this world, they hand you a little box. It's invisible, of course, and it's got a few talents in it. And if somethin' happens that you can't lean on one, why, you got two or three more you can get hold of." Watson's particular "talent box" produced a musician who has helped to retain, re-establish, and revitalize a vibrant form of American expression—the old-time country sound.

Selected discography

LPs

Folk City, Folkways.
The Watson Family, Volume I, Folkways.
The Watson Family, Volume II, Folkways.
Old Time Music at Clarence Ashley's, Volume I, Folkways.
Old Time Music at Clarence Ashley's, Volume II, Folkways.
Jean Ritchie and Doc Watson at Folk City, Folkways.
Doc Watson, Vanguard, 1964.
Elementary, Vanguard.
The Essential Doc Watson, Vanguard.
Home Again, Vanguard.
Old Timey Music, Vanguard.
Doc Watson in Nashville, Vanguard.
Doc Watson on Stage, Vanguard.
Southbound, Vanguard.
Doc Watson and the Boys, United Artists.
Memories, United Artists.
The Watson Family Tradition, Rounder.
Riding the Midnight Train, Sugar Hill, 1986.
Portrait, Sugar Hill, 1987.

With Merle Watson

Doc Watson and Son, Vanguard.
Then and Now, Poppy.
Two Days in November, Poppy.

Red Rocking Chair, Flying Fish.
Guitar Album, Flying Fish.
Pickin' the Blues, Flying Fish, 1985.

Sources

Books

The Illustrated Encyclopedia of Country Music, Harmony Books, 1977.

Shestack, Melvin, *The Country Music Encyclopedia,* Crowell, 1974.

Stambler, Irwin and Grelun Landon, *Encyclopedia of Folk, Country, and Western Music,* St. Martin's, 1969.

Periodicals

People, August 10, 1987.

—Anne Janette Johnson

Andy Williams

Singer

In an era dominated by the driving rhythms of rock and roll, Andy Williams has risen to superstardom by quite an opposite approach. Singer Williams projects a relaxed, affable style, at once soothing and romantic; his popularity has endured while other more faddish singers have come and gone. In fact, Williams reached the height of his success at just the moment—the late 1960s and early 1970s—when rock music seemed most hysterical. A 1968 campus poll picked him as the top male vocalist of the year, and his 1968 album *Honey* remained on the charts for more than six months. A *New York Herald Tribune* reviewer notes that Williams's appeal stems from his good-natured demeanor and his low-key approach to his songs. "He sings well in a casual style," the reviewer writes, "and doesn't attempt to overpower you with personality."

Williams was a professional singer at an age when most children are still playing in Little League. Born in the tiny town of Wall Lake, Iowa (population less than 1,000), he began performing with his three older brothers at the local Presbyterian church. He was only eight when the Williams Brothers made their radio debut at station WHO in Des Moines. Williams's father quit his job as a railway mail clerk in order to manage his sons' engagements, and soon the whole Williams family hit the road. From Des Moines they travelled to Chicago and then to Cincinnati; eventually they wound up in Los Angeles with a coveted Metro-Goldwyn-Mayer motion picture contract. Young Andy's education was piecemeal due to his uprooted lifestyle, but he did manage to graduate from high school in Los Angeles in 1947.

The Williams Brothers had to disband during the Second World War because the two oldest brothers were drafted. After the war the group reunited, adding comedienne Kay Thompson to the act. The team proved exceedingly successful in night clubs, with the four well-groomed Williams men counterpointing Thompson's buffoonery. From 1947 until 1953 they toured America and Europe and "spent their time making money hand over fist," to quote a *Harper's* magazine reviewer. In 1953 the brothers broke up the group in favor of solo work. Andy was unenthusiastic about his chances, but he began recording songs and making the rounds with them in the competitive New York market.

Williams auditioned for a spot on the Steve Allen *Tonight* show early in 1954. He was signed to a two-week run. When the two weeks ended, he continued to report to the set—and continued to be the featured singer on the show. The two-week contract was stretched into two and a half years, during which Williams appeared in comedy sketches as well as song features. The lengthy stint with Steve Allen offered Williams a wealth of new professional experiences—and it made him a star. He began to record on Cadence Records and earned his first two gold records with the singles "The Hawaiian Wedding Song" and "The Village of St. Bernadette."

Television has proven the perfect medium for Williams over the years. As early as 1958 he starred in his first variety show, the summer replacement "Chevy Showroom with Andy Williams." The next summer he hosted "The Andy Williams Show," and thereafter—for a decade—he starred in numerous specials, especially at Christmas time. Williams also continued to make records, moving to the Columbia label in the 1960s. He regularly placed singles in the Top 40 charts, and most of his albums were best sellers. This was especially true of his late-1960s, early-1970s work, including *Born Free, Honey, Love, Andy, Raindrops Keep Fallin' on My Head, Andy Williams's Greatest Hits,* and *Love Story.* Williams returned to a weekly variety show, "The New Andy Williams Show," for two seasons, 1970 and 1971. He has always preferred more sporadic television work, however, because he likes to rehearse and prepare thoroughly for each show.

Very few of Williams's hits over the years have been songs written especially for him. He is better known for his renditions of already popular numbers such as "You've Got a Friend," "The Impossible Dream," "MacArthur Park," and "Born Free." Williams's untrained voice—like that of Perry Como—is a rich baritone that never shows signs of strain or strays from the pitch. Unlike Como, however, Williams projects a more casual, middle-American persona, comfortable and wholesome without prudishness. A *New York World-Telegram and Sun* reporter has described Williams as an entertainer who "looks and acts like just what he is, a country boy from the Midwest who has made good in the big city." The description is not quite accurate—the suave Williams hardly comes across as a "country boy," nor does he suffer from the squeaky-clean reputation that hounds his contemporary, Pat Boone.

Time has not dulled Andy Williams's popularity, although he rarely places albums on the charts anymore. He still retains a busy schedule of club dates and television appearances, and he hosts the prestigious Andy Williams San Diego Golf Open each year. An avid golfer himself, Williams also enjoys tennis, art collect-

> Andy Williams "sings well in a casual style and doesn't attempt to overpower you with personality."

ing, and reading. Williams told the *New York Herald Tribune* that he ignored rock and roll because "ballads are more welcome on TV." He added: "I wouldn't want to sing solely for teen-agers. Once they go to college, their musical taste changes, and then where would I be?" As Kay Thompson once observed in *Look* magazine, stars like Andy Williams "with a plain niceness about them, are the ones that last."

Selected discography

Andy Williams Sings Steve Allen, Cadence, 1956.
Andy Williams Sings Rodgers and Hammerstein, Cadence, 1957.
Two Time Winners, Cadence, 1957.
Lonely Street, Cadence, 1959.
Call Me Irresponsible, Columbia, 1964.
Great Songs, Columbia, 1964.
Hawaiian Wedding Song, Columbia, 1965.
Canadian Sunset, Columbia, 1965.
In the Arms of Love, Columbia, 1967.
Born Free, Columbia, 1967.

Love, Andy, Columbia, 1967.
Honey, Columbia, 1968.
Get Together, Columbia, 1969.
Happy Heart, Columbia, 1970.
Raindrops Keep Fallin' on My Head, Columbia, 1970.
Andy Williams' Greatest Hits, Columbia, 1970.
The Andy Williams Show, Columbia, 1970.
Love Story, Columbia, 1971.
You've Got a Friend, Columbia, 1971.
Alone Again (Naturally), Columbia, 1972.
Andy Williams' Greatest Hits, Volume 2, Columbia, 1973.
Best of Andy Williams, Columbia, 1986.
Close Enough for Love, Columbia, 1987.
A Christmas Present, Columbia, 1987.

Also recorded *Moon River and Other Great Movie Themes* and *Andy Williams' 16 Most Requested Songs,* both with Columbia.

Sources

Books

Stambler, Irwin, *Encyclopedia of Pop, Rock, and Soul,* St. Martin's, 1974.

Periodicals

Harper's, July, 1948.
Look, September 1, 1959.
New York Herald Tribune, July 4, 1958; July 14, 1958; July 22, 1958.
New York Post Magazine, November 1, 1959.
New York Times, August 24, 1958.
New York World-Telegram and Sun, August 14, 1959.

—Anne Janette Johnson

Steve Winwood

Singer, songwriter, keyboardist

British rocker Steve Winwood was making music professionally at an age when most young men are still attending high school proms. As a member of the Spencer Davis Group, Traffic, and Blind Faith—and now as a successful solo artist—Winwood has produced highly eclectic songs based on a grafting of blues, folk, experimental rock, and rhythm and blues. His best-known pop hits have all been released since 1981, and his self-produced albums, *Arc of a Diver* (1981), *Talking Back to the Night* (1982), and *Back in the High Life* (1986) have all gone platinum. "That Winwood . . . has come through [the 1960s] glory grind with minimal scars is evident in the supple, good-natured funk and romantic electronic-keyboard glaze of his recent work," writes David Fricke in *Rolling Stone* magazine. *"Arc of a Diver* and . . . *Talking Back to the Night* are logical high-tech extensions of Winwood's original fusion of American rhythm and blues and European classical and folk traditions with Traffic."

Winwood can hardly remember a time when he wasn't singing in front of an audience. The son of a foundry worker, he grew up in blue-collar Birmingham, one of a family of amateur musicians. By the time he was six, Winwood was playing the piano; he joined an Anglican church choir the following year for his first "professional" work. "I used to get a shilling for every wedding," he told *People* magazine. "That was when I first realized that one can make money out of singing." Schoolwork held no fascination for Winwood. He was consumed by the popular music of the day, especially American blues and the burgeoning rock and roll sound. At eleven he joined a skiffle band, and at fifteen he dropped out of school permanently to join his older brother in a rock band, the Spencer Davis Group.

The teenage Winwood provided lead vocals and organ riffs for the Spencer Davis Group, guiding it to a pair of hit singles, "Gimme Some Lovin'" and "I'm a Man." According to Lillian Roxon in her *Lillian Roxon's Rock Encyclopedia,* it was Winwood's "voice, his songs, his organ and piano work that made Spencer Davis' band soar. *I'm a Man* and *Gimme Some Loving,* done under the Davis umbrella, were so black and strong it took a lot of adjusting to get used to the fact that they were coming from a seventeen-year-old English kid from Birmingham."

In 1967 Winwood left the Spencer Davis Group to start his own band. With Chris Wood, Dave Mason, and Jim Capaldi he formed Traffic, an experimental psychedelic pop ensemble that drew its musical inspiration from jazz, soul, blues, and folk. Traffic's debut album, *Mr. Fantasy,* included two British hits, "Paper Sun" and "Hole in My Shoe," and by virtue of Winwood's already-established fame, the group quickly became a favorite.

Full name, Stephen Lawrence Winwood; born May 12, 1948, in Birmingham, England; son of Lawrence Samuel (a foundry worker) and Lillian Mary (Saunders) Winwood; married Nicole Tacot (a singer), 1978 (divorced); married Eugenia Crafton, January 17, 1987; one child.

Singer-songwriter, 1964—; member of the Spencer Davis Group, 1964-67, had first two hit singles, "Gimme Some Lovin'" and "I'm a Man"; founder and member of band Traffic, 1967-74, cut first album with Traffic, *Mr. Fantasy*, 1967; member of groups Blind Faith, 1970, and Ginger Baker's Air Force, 1970; solo artist, 1974—; cut first solo album, *Steve Winwood*, 1977, had first top ten single, "While You See a Chance," 1981.

Awards: Grammy Awards for record of the year, and for best male pop vocal performance, both 1986, both for "Higher Love."

Addresses: *Office*—Island Records Inc., 14 W. 4th St., New York, N.Y. 10012.

"At its best, Traffic was a band to be reckoned with," writes a *Rolling Stone Record Guide* contributor. "The first two Traffic albums are late-sixties classics, an eclectic combination . . . that was polyglot without ever becoming overextended." Unfortunately, the members of Traffic had disparate musical tastes, and the band changed personnel frequently during its seven-year run. Winwood himself quit Traffic briefly in 1970 to play with Blind Faith (a "supergroup" consisting of Winwood, Eric Clapton, Ginger Baker, and Rick Gretch), but he returned to cut several session albums, including the 1974 *When the Eagle Flies*.

Winwood went solo in 1974, building himself his own personal recording studio on his fifty-acre farm in Gloucestershire. He seemed almost in retirement as the years passed, but instead he was working hard on new material, laying down every track himself at his studio and accepting help only with an occasional lyric. In 1977 he released *Steve Winwood* to unenthusiastic sales. Winwood told *People* that his first solo effort "got buried," and when time came to cut the next album "it was a make-or-break situation. If it hadn't been for *Arc of a Diver*, I might be a taxi driver." Indeed, the 1980 *Arc of a Diver*, with its hit single "While You See a Chance," was a great success both in England and America—even though Winwood refused to tour.

A reputation for reclusiveness (and drug abuse) hounds Winwood, although he denies both charges at every turn. He spends so much time at his farm, he says, because he is a perfectionist who makes albums very, very slowly. As for the drug abuse, he told *Rolling Stone* that he had no interest in drugs during the 1960s or in subsequent years. "I saw what drugs were doing to people," he said of the psychedelic era, "and in most cases I had to suffer the consequences of their substandard work. . . . I just don't fit into the predominant image of rock and roll. I never quite understood or had the attitude that certain other bands had. We were never really involved with the smashing-up of hotel rooms, the rowdy parties, like the other bands of the period."

The 1980s have been a period of resurgence for Winwood. To quote Lisa Robinson in *Vogue*, the artist "sits comfortably at the top of the rock pantheon, a graceful survivor of . . . [an] extraordinary [number of] years in the music business." Winwood has followed *Arc of a Diver* with two more platinum albums, *Talking Back to the Night* and *Back in the High Life*, and he has even undertaken a concert tour after thirteen years off the road. "More and more," he told *Rolling Stone*, "I see that rock and roll doesn't just need a youthful energy and spirit to it. It also needs a craft, an experience to get it across."

Today, Winwood said, his aim is to make music that *he* likes, hoping that an audience will like it as well. "The point for me is to reach people through what I'm doing," he said. ". . . If I make music that people might dance to, that's fine with me." He elaborated in *High Fidelity:* "I try not to aim at an audience. That can be dangerous—you might just miss, and then you haven't got anything. I basically make albums because I like to make them. I like to make successful albums, too, but I make them for my own ear in the hope that other people will like the same things as me." Rock and roll is entertainment, Winwood concluded, "and really, that's what it always was."

Selected discography

With the Spencer Davis Group

Their First LP, Sonnet, 1965.
Every Little Bit Hurts, Wing, 1965.
Second Album, Fontana, 1966.
Autumn 66, Fontana, 1966.
Gimme Some Lovin', United Artists, 1967.
I'm a Man, United Artists, 1967.
The Very Best of Spencer Davis, United Artists, 1968.
Here We Go Round the Mulberry Bush, United Artists, 1968.
Greatest Hits, United Artists, 1968.

Heavies, Vertigo, 1973.
Somebody Help Me, Island, 1973.

With Traffic

Mr. Fantasy, United Artists, 1967.
Traffic, United Artists, 1968.
Last Exit, United Artists, 1969.
John Barleycorn Must Die, United Artists, 1970.
Welcome to the Canteen, United Artists, 1971.
The Low Spark of High-Heeled Boys, Island, 1971.
Shoot Out at the Fantasy Factory, Island, 1974.
On the Road, Island, 1973.
When the Eagle Flies, Asylum, 1974.
More Heavy Traffic, Island, 1975.

With Blind Faith

Blind Faith, Atco, 1969.

Solo recordings

Steve Winwood, Island, 1977.
Arc of a Diver, Island, 1980.
Talking Back to the Night, Island, 1982.

Back in the High Life, Island, 1986.
Chronicles, Island, 1988.
Roll With It, Virgin, 1988.

Sources

Books

Lillian Roxon's Rock Encyclopedia, Grosset & Dunlap, 1978.
The Rolling Stone Encyclopedia of Rock & Roll, Summit Books, 1983.
The Rolling Stone Record Guide, Random House, 1979.

Periodicals

High Fidelity, June, 1981.
People, November 15, 1982.
Rolling Stone, February 19, 1981; November 11, 1982.
Vogue, July, 1987.

—*Anne Janette Johnson*

Stevie Wonder

Singer, songwriter, keyboardist

Stevie Wonder has been called the "crown prince of pop music" since the late 1960s, when he began to produce hit after hit with staggering rapidity. Blind since birth, Wonder has directed an immense inner vision toward innovative music; to quote *New York Times Magazine* contributor Jack Slater, Wonder's work explores "several layers of experience—music which addresses itself not only to one's romantic needs but to racial grief, urban defeat, religious experience, as well as to such conundrums as transcendental perception." A *Time* magazine correspondent likewise notes that Wonder "has distilled a wide array of black and white musical styles into a hugely popular personal idiom that emphatically defines where pop is at right now. As a result, Wonder has become what the trade calls a 'monster,' a star who can automatically fill any arena or stadium and whose records, both in the stores and on radio, transcend musical categories in their appeal."

Wonder was a genuine child prodigy by virtue of his musical ability and his sheer desire to succeed. Signed to a Motown Records contract at thirteen, he had his first top ten single, "Fingertips Part 2," before he began to attend high school. Since then, he has literally never been out of the limelight, and his fame is such that he is asked to lend his name to a variety of social causes. The *Time* reporter observes that Wonder "has managed the considerable task of establishing himself as both a hot commercial property and an authentic voice. Being black, blind, and up from poverty entitles him, of course, to say that he has been there and back." In *down beat* magazine, W. A. Brower writes that Wonder "has become a world-class moral force—a hero—in a time when the personal villainy of television anti-heroes is celebrated, poverty is glibly rationalized, and the ghastly spectre of controlled nuclear holocaust darkens our future."

Wonder was born Stevland Judkins in Saginaw, Michigan. His birth was four weeks premature, and doctors believe the pure oxygen used in the infant incubator robbed him of his sight. Having never had his vision, Wonder did not suffer the loss of it. He claims that he had a happy childhood—with some restrictions—in Saginaw and Detroit, where his family lived in "upper-lower-class circumstances." Not surprisingly, Wonder gravitated to music at a very early age. At two he began pounding tin pans with spoons in rhythm with radio songs, and at four he learned to play the piano, harmonica, and drums. Wonder also liked to sing, and he was a featured soloist at Detroit's Whitestone Baptist Church until one of the parishioners caught him playing rock and roll music with his friends in the streets.

Young Stevland Morris (his mother had remarried) began hanging around the fledgling Motown studio when he was ten. He played the various Motown instruments and even wrote some songs, earning himself the nickname "little boy wonder." At thirteen he signed an exclusive contract with Motown and was given the name "Little Stevie Wonder" by Motown president Berry Gordy. In 1963 the teenaged performer had his first chart-topping hit with the rousing "Fingertips Part 2," a Motown-generated tune that allowed Wonder to sing and to play the harmonica. Thereafter, "Little Stevie Wonder" travelled with the Motown "family" of entertainers, taking private tutoring and attending high school at the Michigan School for the Blind between engagements.

Stevie Wonder dropped the "little" adjective from his name as soon as he could. Between 1963 and 1969 he recorded a number of hits, including "Uptight," "I Was Made To Love Her," "For Once in My Life," and "My Cherie Amour." All through the period, Wonder was held in tight control by the Motown management. His songs were chosen for him, his money was managed for him, and almost all important career decisions were made for him. Brower writes: "The Little Stevie years were . . . full of entertaining but innocuous stuff: juvenile music. Yet the special quality of his voice was unmistakable. Its charisma was like the Midas touch turning even brass to gold, foreshadowing great communicative power and aching for material equal to its potential."

When Wonder turned twenty-one, he rebelled against the Motown system, calling for complete creative control of his work. Eventually he ironed out a contract that allowed Motown to distribute whatever albums he cared to produce. "I had gone about as far as I could go," he said of his Motown experience in *Stereo Review.* "I wasn't growing; I just kept repeating 'the Stevie Wonder Sound,' and it didn't express how I felt about what was happening in the world. I decided to go for something else besides a winning formula: I wanted to see what would happen if I changed."

As creative master of his work, Wonder did indeed change. His songs challenged social conditions, celebrated religious ecstasy, and revealed his most personal joys. According to Brower, Wonder's maturing music "reached beyond infectious yet puerile reverie to the level of art and deeper meaning. Perhaps because his own maturation was so literally entwined with the development of soul music, he was eager and able to incorporate the broader issues of his life and his time into music as few others in the genre have. That this point of view was vested in such a uniquely well-rounded artist—singer, multi-instrumentalist, recording artist, lyricist, composer, arranger, producer—made his creative thrust all the more powerful."

Every album Wonder released in the 1970s went platinum in sales, and every one produced at least one hit single. These hits varied immensely in style and substance, from the grim "Superstition" and "Living for the City" to the playful "Don't You Worry 'bout a Thing," "Isn't She Lovely?" and "You Are the Sunshine of My Life." By 1979 Wonder had won fourteen Grammy Awards and was well on the way to selling *seventy million records.* Even more astonishing is the fact that Wonder often produced his songs entirely by himself, providing all the background music, writing the tune and lyrics, singing, and arranging. He became one of the first artists to make extensive use of electronic synthesizers, computers, and advanced keyboard technology, and he became renowned for carrying a tape machine at all times in order to record his ideas immediately. Brower writes: "The studio had become an instrument for the self-actualization of his personal vision. He proved himself able to get much more than intriguing and atmospheric textural settings out of his electro-synthetic musical arsenal: he was able to make his instruments sing with both melodic poignance and sweetness." Wonder emerged from the 1970s one of the favorite recording stars of any audience under the age of fifty.

Wonder's creative output has slackened in the 1980s, but his popularity has not waned at all. Indeed, as a spokesman for important social causes, he has done more than any other musician to change American attitudes. He was an outspoken proponent of the creation of a national holiday honoring Dr. Martin Luther King, and his poster against drunk driving—"I Would Drive Myself before I Would Ride with a Drunken Driver"—was posted in schools across the nation. He also recorded a song with Dionne Warwick, called "That's What Friends Are For," that benefitted AIDS research. In 1984 he released a pleasant tune, "I Just Called To Say I Love You," that won the prestigious Academy Award for best song of the year. Still a young man—just nearing forty—Wonder continues to pack arenas of every size with fans of every race and creed. A *Newsweek* correspondent concludes that the star "stands alone among rock composers in the range of his creativity."

Wonder told *Stereo Review* how he likes to work. "There's so much *music* in the air," he said. "You hear this music in your mind first; that's the way it is for me, anyway. Then I go after getting it exactly the way I imagined it. If

---

Stevie Wonder was a featured soloist at Detroit's Whitestone Baptist Church until one of the parishioners caught him playing rock and roll music with his friends in the streets.

---

it doesn't come out the way it is in my mind, it has to come out either better than that or equivalent to it. If it's in a different fashion, it's got to be just as good." Wonder is a near-teetotaler who never touches drugs; his well-known head-swaying is a "blindism"—a release of energy that others release through vision. The father of three children, he has been musically inspired more than once by paternal love. Brower concludes that whatever Stevie Wonder does, "one hopes he continues to represent the possibility of the fulfilled life, the power of self-determination—merging what one does for daily bread, with what one enjoys, and sees as one's responsibility."

Selected discography

Little Stevie Wonder: The Twelve-Year-Old Genius, Motown, 1963.

Tribute to Uncle Ray, Motown, 1963.
Jazz Soul of Little Steve, Motown, 1963.
With a Song in My Heart, Motown, 1964.
At the Beach (Hey Mr. Harmonica Man), Motown, 1965.
Uptight, Motown, 1966.
Down to Earth, Motown, 1966.
I Was Made To Love Her, Motown, 1967.
Stevie Wonder's Greatest Hits, Motown, 1968.
Someday at Christmas, Motown, 1969.
For Once in My Life, Motown, 1969.
Elvets Rednow, Motown, 1969.
My Cherie Amour, Motown, 1970.
Stevie Wonder Live, Motown, 1970.
Talk of the Town, Motown, 1970.
Signed, Sealed, Delivered, Motown, 1970.
Where I'm Coming From, Motown, 1971.
Stevie Wonder's Greatest Hits, Volume 2, Motown, 1972.
Music of My Mind, Motown, 1972.
Talking Book, Motown, 1972.
Innervisions, Motown, 1973.
Fulfillingness First Finale, Motown, 1974.
Songs in the Key of Life, Motown, 1976.
Portrait, EMI, 1976.
Journey through the Secret Life of Plants, Motown, 1979.
The Woman in Red, Motown, 1984.
In Square Circle, Motown, 1985.
Hotter Than July, Motown, 1986.
Characters, Motown, 1987.

Sources

Books

Stambler, Irwin, *Encyclopedia of Pop, Rock, and Soul,* St. Martin's, 1974.

Periodicals

down beat, May, 1981.
Esquire, April, 1974.
Newsweek, October 4, 1976.
New York Times Magazine, February 23, 1975.
People, March 3, 1986.
Rolling Stone, April 10, 1986; November 5-December 10, 1987.
Stereo Review, May, 1980.
Time, April 8, 1974.

—*Anne Janette Johnson*

Tammy Wynette

Singer, songwriter

Tammy Wynette, the "Heroine of Heartbreak," became a country music superstar almost overnight in 1967. At a time when traditional values were being challenged and overthrown, the wholesome-looking blonde Wynette sang of the perils of divorce and urged listeners to "Stand By Your Man." With a string of twenty-one number one songs and a host of personal appearances, Wynette established herself in the early 1970s as the one country star that most non-country fans could name. Rural women especially seemed drawn to the performer who, according to Alanna Nash in *Behind Closed Doors: Talking with the Legends of Country Music,* epitomized the image of "a long-suffering, somewhat masochistic housewife, feigning complacency, but aching for release—though certainly not for divorce."

Observers have likened Wynette's life to a soap opera, and the star herself hardly cares to disagree. Her ascent in the country music business has the elements of drama, as does her personal life, with five marriages, a kidnapping attempt, and numerous hospitalizations. Tammy Wynette was born Virginia Wynette Pugh, the daughter of guitarist William Hollis Pugh. Her father died when she was only eight months old, so she was turned over to her maternal grandparents while her mother did wartime factory work in Birmingham, Alabama. Young "Wynette" grew up calling her grandparents Mommy and Daddy. She earned money by picking and chopping cotton on her grandfather's farm and thus was able to afford music lessons for five years. The instruments she favored were those her father had played—piano, mandolin, guitar, accordion, and bass fiddle.

Wynette wanted to become a professional performer even though her family discouraged the idea. At first the possibility seemed highly unlikely—she married at seventeen and had three children and a divorce at twenty. In order to support her children, one of whom had serious spinal meningitis, Wynette worked as a hairdresser in a Birmingham beauty shop. She also won a part-time job as a backup singer on the "Country Boy Eddie Show," a local television production. The exposure to show business re-awakened her desire to perform as a solo artist. Eventually she made several appearances on the "Porter Wagoner Show," and she used these as an entree to Nashville's recording companies.

Each visit Wynette made to Nashville proved slightly more encouraging than the last, but no company was willing to sign her to a contract. Finally, in 1967, she met Billy Sherrill, a shrewd music producer who immediately sensed her potential. Sherrill signed the young singer for Epic Records, changed her name from Virginia

Wynette Pugh to Tammy Wynette, and set about providing her with top-rate material. To quote Nash, Sherrill knew that if he found the right songs for her, the divorced beautician and mother of three "could move out of a government housing project and into the psyches of millions of frustrated and lonely blue-collar women."

With Sherrill's coaching, Wynette quickly made her mark on the country music scene. Her first single, "Apartment Number Nine," made the charts, and her next one, "Your Good Girl's Gonna Go Bad," was one of 1967's best-selling country tunes. She is remembered, however, for two songs that practically became blue-collar anthems: "D-I-V-O-R-C-E," a lament about a broken marriage, and "Stand By Your Man." The latter number sold more than two million copies and became the biggest single by a woman in the history of country music. Wynette is quoted in *The Country Music Encyclopedia* as saying that "Stand By Your Man" was such a blockbuster "because country people aren't attracted to women's lib. They like to be able to stand by their man. And of course the men liked the idea that their women would stand by them." She added: "I try to find songs that express down-to-earth, honest feelings."

In addition to her solo career, Wynette teamed with singer George Jones both professionally and personal-

ly. For more than five years Wynette and Jones were a favorite country duo, but their marriage was a trial for both of them. Wynette told Nash that they divorced in 1975 because she was "naggin'" and Jones was "nippin'," referring to his drinking. From time to time the two singers reunite to produce music; Wynette told Nash that they have been working together better since they divorced. "Somehow," she said, "that always seems to happen." Uncharitable critics claim that Wynette tends to ride on Jones's coattails when her own career begins to sag, but Wynette counters that she has helped save Jones several times from lawsuits and bankruptcy.

Tammy Wynette has been a favorite target of the national tabloids since she and Jones married in 1968. She has been divorced five times, her home has been vandalized, she has been given shock treatments for depression, and she was even the target of a kidnapping attempt (discredited by some as having been "staged" for publicity). "Tammy Wynette has had her trials," Nash writes. "And continues to have them,

> *Observers have likened Wynette's life to a soap opera, and the star herself hardly cares to disagree.*

bruises of one kind or another showing up just as the last ones have faded." Ironically, as Nash points out, these dramatic difficulties only serve to heighten Wynette's appeal—her listeners like to perceive her as a suffering heroine, unhappy in love and besieged by her fame.

Wynette herself draws upon her tribulations for song material. Though not prolific, she does write some lyrics—and she constantly searches for material that mirrors her own despair. She told Nash that she is not ashamed of the personal nature of her music. "I had rather tell the public what the truth really is than for them to hear somethin' from somebody else and it be totally untrue," she said. "Because my life has not been a bed of roses. I have been no saint, and I have not ever tried to imply that I ever was, or ever will be. And I couldn't have written a book, or song, or anything, had I not been totally honest with myself first." Wynette describes her voice as "average," and indeed it is the substance of her material, rather than the sound of it, that draws listeners. Reflecting on her turbulent career, she told Nash that performing has given her a "better life," but it has also been "more of an escape from the real world. Because I could go out on the road and leave my problems behind me, and sing and enjoy what I was doing. Come home, and the problems were still there, but I'd had a little time to work on 'em." She concluded that performing "is a great escape, because you're in another world."

Selected discography

LPs

Another Lonely Song, Epic.
Anniversary: Twenty Years of Hits for the First Lady of Country Music, Epic.
Bedtime Story, Epic.
The Best of Tammy Wynette, Columbia.
Christmas with Tammy, Epic.
D-I-V-O-R-C-E, Epic.
Encore, Epic.
The First Songs of the First Lady, Epic.
From the Bottom of My Heart, Epic.
Higher Ground, Epic.
Inspiration, Epic.
I Still Believe in Fairy Tales, Epic.
It's Just a Matter of Time, Epic.
Kids Say the Darndest Things, Epic.
My Man, Epic.
No Charge, Embassy.
Sometimes When We Touch, Epic.
Stand By Your Man, Epic.
The Superb Country Sounds of Tammy Wynette, Embassy.
Take Me to Your World, Epic.

Tammy's Touch, Epic.
Tammy Wynette, Epic.
Tammy Wynette's Greatest Hits, Epic.
Tammy Wynette's Greatest Hits, Volume 2, Epic.
Tammy Wynette's Greatest Hits, Volume 3, Epic.
'Til I Can Make It on My Own, Epic.
We Sure Can Love Each Other, Epic.
Woman to Woman, Epic.
The World of Tammy Wynette, Epic.
You and Me, Epic.
Your Good Girl's Gonna Go Bad, Epic.

With George Jones

George and Tammy and Tina, Epic.
Greatest Hits, Epic.
Let's Build a World Together, Epic.
Me and the First Lady, Epic.
Together Again, Epic.
We Go Together, Epic.
We Love To Sing about Jesus, Epic.
We're Gonna Hold On, Epic.

Sources

The Illustrated Encyclopedia of Country Music, Harmony Books, 1977.
Nash, Alanna, *Behind Closed Doors: Talking with the Legends of Country Music*, Knopf, 1988.
Shestack, Melvin, *The Country Music Encyclopedia*, Crowell, 1974.
Stambler, Irwin and Grelun Landon, *Encyclopedia of Folk, Country, and Western Music*, St. Martin's, 1988.

—Anne Janette Johnson

Neil Young

Singer, songwriter, guitarist, composer

Neil Young's career has spanned over twenty years, from his early days with Buffalo Springfield and Crosby, Stills, and Nash to a solo history that includes over twenty albums of extremely varied styles. "Every one of my records, to me, is like an ongoing autobiography. I can't write the same book every time," he told Cameron Crowe in *What's That Sound?* "My trip is to express what's on my mind. I don't expect people to listen to my music all the time. Sometimes it's too intense."

Born in Canada, he formed his first band, Neil Young and the Squires, in Winnepeg and began bashing out instrumentals by groups like the Ventures and the Shadows. After hearing Bob Dylan and the Beatles, Young began to concentrate on writing his own lyrics. In Dylan he found not only an incredible poet, but also a mysterious persona that was just as interesting as the words. In *The Rolling Stone Illustrated History of Rock & Roll*, Dave Marsh calls Young Dylan's greatest disciple, having mastered "the art of self-mythology."

After the Squires he played with Rick (then known as Rickey) James and the Mynah Birds, working the rock and blues clubs of Toronto. In 1966 James ran into trouble with the law and the band was forced to break up. Young, just 21 years old, sold all the band's equipment, bought a Pontiac hearse, and, along with bassist Bruce Palmer, drove cross-continent to California. While driving through Los Angeles, the car was recognized by Stephen Stills and Richie Furray, who had jammed with Young back in Canada. After talking awhile the four musicians decided they should form a band together and within a few weeks they had a six-week gig at the Whiskey A' Go Go, calling themselves Buffalo Springfield (named after a lawn tractor).

The group became one of the seminal folk-rock bands of the 1960s and pioneers of the California Sound that would influence later groups, including the Eagles. Young, in the United States illegally, worked without the proper papers or a union card while recording the classic tunes "For What It's Worth," "Mr. Soul," and "Broken Arrow." Tensions and egos in the band were a problem, causing Young to quit and rejoin the band more than once, citing his own lack of maturity and tremendous pressure as the reasons. In May 1968 Stills called it quits and left to record a solo album, during which he teamed with David Crosby and Graham Nash. Young split also, heading to the hills of Topanga Canyon to start working on his own album, *Neil Young,* released in the beginning of 1969 and featuring "The Loner."

After hearing a stomping bar band called the Rockets playing on the West Coast, Young asked them to back him up on his follow-up LP, *Everybody Knows This Is*

For the Record. . .

Born November 12, 1945, in Toronto, Ontario, Canada; son of Scott (a sports reporter) and Edna (a television celebrity) Young; first wife's name, Susan (divorced, 1970); second wife's name, Pegi; children: Zeke.

Songwriter and performer in rock groups, including the Squires, 1962-64, Rickey James and the Mynah Birds, c. 1965, Buffalo Springfield, 1966-68, Crosby, Stills, Nash & Young, 1969-71, and the Stills-Young Band, 1976; solo artist (and with accompaniment from band Crazy Horse), 1969—; composer of soundtracks for films, including *The Landlord,* 1970, *The Strawberry Statement,* 1970, *Celebratin at Big Sur,* 1971, and *Where the Buffalo Roam,* 1980; director of films (under pseudonym Bernard Shakey), including *Journey Through the Past,* 1972, and *Rust Never Sleeps,* 1979.

Awards: Winner of *Rolling Stone* Music Award for album of the year, 1975, for *Tonight's the Night;* awards from *Rolling Stone* Critics' Poll for best rock artist, best male vocalist, and for best album, 1979, for *Rust Never Sleeps.*

Addresses: *Office*—c/o Lookout Management, 9120 Sunset Blvd., Los Angeles, CA 90069.

Nowhere. Switching their name to Crazy Horse, the trio (Ralph Molina, Billy Talbot, and Danny Whitten) provided solid support for Young as some of his finest songs, "Cinnamon Girl," "Down by the River," and "Cowgirl in the Sand," began to dominate the FM airwaves. At the same time, Stills had asked Young to join his trio and in 1970 Crosby, Stills, Nash & Young released *Deja Vu,* containing another Young pop classic, "Helpless." The group enjoyed an AM radio popularity that Young's solo work hadn't established.

Guitarist Nils Lofgren joined Crazy Horse in September of 1970 to help record Young's *After the Gold Rush* LP. Young broke up with his first wife just before its release and spent the next two years in and out of hospitals with back injuries, playing only a small-halls tour by himself before recording a second album with Crosby, Stills, Nash & Young, *4-Way Street.* Hot on the heels of *Gold Rush*'s success came *Harvest,* the top-selling LP of 1972. Young utilized a pickup band called the Stray Gators (Jack Nitzsche, Ben Keith, Tim Drummond, and Johnny Barbata) and Crosby and Nash's vocals to come up with his only top ten hit, the number 1 "Heart of Gold," a blueprint for future Californian light-rockers.

Young made a movie and released its soundtrack in

1973. The somber *Journey Through the Past* baffled viewers who tried to figure out the message Young was trying to convey. "I don't think I was trying to say that life is pointless," he told Crowe. "It does lay a lot of shit on people though. It wasn't made for entertainment. I'll admit, Young began to work on a studio LP, *Time Fades Away,* and an ensuing tour. During rehearsals he sent guitarist Danny Whitten home to Los Angeles because his drug habit began affecting performances. Back in L.A. Whitten overdosed. The news shocked Young, who felt responsible and became depressed for nearly two years. His next LP, *On The Beach,* was released in 1974 and Young performed a tour with C,S,N & Y right afterwards. Tragedy struck again as Bruce Berry, a C,S,N & Y roadie, also died from a drug overdose. Young's LP, *Tonight's the Night,* was dedicated to Whitten and Berry and contains some of the most haunting, albeit alcohol-induced, recordings ever made. Young had another album, *Homegrown,* prepared for release, but after listening to both he decided to go with the starker one (nine of the tunes were actually record-

---

"I don't expect people to listen to my music all the time. Sometimes it's too intense."
—Neil Young

---

ed before *Beach*) which won the *Rolling Stone* Music Award for Album of the Year.

Young emerged from his dark period with *Zuma,* an LP of piercing guitar licks and pounding rhythms. Crazy Horse once again was a springboard for Young's primitive, yet gut-wrenching, fretboard onslaughts. "I really get free with Crazy Horse. They let me zoom off," he told *Rolling Stone.* "They're the American Rolling Stones, no doubt about it." Young also began a three-month tour with Stills to support their duo effort, *Long May You Run,* but had to back out after two weeks due to throat problems. His guitar playing was fine, though, as his next solo LP, *American Stars 'n Bars,* contained the rockers "Bite the Bullet" and "Like a Hurricane."

His 1978 tour a year later featured giant stage props (amplifiers, a harmonica, and microphone) assembled for the audience by scurrying, hooded creatures with glowing red eyes called Road-eyes. Young played a child dreaming about rock and roll as he awoke atop the huge amp system. The first half of the show was acoustic while the second part was sonic warfare.

During the middle of the tour, Young's mellow *Comes a Time* was released, catching fans, whose ears were still ringing, off guard. The half-acoustic, half-electric *Rust Never Sleeps* LP followed to rave reviews. The album "tells me more about my life, my country and rock and roll than any music I've heard in years," wrote Paul Nelson in *Rolling Stone*. "Neil Young can outwrite, outsing, outplay, outthink, outfeel and outlast anybody in rock and roll today." Standout tracks included "Welfare Mothers," "Thrasher," "Powderfinger," "My My, Hey Hey," and its counterpart, "Hey Hey, My My."

Young followed with *Live Rust,* a double-LP that Tom Carson in *Rolling Stone* called "rock and roll emotional superspectacle." That in turn was followed by *Hawks and Doves,* a 30-minute collection of acoustic and electric tunes, including "Union Man" and "Homestead." For the next nine years, however, Young would release an assortment of LPs that seemed to follow current trends instead of setting them. *Reactor* was heavy metal, pure and simple; *Trans* rode the techno bandwagon with elaborate electronics like the vocoder; *Everybody's Rockin'* gave a half an hour's worth of pseudo rockabilly; back to the country format on *Old Ways* and a tour with the International Harvesters band; and then an album of blues with *This Note's For You* in 1988. His 1986 tour to support *Landing on Water* was billed as the "Third Best Garage Band in the World."

Obviously Young likes to keep his audience guessing about his next move while avoiding any chance of prejudgment. "I'd rather keep changing and lose a lot of people along the way," he explained in *What's That Sound?* "I'm convinced that what sells and what I do are two completely different things. If they meet, it's coincidence." Reportedly, Young has anywhere from ten to twenty albums worth of unreleased materials in the vaults. While his recordings in the 1980s seem to some to lack focus, the triple-LP *Decade* is an excellent documentation of Young's best work prior to 1978.

Selected discography

Solo LPs

Neil Young, Reprise, 1969.
Everybody Knows This Is Nowhere, Reprise, 1969.
After the Gold Rush, Reprise, 1970.
Harvest, Warner Brothers, 1972.
Journey Through the Past, Reprise, 1973.
Time Fades Away, Reprise, 1973.
On the Beach, Reprise, 1974.
Tonight's the Night, Reprise, 1975.

Zuma, Reprise, 1975.
American Stars 'n Bars, Reprise, 1977.
Comes a Time, Reprise, 1978.
Decade, Reprise, 1978.
Rust Never Sleeps, Reprise, 1979.
Live Rust, Reprise, 1979.
Hawks & Doves, Reprise, 1980.
Reactor, Reprise, 1981.
Tans, Geffen, 1982.
Old Ways, Geffen, 1985.
Landing on Water, Geffen, 1986.
Life, Geffen, 1987.
This Note's For You, Reprise, 1988.

With Crosby, Stills, Nash & Young

Deja Vu, Atlantic, 1970.
4-Way Street, Atlantic, 1971.
So Far, Atlantic, 1975.

With Stephen Stills

Long May You Run, Reprise, 1976.

With Buffalo Springfield

Buffalo Springfield Again, Atco, 1967.
Last Time Around, Atco, 1968.
Retrospective, Atco, 1969.

Sources

Books

Christgau, Robert, *Christgau's Record Guide,* Ticknor & Fields, 1981.
Dalton, David, and Lenny Kaye, *Rock 100,* Grosset & Dunlap, 1977.
The Illustrated Encyclopedia of Rock, compiled by Nick Logan and Bob Woffinden, Harmony, 1977.
The Rolling Stone Illustrated History of Rock and Roll, edited by Jim Miller, Random House/Rolling Stone Press, 1976.
The Rolling Stone Record Guide, edited by Dave Marsh with John Swenson, Random House/Rolling Stone Press, 1979.
What's That Sound?, edited by Ben Fong-Torres, Doubleday, 1976.

Periodicals

Rolling Stone, February 12, 1976; August 26, 1976; September 9, 1976; June 2, 1977; August 11, 1977; July 27, 1978; November 16, 1978; November 30, 1978; February 8, 1979; October 18, 1979; January 24, 1980; February 7, 1980; December 25, 1980; September 25, 1986.

—Calen D. Stone

ZZ Top

Blues/rock band

That "little ol' band from Texas," ZZ Top, has been together for over two decades now, making more music, and money, than bands twice their size. Although many people may consider the three-piece unit just another boogie band from the South, the Top has some pretty impressive credentials. Their 1976 tour broke attendance records previously set by the Beatles; they were one of the first bands to realize the potential of music videos; and they were arguably the first *blues* band to successfully incorporate advanced electronics (e.g. synthesizers and drum machines) into their sound. But, regardless of these accomplishments, the band has stuck to their original philosophy: "Our message remains pretty much clear cut," guitarist Billy Gibbons told *Guitar Player*. "We're not attempting to deliver any sociological breakthrough other than, 'Have a good time.'"

Gibbons was born in Houston, Texas, and, after being bitten by the Elvis bug at the age of seven, began playing guitar. He formed his first band, the Saints, when he was fourteen and eventually moved on to the Coachmen. It was only a matter of a few years, however, before Gibbons was fronting his own James Brown-styled rhythm and blues group, Billy G and the Ten Blue Flames. By 1967 he was working with a trimmed-down, four-member psychedlic combo called the Moving Sidewalks. Their single "99th Floor" stayed on top of the Texas charts for five weeks and earned the band a spot as opening act for the Jimi Hendrix Experience in 1968. Hendrix was so impressed with Gibbons's fretwork that he cited the Texan as one of America's best guitarists on a "Tonight Show" television appearance.

Gibbons's unique style also caught the attention of Bill Ham, a local record promo man who knew a money-maker when he heard one. Due to the Vietnam War, members of the Sidewalks were drafted and Gibbons was forced to disolve the band. He and Ham began auditioning drummers and bassists before settling with two veterans of the Texas blues scene, Dusty Hill and Frank Beard. Hill, a Dallas native, also entered music after seeing a Presley performance on television and began playing the bass when he was thirteen. Along with his brother, guitarist Rocky Hill, they formed the Deadbeats before playing in Lady Wild and the War-locks. After that band folded in 1967, the two joined drummer Beard's American Blues Band. They picked up priceless experience backing up blues legends like Lightnin' Hopkins, Jimmy Reed, and Freddie King.

When the band broke up, Beard hooked up with Gibbons and told him of Hill's availability. On February 10, 1970, the three musicians were united. "We threw a jam session together that fateful day," Gibbons informed *Guitar World*. "We started off with a shuffle in C and

"Tush" is a fine example of the warped lyrics that have helped ZZ Top become a party favorite. The song, along with "Blue Jean Blues," helped to keep their 1975 release *Fandango* on the charts for an amazing eighty-three weeks and to eventually sell more than a million copies. The album contains one studio side and the other recorded live at New Orleans's Warehouse. Their next tour, the 1976 World-Wide Texas Tour in support of *Tejas*, was an enormous undertaking that established ZZ Top as one of rock's premier live acts. With a giant Texas-shaped stage adorned with actual cattle, bison, rattlesnakes, coyotes, and tarantulas, the tour proved to be one of the most successful ever by grossing over $11.5 million.

In what may have seemed like an unwise business move, the band took the next three years off as Ham tried to break away from London Records. Gibbons spent time working on his guitar collection, which totals over 300 instruments. In addition, the former University of Texas art student has nine design patents and is a board of trustees member for the Contemporary Arts

didn't quit for a couple of hours. We decided that it was so much fun that we kept on cookin'." They knew they had a great sound together, but they also realized that it takes even more to make it in the music world. Ham convinced the trio that his strategies would make ZZ Top a household name and he became their manager, controling every move and aspect of their careers. "We played a lot of the out-of-the-way places, playing for the people at people's prices," Ham told Chet Flippo in *Rolling Stone*. "It's harder that way and takes much longer, but once the band has established itself as a people's band, the people won't leave you."

The Top had a regional hit with "Salt Lick" on Ham's Scat label, which prompted London Records to sign them. Their *First Album* LP received little fanfare as the band continued to hone their live show in juke joints throughout the South. Things began to pick up with their second album, *Rio Grande Mud,* which produced another Lone Star hit with "Francine." Word began to spread as the Rolling Stones asked the boys to open for their 1972 tour. They scored a national hit with "La Grange" from the platinum-selling *Tres Hombres.* "Waitin' For the Bus/Jesus Just Left Chicago" included some harp work by Gibbons, but it was his incredible guitar playing that was drawing the people in. It was obvious by now that ZZ Top could play the blues as well as anyone, but they approached it without the scholarly attitude that causes so many other groups to sink. "See, for white boys playing the blues, you can only get away with it if it's amusing," Gibbons told *Rolling Stone*'s Daisann McLane.

> *"For white boys playing the blues, you can only get away with it if it's amusing."*
> *—Billy Gibbons*

Museum in Houston. As they travelled the world and enjoyed their time off, Ham secured a contract with the prestigious Warner Bros. label. They returned to the studio to record 1979's *Deguello,* perhaps their finest effort yet. "[Deguello] sounds as if they spent all three years playing the blues on their front porch," wrote Robert Christgau in his *Record Guide.* "I've heard a shitload of white blues albums in the wake of Belushi and Aykroyd (the Blues Brothers). This is the best by miles. A-." From the sweetness of "A Fool For Your Stockings" to the raunch of "Hi Fi Mama," the Top's palette of different sounds was remarkable for just a trio, prompting Lester Bangs to describe their sound in *Rolling Stone* "as truly violent music and whang-dang beyond mere professionalism."

Their next album, *El Loco,* was very similar to *Deguello* but not quite so strong. The band opted for a radical change in 1983 for their *Eliminator* LP. With the aide of Tom Scholz's Rockman (a guitar effects unit), Gibbons decided to turn up the heat. "Basically it was a more vicious sound I was after," he told Steven Rosen in *Guitar World.* In addition to the extra crunch, the band's lyrics had progressively been moving away from the typical rock fare while still maintaining their trademark sick edge. "I think that we may have been able to refine our music writing abilities to more genuinely reflect a truer sense of our honest emotions," Gibbons said to Rosen. The new moves were supported by the group's humorous use of videos—"Gimme All Your Lovin'," "Sharp Dressed Man," "TV Dinners," "Legs"—through the then-untested MTV market, which helped to boost *Eliminator* sales to ten million copies, peaking in Billboard's charts at number 9 and remaining in the Top 20 for over a year. The ensuing tour included a giant replica of Gibbons's hot rod's dashboard and a huge Sphinx that engulfed the stage.

After dabbling with the Moog synthesizer on *Eliminator,* they dove headfirst into the electronic age on *Afterburner.* The group employed drum machines, sequencers, and computer sampling (like the slamming of a 1968 Buick Electra 225 car door) while still maintaining the crunch of Gibbons's six-string. "All of a sudden you've got a second generation wave of synthesizers that offer the kind of manipulations where a more human touch can be put into it, to make it pliable for a ZZ Top-styled band not to lose their integrity," Gibbons told *Guitar World.*

The band paid tribute to their roots in 1989 with the Muddywood Tour. After visiting the late Muddy Waters's birthplace on Stovall's plantation in Mississippi, Gibbons took a plank of wood from the cabin that Waters was raised in and had it made into a guitar. It was displayed in cities throughout the world with proceeds going to the Delta Blues Museum in Clarksdale, Mississippi. ZZ Top had played with Waters several times in the late seventies and decided to pay back a little to the music they owe so much to. "Try as we might to spice it up with synthesizers and high-tech thises

and thats, it basically comes down to a few moments of bluesiness that we want to at least make an attempt to hold onto for as long as we can," Gibbons told Jas Obrecht in *Guitar Player.*

Selected discography

First Album, London, 1970; Warner Bros., 1980.
Rio Grande Mud, London, 1972; Warner Bros., 1980.
Tres Hombres, London, 1973; Warner Bros., 1980.
Fandango, London, 1975; Warner Bros., 1980.
Tejas, London, 1976; Warner Bros., 1980.
The Best of ZZ Top, London, 1977; Warner Bros., 1980.
Deguello, Warner Bros., 1979.
El Loco, Warner Bros., 1981.
Eliminator, Warner Bros., 1983.
Afterburner, Warner Bros., 1985.
The ZZ Top Sixpack, (digitally remastered versions of the first five albums and *El Loco*), Warner Bros., 1988.

Sources

Books

Christgau, Robert, *Christgau's Record Guide,* Ticknor & Fields, 1981.

Periodicals

Guitar Player, February, 1981; August, 1984; March, 1986.
Guitar World, May, 1984; March, 1986; November, 1986; April, 1988; March, 1989.
Rolling Stone, August 26, 1976; March 10, 1977; March 6, 1980; May 1, 1980.

—Calen D. Stone

Subject Index

Volume numbers appear in **bold**.

Townshend, Pete **1**
Vandross, Luther **2**
Vox, Bono
  See U2 **2**
Waits, Tom **1**
Waters, Roger
  See Pink Floyd **2**
Williams, Deniece **1**
Williams, Hank Jr. **1**
Wilson, Brian
  See Beach Boys **1**
Winwood, Steve **2**
Wonder, Stevie **2**
Wynette, Tammy **2**
Yoakam, Dwight **1**

Young, Neil **2**
Zappa, Frank **1**

Soul
Brown, James **2**
Charles, Ray **1**
Cooke, Sam **1**
Franklin, Aretha **2**
Knight, Gladys **1**
Little Richard **1**
Reid, Vernon **2**
Robinson, Smokey **1**
Ross, Diana **1**
Vandross, Luther **2**
Wonder, Stevie **2**

Trumpet
Berigan, Bunny **2**
Davis, Miles **1**
Jones, Quincy **2**
Severinsen, Doc **1**

Violin
Acuff, Roy **2**
Anderson, Laurie **1**
Hartford, John **1**
Hidalgo, David
  See Los Lobos **2**
Lindley, David **2**
O'Connor, Mark **1**
Perlman, Itzhak **2**

Musicians Index

Volume numbers appear in **bold**.